The Goatman

By

Jeff Fuell

The Goatman

Copyright 2011 by Jeff Fuell

All rights reserved. No part of this book may be used or reproduced in any manner whatsoever without written permission of the publisher, except in the case of brief quotations embodied in critical articles and reviews.

This book is a work of fiction. Names, characters, places and incidents are either products of the author's imagination or are used fictitiously. Any resemblance the actual events or locales or persons, living or dead, is entirely coincidental.

PRELUDE

It was the summer of 1983, and I thought I knew everything…as I suppose all kids do when they're young. They find out when they look back, though – which they tend to do as they grow older – that they really knew nothing…or at least, next to nothing. I was thirteen years old in 1983. Like most kids at that age, I was under the incorrect assumption that I had quite a bit of worldly experience. I had even travelled to a couple of tropical islands with my parents on vacations, something that no other kids in my neighborhood had done. It was only after the little adventure that the three of us had that summer that I realized how naïve I really was.

I suppose there comes a time in life when you can look back and pinpoint that exact time when you felt you became an adult. For some people, it's when they have sex for the first time. That's the common answer for boys. Or perhaps it's graduating high school or college, maybe even getting your first full-time job. For others, it's getting married or, beyond that, finding out that you're soon going to be a parent. Those are normal situations that come when a person is better equipped to handle it, more or less. Although some things people are never able to handle, no matter how old they are.

For me, though, it was in 1983, when we were all thirteen years old and I encountered the Goatman.

It was summer, and like any teenage boy who was getting a break from the terrorist organization that is known as school, I was as happy as a boy could be. I was living in Corpus Christi, Texas, and I have to say it was pretty nice. Most kids usually say that they can't stand where they live, and as soon as they're old enough, they're going to move away to a better place—preferably without parents in tow.

Some of the places usually mentioned are California or New York, maybe even Miami. There are some kids who are even more creative and say that they're going to move to somewhere in Europe, Paris being a very common answer. But no, Corpus Christi was fine with me, at least for then. Nobody ever knows what life has in store for them, but I was perfectly happy where I was in my life at that time.

My grades were actually pretty good that year, and I didn't have to attend summer school, which would have been a fate worse than death. It killed me merely to think that while all my friends were out having a good time, I might be sitting in class doing the same old thing that, in a world with any justice in it whatsoever, should have been against the law during the summer. That's what I think, at least. That's what most kids think. Ask them.

It makes me wonder, though: If things had turned out differently and I had gone to summer school, I might never have gotten the worst shock of my young life and grown up a lot faster than I had to. On the other hand, it was also a good thing because eventually all the missing kids were safely returned home. I guess I will never know. Anyway, this has been on my mind lately, and I suppose I should tell you all about it and see what you think.

BEFORE THE GOATMAN

I woke up at almost eight o'clock on a Monday morning, which was kind of early for me, seeing as how I usually drifted awake sometime between eight-thirty and nine. It was actually very rare that I slept late on a weekday. I would have liked to be able to, but a lifetime of programming, having to get up for school, had already ruined me. Weekends, however, I had no problem.

As I opened my eyes, I looked down and saw Zock already awake, sitting on the floor staring up at me, his tongue hanging out and a happy look spread across his furry face. Zock was my dog, a Golden Retriever my dad had gotten for me about two and a half years earlier, and he was awesome. I know what you're thinking: Why did I name my dog something weird like "Zock"? Why not something more common like "Rex" or "Rover" or "Butch" or "Spike"? Well, first of all, Zock did not look like any one of those names, if you know what I mean. Some people just have a look that suggests a name. Looking at him or her, you can just imagine that he is a "Chris" or she is a "Jane" and so on. It's usually something very generic, although there are exceptions. The same thing goes for dogs.

Anyway, I named him Zock because that's the name of one of the characters in what was then my favorite book, *The Temple of Gold* by William Goldman. My English class had been assigned to read it a couple of years earlier, and I loved it. It was a very sad book because nothing was working out for the main character and, in my opinion, was a little bit grown-up for kids, but I understood everything that it was saying, and I especially grew attached to the character of Zock. Actually, his full name was Zachary Crowe, but everyone just called him Zock. Well, when my

5

father brought the dog home as a surprise for my eleventh birthday and said I had to name him; Zock was the first name that came to mind. That's my Zock story.

I got out of bed and slowly wandered to the bathroom to wash up. That's what my mom calls it – washing up. Not taking a bath or a shower or washing your hands or even…the other things…but washing up. It means all of it, really, from washing your hands to a full-fledged bath. Mom has always been a stickler for washing up. If you wanted to live in my house, you had better get used to it right quick. (By the way, in case you're interested, when I washed up, I took a shower. I hadn't taken a bath since I was a kid.)

Speaking of washing up, I had noticed that I was growing hair in a certain place, that place being…down there, if you know what I mean. I knew that men had hair on their bodies, usually on their chest and in their armpits, but that kind of hair hadn't started growing yet. Just…down there. It looked weird to me because I had spent my whole life looking at a thin, hairless body that was in dire need of some muscles. I wondered now how long it would be before I had to start shaving. I saw my dad doing it every now and then, and it looked like it would be fun. It would certainly mean that I was a grown-up. I mean, more grown up than I was at the time, since I was currently in the two digits. They may be in the lower spectrum of the two digits, but they were still two digits, and that's what counted.

Eventually, after I was properly washed up, I wandered downstairs and found my dad at the kitchen table doing the usual – reading the newspaper and drinking a cup of coffee. I didn't know how he stood it. The coffee I mean, not the newspaper. He had let me try some of his coffee a couple of years earlier because he saw that I was curious about it. I figured that if a person drank a certain drink every day without fail, it must be pretty good. I was, am, and probably always will be that way with Dr. Pepper. My mom is that way with Pepsi. My dad is that way with coffee. So he let me have a sip of it, and it was the most wretched stuff I had ever tasted! How could anyone drink this crap? It was awful! Even trying it again with a little sugar didn't help much, and he actually drinks it black! My dad just laughed and said, "It's an acquired taste." I had to ponder that for a moment.

Now, think about that. I mean really think about it. I considered myself a pretty smart kid, and since I read a good deal, I knew what the word "acquired" means. What really struck me was the definition of it. "Acquired" means that you have developed a taste or liking for something that you initially didn't like, and that even though you knew you didn't like it, you forced yourself to keep trying it over and over until you learned to like it. Why would you want to do that? Why would you want to force yourself to keep drinking a certain beverage over and over again that you know you don't like, in the hope that you might come to like it? Why not just drink something that you know you do like, like Dr. Pepper? Wouldn't that be so much better? Anyway, that was my opinion on the subject. In regard to the newspaper, the only section I read at that age was the comics, and sometimes the movie page.

"Hey, Dad!"

"Morning, Dan."

My dad was wearing a nice suit and tie, and his dark hair was combed very neatly, as usual. I have to say that my dad was (and still is) a good-looking guy, like someone you would see on television announcing the news. At that age, I thought I had dashing good looks and guessed I got them from him.

Oh, I forgot to tell you, my name is Dan. Actually, my full name is Danny, but by thirteen I preferred to be called "Dan." "Danny" sounds like something you would call a kid. As you know, I was by then a two-digit number, which meant I was no longer just a kid. My dad called me Dan, which I really appreciated. My mother still called me Danny, which made me cringe every time I heard it. I especially hated it when she calls me Danny in front of company, especially when said company was girls. I could have just died.

"Have any plans for today?"

I went the refrigerator, got a can of Dr. Pepper, and cracked it open.

"I was thinking of tracking down the Bluesman and seeing what he wanted to do," I replied while taking a drink from the can. The refrigerator was usually fully stocked with Dr. Pepper and Pepsi. Also, other beverages like milk and orange juice, but the Dr. Pepper was the most important.

"Well, I hope you and the Bluesman have fun," he said, grinning, as he got up from the table with the now empty cup of coffee. He drew out the word "Bluesman." Rest assured, the entire pitcher of coffee was now gone and in my dad. "I have to hit the road. Some of us don't have summers off. Tell the Bluesman I said hello."

"I will."

"And how's my little Dannykins this morning?" my mom said as she entered the room and then kissed the top of my head.

I cringed.

Dad grinned.

I should have mentioned something else: Besides calling me "Danny," my mom also had a habit of calling me "Dannykins," which made me feel like I should be in a stroller being pushed around while I played with a rattle. If I had to pick between the two I would rather be called "Danny." Thankfully, she never called me "Dannykins" in front of company—though I lived in constant fear that sometime she would. I decided that if she ever did, I would give serious thought to having my name legally changed.

I have to say, my mom was (and is) very beautiful. She looked almost exactly like Connie Sellecca, the main girl on one of my favorite shows, *The Greatest American Hero.* Sometimes when my friends came over, all they did was stare at her. It was embarrassing! I mean…my mom!

"Hey, Mom!"

"So, you're going to track down the Bluesman?" she inquired in the same way my dad had just said it and then went into the kitchen to pour herself a glass of orange juice.

"Yeah."

"Honestly, Danny, why do you hang out with that boy? He sounds like nothing but trouble."

"He's funny, Mom!"

"And whoever heard of calling someone something as ridiculous as 'The Bluesman'?"

"That's his name, Mom. He's famous! Someday he's going to be really famous."

"From what you tell me about that boy, I don't know how his parents put up with him," she said while rolling her eyes as she came over to sit next to me at the table.

"He's not so bad, Mom. He's just honing his act all the time."

"Well, he acts like nothing but trouble."

"This sounds like an interesting discussion, but I have to hit the road," my dad announced while looking at his watch. He kissed my mom and then ruffled my hair with his right hand. "You be good…and give the Bluesman my best," he said drawing it out again while smiling at my mom before he was out the door, briefcase in hand.

"I guess I should be off, also," I said as I downed the rest of my Dr. Pepper and then let loose with an enormous belch.

"Danny!"

"Sorry, Mom."

"What do you say?"

"Thank you and good night?"

9

"Danny!"

"I don't know – what do I say?"

"Danny."

"Excuse me."

"Thank you. Now, run along…and be careful. I don't want you trying to do any more tricks on that bike again."

"Okay, Mom," I said as I retreated to my room.

I belched like that on purpose just to get a rise out of her. It was fun. It was like a game that we both played. She'd given up on asking me to quit it, and I knew that she was thinking I'd eventually just grow out of it and stop on my own if she stopped asking me to quit. But I knew that she knew that her not asking me to quit it was part of her plan to get me to quit it, so I kept doing it. Now, about the bike thing: I'd crashed and almost broken my leg a couple of months earlier, trying to pop a wheelie on my bike. Since then, she'd been a nervous wreck every time I mounted my steed. I told her that my trick days were over, but in reality I was still trying to pop a perfect wheelie when she couldn't see me. The Bluesman could pop wheelies like nobody's business!

While in my room, I gathered my wallet, which was sorely in need of replenishing the funds in it, and my Star Wars watch. That reminded me: I needed to talk to my dad about raising my allowance. It had been the same amount for over a year and was now out of sync with the current inflation rate. If I approached it in an adult manner and explained the situation, I was quite sure he would relent.

Zock was looking at me with expectant eyes.

"You ready to go, boy?"

Zock barked his enthusiasm.

"Let's go."

We headed out to the garage, and I mounted my Mongoose, which I'd got for the previous Christmas. Actually, as grateful as I was to finally have a real bike, I was not surprised to find it under the tree on Christmas morning. I had certainly dropped enough hints about it, including leaving pictures that I found in the newspaper of it from time to time all around the house, not to mention bringing it up almost every day for three months prior to Christmas. I could fit it into practically any conversation, an art form that I mastered fairly quickly. My mom could ask me about what kind of sandwich I wanted for lunch and I could fit it in. I was that good. Obviously I was good because here I was riding the bike that I had dreamed about for so long.

As Zock and I were making our way down the sidewalk I carefully attempted another wheelie. I got up some speed, held my breath, and when I felt I was ready, pulled up on my handlebars with everything I had. As usual, all I got was a couple of inches in the air, and then my front wheel fell back to the ground. This really depressed me. I had been trying this for so long, yet I seemed to be the only kid in the neighborhood who couldn't pop a proper wheelie. I was a laughingstock! This was going to have to change. Even the ten-year-old kid who lived a couple of houses down could do one, and his bike was nowhere near as good as mine. How embarrassing!

Soon I arrived at the Bluesman's house and dismounted my bike – the bike that I could not pop a wheelie on – and knocked on his door in our secret code. Zock was sniffing around the bushes, and I hoped that he was not going to pick this time to unload. Anywhere else, but not here. Marie answered the door a few moments later and just stared at me, not saying anything. Marie was the Bluesman's little sister.

"Well, what do you want?" she asked in a direct manner, as though I were the last person on the face of the earth she wanted to talk to. She was always this adorable. Living with the Bluesman, I could imagine why.

"Um, is Keith here?"

"No, the idiot is not here!" she stated in the same tone.

11

"Do you know where he is?"

"Where do you think that idiot is?"

About a dozen different places popped into my mind, so I just looked at her.

"The idiot is up at the store, feeding quarters into the stupid machine again!"

That had actually been my third guess.

"Oh. Okay. Thanks," I said and then playfully raised my hand above her head.

"Don't you dare!" she screamed. She slammed the door.

I grinned and then mounted my steed once again, a quest in front of me.

"Well, boy, we're going to the store. You up for it?" I asked Zock.

Zock barked his enthusiasm, and we were off. Also, I was happy to see that he had not relieved himself on the Bluesman's lawn.

After a short ride down through the neighborhood, I soon arrived at Maverick Market, the neighborhood convenience store. After instructing Zock to stay, I walked in and immediately saw Jerry smiling at me from behind the counter. Jerry was an older guy who was kind of short and always very jovial. I had never seen him in a bad mood about anything. I really liked him because he would sometimes give us free Slurpees if we hang around long enough and played the video games. He wasn't supposed to do that, but he did. I thought he was really pretty cool for an old guy. Like most kids, I did not like to hang around old people. Some of them I could deal with, but not the ones who talked down to me and treated me like a kid. Jerry usually always had a good joke handy and was always smiling, unlike most grown-ups I encountered, who I was almost positive hated kids once the kids entered the double digits because then they are no longer nice, sweet children. They are teenagers. Teenagers are monsters. A completely different species.

12

"Hey, Jerry!"

"Hey, Dan! How are things going?"

That's another thing I liked about Jerry: He called me "Dan."

"Pretty good. How about you?"

"Can't complain, my boy, can't complain," he laughed. This was our usual standard greeting to each other.

I walked the length of the store and saw my friend playing Defender.

"Hey, Bluesman!"

"Hey, Dan," he said as he quickly looked over at me and then back at his game.

I looked at the screen and saw that he had already beaten my high score. The night before, my dad and I had come up here when my mom had sent him out for some things, and he had waited patiently while I played a game of Defender. My dad was really cool about important things like that. I was really excited because I had beaten my own high score, and I was flying high for the rest of the night. Now, though, the Bluesman had already beaten it, and he still had one guy left! I watched in silence as he played the rest of the game and, not surprisingly, he now had the top score on the machine. I, however, was still number two.

I should point out right now that while I was pretty good at Defender; my main game of choice was Tron. Nobody could beat me at Tron. Nobody! Not even the Bluesman. Unfortunately, the nearest one that I knew of was all the way at the arcade inside Sunrise Mall. We had to get a ride to go out there because it was way too long a bike ride. I mean, we could do it, but who wanted to spend over two hours riding our bikes to the mall when we could usually just get a ride? At any rate, even if we did ride our bikes over there, which we had done on occasion, we were usually too tired to do anything when we got there, plus we knew that we were going to have to ride all the way back, and even though it was the same distance either way, the ride back always seemed longer. It kind of killed the fun of it. At any rate, I was the master at Tron. I also happened to be pretty good at Galaga and Tempest. Just thought I would let you in on some of the skills I had at thirteen. Even though I couldn't pop a wheelie, I don't want you to think I was lacking in other areas.

"Looks like you got the high score, again," I said.

"It took a lot out of me. I'm thirsty," he said as he wiped away a light bead of sweat that had appeared on his forehead.

"Think Jerry will hook us up?"

"He always has in the past."

"Let's go find out."

Once the Bluesman was done defending the universe, we walked toward the counter, where the smiling Jerry was watching us approach. Then he got two small cups, filled them up, and gave us each a small cherry Slurpee.

"I really shouldn't be doing this, boys," he said nervously as he handed us the cups and looked around the store, then out the glass door to see if anyone was spying on us. Really. As if anyone would care. They were just Slurpees. Still, as much of a pushover as Jerry was, we didn't do this every time, just once a week. Maybe twice.

"Thanks, Jerry. We appreciate it. You're the reason why we keep coming in here," I said.

"The reason you keep coming in here is because of Defender and free Slurpees," he said, laughing, and we joined him. What could I say? He was right.

The Bluesman and I tapped our cups together in celebration and began to drink through the straws. I loved Slurpees. I really did. If I could somehow have installed a Slurpee machine at my house, I would have. I thought that maybe I should ask for one for my next Christmas present. I considered it seriously.

We were making our way back down the aisle to thumb through the magazines when the door opened, the bells above it jangling as it hit them. We both stopped in our tracks and looked at the weird-looking guy who had just walked in.

He was the oddest-looking guy I had ever seen. The guy did not have any hair at all, and he was constantly blinking. He was wearing a giant smile on his face, but it looked vacant, as if he did it all the time and not because he actually saw something from time to time that made him smile, like most people do. It was just there as a permanent fixture. It really looked weird. I would think that would hurt, wearing a smile that large all the time. What made him seem even odder was the fact that while his head seemed a little small for his body, if you know what I mean, the rest of him was huge! He was wearing a black biker jacket, which seemed kind of odd because it was summer, but you could tell that he was a muscled-up guy. His shoulders alone made his head seem really small on him. And the way he walked — a childlike shuffle instead of taking full steps. What a sight. Even Jerry could not help but stare at him.

He picked up one of the little shopping baskets that was sitting by the door, then proceeded toward the candy aisle and began to just grab handfuls of candy bars and drop them in his basket, all while hardly even looking at them. Still, I recognized some of the wrappers as Snickers, Milky Way, Hershey's, Mr. Goodbar, Twix, Baby Ruth, and Kit Kat. Then he proceeded to the next aisle and picked up some desserts like Twinkies and Ding-Dongs. Once his basket was full, almost overflowing, he walked up to the counter and dropped his basket on it. Jerry looked at it, shocked. It was really full. Even my last Halloween sack had been nowhere near that full, and it had taken me hours of walking around the neighborhood just to get that much.

"Uh, is this going to be all for you?" Jerry inquired while still staring at the full basket in a mixture of shock and amusement.

"MynameisGordon!" the man said.

"I'm sorry?"

"MynameisGordon," he said again, running all the words together as he stood there and blinked with that happy look still on his face.

"Oh. Okay. Your name is Gordon?" Jerry said, trying not to be rude, which was difficult because this guy just kept getting more and more weird.

"MynameisGordon," he repeated.

"The guy's a retard," the Bluesman whispered to me while still looking at him in awe.

"I guess so," I replied, captivated by him. He certainly was a character, and I could not help but stare. I don't know why I did that at times. Sometimes when I would see a person who looked odd, or something about them stood out in some way, I would just look at them and make up some kind of story about who they were or where they were from. It was a habit I had fallen into about two years earlier, and I had no idea why I did it. Early on, my mother would catch me doing it and scold me for being rude because it's crass to stare at someone. I didn't mean to be rude; I was just captivated with...characters. Anyone who stood out, I had to look at them.

Even if it was just something a little bit out of the ordinary like a certain kind of a walk, or a birthmark, or maybe even a pair of eyeglasses that were kind of odd, I had to see it. I would even say absorb it. I know that sounds odd but that's what it felt like. That's what I was doing now. I was trying to imagine who this guy was and where he was from...but he was just too way out. I had never seen anyone like him. And judging from the Bluesman's reaction, neither had he.

"Okay," Jerry said, being friendly, even though it was completely obvious that he also thought the guy in front of him was really weird. "Let me just add all this up for you. Will this be all?"

I saw Jerry flinch, and I knew the reason why. He probably thought he was going to be hit with another, "MynameisGordon," since it seemed to be all the guy knew. Instead, "Thatwillbeallthankyou."

"Okay, let me just add all of this up for you." Jerry grinned, starting to turn back into his usual jovial self. "This is going to take a while. You planning a party or something?"

The man just stood there and blinked at him, the large smile still stretched across his face.

Ten minutes later, when everything was totaled up and in a couple of bags, Jerry turned his attention from his cash register to the man and gave him the total amount.

The man just stared at him for a moment, and you could tell from the expression on Jerry's face that he thought that the guy was probably so dumb; he probably didn't even know how to count. He probably didn't have any money, and Jerry had just spent all this time adding up all this candy for nothing. Who could blame him? I thought the same thing.

Instead, the man pulled out a large wallet from the back pocket in his jeans and withdrew a giant wad of money. It was so thick, the Bluesman and I just turned our heads and looked at each other and then back to the man.

Jerry took the wad of bills and selected the amount he needed, rang it up on the register, and then gave the man back his wad and some change. Once he had placed his wallet back in his back pocket and his change in his front pocket, the man took the large, heavy-looking bags from the counter and looked at Jerry. "Thankyouhaveaniceday," he said.

"You too, son," Jerry said to the man, whose age I would guess was around thirty. It was really hard to tell because he had no hair. Now that I thought about it, hair was a very essential factor in determining a person's age. I had never really thought about it before or why I was

17

thinking about it now. I guess it's because I was just used to seeing most people with hair. Sure, there were a few teachers at my school who didn't have much hair because they were old, but then at that age I wouldn't have really classified teachers as human beings.

The man shuffled out the door as the bells rang again, signaling his departure.

"Well, that was certainly weird," the Bluesman announced.

"It sure was," I said still staring at the door, and then took a sip from my straw.

At any rate, we quickly forgot about him as we looked through the various magazines while finishing our Slurpees. The Bluesman tended to look through the biking magazines, *like BMX,* while I concentrated on the music magazines, like *Circus* and *Hit Parader.* Both of us were really into music, especially since a couple of years earlier this channel called MTV had begun airing, and all they did was play music videos all day and night of songs from various musical artists. It was really pretty cool...like watching the radio. I figured they must not have a lot of them to go around because they tended to play the same ones over and over again. Some of the people they played were *Duran Duran* (which they played a lot!), *Loverboy, Pat Benatar, The Go-Gos, Culture Club, A Flock of Seagulls, Huey Lewis & the News, Michael Jackson, Prince*, and some others whose names I can't think of. Some of them looked really weird.

All of them were pretty good, but, lately they'd begun to play some other people who had a different, harder sound that I thought was really cool. There were some bands with names like *Iron Maiden, Judas Priest, Def Leppard, Quiet Riot, ZZ Top, Rush, Rainbow, Saxon, Ronnie James Dio, Motley Crüe, Ozzy Osbourne,* and Triumph that were all so good, they were incredible! Also, they looked cool. They all had long hair and wore cool clothes that just made them look…well, cool. I wanted to get my hair as long as those guys', but I knew there wasn't any real hope of that happening. My mom made sure I got a haircut every six weeks, and she was always there to supervise it. I didn't look like a nerd or anything, but I also didn't think I looked as cool as I would have if I'd had long hair.

Even though I liked all of those new groups, and I was always scouring music magazines to read about them, my favorite group was still *KISS*. I'd been a fan of theirs ever since I was a kid. In fact, they had just released an album called "Lick It Up," and I was shocked to see that they were no longer wearing makeup! It was actually a picture of four guys on the cover and not the Demon, the Starchild, the Spaceman, and the Cat. When I was a kid, I had thought that that was really them! That they really looked like that! Still, even without the makeup, they looked cool. It was just going to take a while to get used to. The Bluesman's favorite group was *Duran Duran*, but that was kind of a secret because guys were not supposed to be into *Duran Duran* that much. It wasn't considered cool. *Duran Duran* was primarily for girls.

Speaking of music, I suppose I should let you in on something. The Bluesman's real name was *Keith Richards*. I know what you are thinking and, no, he didn't have anything to do with *the Rolling Stones*. I could only assume that his parents were fans because *the Rolling Stones* had already been around for a hundred years. Out of all the names that they could have given their son, they chose Keith. Keith Richards. He hated it because people made fun of him all the time. Personally, I never understood why people liked *the Rolling Stones* so much. They really didn't do anything for me. I thought Mick Jagger looked and acted like an ugly girl.

It just occurred to me that you probably have no idea whatsoever what I am talking about when I refer to Keith as "The Bluesman." It really is quite an interesting story, and it's what made him famous. I would even say infamous. Everyone knew "The Bluesman." And, no, it was not because Keith was a fan of the blues. In fact, off the top of my head, I could not even name one blues artist. I mean, I had heard the blues before, but frankly it all sounded alike to me. Everyone sounded depressed and down all the time. Who would want to listen to something like that? Put on some *Van Halen*!

Like most kids, Keith did not like school. He thought it was boring, and I had to agree, at least most of the time. When not having summer freedom, we both attended Tom Brown Junior High School. I guess it was a pretty nice school as far as schools went. We even had a gang. I was not in the gang, but we did have one, called the Piranhas. The Piranhas were basically a group of Mexicans who roamed the school looking tough. It's not like they had matching jackets made or anything, just a group of kids who looked scary as hell. Legend had it that they kept their death list written on the roof of the gymnasium. I don't know if this was true or not since I never went up there. There had never been a death at our school. Still, I really did not want to go up and look at the list because I might be on it. There was no reason why I should have been, but why take the chance? That was my opinion.

Anyway, I was about to tell you how Keith became "The Bluesman." One day the previous year, Keith was sitting in class and bored out of his mind. It was a math class, so his boredom was quite understandable. While sitting in class, Keith, from out of nowhere, decided to burst into song.

"Da Da Da Da Da!... da da-da da... Da Da Da Da Da!... da da-da da... Da Da Da Da Da!... da da-da da... Da Da Da Da Da!... da da-da da."

"Keith? Is something wrong?" Miss Littleton asked, looking at him with a baffled expression. Miss Littleton was the math teacher, and I had to say she really was kind of cute. Not like the rest of the teachers I had, believe me. She was a rare breed.

"Da Da Da Da Da! Sitting in this class! Da Da Da Da Da! Bored out of my mind! Da Da Da Da Da! Feel like I'm going crazy! Da Da Da Da Da! Get me outta this bind! Da Da Da Da Da!"

I suppose you can see what was happening. Keith was singing the blues. He was supplying both lead and back-up vocals.

"Keith, I need you to stop that," Miss Littleton said, getting up out of her chair.

"Da Da Da Da Da!"

"Keith, stop it!"

"Da Da Da Da Da!"

"Keith, I'm serious. Stop that."

"Da Da Da Da Da!"

Because of Keith, Miss Littleton was now unwillingly singing the blues. Keith now felt like he had gotten his little concert started and sensed that his amused audience wanted to have a sing-along.

"Can't sit here no longer!" he said as he raised his hands to cue them.

"Da Da Da Da Da!" the class chimed in.

"I'm losing my mind!"

"Da Da Da Da Da!"

"I gots to get out of here!"

"Da Da Da Da Da!"

I gotta unwind!"

"Da Da Da Da Da!"

"Stop that! All of you! Stop that!" Miss Littleton barked, trying to regain control of her classroom.

"Da Da Da Da Da!" the class chimed back.

"You are all going to be in serious trouble!"

"Da Da Da Da Da!"

"I'm going to go get the principal, Mr. Mendez, and bring him in here!"

"Da Da Da Da Da!"

"I'm going to give you one more chance and then I'm leaving."

"Da Da Da Da Da!"

"Fine!" she said in a huff and walked out the door.

"Da Da Da Da Da!"

By now, all the surrounding classrooms had heard what was going on and some of the other teachers and students had wandered in to see what was happening. Now, with an even larger audience, the blues continued onward, with Keith as the conductor. The blues continued on for about ten minutes until Miss Littleton arrived with Mr. Mendez in tow. A look of astonishment covered his face as he surveyed what was happening.

"What is going on in here?" he demanded.

"Da Da Da Da Da!"

"Shush! Be quiet!"

"Da Da Da Da Da!"

"Who is responsible for this?" he yelled.

"Da Da Da Da Da!"

The blues continued, and outside the window there were now other students who wanted to participate…and did. Everything was now so loud that it seemed as if the entire student body of Tom Brown Junior High was singing the blues. And Keith had been the orchestrator of it all. It was really not hard to determine that Keith was the leader, and Principal Mendez grabbed him by the shoulder and led him out of the classroom to his office. Even as they were walking down the hall, the blues could still be heard ringing through the halls.

Well, things being the way they were, everything worked out in Keith's favor. When Mr. Mendez, still fuming, had gotten Keith's father on the phone and explained what his son had done, Mr. Richards burst out laughing, leaving a stoic Mr. Mendez on the phone waiting for him to finish.

Keith was already known around the school for being a likeable, funny guy, who was always quick with a joke, but spontaneously singing the blues had turned him into a legend. And it didn't stop there. For the rest of the year, Keith would randomly give a lucky class the blues every week. Nobody knew when he would suddenly be inspired to burst into song, but he did it once a week, a different class every time, and the class would always join in.

This did not occur without his having to pay a penalty, however. Guaranteed, every Friday, Keith would have to spend a half hour after school in detention as punishment for his music. But that didn't matter; the Bluesman was willing to suffer for his art. I suppose things could have been worse but, truth to tell, I think some of the faculty found it as funny as the kids did. It was a nice break in an otherwise boring day. And thus, the legend of the Bluesman was born.

Anyhow, back to the day I was telling you about. Once we had finished our Slurpees and had pored over every magazine available, I decided to see if the Bluesman wanted to stop off at H.E.B., which is the neighborhood supermarket. I have no idea what "H.E.B." stands for, so don't ask.

"So how about we head on over to H.E.B.?" I said nonchalantly.

The Bluesman looked over at me with a wide grin.

"What?" I challenged him.

"I know why you want to go over there," he intoned.

"What do you mean?" I turned slightly red.

"You want to see if Kelly is working today."

"What? I could care less!"

"Oh, if you don't care, how about we just head back then?"

I was stuck. Every time I had an opportunity to go to H.E.B., I looked forward to seeing Kelly. I was hoping to see her right now, seeing as how she might be across the

23

street right at this moment. I liked Kelly so much, I practically ran to the car whenever my mom announced she was going up to the store to pick up a few things.

"Fine. You win. I'm hoping to see Kelly."

"I just wanted to hear you say it, man," he grinned. "Let's go!"

We said goodbye to Jerry and mounted our bikes. As I mentioned, I rode a Mongoose, which was really cool. But the Bluesman rode a Supergoose, which was even cooler. Plus, as I mentioned, he could pop a wheelie on it like nobody's business. We headed over to the store, Zock happily following.

I guess some sort or explanation is in order. A couple of years earlier I had discovered girls. I mean, they'd always been around; it's just that now I really noticed them a lot more. I forgot the first girl I was really sparked over. However, I do remember Jeannie and Wonder Woman. All the guys liked Jeannie and Wonder Woman—that's like a rite of passage. I didn't fully understand why I liked them so much at the time because I had previously found them to be annoying, but I really enjoyed looking at them on television. However, there were two certain girls I was really hooked on at the time due to two movies that I had recently seen.

One of them is *Fast Times at Ridgemont High*. You probably know where I am going with this because the scene is very famous. I had a crush on Phoebe Cates. For those of you who somehow missed the movie, she was the beautiful girl with the long, black hair, and she had a couple of scenes where she was wearing a red bikini. In one of them, she was topless! Those scenes drove me crazy! I couldn't stop thinking about Phoebe! I also couldn't believe that she was just a few years older than me. Hardly any of the girls in my school looked like that! Then again, I suppose four or five years can make a world of difference, especially going through the teenage developmental years. They usually affect girls in a more dramatic way than boys.

Oh, by the way, my parents didn't know I'd seen this movie because the Bluesman and I sneaked into it when my parents dropped us off to see another one. If they had found out I saw a movie with so much sex in it, they would have freaked! Still, it was a really good, funny movie. Mainly because of Phoebe.

However, I had my parents to thank for my other crush. A while back, we had all gone to see a movie called *The Best Little Whorehouse in Texas*. At the time, I had no idea what a whorehouse was. I thought it was a place where horses were kept. I know how weird that sounds, but that's what I thought. My dad tried to explain to me what it was, but he didn't do a very good job. Once I saw the movie, though, I understood. Man, did I understand! I suppose the reason my parents took me with them to see it was because it was a movie that was based on a stage musical from New York, and they thought it would be a nice, family film.

I guess it was funny, and it had a lot of singing and dancing in it, but I wasn't really into it. To me, it seemed too apart from reality. A couple of people would be having a scene and then, all of a sudden, fifty people would pop out of nowhere and put on a perfectly choreographed dance routine, all of them singing a song where they knew all the words and music seemed to be playing from out of nowhere. Now, tell me, how is this in any way reality? Where would you see something like that happen except on a stage or in front of a camera without a lot of preparation taking place beforehand? Maybe I was just being too critical, but I liked things to be a little more realistic. Even the *Star Wars* movies and *Battlestar Galactica* were more realistic than this because they were more grounded in their own reality, if you know what I mean.

At any rate, the main thing I liked about this movie was that it was the first time I ever saw Dolly Parton. What a woman! I had never seen a girl before with such huge boobs! They really were enormous! I loved them! I especially liked the scene where she was wearing that black lingerie and she and Burt Reynolds were singing something about sneaking around together. I kept hoping that they would show her naked like they did with Phoebe Cates in *Fast Times at Ridgemont High,* but no luck. After that I became a huge Dolly Parton fan. Musically, though, I can't say I really liked it. It was too cutesy. I kept hoping they would play something harder like some AC/DC or some Ozzy. That would have made the movie better in my opinion.

Which brings us up to Kelly. Kelly was a checker at H.E.B., and I had a crush on her. She had long, light brown hair, blue eyes, an adorable face, and a fantastic body! Even under those tacky uniforms that they made the checkers wear, I could still tell she had a body to die for! I estimated that Kelly was at least nineteen, and way out of my league, but I hoped she'd still be there in a few years because when I turned sixteen I planned to apply for a job there. I figured, who knows what might happen then? She might turn out to be one of those girls who were into younger boys. It wasn't impossible. If I could get a car by then, I was sure that that would help out a lot because girls liked boys with cars.

We parked our bikes outside and wandered into the store, me instructing Zock to stay. There was this one time not far back when Zock came up with us and didn't listen to me when I told him to stay outside because he was too curious to see what was going on inside the store. Also, I think he smelled food inside because the deli was directly to the left once you walked in. Zock went wild! He was running all over the store with me, the Bluesman, and employees of the store chasing him. And believe me, Zock is fast! It really was quite an adventure because every time he turned, he would slide a little bit on the smooth linoleum floor. This one older lady with rollers in her hair and wearing a dress that looked like a tent because she was so fat screamed so loud when she saw him approaching, I had to cover my ears. I thought she was going to have a heart attack! That was really silly because Zock would never hurt anybody. He just wanted to have some fun. Unfortunately, his fun was causing people to panic. We eventually caught him in a corner and got him back outside before he could cause any more trouble. Still, despite all the confusion, it really was funny. For us, I mean. Not the employees or customers of the store. At any rate, I think Zock learned his lesson because he usually just lay down on the sidewalk when I told him to from then on.

We proceeded in and walked down the main aisle… and there she was on checkout number 6… Kelly! My heart soared.

"Well, there she is," the Bluesman indicated while looking at me with a smile on his face. He was quite aware of how enamored I was of Kelly. She was busy checking out a small, older man who was buying a large cart full of stuff. It was going to take her a while. "Why don't you go up and say hello?"

I looked at the Bluesman as if he were an alien who had just landed in his flying saucer. "I can't do that!"

"Why not?"

Yeah, why not? I thought to myself. "Because…because she's working. I can't just go up and talk to a girl while she's working!"

"Why not? It's her job. If you go up and talk to her she has to talk to you. It's her job to be nice to customers."

"Yeah, she has to be nice to customers. I'm just some kid going up to talk to her. That's not the same thing."

"So, buy something."

"What do you mean, buy something?"

"Pick something up and let her check you out. While she's doing it, talk to her. She has to talk back to you to be nice."

I thought about it. He was right. This was a perfect opportunity to be able to talk to Kelly. I'd been watching her for months, and yet I was only vaguely aware of what her voice even sounded like.

Before I go any further, I don't want you to get the wrong idea. It's not like I'd been following her around and know where she lived or anything. I wasn't crazy. I just liked her. I saw that she was almost finished totaling up the groceries for the old guy, and there was a perfect opportunity to talk to her. It was still kind of early, so the store was not very crowded. I would have her all to myself!

"Okay. I'm going to do it!"

"All right!" the Bluesman said, cheering me on.

I looked around and saw a mini-cooler where bottles of soda were kept. Perfect! Plus, I was thirsty. I opened the glass door and was about to reach in when my face fell.

"I can't do it," I said glumly.

"What do you mean you can't do it? She's right there. This is a perfect opportunity!"

"There's no Dr. Pepper."

"So?"

"So, I always drink Dr. Pepper."

"Dan, are you listening to yourself? You are going to blow a good opportunity here just because of a brand of soda. Get a Coke. Get a Mountain Dew. Anything! It doesn't matter."

The Bluesman was right. I was just making excuses. I grabbed a bottle of Coke and then slowly proceeded up the aisle. The older man had all of his things bagged in a cart, and a sacker who was only a few years older than myself was following him as he slowly made his way down the aisle. I couldn't help but stare at the old guy. He had such

28

a weird walk, the way he seemed to go at a normal pace and then slow down as if he were about to lose his balance and then speed up again. Also, he was wearing this weird kind of cloth hat that I had never seen before. It wasn't like the kind I had seen in most old movies or even in that old black and white series *The Untouchables* about Elliot Ness, but kind of similar. It kind of reminded me of Sherlock Holmes, but that wasn't quite it. Also, he was smoking a pipe. I couldn't tell if it was lit or not. I'm assuming it was. I mean, why bother having a pipe in your mouth if it isn't lit?

My dad said he tried to get into the habit of smoking a pipe once, but it was a pain because he had to keep relighting it, so he gave it up, much to my mom's appreciation. And why was this old guy so dressed up? He was wearing a suit with a vest. A vest! Who wears a vest? Even my dad doesn't wear a vest, and he wears suits all the time! What a weird guy. I wondered what he did for a living? I wondered what kind of house he lived in? I wondered....

"May I help you?"

I glanced up. Kelly was looking at me with a nice smile spread across her full, rosy lips. She was talking to me! A quick glance behind me proved it because there was nobody behind me. The Bluesman had disappeared so that I would have some privacy. Part of me wished that he were here, but the other half was glad he had vanished. Now I had Kelly all to myself!

"Uh...I would like to get this Coke, please," I muttered as I placed it on the black conveyor belt. It was only when I pulled my hand away that I realized how far away from her it was. She pushed a button on her counter, and the conveyor belt hummed to life. My Coke began its long journey toward her.

That was stupid, I thought. *I should have placed it nearer so she wouldn't have to push the button and use the*

29

conveyor belt. It looks really dumb — a lone bottle of Coke having to travel all that way by itself. It probably won't even be cold anymore by the time it reaches her. In fact, I could have even handed it to her. I might have even been able to hold her hand for a brief second and see what it feels like! Stupid! I bet she has really soft hands. I blew it! I really, really blew it! I should have thought this through more before just jumping in like this. Everything is going wrong! It's probably taking everything she has not to burst out laughing. She has to know I have a crush on her. She has to! How many times have I come up here with my mom and stood as close to her as I am now and never said a word, just stared when she wasn't looking? How embarrassing. I should never have done this. Why can't the day just go away and start over?

She took the Coke and rang it up. I reached into my pocket, and I was immediately shocked. I had forgotten my wallet! *I left my wallet at home! How could I do something so stupid like that? Now she's going to have to close the sale or void it out or whatever it's called. She's probably even going to have to call the manager over because she's going to need some type of approval code to get rid of the charge. It's going to turn into this whole big thing, and a giant line is going to form behind me with at least thirty people and then something is going to go wrong with the register and they are going to have to take it apart and everyone is going to stare at me, and Kelly is going to hate me, all because of not having enough money for a lousy Coke, and this wouldn't have happened if they had Dr. Pepper because Dr. Pepper is better and—*

Wait a minute! I'm searching in the wrong pocket. I keep my wallet in the other pocket.

You could not imagine the sigh of relief I made as I took a dollar from my wallet and gave it to her.

"Here you go, Kelly," I said holding the dollar out for her. Immediately, I turned red. I had said her name. That's something you're never supposed to do! *I've been up here dozens of times with both my mom and my dad, and neither one of them has ever said her name when paying her. Now she's going to think I'm flirting with her like I'm some kind of letch or something. She's going to hate me because women don't like letches. I blew it! I really, really blew it!*

"Thank you, Danny," she said.

Did I hear her correctly? Did she say my name? "Did you say my name?" *Stupid! Of course she said my name, and I just asked her if she said my name! I'm blowing it! Still, she did say my name.*

"I see you up here all the time when you come up here with your parents."

Great. My parents. I feel like I'm six years old. I could just die. "Oh. Okay."

"Your mother told me that you have a crush on me," she said, grinning.

I'm going to run away. Right now, I am going to run away, and I am not going to stop until I get to Dallas. Maybe I can meet J.R. Ewing while I am there. He's cool, the way he always has that devilish grin.

"Um, she did? That's... that's kind of embarrassing," I said sheepishly.

She smiled at me because she could see how embarrassed I was, and she loved it. Girls love to tease boys. I was old enough to know that. She also had the most beautiful, radiant smile I had ever seen. A person could lose themselves in a smile like that. It felt like I was soaring through the clouds, unable to see anything in front of me with only the vision of her lovely face in front of me, keeping me aloft and guiding me through to the other side of Heaven.

"Don't be embarrassed. I think it's cute," she teased as she took my hand and then patted it as though I were a puppy. I had been right. Her hand was so soft. I immediately reacted and squeezed hers.

Stupid! She probably thinks I am going to pull her away and put her in a cart and try and kidnap her, and an image of me pulling her yelling and screaming out of the store is in her head as she is screaming for help from anyone. Stupid!

"You remind me of my boyfriend. I bet he would look just like you if he were your age."

I immediately deflated. I was already picturing how she would look in a wedding dress, and now she's telling me she already has a boyfriend. He probably even has a car, a fancy one like the one Burt Reynolds drove in *Smokey and the Bandit*, or at least like the one that Jim Rockford drove in the *Rockford Files*.

"Oh. I guess that's nice."

She laughed at that, but it wasn't a laugh to be cruel. It was the kind of laugh where she could understand my disappointment and she thought it was cute because she knew I had a crush on her.

"You're such a nice young boy. I bet you have a girlfriend."

Someone immediately came to mind, but I wouldn't necessarily have called her my girlfriend. I mean, it wasn't like we'd ever kissed or anything. I'd thought about it but...well, you know what I mean.

"Uh, well, not really," I said, unsure.

"Do I detect a little bit of hesitation there?" she said flirtatiously, one eyebrow arched.

"Well, to tell you the truth, I don't really know," I said honestly, and I meant it because I really had nothing to compare it to.

"Sounds to me like you should find out. A handsome young man like you should already have a girlfriend."

Did she just say that I'm handsome? Did I hear her correctly? "I...I guess I should." *I never really thought about it. After all, she was a girl and she thought I was handsome, so she must know what she's talking about.*

32

Some people had lined up behind me. Kelly gave me my Coke plus the change.

"Well, Danny, it was nice to finally meet you and talk with you. You should talk more often the next time you come up here. There's no reason to be shy."

"Um, okay. Well, it was nice meeting you, Kelly."

She smiled at me one last time and then went to work ringing up the items for the customer behind me. She was really good at ringing up items.

I walked away holding my Coke and immediately thought about the conversation that we had just had. The first thing that came to mind was the image of my mom telling her how much her son had a crush on Kelly and how he always looked forward to going up to the store so he could see her. Wasn't that adorable?

I immediately wanted to scream at the very thought of it.

Also, she had called me Danny. Obviously my mom's work. My dad would never have done such a thing. He would have introduced me as Dan because Dan sounds more grown up and sophisticated. Still, coming from Kelly's mouth — and she did have such a lovely voice, like listening to a beautiful melody drifting on the wind — I didn't mind it one bit. In fact, she probably even preferred Danny to Dan because it sounded, I don't know…cuter. I could live with that. And now that I thought about it, maybe Danny wasn't so bad. Only in certain situations, of course. Still, it was too bad she had a boyfriend. Although, I would be surprised if she didn't because she was so beautiful. Despite all of it, I had gotten to meet her. I had actually held a conversation with a woman. I was definitely on my way! Even the Bluesman had never held a conversation with a grown woman. I'm not counting teachers or our moms' friends, of course. This was a real woman.

"So how did it go?" the Bluesman asked.

33

I looked over, and he was now right beside me, popping up out from of nowhere.

"Uh, pretty good," I said putting on a confident face. "We talked for a while and had a nice conversation. She's a really nice girl."

"I'll bet," he said chuckling.

"What?" I said looking at him.

"Nothing."

"No, what?"

"'Did...did you just say my name?'" he said imitating me perfectly and then burst out laughing.

I immediately turned red. "How did you hear that? Where were you?"

"I was crouched down behind the barrier on the next check-out. I heard the whole thing," he said and then laughed again.

I was mortified. He had heard my entire conversation, which meant he knew how much of a nerd I must have sounded like.

"Oh yeah? Well, then you heard that she called me a handsome young man and said I should have a girlfriend because I'm so handsome," I said, thinking quickly. That immediately shut the Bluesman up. He had his share of casual girlfriends, but none of them was a woman. I had him beat, and he knew it.

We stopped and looked at each other for a moment...and then started laughing and walking down the aisle again.

"You did it, man. You finally got to talk to her. I bet that just made your day."

"It did. It really did," I said thoughtfully.

I opened my Coke and began to drink it. It was the first time in months that I had had a Coke, and I had forgotten how good it really was. Still, I was a Dr. Pepper man, and I always would be. I drank half of it and then gave the other half to the Bluesman, which he quickly made disappear.

By now, we were outside the store, where our bikes were parked, Zock faithfully guarding them, and nobody messed with Zock. As we were about to pick them up and ride off, I saw something that caught my attention.

Parked near the front of the store was the largest pick-up truck I had ever seen. It was huge! It was so huge, I bet it could have been used on one of those construction sites we always wander around looking for anything good.

That reminded me about something. There was this one time the summer before — and I had never told anyone about this, especially my parents — when the Bluesman and I climbed into one of those big machines that was parked on a site where some work was being done. It was really big and similar to a bulldozer but larger and with a longer front end, if you know what I mean. I climbed into the seat and started playing with all the little gears that were sticking up out of the floor. It certainly was different than any of the cars my parents drove. How could anyone drive something like this if you constantly had to play with the gears? It seemed dangerous to me because there was so much to do.

Anyway, I noticed there was a big black button near the large, worn wheel, and I unthinkingly pushed it, not expecting anything to happen. From previous experience, I knew that you usually had to have a key to get one of these things going, just like a car. But this time the machine started up with a giant roar and slowly started to move! The Bluesman and I looked at each other in shock! We gazed ahead, and there was a row of houses ahead of us about a hundred yards away.

"Oh, crap!" we both yelled at the same time.

"We need to jump!" the Bluesman exclaimed.

"We can't! If we jump, the machine will keep going and smash into the houses!"

I immediately thought of what would happen if the machine kept up its progress and, I have to admit, I thought the image of it was pretty cool, but then I realized how wrong it was and that I had to stop this thing before any smashing could take place, not to mention the possibility of anyone getting hurt. After all, it was my fault the thing was even moving in the first place.

The Bluesman must have agreed with me because he didn't jump. "Well, do something!" he yelled in a panic.

"What?" I yelled back. It's not like I knew what I was doing or anything. I didn't even have a car yet, and this was a lot more complicated than a car.

"Move the gears around!" he screamed.

Good idea, I thought. *It's not like anything could get any worse.*

I moved the first gear that I could grab onto and pushed it forward. The giant shovel that was at the front of the machine suddenly started moving upward until it was now above us. It looked like the fist of an angry giant that was about to smash somebody.

I was wrong. Things had gotten worse. And we were getting closer to the houses!

"Try another one!" the Bluesman loudly suggested.

I moved another gear, and the machine suddenly twirled around in another direction, but we were still moving forward. Still, we had saved the houses. Actually, that was not necessarily true because the houses had been in no trouble to begin with until we came along. Still, we had saved them.

The crisis was not over, however, because we were still moving forward and picking up speed!

I frantically moved some other gears, but nothing was happening. Then I noticed some pedals in front of me and started stomping on them, thinking that one of them had to be the brake. Nothing was happening. The Bluesman and I looked at each other again and then in front of us.

There was a ditch coming up.

It wasn't like it was really deep or anything. We had seen it earlier, and it was maybe around twenty or thirty feet, but it would still cause a heck of a mess if the machine kept going. I played with some more gears and stomped on the pedals some more. Nothing.

The ditch was closer.

"It's time to go!" I yelled, getting out of the seat, and the Bluesman must have agreed with me because he got out of my way so that we were now standing on the side of the cab and looking down at the ground.

We were pretty high up. It seemed even higher than before because we were now moving. Also, the tires on this thing were like the treads on a tank and not regular wheels, so we were both pretty scared of getting caught in the tread and getting mangled up. That's how they would find us if we weren't careful – mangled up.

Still, we knew what we had to do, especially considering that the ditch was coming up pretty quickly and we didn't want to be around when it showed up.

We counted to three and jumped, hitting the ground and rolling. I don't want to get off topic here, but at that moment I felt exactly like Buck Rogers. Speaking of Buck, I was always kind of mad at him that he never tried to hook up with Wilma, who obviously liked him. She was really cute.

Once we made sure that each other was okay, we looked back at the machine in horror as it was chugging along until it came to the ditch. It suddenly went diving down and made a horrendous crashing and clanging noise that sounded louder than a gunshot! And it was still going! I mean, it wasn't moving—those days were over—but it was still making noise.

The Bluesman and I gazed at each other and then looked around the field. There was nobody around and, surprisingly, nobody seemed to have heard it and come running to see what the fuss was all about, which really was pretty incredible. I mean, if you heard something like that, wouldn't you go see what it was?

Since we were alone, we decided to refrain from running – for the moment – and go look at the machine. Once we got to the ditch and looked down, we both thought the same thing: *What a mess.*

The poor machine was almost completely on its side and looked like a dying animal that was whining in pain. I had no idea whatsoever how they were going to get it out once the workmen showed up on Monday, especially considering that they were going to need a machine even bigger than that one to pull it out. Boy, were they going to be surprised. I bet they were also going to be pretty mad. Wouldn't you be?

There's really not much to say after that because we did the only logical thing we could think of.

We ran.

Anyway, back to the giant pick-up truck. It was huge. It wasn't near as large as the machine, not by a long shot, but it was certainly larger than most of the other cars you usually see on the road.

I did remember seeing a truck similar to that one a few months earlier when it pulled up next to us while my dad and I were at a red light. My dad looked at it and grunted. He said, "The only reason a guy would drive a truck that big is because he's compensating for having a small wiener." I didn't really understand what he meant, but it must have been a joke because he was grinning when he said it. What did he mean? If a person did not like the size of their wiener, was going out and buying a truck that big suddenly going to make it grow for some reason? What difference did it make anyway, how big it was? Why would anyone want a large wiener, anyway? Wouldn't it just get in the way when they were trying to walk? That's what I thought. Besides, at that age I really didn't know what was considered a big or small one, anyway. Who cared? I figured it was just something to pee with, as if that's so important. Yes, I kind of knew about sex already, at least a little bit, and I knew the wiener came into play somehow, but I really wasn't clear on the facts and, for some reason, I felt too embarrassed to ask my dad about it…and I certainly wasn't going to ask my mom.

Anyway, about the truck. The truck itself was really no big deal—I had seen big ones before; it was the two guys standing in front of it, talking and drinking beers, who caught my attention. I looked at my watch and saw that it wasn't even ten o'clock yet. I was not sure of the proper etiquette, but I didn't think you were supposed to drink beer that early in the day. My dad hardly ever drank beer. He said beer was for rednecks and hillbillies…the kind of people you saw on *Hee Haw*. Personally, I didn't think the people on *Hee Haw* were so bad. In fact, I told Dad that I thought they were really funny, but my dad said that those were not real rednecks and hillbillies; they were friendly rednecks and hillbillies. *Real* rednecks and hillbillies were ugly, smelled bad, and were usually unemployed. That's how you could tell.

The two guys looked kind of like the people on *Hee Haw* except they were mean looking and not wearing cowboy hats and overalls, even though they were talking with southern accents. Instead, they were fat and ugly. I decided my dad was right. These guys were wearing dirty baseball caps, had beards, and were wearing clothes that looked hopelessly dirty. One of the guys was wearing a t-shirt that was too small for him. His giant, hairy belly was hanging out over his belt, and it was really quite gross to look at.

I had seen enough television shows and movies to recognize people like this, and I couldn't help but stare at them and wonder who they were or what they did with their lives. They looked like the kind of guys who would hang out all day at a low-dive bar with bad lighting and drink beers and smoke cheap cigarettes while surrounded by ugly girls with no teeth because they did not have jobs, while everyone else in the world was working, and thought there was absolutely nothing wrong with this picture.

They looked like the kind of guys who were divorced and never had any money to pay alimony and child support but could somehow always find money to go see an illegal cockfight somewhere and bet on the outcome and would think there was nothing wrong with this picture.

They looked like the kind of guys who would spend all day "fishin'" — not "fishing," but "fishin'" — on an old, tattered boat somewhere with a cooler full of warm beer as they idly joked and talked the day away while listening to the Charlie Daniels Band on a radio while everyone else was working, and would think there was nothing wrong with this picture.

They looked like the kind of guys who only liked a dumb, mindless show like *The Dukes of Hazzard* and thought it was God's gift, instead of appreciating good shows like *The A-Team* or *Knight Rider*. The only good thing about *The Dukes of Hazzard*, besides the General Lee, was Daisy Duke, who was really cute. Daisy wouldn't give these ugly guys the time of day. These guys would probably go up to her and try something only a louse would do like pinch her butt and say....

"Hey, asshole! You got a problem?"

I shook my head for a moment because I was deep in thought. Then I realized that the guy with the fat, hairy belly was talking to us – me, specifically. I looked at him and then pointed at myself.

"Yeah, you, asshole. You got a problem?" the guy said again but louder.

"No, sir," surprised that he was talking to me, even more surprised that he was cursing. You're not supposed to curse at kids. There are certain instances when it is considered okay to curse, like when your favorite football team loses the Super Bowl, but never at kids. At least that's what my dad said, and he was usually right.

"Then why are you starin' at us? You a queer boy? That it? You a queer boy?"

Now I was even more shocked and even more scared. I glanced over at the Bluesman, and I could tell he was just as scared as I was. We both knew what a queer boy was, and that was probably the worst insult you could call a guy, because it was wrong. The Bible said so. Not to mention that the very thought of it was gross.

"No, sir. I'm not one of...those."

They both walked toward us. As the guy with the giant belly moved, I could see the bottom half of his hairy mass jiggling and quaking. It might have been my imagination, but I thought I heard something swishing around inside of it. If his gut were not so flabby and doughy, I would have thought he was pregnant. We just stood there, petrified. We didn't know what they were going to do. We were hoping that they weren't going to beat us up because we were kids and we really had not done anything wrong, but these were brainless rednecks with hygiene problems, so the usual rules did not apply. Rednecks were barely human. Not only did my dad say that, my mom said it also.

Then, as they got closer, Zock, sensing trouble, walked in front of us, bared his teeth, flattened his ears, and started to growl at them. Zock was a really nice dog, but he had a temper. And if you pissed off Zock you had better watch out.

The two rednecks stopped where they were and just looked down at Zock. Then they looked at us as they assessed the situation. I am pretty sure that if they would have moved one inch closer to us, Zock would have been on them like bees on honey.

"You just best watch yourself, boy," the guy said in a mean tone, even though I could tell he was really scared of

Zock. He and his friend then slowly moved around us and walked into the store.

Once they were both gone, both the Bluesman and I let go with a sigh of relief and started breathing regularly again. Also, Zock turned back into his regular, friendly self.

"Man! That was close! I thought we were done for! Those guys were real dicks!" the Bluesman exclaimed.

"Those guys were major dicks," I said.

"I think we should get out of here before they come back," the Bluesman stated as he picked up his bike and sat on the seat.

"Wait a minute," I said getting an idea. I looked at Zock. "Zock, do you have to poo?"

Zock barked twice, which was Zockspeak for yes.

I quickly looked into the store to see if they were around the corner waiting to pounce on us, and when I saw that they weren't, I turned back around.

"Come on, Zock. Come on, boy," I cooed as I walked toward the truck with Zock trailing behind. I got behind the truck, stood on the back bumper, and then patted the top of the door, signaling Zock that I wanted him to jump up and into the truck. He easily made the leap and started sniffing around the carriage of the truck and then looked at me.

"Okay, Zock. Poo."

Zock immediately hunched into a ball and started to do his business as I looked away and smiled at the Bluesman.

He smiled back at me while shaking his head back and forth. I could tell it was taking everything he had not to burst out laughing.

A few moments later, Zock jumped out of the carriage and back onto the ground. I quickly looked at the steaming, piling mess of a present that Zock had left, grimaced, and lowered myself from the bumper and mounted my bike. We quickly rode off as we both started laughing. Even Zock, with his tongue hanging out and keeping pace with us, seemed to be laughing, also.

As we were cruising down the sidewalk next to each other, which is a pretty hard feat, and you have to be a master bike driver to even attempt it, the Bluesman looked over at me. "So, what do you want to do now?"

"Well, do you feel like going swimming?"

The Bluesman looked at me and grinned. He knew how much I like to go swimming at the club, and he had me up on this particular one. His family were members of the local country club and could go there whenever they want to swim, play tennis, eat, whatever. The club even had a small arcade. It wasn't as good as the one at Sunrise Mall, and it didn't have a Tron machine, but it was still very nice. I had to depend on the Bluesman to get me in as a guest because my parents believed it was a waste of time to join a country club. The reason was that, except for the summer, they would hardly ever use it and, besides, the Bluesman could get me in for free, anyway. It wasn't really a matter of money. My dad was an insurance salesman, so we certainly weren't hurting. In fact, ever since I could remember, we'd gone to Las Vegas every year.

That might not sound like a lot of fun for someone the age I was, but it really was. We used to stay at the MGM Grand before it burned down. They had a nursery there for parents to drop their kids off while they went about doing their daily gambling. It was pretty cool because I always met some nice kids from all over the country to play with. And when I wasn't there, my parents always took me to *Circus Circus* and some other neat places to see. I wasn't old enough to get into any of the shows yet, but I still had fun. In fact, my favorite part out of all of it was the plane ride. Anyway, I don't want you to think we were destitute or anything.

"Sounds like fun. Why don't you go home and change and then head back over to my house so we can cruise over?"

"Sounds cool."

We came to a certain street and I veered left while the Bluesman kept going. We waved to each other, and I raced home as quickly as I could. I was going so fast you could hear the loud hum of my tires on the street, though Zock was still easily able to keep up with me. In fact, he could probably have beaten me if he'd wanted to.

I parked my bike in the garage and headed inside to my room. Looking through my dresser, I found my swimsuit and quickly put it on and then looked down at myself. I really hated how my body looked when I wore my swimsuit. At thirteen I was very thin and had no muscles at all. The fact that I had no hair anywhere except for what was on my head (and down there) just seemed to make it worse. It would have been nice to have some muscles. I kept meaning to start exercising, but then something more interesting to do always came along. I figured I'd worry about it later.

I went to the closet in the hall and pulled out my Superman towel. It was my favorite towel, and I used it only on special occasions like going to the country club or the beach. After that I walked into the living room, where my mom was sitting on the couch reading a book. This would not last long because the soap operas would be coming on soon. I think her favorite one was called *As the World Turns*. To me, though they were all the same. Everyone was good-looking, and the girls were always crying about something. She liked soap operas so much, she even watched them at night – *Dallas* and *Dynasty*. Just more of the same. Although *Dallas* was better because it had J.R. Ewing, who had to be the best bad guy ever!

"Hey, Mom. I'm going to go meet the Bluesman at the club. I'll probably be gone for a few hours."

"Okay, dear. Be careful and stay out of the sun or you'll get burned."

"Okay, Mom."

I looked down at Zock, who was looking up at me expectantly. I felt sad that I had to break the news to him. "Sorry, boy. No dogs allowed at the club. I don't want to take you with me —you'll just get bored waiting for us in the parking lot."

Zock seemed to understand because he just looked at me for a moment and then went to lie down in his favorite spot in front of the television. I think he was tired from all that running, anyway. Besides, I think he preferred to watch the soap operas. Sometimes he just lay there and watched television, and sometimes I really believed he understood everything that was going on. Whenever there was another dog on the screen he really took notice and sometimes even sat up.

I had everything I needed, so I headed back to my bike and raced through the neighborhood with my towel flapping around my neck like a cape. Soon, I was back at the Bluesman's house. I parked my bike by the door and looked at it. The door was cracked open, which he always did when he knew I was coming over. It was so that I could just walk in and wouldn't have to bother ringing the bell or knocking on the door. I walked in and looked around. "Hey, Bluesman! I'm here!" I yelled. I didn't yell it too loud. I didn't want to be rude, but I yelled loud enough that anyone in the house could hear me wherever they were.

A moment later, Marie walked into the room with a mean look on her face, with the Bluesman walking behind her. He was repeatedly patting her on the head. She walked all the way around the room, and the Bluesman kept up with his patting, all the while with a grin on his face.

Several months earlier, the Bluesman had gotten into the habit of patting his little sister on the head all the time,

45

much to her annoyance. It wasn't enough to hurt. I mean, it wasn't like he was hitting her or anything, just patting. I don't know where he'd gotten the idea to do it, but I thought it was genius! It annoyed her so much at first that she would go ballistic whenever he did it, which just encouraged him to do it even more. By now it had become a common ritual, and nobody knew how long it would last. As I watched them, I had a funny image in my mind of both of them old and gray, sitting on a porch somewhere, and he was still patting her on the head.

Eventually, he stopped, and she just went to the couch and picked up the remote control so she could watch television. I don't know why she bothered. There was absolutely nothing good on at that time of day, daytime television being atrocious. All that was on was soap operas. If you didn't have cable, you were pretty much sunk. Fortunately, they had cable. As she was flipping around the channels, she came to HBO and I recognized *Star Trek II: The Wrath of Khan.*

"Stop!" the Bluesman and I yelled at the same time, so loudly that it made Marie jump in her seat.

"You two idiots are about to go swimming, so leave me alone! Besides, that's a stupid movie. All those space movies are stupid!" she yelled back.

I could think of at least a dozen space movies off the top of my head that were definitely not stupid. Girls just did not appreciate good drama unless it involved a lot of kissing and hugging with bad music in the background, and too much of that was, in my opinion, gross. I liked action!

We decided to let her have the television because she was right. About us leaving, that is, not about space movies being stupid. Besides, if we got involved in the movie, we wouldn't be leaving for at least an hour.

"Hey, Ma! I gotta take a whiz!" the Bluesman yelled.

"Okay, dear," an adult voice came from somewhere in the house, and Marie grimaced in disgust.

46

For some reason, the Bluesman had gotten into the habit of announcing his bathroom activities. I think the main reason was just so he can find something else to annoy his parents with, as kids tend to do. But this had kind of backfired on him because his parents just ignored it. Here's what I had decided: I decided that his parents were attempting to pull some reverse psychology on him. If they just ignored it, then he'd see that he wasn't getting any attention or any reaction, and he'd stop doing it. Well, they were wrong. The Bluesman had easily figured out what they were doing, and now he just did it out of habit. What's more, he did it every time he had to use the bathroom, for anything, no matter what. He even announced when he was about to brush his teeth or cut his fingernails or toenails. To add insult to injury, he called his mom and dad "Ma" and "Pa." Now, this was something that only rednecks did, like on *The Beverly Hillbillies*. Kids who lived in the suburbs did not call their parents "Ma" and "Pa." It sounded disrespectful...or at least, that's what I thought.

Still, the Bluesman was doing it all in good fun, so there was really no harm. The only person who seemed to be annoyed at all times by the Bluesman was Marie. She even thought the name "The Bluesman" was stupid. Personally, I thought she was jealous of him. The Bluesman was so naturally funny and quick-witted, it really was striking. But every time Marie tried to tell a joke, it fell as flat as a pancake. It infuriated her because the Bluesman could take anything and make it funny. In fact, I was willing to go out on a limb and say that the Bluesman was almost as funny as Robin Williams. Now, *that* is funny!

As the Bluesman was doing his business – I could hear him because he purposely left the door open to get a reaction, which never came – I walked around the living room and looked around. There were model airplanes everywhere. Before you get the wrong idea, the Bluesman did not leave toys lying around the house. These models were all built by his father, which was one of his hobbies, and they really were incredible to look at. The details were so intricate it was astounding! Most of them were WWII planes like a B-17 Flying Fortress, a B-24 Liberator, a P-51 Mustang, a Spitfire, a Corsair, and a Messerschmitt. Some of them even had their own detailed crash sites made for them, and they looked completely real, even leaving a trail behind the plane in the makeshift dirt so it gave the impression that when the plane crashed, it slid along the ground until it finally came to a stop. Mr. Richards was really talented.

The Bluesman showed up a few moments later.

"Ma! Everything came out okay! I lost six pounds!"

"Okay, dear."

Marie grimaced in disgust and kept switching the channels.

"You ready to go?" he asked.

"Ready and willing."

He walked behind the couch and patted Marie on the head a few times, and then we were off.

After a short trip, we arrived at the club and parked our bikes on the bike stand, which was already more than partway full. Apparently, a lot of the other kids had had the same idea as us. Considering how hot it was, I couldn't blame them. There were even a good number of cars in the parking lot.

We walked up to the front booth and saw the same older woman who's usually there, sitting behind a window. I estimated she was about fifty, but I could have been wrong. The Bluesman showed her his club card, and all he had to do was sign in.

Now, there was a problem because a member could invite the same guest only three times in a one-month period, no more. I sometimes used up my guest passes in a week, never mind a month! So, we had devised a plan —

and to my knowledge, a lot of the other kids used this same method. Every time I came up to the club, I changed my name. She never asked for my identification. All she did was look under the Bluesman's name, Keith Richards, and check to see when the last time he'd had a guest was, to see if my name was on it. If I wasn't there, I could go in. Simple. In fact, it was so simple; I started having some fun with it. Some of the names I'd given her were: Rob Halford, Eddie Van Halen, David Lee Roth, Randy Rhoads, Joe Elliott, Bruce Dickinson, Angus Young, Paul Stanley, and Gene Simmons. She never even flinched. She was so old, she'd probably never even heard of any of them, which was astounding! That's what I thought, anyway. There were so many kids going in and out on a daily basis, she never remembered any of them. Or, if she did, she surely didn't seem to care.

Once we were in the club, we made our way to pool area and, not surprisingly, it was the most populated place of the club. I loved going to the pool area because besides getting to go swimming and cool off, there were usually some girls who were older than us wandering around, and they tended to wear bikinis. I always hoped to see Kelly there, since I assumed she lived in the same neighborhood as the store she worked in, but no luck. I was willing to bet she looked incredible in a bikini!

Looking around, I was not disappointed. There were beautiful girls everywhere! Summer at the club was always heaven! Even the Bluesman had a grin on his face as we traded looks. This was going to be a great day! The only thing that made me sad was the fact that not only was I so much younger than them, my skinny, muscle-deprived body looked like something you would find in a toy store. If I'd had some hair on my chest, that would have at least helped a little.

That reminds me, I have been so busy telling you about the girls I liked, I've completely neglected the Bluesman's tastes. Like me, he liked attractive, sophisticated women, and he tended to prefer blondes more than anything. In fact, to give you an example, he was a fan of the Heathers. I say "the Heathers" because there were at that time two Heathers on television who he liked: Heather Thomas and Heather Locklear. Heather Thomas was famous for being on *The Fall Guy*, which was a show I thought was great, and Lee Majors was cool. Before that, he had been the Six Million Dollar Man, which was also a cool show. Heather Thomas was a beautiful blonde, and I could perfectly understand why the Bluesman liked her. I especially liked the episodes when she wore a bikini, like in the opening credits when she appeared opening some small bar doors.

The other Heather he liked was Heather Locklear. Heather Locklear was famous for being on two shows, which I had no idea how she managed to do – *T.J. Hooker* and *Dynasty*. Now, to me, *T.J. Hooker* was the better show because it was about the police and there was more action. Also, *T.J. Hooker* had Captain Kirk in it. I knew his name was really William Shatner, but he would always be Captain Kirk to me. The other show, *Dynasty*, was a sleeper because it was just a soap opera. Although, I kind of liked the lady who played Alexis, though I could never think of her name. There were some other cute girls on the show, but Heather was the most beautiful. I thought they were both attractive and they both seemed nice, but I would have liked to combine them somehow. If I could have taken Heather Locklear's face and hair and put it on Heather Thomas's body, the result, to my thinking, would have been the perfect woman!

I wondered if they might be able to do that in the future sometime, a guy wanting to have his perfect mate built for him, both mentally and physically, and she would be the perfect match for him because she would be made just for him…using his brainwaves or something. That would be the perfect woman! There would be no reason for them to fight or anything because she would basically be the same as him because of the brainwaves, and who would want to fight with yourself? It's not impossible. Still, I figured that would have to be…at least fifty years in the future. I was sure it would make a great book or movie.

We found an empty lawn chair to put our stuff on and then proceeded to the pool. I stuck my toe in to gauge the temperature, and it was perfect! Not too cool, not too hot. Perfect! Since we were already at the deep end, we sat down on the edge and slowly lowered ourselves in.

This was really cool because I had recently taught myself to be able to open my eyes underwater. I had been trying and trying for months because I knew the summer was coming up. I wanted to master the art of it so I wouldn't have to wear a mask or goggles all the time and look like some sort of creature. Every chance I got, I practiced opening my eyes in the water by sticking my face in the sink after I filled it up, or when I took a bath. I usually took a shower, but every now and then I would take a bath for the express purpose of practicing. I just could not get it down, and I was getting really frustrated because everyone could do it except me. I bet even Zock could do it if he had to. Then, one day, it just happened. All of that practicing had finally paid off and I was doing it! I was ecstatic!

On the edge of the pool, I found a penny, and I showed it to the Bluesman. We took turns letting it float to the bottom and then seeing who could swim all the way to the bottom, grab it, and then make it back to the surface faster. We were pretty close, but he won three out of five. The only reason was because I was still getting used to the sensation of opening my eyes underwater. That's what I think.

Once we were done with that, we just swam and floated around while the sun shone down on us. The popular pop radio station was playing from the speakers in the area and

"Centerfold" from the J. Geils Band came on, which used to be my favorite song before I discovered hard rock. I had seen the video on MTV a hundred times, and it was really cool because it had all of those girls in it.

For a while, we just floated off to the side of the pool and watched some people dive from the diving boards, and a lot of them were pretty good. There were two boards, one that was just hovering a few feet over the water, and the other one that was really way up there. I'd gone off the smaller one numerous times, and I was okay at it. The other one I was scared of and had jumped from it only once. And I held my nose and jumped feet-first when I did it, so it wasn't very graceful. As bad as that was, the Bluesman had never jumped from it at all, so I had him there.

"So what do you want to do tomorrow?" he said as we floated.

I had not even thought about what to do the next day. I had just assumed we were going to go swimming again. In fact, I had already picked the name I was going to use – Jimmy Page.

"I don't know. What do you want to do?"

"I was thinking about riding out to Goatman's and doing some exploring."

That actually sounded like a good idea because we had not been out to Goatman's in at least six months. We would usually spend up to the whole day there exploring because there was always so much to see. The only thing bad about it was that it took over an hour and a half to get out there, and after doing that, exploring, and then riding back, it made for a very exhausting day. Still, it sounded like fun and I was up for it. "That sounds cool."

"We should pick out at least one other person to go with us this time."

"Why?"

52

"Just to make it more fun. We usually go alone, and we should include some other people to make it more of a...what do you call it? Not an adventure...an expedition."

"We can take Zock."

"I meant a human being."

"Oh. Have anyone in mind?"

"I'm not sure," he said as we began to look around to see if we could get any ideas, since there were some kids there who we knew.

On the other side of the pool, floating with some friends, we saw Matt Distler, who was known as "The Thunderer." Matt was famous for being able to belch on command. It really was incredible because he didn't need a soda or anything — he could just do it anytime he wanted. And when I say belch, I mean he could really unleash! Legend had it that if he was on one side of the school and the wind was just right; he could unleash and be heard all the way to the other side. THAT, ladies and gentlemen, is talent. There was this one time when we were crank-calling people, and this old woman picked up the phone, and he belched at her. It must have frightened her something fierce because she immediately screamed in horror and then the phone went dead. We both looked at each other, wondering what had happened. I hoped she was alright. All the guys thought it was great, but, for some reason, the girls were not in awe of it as much as we were. Some people just do not appreciate real talent. As far as we were concerned, he was a better athlete than anyone on the football team.

Walking down by a row of chairs with his little brother was Jason Hawkins, whom we christened "Sperm Cell." The reason he was called "Sperm Cell" is that one day the year before, he got bored in class and got caught drawing a giant sperm cell on his desk. I mean it was huge and had a giant, swirling tail! It took up the whole desk! Also, it was drawn with a permanent marker, so the custodian was never able to get it off. The teacher took him to the office and, schools being what they are, news travelled fast, and before the end of the day everyone was calling him "Sperm Cell." Yet again, all the guys thought he was cool, but the girls avoided him like the plague because they thought he was weird. I mean, who would draw a sperm cell of all things on a desk? A sex maniac, that's who. It really was a shame because I knew him and he was really a pretty nice guy. He was also a very gifted artist and could draw all the superheroes like nobody's business! I'd seen his stuff, and he was really that good, believe me! It wouldn't have surprised me if he'd grown up to draw for one of those comic book companies.

On the far side of the pool, walking toward the area where you can buy hamburgers, hot dogs, and other cool stuff was Larry Zimmerman. Larry Zimmerman was a sight. At thirteen years old, Larry Zimmerman was already 6'2" and probably weighed just a little more than us. He was incredibly thin, had buck teeth, severe acne, and a concave chest, and because he was so tall and not used to dealing with his height, he walked bent slightly forward and hunched over, as if someone had attached an invisible piece of string to the top of his head and he was being pulled along against his will. Plus, his skinny arms looked longer than they should and hung beside him like long strips of uncooked bacon.

Larry liked Bea Peters.

Bea Peters was a really cute and friendly Mexican girl who had sat in front of me in Science class the year before. Bea was the same age as us and already had huge boobs. They were not as big as Dolly's, but they were pretty darn close. They were certainly the biggest boobs I'd ever seen in real life. For some reason, Mexican girls seemed to develop earlier than everyone else, and there were certainly a lot of cute Mexican girls at our school. Legend had it that Bea had a boyfriend who was in high school and even had his own car. Because of her unique and high standing, none of the boys at our school had even considered trying to get friendly with her. For all we knew, her boyfriend was a knife-wielding maniac with a prison record. We'd heard the rumors of people who went to high school and how it drove most people crazy before they reached their senior year. My dad said it wasn't true, but I was still dreading it. School was already hard enough as it was without my being driven crazy.

One day, Larry made the drastic error of telling someone that he had a crush on Bea Peters. Big mistake. It was all around the school before lunch. Bea eventually found out about it and did everything she could to avoid him. Because of his appearance, most of the girls considered Larry a monster. I knew Larry, and he was really a nice guy. He was also very smart and had already started a business. A couple of years earlier he'd been playing around in the attic of his house and discovered a rather sizeable collection of porn magazines that belonged to his dad, which he had probably forgotten about. There were probably close to a hundred! *Playboy, Penthouse, Hustler*...you name it, and it was there!

Anyway, Larry, being a really brainy guy, saw this as an opportunity to make some money. He moved the collection of magazines and kept them stacked neatly in some boxes in his closet that he kept hidden under some old clothes. Once he was ready to open his business he announced what he had discovered, and word quickly got around. When his parents were not home, you could come over to his house and, for a dollar, you could spend a half hour in his room looking through porn magazines all you wanted. There were only two rules: 1) You had to keep everything nice and neat and 2) No "funny business," if you know what I mean. If you felt the need to...take care of yourself...you would just have to wait until you were at home. Larry made a fortune, and word spread everywhere! The previous summer he must have made somewhere over a hundred dollars and was on his way to building an empire. It would not have surprised me in the least if he'd become the first of all of us to own a car. I always figured, who knows what he'll be capable of when he grows up. I figured he'd probably even wind up being a millionaire, and then he'd be able to get any girl he wanted. He might even have been able to get Bea Peters. It didn't seem impossible.

Walking behind us and staring up at the sky was Alex Martinez. Alex was known as "The Wanderer." The reason was that he was always staring up at the sky. Alex had this habit of always walking around and staring upward, with his hands in his pockets. He hardly ever looked straight ahead. Even when you were standing right in front of him and talking to him, he kept staring up at the sky. In class, he tended to unnerve the teachers because while they were lecturing, he stared up at the ceiling the whole time. This alone was weird enough, but on top of that was the fact that he hardly ever said anything. For the first couple of weeks that I had a class with him, I didn't even know if he could speak English. Also, at thirteen, he already had a moustache. Now, I had no clue why he stared up all the time. I figured maybe he was looking out to see if aliens were going to land. If aliens ever did invade the earth, I was sure he'd be the first person to know about it. It would not have surprised me one bit if Alex had grown up to be an astronomer.

The Bluesman and I talked about it and considered all of them but decided that none of them was really suitable for our little trip. Some of them might be fun, but all of them had the common trait of being the kind of person who would get on your nerves if you were around them for too long. My dad said that about a lot of the people at his office, so you probably know what I mean.

We were starting to get kind of hot lying out in the sun, even though we were in the water, so we decided to go spend some time in the arcade. The arcade at the club had some pretty good machines, including a Defender. Unfortunately, they didn't have a Tron. As I stated earlier, I was the best there was at Tron, though I was only pretty good at Defender. This meant that I was probably going to be taking some punishment from the Bluesman. We toweled off and headed for the arcade. Fortunately, the Bluesman always kept a little pouch of quarters handy when we came to the country club.

As we were heading to the arcade we passed near the entrance, and I stopped in my tracks. There, walking in with a few friends of hers was Amelia Shutterbug.

I had a crush on Amelia Shutterbug like you could not believe! In fact, I liked her just as much as, if not more than, Kelly. That was her name – Amelia – which I thought was a really beautiful name, but everyone called her Amy, which I thought kind of cheapened it. It's the same type of thing with a person called...well, Thomas/Tom, for example. When you think of a Thomas, the person who comes to mind is a very handsome, sophisticated man with perfectly combed blond hair, in a nice suit, who has an air of confidence that is unmistakable and has a knack for hooking up with the ladies. When you reduce it to Tom, though, you think of a fat idiot wearing a straw hat and a pair of overalls who scratches his butt all the time, has a drooling problem, and has a laugh like a hyena... if you know what I mean.

Amelia had been living here for only about a year because her family had moved up from San Antonio. She really was a sight to see because not only was she so beautiful, she was a few inches taller than all of the girls and almost all the boys. She was certainly a little taller than both the Bluesman and I. Amelia had long blonde hair, beautiful blue eyes, nice creamy skin, and a melodious voice. Also, even as young as she was then, a body to absolutely die for! She looked exactly like some of the beautiful girls on television, the ones that they made out in California. A friend of mine said that they actually breed them there through a special technique. While I didn't know if that was really true or not, it wouldn't have surprised me. My mom said that California is where all the crazy stuff always happened, and if you lived there for a certain number of years, you'd flip out. California is also where both of the Heathers are from. I would never have said it to her face, but I thought Amelia could easily grow up to be an actress or a model or something. It wasn't impossible.

Amelia was really beautiful, but there was one thing that you immediately noticed about her when she smiled: her braces. She had them on when she moved to Corpus Christi, and she still had them on when school ended. I was assuming she still had them on when I saw her at the club, though I hadn't seen her in about a week.

The first time I met her, I was really nervous because she was so beautiful and I had to concentrate to keep from staring at her because I didn't want her to think I was a weirdo or anything. I guess I shouldn't have been so nervous because she was probably used to being stared at. Someone told me that she even had one of those talent agents who help you get on television. It wouldn't surprise me. To me she was even more beautiful than both of the two Heathers put together. Although, the braces could be a problem. Still, I knew she wouldn't be wearing them forever.

When we first met, I wanted to do something different from all the other guys who she probably always talked to. I was sure that most guys said the usual things like complimenting her on her eyes or hair or something like that. I wanted to do something different to stand out. A friend of hers and I were walking up to her, so she could introduce me to her, and my mind was racing with something to say, and my ideas were all mixing together because I thought they were all good but all terrible at the same time, if you know what I mean. We were getting closer, and I was thinking really hard about exactly what to say because this was going to be my one chance to make a good first impression, and making a good first impression is really important, especially with girls. I was really nervous, and I was finding it difficult to think straight because she was so beautiful and everything. Finally, we were standing in front of her, and her friend introduced me to her, and she smiled at me with that beautiful smile of hers.

"How's it going, Track Tooth?" I said. *Stupid! I'm blowing it!*

She immediately beat me up. Literally! Apparently, Amelia had a "thing" about her braces.

It was the first time I realized how strong Amelia really was. She also said it was the most original opening line she had ever heard. Since then, we'd become pretty good friends, and we usually saw each other all the time. I don't know if you could have called her my girlfriend or anything like that because we had never kissed or anything, but she was certainly more than just a casual friend. Remember when I told Kelly that I wasn't really sure if I had a girlfriend or not? Amelia was who I had been referring to.

After we first met, I would always say something to get her attention. I would call her things like "Track Tooth," "Metal Mouth," "Iron Fang," and "Rail Tooth." This may sound cruel, but it was really our little game because nobody called her names like that. The few who tried received such a beating that they never did it again. When she beat me up, she just did it in a rough but playful way, and I loved it. I think we both did. This was really the beginning of our strange but beautiful and more than casual relationship. When we were playing outside somewhere, I would call her whatever name I had handy, and then she would beat me up. Afterward, I would invite her over to my house so we could watch television or whatever. It was really my way of asking her out, and it worked every time, because she would feel guilty about beating me up. Frankly, I thought it was pretty smooth. It was certainly original, and originality is what it's all about when it comes to women. I learned that on television.

I think the reason she beat me up all the time was because she was my unofficial girlfriend, and that's what girlfriends are supposed to do. She didn't seem to object because she could have easily been spending her time with any guy in the school. So, I guessed she was my girlfriend, technically speaking. Relationships can be complicated. That's what my dad always said, and he was pretty smart.

The Bluesman looked over at me and grinned.

"There's your girlfriend," he informed me, and I blushed. He knew how much I liked her, and my holding back how much I liked her makes it even more obvious how much I liked her. "Let's go up and say hello."

"Okay," I said, not objecting, acting as though I were just doing it as a favor for him, even though we both knew that I wanted to. I was wearing nothing but my swimsuit, and now more than ever, I really wished I had some muscles.

As we drew closer to her and her friends, I really took in the one-piece swimsuit she was wearing. I mean, I had seen her in a swimsuit before, of course, but now...something was happening. She was starting to grow boobs. I tried to remember if they had been there the previous week. They must not have been because I surely would have noticed them.

We were now standing in front of them, and when she saw me, she smiled in pleasant surprise. Yep, she was still wearing her braces.

"Oh, hi, Danny," she said. Yes, she called me Danny, and you know how much I loved that. Still, coming from her, I didn't mind it one bit.

"Hey, Amelia," I replied. Yes, I called her Amelia. I was one of the few people who did. "So, you're at the club, today?" I asked, which was really stupid because she was standing there right in front of me, so she obviously was. Despite the length of time that we'd known each other, I was still always kind of nervous around her. I was even more nervous than usual right then because she was wearing her swimsuit and had the beginnings of boobs.

"Yeah, it's a nice day, so we all decided to get together and spend the day in the pool," she said, looking at her group of friends.

"That's cool," I intoned, and I really thought it was because I always enjoyed being around Amelia. We actually did have a lot in common, although she didn't really like hard rock, which I couldn't understand at all. She didn't even like *KISS*, which I thought should be against the law. Like the Bluesman, her favorite band was *Duran Duran*, which seemed to be the favorite of most girls. She really liked that Simon LeBon guy. That kind of burned me up because he was a good-looking guy, and he probably had muscles.

"Hello, Keith," she said, and the Bluesman's face fell. Amelia was one of the few remaining kids who called the Bluesman "Keith," and I knew she did it to burn him up. Personally, I thought it was a sign of disrespect. Keith was the Bluesman for one reason – he was famous — and famous people should be respected. Still, she did it in a playful way because she knew what he wanted to hear and wasn't giving it to him, so I guess it wasn't cruel, technically speaking. Girls have always been real good at driving boys crazy.

"Hey, Amy," he said, and this didn't bother Amelia at all because she's fine with either "Amelia" or "Amy." You probably noticed that the Bluesman did not open up with any of the names that I mentioned when referring to Amelia's braces. The reason for this is simple – the Bluesman did not have a death wish. He actually tried it once, and he received a beating that was so severe he actually didn't come to school the next day. I really didn't think it was that bad. I mean, it wasn't like he had to go to the hospital or anything; it was just the fact that he was beaten up by a girl, and he didn't want to show his face and thought that if he gave it a day everyone would forget about it. It didn't work, though, and when he arrived, laughter abounded. Still, it made me feel kind of special that I could call her a name once in a while and get away with it. I mean, I still got beat up, but it was in a playful way. I loved it.

"So, how long have you guys been here?" she asked.

I said, "I guess about forty minutes."

"Do you want to go swimming?"

We had just gone swimming and were about to go play in the arcade, which I was really looking forward to, so I said…

"Sure, that sounds good."

I could play in the arcade later. Relationships are all about making sacrifices. I learned that from either my dad or watching television — I forget which.

The Bluesman didn't really seem to mind either. He now had Amelia's two girlfriends to spend some time with, and both of them were kind of cute. Not as cute as Amelia, but pretty darn close. The Bluesman had a way with the ladies. He was not only a funny guy who everyone liked, he was also famous, and so he had the best of both worlds going for him. He didn't have a girlfriend yet, but I was pretty sure that situation was going to change soon. As long as he stayed away from Amelia, there wouldn't be a problem, but I didn't think he would really go after her anyway because he knew how much I liked her. Besides, I didn't think he would ever be comfortable being around a girl who had beaten him up.

Because we were with the girls we had to walk all the way to the other side of the pool, which is the shallow end, so they could slowly walk into the water instead of just lowering themselves into the deep end from the steel ladder like we did. I don't know why we bothered because we were more than likely going to end up in the deep end anyway, but it wasn't really a big deal or anything.

Once we were in the pool and swimming around, we started playing with the beachball that one of Amelia's friends had brought and started getting a game going on of throwing it around to each other, which was pretty fun. After a while, Amelia started getting kind of tired and drifted off to the side. I didn't want to leave her all alone, so I drifted along beside her. I still wanted to play the game, but it wasn't really a big deal if I stopped. We eventually drifted off to the deep end, like I knew we would, and leaned against the wall by the ladder as we talked and watched people dive from the boards.

She looked really beautiful with her hair wet. In fact, she looked so beautiful I was glad that we were floating in the water and not standing up walking around the club, if you know what I mean. Plus, in the water, we were exactly the same height. It's not like I had a complex about it or anything; she just happened to be a little taller than I was, which I thought was really kind of cool for some reason.

The diving seemed to be over for a while, and we just looked at each other and talked as we held on to either side of the ladder.

I'm not really sure how to explain what happened next, but I'll do my best. As we were talking, we each started drifting closer to one other until we were now right in front of each other. I think she wanted me to kiss her. It's not like I was really sure or anything because we had never kissed, and I had never kissed a girl before and, to my knowledge, she had never kissed a guy. If she had, I never found out about it. Then again, if she had kissed another guy, I doubt she would have told me anyway. I mean, why would she? Just like if I had ever kissed another girl, I would never have told her about it. Then again, she probably would have found out about it if I had because girls can find out anything. I don't know how they do it, but they do. Anyway, I really got the strong impression that she wanted me to kiss her. The way she had drifted closer to me and especially the way that she was looking at me and being kind of quiet was a pretty good indication. I mean, the only times girls are ever quiet is when they want something because they are usually always talking. So, I was pretty sure she wanted something and that the something she wanted was for me to kiss her.

I have to say, it was a pretty romantic setting. We were both wet and floating in the pool, and it was such a nice day and everything, it seemed like it was the perfect time for a kiss. She drifted a little closer to me and was still looking at me. Usually when someone is staring at you, it can creep you out, but coming from her it was pretty cool because she was beautiful and everything. I made up my mind right there that since everything was perfect; I was going to kiss her. It was going to be the best kiss that she had ever had…if she had ever been kissed before, I mean…and the very thought of that burned me up; this one was going to be even better. It's not like I had any experience or anything, but I was determined that it was going to be a really good kiss. There was only one thing that stopped me.

The braces.

I don't really mind them or anything, and they're certainly ripe material for jokes as long as I don't push it too far and hurt her feelings, which is something that I would never do. I was just worried about what would happen if I kissed her. I had heard stories of boys kissing girls with braces and their lips getting caught in them and getting them hung and mangled up. In fact, I remember this one story about how a boy and a girl had to go to the emergency room because they were stuck together, and by the time the doctor had finally gotten them apart, his lip was all mangled up. I don't think any kind of kiss would be worth all of that. I mean, I'm sure it would be nice at first, but the end result could be very dangerous. Speaking of which, I wonder what would happen if two people who had braces kissed. I suppose they would get locked together, and they would have to go to the hospital so the doctor could use some special equipment to pry them apart. I bet that would something pretty funny to see, two people stuck together like that.

Amelia was waiting.

Fine. I'm going to kiss her. I was sure that if I was really careful, my lip would not get caught and get mangled up. Maybe that boy had kissed her in the wrong way. I knew there was a type of kissing called French kissing, where you're supposed to stick your tongue in each other's mouth as you're kissing. It sounded gross to me and, from what I'd heard, it seemed to be popular only among people who were dating and not married. So far as I knew, once you got married you weren't supposed to kiss like that anymore. I had never asked my dad about it, though, because he would only have asked why I wanted to know, and I wouldn't really have had an answer for him, and then he would have asked me where I had heard about it, and I didn't really want to go there. He still hadn't given me the talk about the birds and the bees yet. I mean, I already knew about all of that, I thought. I had half an idea about how the guy was supposed to stick his wiener in the girl's bellybutton to make a baby. Still, that's something that fathers are supposed to tell their sons, and as far as I knew, they looked forward to it, and I didn't want to spoil it for him.

I think Amelia was getting annoyed that I was taking so long.

Fine. Here I go. I just had to remember to be careful.

I drifted closer to her as we looked into each other's eyes, and I was about to finally kiss her, something that I had been thinking about for some time, and this was it an-

"Hey, you guys want to head to the arcade?"

We looked up at the Bluesman. He had a smile on his face, and I could tell that he had no idea that he had appeared at the most inopportune moment. Just a few more seconds was all I would have needed.

We gazed at each other and then laughed like we had just been talking and joking around, even though we weren't at the time, and then looked back up at him.

"Sure. Sounds like fun," I said.

We climbed out of the pool on the ladder, me letting Amelia go first because I am a gentleman, and then I got out.

Stupid! I blew it! It was a perfect opportunity and I blew it!

Once we were all toweled off, we proceeded to the arcade and started looking around at the various machines. The arcade was really nice and cozy, and we were the only ones in there at the time, for some reason. The entire room was brown with wood paneling on the walls, and the carpet was a lighter shade. As soon as you walked in, you were in the sitting area, where there were four plastic tables surrounded by chairs. Off to the right by the food window were several high tables and chairs. There were about eight machines and also a pool table, a foosball table, and an air hockey machine. The air conditioner in the room was kind of loud, but it gave off a nice humming noise that I thought was actually kind of pleasant once you got used to it because it seemed to have its own rhythm going on. There were even a couple of vending machines on the other side in case you were thirsty or hungry for a snack. It really was a nice little arcade. In fact, I'd been there at night before, and I liked it even more that way. I guess just because it was night and everything. In a strange way, even though it was just an arcade, it made it even more…romantic. I know how weird that must sound. I had never done anything remotely romantic there or anywhere, but it was romantic just the same.

As I stated earlier, they did not have a Tron, which was annoying. I wanted to show Amelia how great I was at Tron because I was quite sure she would have been impressed. I really did not want her to see me play Defender against the Bluesman because he would slaughter me, and that would be embarrassing.

Also, I wasn't really sure, but I think she was disappointed that I hadn't kissed her. The way she was looking at me, it was kind of weird. There seemed to be a kind of sadness in her eyes. It was not like it was really obvious, but I could see it. Now I felt terrible. I should have stopped taking so long and just done it. Even if my lip had gotten caught in her braces, it would have been worth it. Now, it seemed as though I had hurt her feelings, and that made me feel lousy because I really liked her and everything. I didn't want to just do it now because it wasn't romantic or anything like it had been back then in the pool. I wanted to make it up to her, so I said the only thing I could think of, and I was hoping she would appreciate me trying to be romantic again: "Would you like me to buy you a hot dog?"

"Sure. That would be nice." She smiled, and I smiled back at her. I walked over to the window where a person could order food and ordered two hot dogs and sodas. Once I received them, I gave her one of each, and then we sat at the high table and ate and talked while we watched the Bluesman and Amelia's friends play games.

That was one of the most beautiful moments of my life. I didn't know how Amelia felt about it, but I was treasuring every second of it. We had that whole nice arcade to ourselves, and everything just felt…so right. Here I was in one of my favorite places, and I was sharing it with the person I liked most in the world. I mean, I also liked the Bluesman and my parents, of course, but Amelia was special to me in a way that they weren't. We could hear the radio in there, and a song called "Waiting for a Girl Like You" by a group called *Foreigner* came on, which was one of my favorite songs. I was still mainly into hard rock, but that was one of my favorite songs and had been since I'd first heard it a couple of years earlier. I'd never told the Bluesman that because I wasn't sure if he would laugh or not. Anyway, sitting there like that in the arcade and looking at Amelia and with the song playing, I felt really good. I almost thought of trying to kiss her again because it felt like the thing to do…but I didn't. Even though I wanted to and it seemed like the right thing to do, it didn't seem like the right time anymore. That moment had already passed, if you know what I mean.

"This is one of my favorite songs," I said, and she looked at me. I almost expected her to start laughing at me because guys are not supposed to like love songs like this. Instead, she said…

"Mine, too."

It was right then that I thought that she was feeling exactly the same way I was. I wasn't totally sure, but I liked to think so.

We smiled at each other and proceeded to eat our food as we talked for a while. I don't want you to think that we were being rude or anything by not including the Bluesman or Amelia's friends in with our conversation or joining in with them. They were having a good time playing games and cheering each other on. I also got the sense that they wanted to leave the two of us alone because they knew we wanted to spend some time alone together. It was an unspoken but realized thing, if you know what I mean.

After we were done, I asked Amelia if she wanted to play air hockey, which I was pretty good at, and she agreed. We walked to the opposite sides of the table and, after I put some money in, we were off. I easily made the first score. However, Amelia came into her own very quickly, and we had a really good game going, the area around us filled with nothing but the sound of the clacking of the puck going up and down the table as it hit our paddles. Still, I was better. However, near the end of the game, which I could tell because there was a timer on the rim of the table, I decided to be a gentleman and let Amelia have the last score. So, she beat me, but it was because I let her beat me. However, she knew I let her beat me and I knew that she knew that I let her beat me. It was that kind of thing.

The Bluesman and the girls were now on a different machine, and I decided to ask Amelia if she wanted to go outside and walk around since it was such a nice day. She agreed, and we began to walk down the cement trail together, so we could watch some of the people play tennis, something which I had never played, but I thought it might be fun to watch.

As we were walking, something strange happened. Without even thinking about it, I grabbed her hand as we were strolling along, and suddenly I realized that I was holding her hand. I almost expected her to pull it away because, even though we had known each other for a long time and she was kind of my girlfriend, we had never held hands before. You already know that we had never kissed, and I had just blown that, but we had never even held hands before. In fact, now that I think about it, the most intimate thing we had ever done was whenever I gave her an excuse to beat me up. I figured that this was the next step, and I was on my way. I realized that I could have kissed her earlier and skipped a complete step, but I wasn't complaining about this. Besides, her hand was really soft, and she looked beautiful.

69

We arrived at the tennis court and sat on the grass under a large tree to watch the people play. I wished I had remembered to bring towels for us to sit on, but it wasn't so bad because the grass was healthy and green and the entire layout of the club was always really nice. The two people playing the game in front of us were really good, especially for being so old. I think they were around my parents' age, maybe a little older.

Suddenly, I had a great idea. I just remembered that on the other side of the courts, the club had a small miniature golf course. I asked Amelia if she felt like playing, and she said yes. I helped her up and then we proceeded along the trail until we were at the hut where you could get golf clubs and balls.

"Excuse me, sir. Could I get a couple of clubs and some balls, please?" I asked the man who was standing behind the counter and putting some orange golf balls into a large, glass jar.

"Sure, I need to see your membership card."

"I'm a guest of the Bluesman."

"Excuse me?"

"I mean Keith Richards."

The man checked his large list of club members and found it.

"Okay, is he here with you? Only a member can rent clubs."

"Oh, not at the moment. He's back at the arcade," I said turning around and pointing at it, which was really pretty foolish because the man worked there so he probably knew where the arcade was.

"I'm going to have to get permission from him to loan you the clubs."

"Oh," I said disappointedly. I mean, I supposed it would not be a big deal to go all the way back and get Keith and bring him here so we could get the clubs, but then he and the girls would probably want to join in on the

70

game, which I really didn't want right now. I don't mean to sound like I was being selfish or ungrateful or anything because Keith is my best friend and everything, but I wanted to share this time alone with Amelia, if you know what I mean. We were having a really good time together, and I didn't want it to end, not to mention the fact that I thought she would really enjoy playing miniature golf.

The man must have taken pity on me because he saw how disappointed I was, and his eyes wandered to Amelia and then back to me. He smiled as he took two clubs from the bin behind him and then got a couple of balls from under his counter and gave them to me.

"Gee, thanks, mister."

He winked at me, and I felt myself turning red with embarrassment because I'm quite sure that Amelia had seen the wink, also. The man had just assumed that she was my girlfriend, which I guess she was, technically speaking in a weird way, and wanted us to have a good time.

I gave Amelia a club and a ball, and we were off. When we arrived at the first tee, I let her go first and, to my surprise, she gave the ball a good, solid whack that went all the way down the center of the lane. The ball hit the wall just perfect and then went to the right and stopped almost by the hole. The first lane was really pretty easy, but still it was a great shot. That was going to be hard to top. I placed my ball down and then hit it. It was a good hit, but when it smacked the wall, it didn't go as far as Amelia's. Needless to say, she won that hole, and not because I let her but because she was really good. She was a member of the club — if I had thought about it, maybe she could have gotten the guy to give us the clubs and balls, being a member herself and all — so she had probably played there a good many times. There were a dozen holes in all on the miniature course, and each one got harder, some of them even having to go over bridges or into a certain opening at a specific time before it was blocked by a rotating shield of some sort.

My ball went in the water once, but she let me pull it out and didn't hold it against me when we were totaling up points, which was very cool of her. I think we had a lot of fun, certainly the most fun that we had ever had together, and I didn't even have to get her to beat me up to go out with me. You could say, in a weird way that I had not even planned, that this was a date. I mean, some adults would certainly have considered coming here and doing the things we did as some sort of date, so...I guess it *was* a date, technically speaking. All in all, she beat me by a total of five strokes. The reason she was able to do that, I decided, was that she was taller and had longer arms, which enabled her to aim better.

Once we were done, we gave the clubs back to the nice man who had loaned them to us and then made our way back to the arcade. When we got there, the Bluesman and his audience were sitting at a table with empty cups and the remnants of lunch before them.

"Well, well, look who decided to return," the Bluesman announced as all three of them were now looking at us.

We both blushed because we knew what they were thinking: that we had sneaked off together so we could have some alone time. We pulled some chairs over from another table, me seating Amelia first, and then sat down.

"So, where did the two of you disappear to?" the Bluesman said.

"We went to go play some miniature golf," I replied.

"Really? Who won?"

I didn't say anything, and Amelia grinned, which made it completely obvious.

"Now, that is hilarious!" he laughed.

"What's hilarious about it?" Amelia inquired.

"What's so hilarious about it? Being beat by a girl. That's hilarious! That is beyond hilarious!"

Oh, boy, I thought. Amelia was not your typical girl, which was one of the things I liked about her. She never walked away from a challenge, and that's what this was. I don't think that the Bluesman realized he was flirting with death. Or, at least, a beating.

"I bet I could beat you," she said in a playful but still challenging, way.

"At miniature golf? That's no big deal," he scoffed.

"Well, then, what would you suggest?" she said as we all watched and wondered what was going to happen.

"Something that we can really sink our teeth into."

"Like what?"

"Well...I don't know off the top of my head."

"How about...arm wrestling?"

We all looked at her incredulously. Not just me, not just the Bluesman, all of us.

"You want to arm wrestle me?" the Bluesman giggled, having to make sure that he had heard her correctly.

"Sure."

"I would wipe the floor with you. You're a girl."

"So?"

"So, I don't want to hurt you."

"Sounds to me like you're backing down," she said with a small, challenging grin.

The Bluesman was stuck. Now he had to take the challenge. If he backed down, especially in front of her friends, she would rib him about it every chance she got. He was still smarting that she'd beaten him up, even though that had been a year before. This would just be too much.

"Okay, it's your funeral," he said, shaking his head sadly as he picked the remnants of lunch from the table and then got up and placed them in the garbage. "I'll try to go easy on you," he mocked as he put his arm up in the standard position.

Amelia didn't say anything as she took the Bluesman's hand, and they looked into each other's eyes.

"Okay, on the count of three. One… two… three!"

Nothing was happening. Actually, that was not completely true. A lot was happening. You could see their arms slightly quivering as they were straining to put each other down. They were just so evenly matched that it appeared that neither one of them was moving. I looked at Amelia's arm and saw how big her muscle was. I knew she was strong, but geez! It was about the same size as the Bluesman's. It was hard to imagine how that skinny arm of hers had so much muscle in it. The Bluesman had a slightly strained look on his face, and Amelia was still grinning. I honestly could not tell if she was playing with him or if she was just really good at covering up the effort that she was making. A full minute passed, and neither one of them had really moved the other.

"Guys?" I said.

They kept straining.

"Guys, we're going to be here all day."

Nothing.

I sighed. Actually, I was getting worried, and so were the two girls, who were anxiously watching. I knew Amelia was tough, but she was still a girl. I was worried that she might get hurt somehow. The Bluesman was getting tired, I could tell, and when that happened, she would be able to slam his hand against the table, and he would never be able to live it down – being beat by a girl. I couldn't let that happen to my best friend. I needed to put a stop to this before any one of these things could happen.

"Look, why don't we call it a draw?"

Straining.

"I'm going to count to three, and on 'three', I want both of you to let go, okay? One… two… three!"

They both let up at the same time and let go of each other's hand, each of them wiggling their fingers.

"Okay, fine," the Bluesman said. "You're strong. If we would have had more time, I would have beaten you. I just decided to let you off easy."

Amelia immediately put her elbow on the table and opened her hand again.

"No!" all three of us said at the same time.

"Let's just call it a draw. Nobody won, nobody lost," I suggested.

This seemed to satisfy them and they sat back in their chairs as they regarded each other. Then, slowly but surely, we all started laughing at the absurdity of it all. If you just looked at it objectively, it actually was pretty funny. The Bluesman was no weakling, and because of what Amelia has had to put up with practically every day for the past several years, she was certainly not your average girl.

Amelia looked at her watch. "I should probably head home in an hour or so."

"Why?" I said kind of disappointed. I thought we could…I don't know, but I didn't want her to leave.

"My mother has a hair appointment at Sunrise Mall in a couple of hours. She usually gets her hair done earlier, but the lady who does it had to reschedule it till later. She said I could come with her if she wanted."

"Oh," I said, thinking it would be nice to go to the mall, but I didn't want to just try and invite myself or anything.

"Well, I guess we can talk about what we're going to do tomorrow, then," the Bluesman said.

"What are you going to do tomorrow?" Amelia asked.

"We had talked about going to Goatman's."

"I've heard about that place, but I've never been there."

"It's pretty cool. There's always stuff to explore."

"What time are you going tomorrow?"

"I don't know. I guess we could leave around 10:00 tomorrow?" the Bluesman said while looking at me.

"Can I come?" Amelia said.

We both looked at her in surprise. It had not even dawned on me to ask her because I didn't think it would be the kind of thing that would interest a girl.

"Uh, I don't think you would want to go," the Bluesman begged off.

"Why?"

"Well, because you're a girl," he explained and I immediately cringed.

"And what does that have to do with anything?" she said with an arched eyebrow.

"Well, it's a long bike ride, and you wouldn't be able to keep up with us, for one thing. Plus, it's all the way in the middle of nowhere, and you would probably get scared."

At that moment, I seriously thought that the Bluesman was digging his own grave.

"Oh, so we're back to that, then?" Amelia said.

"Back to what?"

"Back to me being a girl even though I was about to beat you at arm wrestling."

"You didn't beat me. I decided to let you call it a draw because I didn't want you to get hurt and start crying."

Amelia immediately put her elbow on the table again and opened her hand.

"Oh, come on. It's no big deal, really. We were just talking about it. It's not like it's anything definite," I interjected, looking at him and hoping the Bluesman would pick up the hint.

"It was? I thought we had decided to go. We just need one more person," he said, obviously not catching onto the hint.

"Fine. I'll go with you. It sounds like fun."

"Oh, man," the Bluesman moaned, "you'll just slow us up."

"No, I won't."

"Yes, you will. It will take us twice as long to get there."

"I bet I can ride faster than you," she challenged.

"I could blow you away," he scoffed.

"Care to find out for sure, or are you just all talk?"

Yet again, the Bluesman had trapped himself, which seemed to be turning into a habit. If he backed down he would hear about it for the rest of his life. If not...well, I wasn't sure if he could win or not. The Bluesman could really ride like the wind if he wanted to, but I knew for a fact that Amelia had really strong leg muscles because she rode a pretty unusual bike that she could move really fast on.

"And exactly what are you proposing?" he asked with a smirk on his face.

"Let's have a race. If I win, I get to go with you tomorrow. If you win....then you win."

"You really want to eat my dust?" he joked.

"I'll think you'll be eating mine. In fact, I guarantee it."

"Fine. Let's do it. Name the time and place."

"Right now in the alley behind the club. It's long enough for a race, and cars never go through there. If we do it now, I'll have time to make you cry in my dust before I have to go home."

"Oh, ho, ho. Pretty confident now, are we?"

They looked at each other for a moment.

"You're on," he said. They both got up at the same time, followed by the rest of us.

I was worried. It was just a bike race and not like it was anything dangerous, but I still hated the chance of Amelia getting hurt in any way. I knew she was pretty good on a bike, but the Bluesman was almost master class. He could even do a wheelie, as you already know, among a few other tricks which I would never even have attempted unless I were wearing an all-body-padding suit. Finally, I decided to just let it happen. And truth to tell, I was kind of eager to see who would win. It really would be an awesome race to see.

We left the club and walked over to our bikes. I mounted mine, and Amelia's friends got on theirs, both of them riding ten-speeds, which were nothing fancy. The Bluesman mounted his Supergoose, and Amelia climbed on her bike. Amelia's bike was a bit unusual. Have you ever heard of a Baja? Basically, a Baja is a ten-speed bike with thick, dirt bike tires, the kind you would find on a racing bike like the ones that the Bluesman and I rode. A regular ten-speed bike has such thin tires, they're useless on anything other than a smooth surface like a sidewalk or a street. A Baja remedies that problem. This added with the fact that Amelia was stronger than the regular girl made me believe that this was going to be a very interesting race.

We rode into the alley and saw that there was nobody there. It was pretty wide, which relieved me because there would be no chance of them having to be so close together that they might crash. I supposed it could still happen, but I tried not to think about that.

I stayed near the front end of the alley with Amelia's two friends, and she and the Bluesman rode all the way to the other side, which was about fifty yards. Once they were there, they turned around and got ready. Because of the size of Amelia's bike, she towered over the Bluesman. This was going to be a killer race!

Connie got off her bike and hit her kickstand. (Oh, by the way, Amelia's other friend was Nicole.) I knew them both from school, and they were both cool. Nicole was even one of the few girls who liked hard rock. In fact, her favorite group was Def Leppard. Connie was really into Pat Benatar, which was cool. Anyway, Connie was now standing in the middle of the alley and looking down at them.

"Ready?" she yelled

Both of them gave her a thumbs-up sign.

"Okay, on the count of three. One... two... three!"

The Bluesman and Amelia immediately took off, and it was already starting off to be a good race. Then Amelia started to pull ahead. I saw the look of shock on the Bluesman's face, which immediately turned into an expression of determination, and he started pedaling faster. They were now neck and neck again. Amelia looked over at him and smiled and then put on an extra burst of speed and pulled ahead. She was now going so fast, her bike was slightly rocking side to side as she pedaled. Amelia was the first one to sail past us, followed closely by the Bluesman before they came to the end of the alley and stopped.

I have to admit, I was really surprised. I mean, I knew it would be a good race, and I was glad that nobody got hurt, but I was really surprised that she had won. Arm wrestling was one thing, but bike racing? That was strictly something for the guys.

Looking at him, I could tell that the Bluesman was devastated. He simply could not believe it. Beat by a girl. I didn't know if he was ever going to live that down.

We rode up to them, and Amelia's friends were congratulating her, of course, and I said something along those lines, also. I mean, I had to. Then I looked at the Bluesman, and the disappointment on his face really was tragic. "Hey, don't worry about it. It's just a dumb race," I said in an attempt to make him think it was really no big deal.

"Yeah, you're not the one who just lost," he said disgustedly.

Amelia saw how hurt he was, which was something that was completely understandable because boys have a much bigger ego than girls. When it gets broken, it's hard. She got off her bike and walked up to the Bluesman. They regarded each other for a moment. She could have said anything at that moment and gotten away with it because she had won the race fair and square. The way the

Bluesman had been playfully making fun of her, she would have been entitled to say anything to him to make him eat crow. Instead, she put out her hand and said…

"Nice race, Bluesman."

He looked at her a moment, surprised, and then took her hand as they smiled at each other.

"Nice race," he said.

It was at that exact moment that I knew they would be friends for life.

"So, I guess this means that I'm going with you two to Goatman's tomorrow."

"I think you've earned it," he said and meant it.

As sad as I was that the Bluesman lost the race, I was also kind of glad. This meant that I would be able to see Amelia again the next day.

"So, what time are you going to stop by tomorrow?" she asked.

"Well, how about ten o'clock?" I said, looking at her and then the Bluesman and then back to her.

"Okay, I'll see you tomorrow," she said getting back on her bike. "Oh, by the way, do you want to go to the mall with me and my mother today?"

"Um, sure," I said almost immediately, and the Bluesman just grinned at me, which was his way of agreeing with me.

"Great. We're going to leave pretty soon. Why don't you go home and change and then come over. Connie? Nicole? Do want to come?"

"No, thanks," Nicole said. "I think we're going to head back into the club and do some more swimming."

"Okay, I'll call you both later, and I'll see you two in a couple of hours," she said, waving, and then raced off down the street. It may have been my imagination playing tricks on me, but I thought she winked at me before she took off. But, like I said, it may have just been my imagination, if you know what I mean.

We talked with the girls for a bit to catch up on things before they headed back into the club, leaving the two of us alone.

"Well, you must be a happy camper," the Bluesman said.

"What do you mean?"

"Now you get to spend even more time with your girlfriend."

"Who said that she's my girlfriend?" I said, turning red.

"Oh? So you don't want her to be your girlfriend?"

"Well... I... I didn't say that," I stammered.

"So, then, she's your girlfriend."

"If you say so."

"I think you say so."

"Well, if you think she's my girlfriend, then...then I guess she's my girlfriend," I said, not knowing what else to say.

"That's what I'm saying."

We looked at each other and grinned. I guessed it was official then — I had a girlfriend. I mean, I guessed so. It wasn't like we had kissed or anything. But, we had held hands and gone on a date, technically speaking, not to mention the fact that we had known each other for a while. So, yes, I guessed she was my girlfriend. And, you know what? It was pretty cool.

"So, how about we go home and change?"

"Okay."

"Okay. Since Amy's house is on the way to mine, why don't you go change and then stop off at my house and then we can head on over to hers?"

"Sounds cool."

We headed off and, once we got to the Blueman's street, we waved each other off and then I was soon at home running into the house.

81

"Whoa! Where's the fire?" my mom blurted in surprise as I almost barreled over her, almost causing her to drop her drink.

"The Bluesman and I are going to the mall with…a friend," I said quickly as I rushed to my room, and she followed me. Zock was now standing beside her and wagging his tail, happy to see me back.

"Wait a minute! Slow down. You and the… you and Keith and are going to the mall? Who with? Who's taking you to the mall? You just got back from the country club and now you're going out again?"

"It's… it's just a friend," I said pulling some clothes out of my dresser and trying to decide what to wear. I had a Judas Priest shirt that my dad had bought me a couple of months earlier that I really liked because it was the cover of their album *Screaming for Vengeance*, but I didn't think that that would really be appropriate for this occasion.

"Young man, you are not leaving this house until I get all the details. Now who are you going with?"

"Mommmmm…it's just a friend," I said, turning red, which must have been a good tip-off because her next question was…

"Is it a girl?"

I didn't say anything and just stood there.

"Is it Amelia?" she beamed.

"Yes," I finally said, moaning.

She smiled at me for a moment and didn't say anything.

"She's such a nice girl, and I can tell how much she likes you."

"Mom, she's just a friend."

"The way you two spend so much time together and watching television over here, I think she's more than just a friend, don't you think?"

"Mommmmmm…"

"I think it's adorable," she practically sang. Then she walked up to me and took my face in her hands. "I guess my little boy is growing up."

I really didn't know what to say, but it sure felt good to be called a grown-up and not a kid. Well, she didn't actually call me a grown-up, technically speaking, but it was just the same, almost, if you know what I mean.

"So, I guess you better take a shower before you head out and meet her," she said.

"Why? I was just in the water. I'm clean."

"You were in a swimming pool. It's not the same thing. I can smell the chlorine in your hair."

"Mom, it's no big deal."

"Yes, it is. You want to make a good impression, don't you? Now, go take a shower and get cleaned up. It will only take a few minutes."

Without saying another word because I knew it would be a waste of time, I walked to the bathroom, jumped in, and took a quick shower, and then jumped out and toweled off. She was right. I already felt better and cleaner. I went to my room and put on my favorite shirt, not a rock shirt, and a pair of pants. Then I went back to the bathroom and dried my hair some more and combed it. Hopefully it would be dry by the time I got to the Bluesman's house.

I was about to leave when something caught my eye. Sitting on the counter was my dad's cologne. I had never worn cologne before, mainly because I'd never shaved because, as you know, I was hairless except for down there. Still, I wondered if I should put some on. This was, technically speaking, a date. I mean, her mom and the Bluesman were going to be with us, also, but it was a date, I guess. I stared at it for a moment and then grabbed the bottle and took the lid off so I could smell it. It was nice. *Fine, I'll put on some cologne.* I poured some into my hands and a lot more spilled out than I had planned on pouring. I didn't want to waste any of it because I probably shouldn't have been using it anyway, so I just smeared it all over my face and wiped the excess off with a towel. Okay, I was ready. I went to my room to get my watch and my wallet, which reminded me that I needed to talk to my dad about my allowance later on, and then went to the living room to tell my mom I was leaving.

"Mom, I'm leaving, now," I announced.

"Okay, dear. Have fun and – what in heaven's name is that smell?" She looked at me with a shocked expression. Even Zock was looking at me like I was some kind of alien.

"Oh. Uh…I put on some of Dad's cologne."

"Oh, honey, that's way too much. They can probably smell you all the way to Padre Island. Go wipe some of it off before you go."

"Mom, I'm going to be riding my bike over there. The wind is going to take most of it off. If I wipe it off, there won't be any left by the time I get to her house."

"Oh, all right," she sighed. "You'll be sorry. Have a nice time, and call me if you need me."

"Okay, Mom," I said, turning away and anxious to leave. As I opened the door to the garage, I looked down and noticed Zock standing there, staring up at me with a smile on his furry face. I was going to have to break the news to him. "Sorry, Zock. No dogs allowed in the mall. Maybe next time."

Zock looked at me with a hurt look on his face and then walked away. His tail was hanging down, so I knew he was hurt. Poor Zock. I was probably giving him a complex, and I felt terrible because he was my best friend – well, him and the Bluesman, and Amelia. I would make it up to him because I decided right then and there that he would be going with us to Goatman's the next day. He would like that, especially since he had been there before and always had a good time. There were all sorts of places to explore and for him to sniff.

I mounted my bike and was soon streaking along the sidewalk. I felt really good because this had been such a great day and it was going to get even better. I felt so good; I decided that this was going to be the day that I finally popped a decent wheelie. I tightened my grip on my handlebars, sped up a little more, took in a deep breath, pulled up on my handlebars, and now I was…about an inch off the ground before I went back down. No wheelie. This was really annoying. I bet if I had more muscles, I would be able to pull up on the handlebars more. At any rate, I kept going with a smile on my face and was soon at the Bluesman's house. I got off my bike and walked up to his front door. As usual, it was cracked open in anticipation of my arrival, and I walked in.

"Hey, Bluesman! I'm here!" I politely yelled.

I heard a loud thumping noise upstairs and then somebody screaming. It sounded like a girl's voice. Then, there was a rumbling and I heard some footsteps coming quickly down the stairs. A moment later, Marie appeared with the Bluesman following quickly behind her. He was patting her on the head again, and she was screaming at him to stop. She was struggling to get away from him, which there was no way he was going to let her do until he was good and ready. She ran to the living room and around the couch, trying desperately to get away from the patting. Then, in the open area in front of the television set, she tripped, and he immediately sat on her back so that she was pinned to the floor and started patting her on her head again.

"Stop it!" she screamed.

More patting.

"Quiiiiiiiiiiiiiiiiiiiiit Iiiiiiiiiiiiit!"

Patting.

Finally, he decided that she had had enough, at least for right now, and then got up and just left her there. Without another word and with an agitated expression on her face, she got up and sat on the couch and used the remote control to turn the television set on. Believe it or not, this was just another typical day in the Bluesman's household.

"You ready to go?" he said.

"Ready and willing," I replied. I could tell that he had just taken a shower, also. I guess Mom really was right.

"Okay. Just give me a moment and then we can go. Hey, Ma! I'm gonna go to the john!" he bellowed. "I gotta do a number two!"

"Okay, dear," an adult voice said, coming from the kitchen.

"I'll be back in a minute," he said and then disappeared down the hall. I went and stood beside the couch and watched the channels as Marie was flipping through them. A moment later, I heard the Bluesman yelling and grunting as loud as he could, which was an indication that he was doing a number two. Marie closed her eyes and grimaced. I almost thought she was going to cry because she was so disgusted. In a way, I almost pitied her because she got tortured on a daily basis…all of it in a playful way, of course. Still, it obviously annoyed her. I thought it was hilarious! A few moments later the Bluesman walked back into the room. "Hey, Ma! Everything came out okay! I lost eight pounds!" he announced.

"Okay, dear."

Marie slammed the remote control down.

"When are you two leaving?" she demanded.

"Right now," the Bluesman said.

"Finally! And don't come back until…what it that smell?"

The Bluesman sniffed the air and then looked at me.

"Yeah, what *is* that smell?"

"Um, I put on some of my dad's cologne," I admitted.

"You sly dog, you," the Bluesman said grinning at me.

"Danny has a girlfriend! Danny has a girlfriend! Danny has a girlfriend!" Marie began to sing, and I blushed.

The Bluesman saw how much his little sister was embarrassing me, and he wasn't going to have it. He immediately walked behind the couch and started patting her on the head.

"Stop it! Stop it!" she yelled as she tried to get away from him, but he was everywhere. Once he attacked, there was no escape. "Go away!"

"Okay, let's go," he said as he suddenly stopped. "Hey, Ma! We're leaving!"

"Okay, dear."

I sometimes wondered if those were the only two words that the Bluesman's mother knew.

We were soon racing down the street together at a steady pace, our tires humming away. The Bluesman veered off and then jumped off a curb. He lifted his bike at the precise moment and was able to get a pretty serious amount of air before he made a perfect landing. Remember when I told you that I had tried to do a certain trick and almost wound up breaking my leg? That was it. I had not tried to do it since. Instead, I just concentrated on trying to do wheelies. If I could just have mastered a wheelie, I would have been more than happy. I would have been ecstatic! Someday it would happen.

Fifteen minutes later we arrived at Amelia's house. We parked our bikes on her front porch beside her white, wooden bench that could swing back and forth. It was really pretty cool. When I had visited her in the past we had sometimes swung on the bench with the radio going and talked and joked around for hours. Nothing romantic ever happened, in case you are wondering, even though it sounds romantic, especially during the evening when everything is calm and the stars are out, sometimes even a full moon. If things kept progressing the way I hoped, I

87

thought to myself, I might have to rethink my future visits on that bench…if you know what I mean.

I rang the doorbell, and Amelia's mother answered a few moments later. She looked almost exactly like Amelia except her hair was shorter and kind of wavy. "Oh, hello. How are you doing, Danny?"

"Okay, Mrs. Shutterbug. How are you?"

"I'm fine, thank you. And you must be… Keith?"

"Yes, ma'am," he said not going into his spiel about how he was really the Bluesman. I guess Mrs. Shutterbug was not aware that she was talking to someone famous.

"Please come in. We're going to be leaving in a few minutes. Amelia is upstairs getting ready; you can wait for her in the living room. Would you like anything to drink?"

"No thank you, Mrs. Shutterbug. We're fine," I said as we walked to the living room and sat down as she walked off. Amelia's house was really beautiful. What with her father being an attorney, you know they were just rolling in it. We sat down, and I was tempted to grab the remote control and turn on the television, but I thought it would be rude to just make myself at home that way, even though I had been there numerous times. It was better etiquette to just sit there patiently and wait; at least that's what my mom would have said if she had been there. Anyway, it was daytime, and you know what I thought about daytime television, so it was really no big deal or anything. The good stuff didn't start coming on until around 8:00. In fact, one of my favorite movies was going to be on that night, and I hoped I'd be home in time to see it.

We heard someone coming down the stairs, and I recognized the sound of the footsteps as Amelia's. When she turned the corner, I was almost completely blown away. She looked beautiful! She was wearing a dark blue shirt and a pair of white shorts. Her hair was still a little bit wet and, even from where we were sitting, I could smell that wonderful mixture of soap and shampoo on her. Plus, as she got closer, I could tell she was wearing something else. Was she wearing…perfume? By golly, she was! Off the top of my head, I couldn't recall her ever wearing perfume before. Wow. It made her even more beautiful! I had to concentrate not to stare at her.

"Hey, guys!" she said as she walked toward us, and we both got up.

She looked different. She looked different because…she was wearing make-up. I mean, she had worn some make-up before, but never to the point where she looked like this. It was a really professional job. I don't mean it to sound like she had always looked like a slob in the past because that wasn't the case, but now she looked like she had put more effort into it, if you know what I mean. Wow. I was suddenly glad that I had taken a shower and put on some of my dad's cologne.

"Hey," the Bluesman strained in a weird voice, and I could tell that he thought she looked as beautiful as I did.

She smiled a little bit because I guess she was getting the reaction she wanted. "You guys ready to go?"

"Yeah," I said trying to sound like it was just another day and still concentrating on not staring at her.

"My mother should be ready in a few minutes, and then we can leave."

"Okay," we both said at the same time because we were both anxious to get to the mall. We had not said anything, but we were both thinking the same thing: the arcade.

Suddenly, Michael appeared from around the corner, stopped, and stared at Amelia. Michael was one of Amelia's two older brothers, both of whom were already in high school, and both of whom I thought were at least a little crazy. Michael raised his hand and pointed at Amelia.

"I'm going to take you to school!" he yelled.

Amelia just stared at him with a bored look on her face.

Michael approached her, and she raised her arms in a boxing stance with her palms open. When he was close enough, he grabbed her shoulders and she grabbed his, so that they were now trying to force each other down, or at least move each other in some way. They struggled for a few moments as they were squeezing each other's shoulders and were beginning to move around the area. Michael was starting to maneuver her down, and then Amelia got a new grip and started to move him to the side as their feet were hitting each other. The Bluesman and I just backed away and gave them room.

"I'm… going to… take you… to school…." Michael wheezed.

Amelia didn't say anything; she let her actions speak for her.

I suppose you are wondering what was going on here. Both of Amelia's crazy brothers were wrestling fans and always used their little sister for practice. This had been going on for several years, she told me. Remember when I said that Amelia was really strong because of what she had to put up with all the time? This is what I was referring to. When it all started, Amelia got beaten up all the time. Not *really* beaten up, but just beaten up, if you know what I mean. They would take turns attacking her and practicing their moves, but throughout the months and years, Amelia had gotten to be pretty strong and learned a thing or two and could now fight either one of them almost to a standstill.

Half the reason was because she was a girl and their sister, so they went easy on her, but the other half was because they were now just having a harder time in defeating her because she was so strong. Needless to say, if she could fight an older guy almost to a standstill, she was a force to be reckoned with. Since I had no wrestling experience at all, she was always able to beat me up whenever I gave her reason to.

"I'm going…to take you…to school," Michael wheezed again.

This was his favorite saying when he was attacking her. I don't know where he picked it up from, but it sounded pretty good. The only thing that was wrong with it was that he was at the moment having a fairly difficult time taking her to school.

Then, Michael swooped his leg under her and tripped her up. She lost her balance, and Michael used this as an opportunity to get her to the floor and almost pin her down. Before he could get all of his weight on her, though, she quickly moved and forced him onto his stomach. She was now trying to get a good grip on his right arm so she could twist it behind him.

As all of this was going on, Amelia's mother walked into the room and looked at them. She was going through her purse. "Amelia, honey, go easy on your brother and don't hurt him," she said nonchalantly in a bored tone, not breaking stride one bit and continuing to walk on into the kitchen.

Apparently, Mrs. Shutterbug was more concerned about Michael's welfare than Amelia's. This led me to believe, as impossible as it sounds, that Amelia had won at least some of the matches. Wow! What a girl!

Michael was able to get himself up and, in a burst of dazzling speed, forced Amelia onto her back and pinned her arms to the floor. He was weighing her down with his body so that she was now completely helpless.

"One... two... three! Whoop!" he yelled in triumph as he got up and looked down at her and pointed at her. "I took you to school! Whoop!" he yelled again as he jumped up and down a few times with his hands in the air enjoying his victory...and then walked off.

Without saying anything, Amelia got up off the floor and walked over to us.

"We should be leaving in a few minutes," she said as if absolutely nothing out of the ordinary had happened.

91

Yes, this was just another day at her house. Can you imagine such a thing? In a way, I was kind of worried. I hoped the Bluesman didn't get any ideas from this. In my opinion, Marie suffered enough as it was.

"Are we ready?" Mrs. Shutterbug asked as she appeared in the room, wearing sunglasses and with her purse over her shoulder.

We all smiled and started walking to the door.

Mrs. Shutterbug drove a nice car. I think it was a Cadillac, which wouldn't surprise me since her husband was a lawyer and everything. She was driving, of course, Amelia was riding shotgun, and the Bluesman and I were in the backseat. After she backed out of the driveway, we were off!

The radio was already driving me crazy, and from the expression on the Bluesman's face, he was having the same reaction. The music was some kind of old, instrumental noise that was guaranteed to put you to sleep at a moment's notice. Frankly, I thought it was dangerous. Music this boring could cause the person behind the wheel to fall asleep while we were in motion and then we would all die and they would find us mangled up in a horrendous wreck. Amelia must have felt the same way because she started fiddling around with the radio and found a good station. I instantly recognized a Stevie Nicks song – I think it was called "Stand Back." MTV played the video all the time and, I have to say, I thought Stevie Nicks was kind of hot. It wasn't KISS but it was certainly better than the horrible noise that had been on a few seconds earlier that would start making dogs whine in pain.

"Ma, are we there yet?" the Bluesman said while looking at me with a grin. I immediately took his cue.

"Ma, I have to go to the bathroom."

"Ma, Dan is bothering me."

"Ma, the Bluesman is trying to push me out the door."

"Ma, Dan is throwing your stuff out the window."

92

"Ma, the Bluesman is making faces at people as they drive by.

"Now, boys, what would your mothers say if they were here right now?" Mrs. Shutterbug said with a soft laugh. I could tell she thought it was funny. With two sons and a daughter, it had probably brought back some nightmares. "Keith? What was it that Danny called you? 'Bluesman'?"

"Yes, ma'am. The Bluesman."

"Why did he call you that? Do you like blues music?"

"Not really, ma'am. I'm more of a rocker. We both are."

"Although he likes *Duran Duran*," I chimed in.

"I like *Duran Duran*," Amelia said.

"Why did he call you 'the Bluesman'?" Mrs. Shutterbug inquired again.

The Bluesman explained the whole story of it and how he was now famous and how hardly anyone ever called him "Keith" anymore. Sometimes even his parents called him "the Bluesman."

Looking at the profile of her face, I could tell that it was one of the most unusual stories she had ever heard, and she wasn't quite sure how to respond to it. I guess I couldn't really blame her, her being a grown-up and all. Except for the radio, the car was silent for the rest of the trip.

We arrived at the mall about thirty minutes later and were fortunate enough to find a parking space that was pretty near the entrance.

"Okay," Mrs. Shutterbug said while checking her watch. "I don't have my appointment for a while, so I'm going to let the three of you run around while I do some shopping. Let's meet here in two hours. Does that sound good?"

"Sounds great!" we said

"All right, then. The three of you be good. Amelia, if you need me, you know where I'll be."

"Okay, Mother."

"You three have fun," she said and then walked off.

The Bluesman and I looked at each other and then to our right. Without saying a word, we rushed over to the arcade, Amelia following.

We were now in heaven! The rings and dings of the arcade were filling our ears! I could finally show Amelia how good I was at Tron. Once she saw that, she would probably be swooning.

"I'm going to head for the Defender," the Bluesman informed them.

"You know where I'm going," I replied.

He smiled and then took off. I looked at Amelia. "How would you like to see a master at work?"

"What?" she asked. There was a confused expression on her face.

I gently took her hand, which was still soft, and led her to the Tron machine. Fortunately, it was not being used at the moment. "Have you ever played this before?" I asked as I put a quarter in.

"No. I usually play Pac-Man or Mrs. Pac-Man."

"This is way better. It has multiple screens and levels. You really have to be a video game master to play Tron."

The game started, and I started with the light cycles and then moved on to the spiders and then the cone and so forth. I must say, I was really tearing it up! I really was playing one of my best games ever, and I was glad that Amelia was here to see it. As I finished another level of the cone, I looked over at Amelia, expecting her to be really impressed with what I was doing.

She was bored.

I couldn't believe it! I was playing one of my best games ever and she looked like she was about to fall asleep. She was trying to hide it, but I could tell that she was about to hit the floor. Then it hit me, what I was doing wrong – I was playing a game and she was just standing there watching. Of course she was going to be bored. How could I be so stupid? I was really playing a good game...but I felt the need to be a gentleman.

"Hey, do you want to take over?"

"What?" she said surprised.

"Move over here," I said so she could get at the controls. "Okay. Get ready."

"What am I doing?" she said as she grabbed the stick.

"This is the light cycle. You have to get the other guy to crash into either the wall or one of the light walls that you are making with your cycle. Get ready. Go!"

Surprised and fumbling, she gripped the handle and started off slowly at first and then began to pick up speed. The other cycle whizzed in front of her and created a wall, which she immediately crashed into. She was dead.

"I'm sorry. Do you want it back?" she said starting to move away.

"No, you're doing great. Get ready! These are the spiders. Try to kill as many of them as you can before you go into that tube there," I said pointing at it.

"Oh...I don't like spiders," she said quickly as she started moving her guy and awkwardly shooting at them, her discs going everywhere. She moved her guy toward the tube, but a spider pounced on her, and she derezzed. She was dead. "I'm killing all your guys," she said in an apologetic tone that I thought sounded adorable.

"Don't worry about it. You're getting the hang of it. Get ready. Here comes the cone. Shoot your way through it and get to the top. Aim at the side and then move up when you have some room."

The cone began, and she started to shoot upward, a few discs firing at a time.

"Squeeze the trigger faster so you can knock out more squares. Once you have enough room, move up to the top," I said, not telling her to try and stay for as long as she could because the more squares you took out, the more points you got. Right now, I just wanted her to survive.

She began to fire faster and then slowly moved her guy up. She was getting the hang of it! She fired some more and, once she felt she had enough room, she quickly moved her guy up toward the top. Unfortunately, one of the squares touched her foot and she derezzed. She was dead. Game over.

"I'm sorry," she moaned. "You were playing a good game and I messed it up."

"You did great! You did a lot better than I did when I first played," I said. Actually, she hadn't, but I thought it would be a nice thing to say to make her feel better.

We walked off, and I was trying to think of something we could play together that she might be good at.

Then, I saw it. Right in the middle of the arcade, and nobody was playing it. Air hockey!

"Care for another match?" I said while indicating the table, and she smiled. We went to opposite sides of the table and started playing, and we started having just as much fun there as we'd had at the club. In fact, it almost felt as if we had never stopped, and we had been playing the whole time. That's how good it felt, if you know what I mean. We were both laughing as we knocked the puck toward each other, back and forth and, let me tell you, she could really slam it when she wanted to! Although, even though I was having fun playing the game, the best part of it was seeing her smile and hearing her laugh the whole time. She was really having a good time now, and you cannot possibly believe how thankful I was that the arcade had an air hockey machine, something that I had completely forgotten about because I am usually concentrating on Tron and a few other machines.

We played a few games and then went to go track down the Bluesman. He was still at the Defender machine and had been playing the entire time we had been there on just one quarter! Although, he was down to his last guy. Still, because he was such an ace at the game and his score was

96

so high, there was a small audience gathered to watch him. I could tell by the expression on his face that he loved it. Amelia and I stepped back and just talked for a while. We came across one of those machines where you can direct a hanging claw over some stuffed animals. I tried to win a small bear for her that she said she liked, but I wound up catching nothing. Still, I guess it was a pretty good attempt, though, since the claw was hard to direct and you only got one try and all. By now, the Bluesman was done with his game and left to some small applause as he walked away from the machine.

"So, what now?" I asked.

"Let's head into the mall and see what's happening," Amelia said.

We walked around the mall and visited the book store, a record store, where we spent quite an amount of time, and a few clothing stores, which was mainly where Amelia wanted to spend some time. The Bluesman and I were bored at those stores, but we didn't say anything. We wandered over to the food court and had some drinks and corn dogs and had a great time talking and goofing around. Amelia saw some friends from another school who she knew, and they joined us at our table for a while.

Something weird happened when she introduced us to her friends. When she introduced the Bluesman, she actually said "The Bluesman" and then explained why he was called that and that he was pretty famous for it. The girls looked at him in awe, and I could tell that he loved it. His legend was spreading. But the weird thing was when she introduced me. She said that my name was Danny and that I was her boy…

And then she caught herself and said that I was a really good friend and my name was Danny and that I was really nice. It was very subtle, but I caught it, and I wondered if her friends did, girls being more perceptive about things like that and all.

97

She had been about to call me her boyfriend.

That really blew my mind. I was already kind of sort of thinking of her as my girlfriend, if you know what I mean, but she was the first one to almost kind of make it kind of official, if you get what I am saying.

Wow! I was definitely going to have to kiss her now. Not now, specifically, because it wasn't romantic or anything just being sitting in the middle of the food court, but soon.

Before we even knew it, it was time to meet Mrs. Shutterbug back beside the entrance by the arcade. We walked over there, and she arrived a few minutes later carrying a few bags from various stores.

"You look beautiful, Mother," Amelia said, and Mrs. Shutterbug smiled. I looked at her closely, and I honestly could not tell any difference from the way her hair had looked before we arrived. I wondered how much she paid just to look the same. My mom got her hair done all the time, but she usually looked different when she came back from the salon, at least a little bit. She went so often, it was hard to tell if there was any real difference. I wondered why girls did that. Guys just got a haircut about every month or so. Girls went every week. It seemed weird to me.

"Did you three have a good time?"

"Great!" both the Bluesman and I said. "Thanks for bringing us," I added.

"You're more than welcome. Well, I guess we should head back. Your father should be home soon," she said, checking her watch.

We were soon in the car and back at her house in no time. We thanked Mrs. Shutterbug again before she went into the house, leaving us standing outside and talking. It was now almost six o'clock. My favorite movie was going to be on in two hours. Plenty of time to hang out some more before heading home. A few minutes later, the

Bluesman said he had to take off to help his dad with something, even though I suspect that he just saying that as an excuse so he could leave the two of us alone.

So now it was just Amelia and me. We went and sat on the bench for a while, and she turned on the radio so we could listen to it while we talked. Even though I didn't want her to go to any trouble or anything, she went into the house and brought back a couple of cans of Coke. I would have preferred they be Dr. Pepper, but I didn't say anything because it wasn't like it was anything important. This reminded me of something my dad said once: "When you are out on a date with a girl, it's not the food that really matters, but the company."

As usual, Dad was right. The drink didn't matter but the company sure did. Also, this entire day had pretty much been a date. I mean, sure, there had been some other people around, but it was still a date. In fact, the date was still happening right now.

The sun was getting lower in the sky, which looked quite beautiful. There was also a light wind in the air, and it took some of the heat away and made everything more cool and complacent.

Suddenly, it dawned on me that this was a very romantic situation and that I was sitting next to my girlfriend. We looked at each other, and I could tell that she was thinking the same thing.

I moved kind of closer to her and, trying to be a smooth as possible (I was pretending that I was James Bond right now because he made everything look so easy, especially when it came to girls), I put my arm around her and moved even closer to her.

She could tell what I was going to do and had to move her head down a little, which was kind of embarrassing, but I tried not to think about that. I also tried not to think about her braces and my lip getting mangled up. I mean, sure I was thinking about it, but I was sure that if I was careful, nothing bad was going to happen.

I moved my lips closer to hers, and I could still smell her perfume, which was really nice. I wondered if she had smelled my cologne at any point. If she had, she never said anything about it.

Our lips were almost about to touch and....

"Amelia?"

We quickly looked over and saw Mrs. Shutterbug popping her head out from the crack in the door.

"Um, yes, Mother?" she said, surprised, and I quickly moved away from her. I was so scared that she was going to be mad at me trying to kiss her daughter; she was going to pull out a gun or call the police or something. Instead, she seemed to really not notice.

"We're about to have dinner. It'll be on the table in fifteen minutes. Oh, Danny? Would you like to stay for dinner, honey?"

"Uh, no, ma'am," I replied automatically. She had already done so much for us, I didn't want to make myself a complete nuisance and intrude during family time. Also, as much as I wanted to stay with Amelia some more, I wanted to make sure I didn't miss my movie. I mean, I knew it was just a movie and all, but it was my favorite movie, and I was really looking forward to seeing it again. "I should probably get back home since I've been gone all day. Thanks again for taking us to the mall."

"You're welcome, dear. Amelia? You won't be long?"

"I'll be right in, Mother."

She smiled and then disappeared back inside.

I took this as my cue to get up, and Amelia got up after me. I had thought about trying to kiss her again, but the moment was gone. Now it would just be a rushed sort of thing and not very romantic since she had to go inside and everything. Yet again, I had blown it. Still, today had been massive progress!

100

"Well, I guess I should take off so you can go inside."

"Okay. I had a nice time today. Are you going to be here tomorrow at ten o'clock so we can go to Goatman's?"

"Ten o'clock."

We stood there for a moment looking at each other and, standing there, I decided that the evening needed some kind of topper before I left her. "Well, so long, Iron Fang."

We stared at each other for a moment, and then I suddenly ran off. I looked behind me, and she was chasing after me. I put on some more speed as I ran across the street and around a car. I looked behind me again. She was trailing. Her legs might have been longer than mine, but I could run faster. I ran across the street again and, as I did so, I looked behind me, and I could tell that she was upset that she couldn't catch me, so I decided to be a gentleman and slow down. She immediately tackled me, and we rolled across her lawn. We wrestled for a while, and she proceeded to beat me up. Once she was satisfied that I had had enough, she got up, and then I got up after her as we brushed ourselves off. Fortunately, her lawn was just as neat as the one at the country club, so neither one of us had gotten really dirty. We stared at each other and started laughing. All in all, I thought it was the perfect topper to the day. In a strange way, I thought it was an even better topper than a kiss. I know that sounds weird, but that's the kind of relationship we had. Although, after this day, I thought, it might now be a little different, which I thought was really nice. I thought she thought it was nice, also.

I said good bye to her and then climbed on my bike and raced home. As soon as I opened the door, Zock was standing there waiting for me. Poor Zock had not had anyone to play with all day, but I was going to spend the rest of the night with him, just him and me. My mom said that dinner was going to be ready in about half an hour, so Zock and I went into the backyard so I could throw a Frisbee for him and he could fetch it. I could tell how excited he was that I was back and he had someone to play with again.

While we ate, Mom wanted to know all about the trip to the mall and I told her, but not giving all the details, if you know what I mean. Once I was done, Zock and I retired to my room, and I flipped on my television.

One Flew over the Cuckoo's Nest was about to come on. My favorite movie.

I had first seen it a couple of years earlier, and I loved it. Jack Nicholson was also my favorite actor, and I had seen a couple of other movies that he has been in, but *Cuckoo's Nest* was my favorite. The whole movie was great, but my favorite scenes were the ones where he is trying to teach the Chief basketball, which is hilarious, and then the fishing trip that he takes the inmates on.

I had a talk with my dad about the movie once, and I said that, in my opinion, the hospital represented America and that Nurse Ratched represented the government. The inmates represented the country's population. My thoughts were that the hospital was essentially a giant prison that was controlled by the government and because of being surrounded by the walls, there was no escape for the population and that Nurse Ratchet was Big Brother, always keeping watch over them because the government does not want free-thinking people who do whatever they want in life to be happy; they want mindless drones who do what they are told to do. The people are helpless because they are completely terrified of the government. McMurphy, which is Jack Nicholson's character, represents a rebellious, Christ-like character who comes to the hospital and tries to orchestrate a change, so that the inmates/Americans are free to think and be themselves once more. Therefore, the movie is a metaphor for good versus evil.

Unfortunately, the government wins when McMurphy is sacrificed and put through electro-shock therapy. He is

102

later lobotomized and no longer able to freely think anymore because the government has taken away his brain and, in essence, his very self. However, the Chief keeps McMurphy's/America's dream alive by escaping and letting the rest of the inmates/Americans know that just because one of their own has been crushed, that is no reason to just give up and let them win, that they should keep fighting because a people should never be afraid of their government. If anything, a government should be afraid of its people.

My dad thought about it and agreed with my assessment, which I really appreciated because it meant he thought of me as an equal and not just some kid.

He also said that I needed to start watching some more cartoons.

By the way, my second favorite movie was the first *Superman*. In fact, I still had a rather large collection of Kryptonite rocks that they were selling at the theater when the movie was playing. I realized that they were just rocks slathered with green, glow-in-the-dark paint, but they were still pretty cool.

Good night.

JOURNEY TO GOATMAN'S

I slowly opened my eyes. Just a few feet away, a certain furry face was staring at me in anticipation. I opened my eyes farther, and the familiar face of Zock came into focus. He must have known something was up because he was right there waiting for me to wake up. After being stranded at home the day before for most of the day with nobody to play with, he was in no way interested in a repeat.

I rolled over onto my back, stretched, and yawned. The day before had been a really long and eventful day, and I had topped it off by staying up until eleven o'clock, watching my favorite movie. Needless to say, I was still tired. However, today was the day the three of us – four including Zock – were going out on our little adventure, and I was going to have to be at my peak because it was going to be a long bike ride.

Not to mention the fact that I was going to be seeing Amelia again.

I was suddenly wide awake and started to roll out of bed.

Zock quickly got of my way but kept me in his sight. He wanted to make sure I did not somehow leave the house without him. I brushed my teeth and took a quick shower. Once I was dressed, I walked into the living room. Dad was just getting ready to leave.

"Hey, Dan," he said. He was checking some things in his briefcase while sitting at the table. As usual, he was wearing a nice suit, and he looked pretty sharp. Wearing a suit didn't really appeal to me, but it also looked nice and grown up. I guess I was conflicted about it since I knew I was going to have to be doing it sooner or later.

"Hey, Dad. Ready to leave?"

"Almost," he said as he ruffled some papers, snapped his briefcase shut, and then quickly drank the rest of his cup of coffee. I honestly did not know how he stood it. I guess once you become an adult your taste buds change or deaden or something. I went into the kitchen and saw Mom drinking a cup of orange juice while looking over what appeared to be a grocery list. Sometimes I added things to it like cookies or candy or donuts or something. Sometimes she picked them up, sometimes she didn't, so it was always a crap shoot on what to expect. However, fruits and vegetables were always a constant.

"Hey, Mom."

"Hey, honey. Got any plans today?"

I panicked. I really didn't know what to say. I'd never told them about Goatman's and, to my knowledge, they had never heard about it. It was strictly something that was known about in the kid underworld, if you know what I mean. I'm sure that if they knew I was riding out to the middle of nowhere to explore a broken-down place that was little more than a jungle, they would freak.

"I just thought I would go over to the Bluesman's house and see what's up."

"Okay. Just be careful. There was another disappearance on the news last night, so I want you to always be on the lookout and stay away from strangers," she said with a mixture of disappointment and disgust. I guess I couldn't really blame her, since she's my mom and I'm her only kid and everything.

That reminds me, I forgot to tell you about something. About five months earlier, some kids had started disappearing from around the neighborhood, and everyone was up in arms about it. I think the last count at that point was six — seven with the one that my mom had just told me about. Nobody knew what was going on or where they were or who was doing it or if it was more than one person or anything. Kids just disappeared, usually at nighttime. I even knew a couple of them – not really well because they were all younger than I was, so I didn't go to the same school with them, just saw them around the neighborhood from time to time, usually at the country club with their parents.

The police were doing everything they could, but it wasn't enough in my mom's opinion. Frankly, I guess, in everyone's opinion. Because of this, and especially because another disappearance had just happened, parents everywhere were really freaked out, and my parents forbade me to be out after dark, even if it was right in front of the house. Even if Zock was with me, there was no way, no how, they were going to let me stay out after dark. I could get away with being in the backward, which has a high fence, and the garage, but that was about it. Mom even kept a list of all of my friends' phone numbers on the refrigerator, and she had met all of them at least several times. If something didn't change soon, grown-ups were going to be taking to the streets with guns and pitchforks like in *Frankenstein*. Who could blame them? I suppose if I were a father and anyone tried to hurt my kid, I would mutilate them. I would certainly have done the same if anyone had tried to hurt Zock, since he was kind of my kid, if you know what I mean.

"Was it anyone I know?"

"I didn't get the name, but I hope not. I just want you to be careful when you're out today."

"Okay, Mom."

Just to make her feel better, I thought about cancelling out on Goatman's, even though it would be fun. Maybe we could just go swimming again. But then I thought about Amelia and how she had never gone and was looking forward to it and all. I sure didn't want to disappoint her, especially now when I was really making some good progress! She might even be so mad that she might beat me up, this time for real!

"Well, I'm off to the office," Dad announced. He kissed Mom on the cheek, ruffled my hair, and was soon out the door.

I decided that it was time to leave. If I hung around, my mom might somehow deduce that I was up to no good. Moms have a way of doing that. Dads, not as much, but Moms can pick up on just about anything like they have some kind of built-in radar. Anyway, I had a quick muffin and a glass of orange juice and then headed for the garage, Zock following.

We were soon off and racing down the street. It was a really nice day and, fortunately, a bit cloudy, which meant that the sun would not be beating down on us unmercifully as we travelled.

Within no time we had arrived at the Bluesman's house, and once I had dismounted from my steed, I rang the bell and waited for him to answer.

To my chagrin, it was Marie I was looking at when the door opened. It's not that I didn't like Marie — I actually thought she was pretty nice once you got to know her — it's just that her brother drove her crazy on a daily basis with all of his antics, her parents seemingly doing nothing about it, and anyone who was a friend of his she looked at as though they were a cockroach. The way she was looking at me right now, she probably wanted to step on me.

"Uh, is Keith here?"

"Unfortunately, yes," she said in a tone of voice that sounded like her best friend had just died. She opened the door. "I'm actually glad that you're here."

"Really?" I said. "So, how has everything been going?"

"Okay, I guess. Keith has been kind of quiet all morning. He's hardly left his room."

"Is he feeling okay?"

"He must be. When he came down earlier to have breakfast, he patted me on the head a little, but not as much as he usually does. He didn't... I don't know... he didn't seem to be into it as much as usual," she said with a trace of intuitiveness.

Now, that was weird. One of the highlights of the Bluesman's day was assaulting his sister as much as possible. If he could get her to go into a screaming fit before noon, he was on cloud nine, plus he still had the rest of the day to go. In fact, several years ago he had started his career with torturing and hiding her dolls, which had eventually evolved into head patting, among other things. Who knew what would be next.

"Is he in his room?"

"Yes. Why don't you go up and see what he's doing? For all I know he's planning some sort of attack on me when I least expect it."

"Okay," I said as I walked up the stairs and looked at his closed door. There was a picture of Andy Kaufman on it, one of his favorite comics, and a yellow sign that said 'I'm not on Earth right now. Feel free to leave a message.' I knocked on the door.

"Hello?"

"Hey, Bluesman! It's me. Can I come in?"

"Sure," he said and I immediately caught on to what Marie had been talking about. There was a trace of something in his voice, as if he were tired or something else, but not sick, if you know what I mean.

I opened the door and saw him sitting at his desk, flipping through a movie magazine. He looked at me with a smile on his face as he flipped the magazine shut. "Hey, man. What's up?" he asked.

"Things are pretty good. How about you?"

"Can't complain. So how did things go last night after I left?"

"What do you mean?" I said, a little embarrassed.

"You know what I mean." He winked. "I saw the way you two were looking at each other all day. The fact that the both of you disappeared for a while at the club was a pretty good tip-off."

"Oh. Well, we just talked for awhile while sitting on her bench before I headed home."

"Oh, nothing else?" he said with a cocky smile.

I just grinned at him and looked away. Telling him that I got beat up wouldn't exactly blow his mind. I mean, it was a game between Amelia and me, but I wouldn't really expect anyone else to understand it, even the Bluesman.

I wanted to change the subject so I inquired, "How are you feeling?"

"Good. Why?"

"Marie said you haven't been driving her as crazy as possible. She's worried."

"She's worried about me? You know, that could be good," he said with a thoughtful expression. "If I leave her alone for a while, it would really rattle her brain, and she would be living in a state of fear. Wow. That's pretty good!"

It did sound funny, especially since I knew it would turn Marie into a nervous wreck, but I also knew he was covering something up. I know the Bluesman too well not to know when he's hiding something or when something is bothering him, especially considering the fact that nothing ever really bothers him. If anything, he can always be counted on for a good joke. He is always the one to pick up someone's spirits whenever they're feeling down, which is one of the reasons he's so well-liked by everyone.

"So, what's up?" I said casually, wandering around his room and looking at his walls, which were dominated with numerous posters. One was of Heather Thomas from the *Fall Guy*, where she was posing and smiling in front of Colt's truck, which wasn't surprising because, as you know, he really had the hots for Heather. Another poster was of some sexy girl named Debora Zullo, whoever she was, wearing lingerie that she was about to pull off, which I thought was really nice. When the Bluesman first put it up, I used to stare at it all the time, whenever I came over. There was no way on God's earth that my parents would have let me hang up a poster like that in my room. The Heather Thomas one, maybe. Debora Zullo, not a chance.

There were also some posters of some sports figures that I had no clue as to who they were. Sports were not really my thing. The posters in my room were the usual kind of thing you would find in a kid's room: Superman, Spider-Man, a couple of rock posters that my parents had let me get away with like *Iron Maiden, Judas Priest*, and, of course, *KISS*. I once put up one of *Ozzy Osbourne* but they made me take it down because they had heard about him. They just didn't understand that *Ozzy* was just a crazy rock and roll guy, and not some wild animal that was born from hell, like he enjoyed portraying. Like *KISS*, it was all an act.

"What do you mean?" he said.

I looked at him and then sat on the bed so we were now facing each other. He regarded me for a moment and then turned away. It was quiet for a moment. Finally, he said, "Dan, do you ever wonder about the future?"

"What do you mean? School?"

"No, beyond that. After that. Do you ever wonder what you're going to be?"

"You mean like when we grow up and school is finally over?"

"Yeah. Do you ever wonder what you're going to do with your life?"

"Well, not really," I said slowly. "I just assumed that I would go to college and then...I don't know...get a job like what my dad is doing or something. I haven't really ever thought about it."

"Well, lately...it's been on my mind, and I just realized that I have no clue as to what I want to do when I grow up. I don't know what I *can* do."

"You sound like every other kid in the world," I kidded. "I really don't have a clue, either."

"Dan," he said seriously, "you can do anything you want to do. You're smart."

"What do you mean, I'm smart? My grades are okay, just like yours."

"No, I mean *really* smart, not just book smart. You have an imagination. All those ideas that you come up with that you say would make great movies or books. And the way you talk sometimes and describe things like an adult or a writer or something... you're going to be famous someday."

"What do you mean, I'm going to be famous? Doing what? Daydreaming all the time? Those are just ideas and things to goof around with."

"That's what I mean. Who else has ideas like that? Most people just see what's in front of them. You see beyond that. Like... when someone sees a mountain in the distance and they say 'Wow, that's a beautiful mountain.' You would say, 'Yes, it is. I wonder what's beyond it.' That's something that most people can't do because they're too...limited, I guess."

In all the time that we had known each other, this was the first time I had ever heard Keith talk like this, a side of him that I did not even know existed. Needless to say, I was worried because, for some reason, he was really depressed about something. The Bluesman was never depressed. Not the Bluesman I knew.

"Keith, I'm not exactly Einstein. You're just as smart as I am. Or, I'm just as smart as you. Take your pick. What do you want to do in life?"

He thought about it for a moment and then just looked at me. "I don't know. The only things I really enjoy besides music and girls are telling jokes all the time. How does a person make a living telling jokes and fooling around and goofing off?"

111

I had to admit, he was right. Off the top of my head I couldn't think of a job description that required telling jokes all the time. Then I remembered who I saw on his door whenever I came to visit him – Andy Kaufman. "Why not get into show business?"

"What? What do you mean?"

"Be like Andy Kaufman. He tells jokes all the time and does that weird character that he plays on Taxi. Do something like that. You're just as funny as he is, and you're only thirteen. I can't imagine what you might be like ten years from now."

"Oh, man," he moaned. "That's Andy Kaufman! He's a legend! I could never be like that!"

"Keith, you're already a legend around here. You're the Bluesman…and nothing can stop the Bluesman."

He looked at me for a moment as he thought about it, then turned around and looked at Andy Kaufman. When he turned back to me, he was smiling. The smile that I was so familiar with that said, "The Bluesman has entered the room."

"Thanks, man. It's… something to think about."

"No problem," I said.

"So, you ready to go?"

"Ready and willing."

We got up and headed downstairs. The Bluesman was about to head for the garage to get his bike when he saw Marie walking across the living room. He immediately ran up to her and started his patting assault. She started screaming for him to stop, and he kept at it. Although I now sensed something different. Even though she was being annoyed again, I could hear a trace of relief in her voice because her brother had returned to normal. The Bluesman was back, better than ever! In fact, looking at him, it gave me an idea for something that I thought would make a great story or movie or something. I could easily imagine Keith doing exactly the kind of thing he was doing right now, but in front of an audience or a camera.

When he had gotten his fill, he stopped and looked back at me. "I'll meet you out front!" he said as he playfully pushed Marie onto the couch and disappeared down the hall. She looked after him with an annoyed expression on her face and then at me. Now she was smiling, and I smiled back at her. While we were gazing at each other, we were having a silent conversation. She was saying, "Thank you," and I was saying, "You're welcome. Hope you can endure it."

Then I left out the front door so I could meet the Bluesman in the front of the house with Zock.

The Bluesman zoomed out of his driveway and did a massive jump off the curb, gained some good air, and then came down perfectly onto the street and kept going. After witnessing that feat, there was no doubt in my mind at all that the Bluesman was back on top and would always stay there no matter what.

The three of us made our way to Amelia's house. We were a little early, but I was hoping she wouldn't mind. I sure wouldn't mind seeing her again as quickly I could. Once we were there, we dismounted and rang her doorbell. I noticed that Zock was sniffing the door with familiarity, and I knew what was coming.

The door opened a few moments later. It was Amelia, and she looked beautiful. She was wearing a red shirt, a pair of white pants, and some white sneakers. She had a big smile on her face when she saw the Bluesman and me, especially me. At least, I like to think so. Then she saw Zock, and her smile faltered.

Zock immediately ran up to her and started humping her leg as aggressively as he could. Amelia was trying to shake and push him off as gently as she could, and then as hard as she could... and Zock held on because he wasn't done.

This happened whenever Zock saw Amelia, and she hated it. I loved it, and so did Zock, obviously. Personally, I thought she should be flattered. Zock was very picky and didn't hump just anyone's leg. She was the only one he aggressively went after when he saw her. I guess, like me, he really liked her.

Once he had gotten his fill, he backed off and then just stood there panting, Amelia looking at him with daggers in her eyes.

"Did you have to bring him?" she asked me. There was an irritated look on her face.

"I had to. He was all by himself at the house, yesterday bored out of his mind, and I felt guilty about it, so I had to bring him with us today."

"I hope he doesn't do that again," she said, looking down at him. He was still panting.

"I don't think he will. It looks like he's had his fun. It's just his way of showing that he's happy to see you."

"I would prefer he showed it in a different manner. Well, come on in. I'm busy in the kitchen making some sandwiches," she informed us as she opened the door, and the two of us walked in. Before she could close the door or we could stop him, Zock ran in.

"Zock!" we all yelled at the same time as he disappeared down the hall and then ran up the stairs.

"Oh, no!" I moaned as we started running after him and up the stairs. This was not how I imagined the day would start when I saw Amelia again. I had expected the humping part, which I thought was hilarious, but not Zock making himself at home and running amok.

"Aiiiiiiiiiiiieeeeeeeeeee!!!"

"Mother!" Amelia yelled in fright.

"Get him off me!" we heard a female voice scream.

"He won't hurt her. He's a good dog," I said to both of them as we proceeded up the stairs wondering what he was doing to make her scream like that. I hoped he wasn't

114

humping her leg. With Amelia, it was funny. With Mrs. Shutterbug, not so much. I seriously doubted he was, because even Zock couldn't recuperate that fast, if you know what I mean.

We ran into Mrs. Shutterbug's bedroom. She was sitting on the edge of her bed, painting her toenails, and Zock was sniffing her with his paws on her lap. She had recoiled back in fear with her hands in the air as he was having his way with her. In a strange way, it looked as though he were proposing to her. A funny image came to mind of Zock wearing a tuxedo.

I immediately ran up to Zock and started pulling on his collar. He must have liked Mrs. Shutterbug a lot because it took a few seconds to pull him away.

"Zock, come on! Stop being such a pain! Sorry, Mrs. Shutterbug. He got inside before we could close the door," I said apologizing, hoping she wouldn't go nuclear.

It's...it's okay," she said, calming down and starting to get control of herself again. "He just startled me for a moment there."

"He's a nice dog. He's just very curious about everything. Come on, boy," I said, pulling him away so I could get him out of the room. Talk about embarrassing. I'm glad that she's a really nice grown-up and not like some of the uptight ones that my mom knows.

We were all eventually downstairs, and I led Zock to the front door. When he saw where I was taking him, he immediately started trying to stop himself. His nails were clicking across the linoleum, all four of his paws in use as he tried to keep himself from being put outside. I first started to push him and had no luck because he was too strong. Eventually, I had to get in front of him and start pulling on his collar with my feet rooted in place, and he was still able to stop himself. He really did not want to go back outside, probably scared that we would be in here all day and he would be left all alone again. The struggle abruptly stopped as his collar slipped over his head and came off. I immediately fell backward, banged my back on the door, and fell to the floor, hurting my tailbone. Zock ran between Amelia's legs and toward the living room. I got up, and we all ran after him. It was not even ten o'clock yet, and I was already tired.

"Zock!" I yelled, wondering what he was doing now. I remembered that Mrs. Shutterbug kept a lot of collectible figurines in the living room, and I was scared that Zock was going to help himself to them.

When we arrived in the living room, it was empty. Where was Zock? We had all seen him run in here. The only place he could have gone was into the kitchen, and we would have seen him if he had. We walked around the couch and found him lying under the glass table with his head between his paws, looking at us. He had a hurt look in his eyes, like he knew he was in trouble, but I could tell more than anything that he just didn't want to be stranded again. I got down and tried to coax him out, but he wasn't budging. Finally, I just got back up and looked at Amelia and the Bluesman. "I think he's fine. Why don't we just leave him there until we go?" I said.

"He won't do anything on the floor, will he?" Amelia asked, looking down at him fearfully.

Actually, I wasn't sure. He was really nervous right now, and dogs tended to let go when they were nervous. I was pretty sure that he wouldn't do anything, because he was a good dog, but the sooner we left the better.

"He'll be fine. He was housebroken a long time ago. Whenever he needs to go he stands by the door and scratches it.

"Okay," Amelia replied slowly. I looked at the Bluesman, and he was doing everything he could not to laugh. He knew that if he did, there was a good chance Amelia would beat him up, and I know that he didn't want that, especially after being defeated in yesterday's race.

"What's going on?" someone yelled.

We looked over and saw Jason, Amelia's oldest brother. He was standing there staring at us expecting an answer.

"I thought I heard barking. And why did Mom scream? Is there a dog in the house?"

"Uh, it's just Zock," I said looking down at the table. He walked over and looked down at the table and saw Zock staring up at him.

"He's not going to take a dump down there or pee on the rug, is he?"

"No, he's a nice dog," I explained. Jason was kind of a big guy, even bigger than Michael, so I was hoping now that his curiosity was sated he would just go away. Instead...

"I think it's time I showed you what's what," he stated as he looked at Amelia.

"Jason," Amelia moaned in frustration as he started walking toward her. Knowing that there was no stopping it, she put her hands up in anticipation. He grabbed her shoulders as she grabbed his. Before he could settle himself, Amelia pushed forward. Jason lost his balance and fell backward. He was able keep himself from going down at the last moment and renewed his grip on Amelia. They started pushing each other as they maneuvered themselves around the room, trying to get the best of one another. They were both grunting in effort, and Jason, as big as he was – I think he played football – was actually grunting louder than Amelia. In a move that could only be described as excellent, Amelia quickly lowered her right shoulder, and Jason lost his grip on her as he toppled forward. She immediately spun him around while grabbing his arm and twisting it as she got behind him and held it in place. While he was struggling to get free, Amelia used her right foot to trip him up, and he fell down, she now on top of him.

117

The Bluesman and I were impressed, to say the least. I looked down, and even Zock seemed to be freaked out about what was going on.

Mrs. Shutterbug was walking down the stairs and then into the living room as she looked at her two children.

"Okay, you two. Play nice. We have company," she said and then continued to walk to the kitchen.

Jason was able to slowly roll himself over and get his arm free. Reaching up and placing his arm against Amelia's head, he maneuvered her down and quickly got up and straddled her as he pinned her arms down before she could do anything about it. From that position, it was obvious – he had her.

"One... two... three!" he said as he quickly jumped up and stood in a victory stance, looking down at her and pointing his finger. "I showed you what's what! That's how it's done! Yeah!" He jumped up and down a few times with his fists in the air and, once he was happy with his victory, walked off.

Amelia lay there for a few moments and then got up. It was just another day. I couldn't help but think of the morning she had woken up to. First she gets her leg humped, then she chases a dog around the house, then she has to put up with her mother being attacked by the same over-friendly canine, and then gets attacked by one of her crazy brothers. All this and we had not even left for Goatman's yet! That would be enough to make anyone lose their temper. Instead, she just got up and smiled as she smoothed out her clothes. Incredible!

"I guess I should finish making the sandwiches. I though they might be nice to have, since it's probably going to be a long day," she said, which I thought was really nice of her, especially since we hadn't asked her to do it or anything. It was a good idea, too. Goatman's was in the middle of nowhere, and if you got hungry or thirsty, that was tough. "Oh, by the way," she whispered to us, "don't tell my mother about Goatman's. As far as she knows, we're just riding out to a park somewhere to spend the day. If she found out we were going to go to some place with a weird name like 'Goatman's,' she would never let me leave the house."

"Okay," we both whispered back.

We all walked into the kitchen, me checking on Zock to see that he was still there. He looked up at me; he had not moved one inch. Even with all of that wrestling happening right in front of him, he was not going to come out until we were all set to go.

A section of the counter was piled high with about a dozen sandwiches. Wow! I thought she was just going to be making four or five. This was enough to feed her entire family, even her big and annoying brothers! Even though it was nice of her to go through all of this, I felt kind of guilty about it. She was such a nice girl, though, she probably thought of it as no trouble at all. Not wanting her to do all the work, the Bluesman and I started helping her put them in plastic sandwich bags and sealing them up.

"Well, I hope you three have a nice time today," Mrs. Shutterbug said as she was pouring a glass of tea for herself at the other counter. "Amelia, I'm going to be home all day, so if you have a problem, I want you to call."

"Yes, Mother."

"You three have fun," she said as she left the kitchen. As she did so, I halfway listened to see if Zock was going to attack her again and get some sniffing in. When I heard her going up the stairs, I let loose a sigh of relief. Once, she had been nice enough about. Twice, I wouldn't think so.

We now had all the sandwiches ready to go, and Amelia was stacking them neatly into a backpack with some small bags of chips. She had really gone all out!

"Okay, we're almost out of soda, so I thought we might stop off at the store and pick up a couple of bottles before we left," she offered.

"That sounds good," I said. I noticed there was another backpack sitting on the counter, and I went ahead and put it on so I could carry the sodas for us after we purchased them.

Amelia zipped up her backpack with the sandwiches in them and put it on. "Okay, I guess we're all set to go," she said, and then we walked out of the kitchen and into the living room. Zock was still there and looked at us as we approached.

"Okay, boy, we're leaving," I announced, holding his collar out for him.

He didn't move.

"Zock, come on. We're leaving," I said reaching under the table and trying to pull him out. After trying to get a grip on him and coax him out, I got up and looked down at him as he stared up at me. "He thinks I'm trying to trick him," I stated as we debated about what to do.

"I have an idea," the Bluesman said. "Why don't we just go but leave the door open? That way, he'll see that if he doesn't come, we'll be leaving him in the house."

Amelia and I regarded each other.

"That sounds like a good idea," I said and, with one last look at him, we walked to the front door, opened it and walked out leaving the door open.

We stood there for a few moments wondering if it was going to work or not. Zock was a smart dog, and he might still be sensing some kind of trick...which *was* what we were doing. Still, we were depending on his getting lonely enough to come out.

A moment later, Zock raced out of the house, looking for us.

"Good boy," I said, as he walked up to me, and I slipped his collar back on.

"Now that that's taken care of, I'm going to go back inside and then go to the garage and get my bicycle," Amelia stated. We mounted our bikes, and Amelia joined us a few moments later.

We were off!

The four of us were racing down the street and through the neighborhood. I couldn't take my eyes away from Amelia, as we were riding side by side. With the wind blowing her hair back the way it was, I thought she looked like an angel soaring through the open sky. What a vision!

We soon arrived at H.E.B and parked our bikes on the bike stand outside, with Zock to watch over them, then proceeded into the store and found the soda aisle. While we were standing there and debating what sodas to buy and whether we should by bottles or cans, we heard some clicking on the floor and looked over to see what it was.

Zock was walking toward us, happily panting, his nails clicking on the floor as he approached.

"Oh, no!" Amelia immediately moaned. "He's going to get us in trouble."

"No, he'll be fine." I was trying to make myself believe that. "He just doesn't want us to get away from him."

I slowly walked up to him and was desperately hoping that he would not decide to bolt, leaving us with another adventure on our hands. He looked up at me as I reached down to get a grip on his collar. If he decided to bolt, he was taking me with him. This was not necessarily a reassuring thought, because I am quite sure that he *could* take me with him if he wanted to.

"Okay, I've got him. Let's get the soda and get out of here," I said.

We decided on cans because they would be easier to stack in the backpack and would probably stay colder for a longer period of time – Dr. Pepper and Coke.

Once that was done, we walked up to the check-out counters and hoped nobody would say anything about Zock before we could pay for the soda and leave. It was still kind of early, and the store wasn't as crowded as it would be in a few hours. Still, we got a few odd looks here and there. We saw a woman pushing a shopping cart with her baby sitting in the seat of it. When the baby saw Zock, it reached its hands toward him and yelled, "Doggie!" in a happy way. Zock immediately tried to run toward the baby, who was happy to see him, and it took everything I had to hold on to him. The mother got nervous and turned into the first lane she came to, whether she needed anything on it or not.

The sooner we got out of there, the better.

We walked up to the first lane where I saw someone standing behind the register. I placed the two stacks of cans on the conveyor belt and breathed a sigh of relief. We were almost done and no incident! Then, as I walked up and looked at the cashier, I realized it was Kelly. I immediately panicked. Not only did I still have a massive crush on her, I was also with Amelia, and I guess she was kind of officially/unofficially my girlfriend, if you know what I mean. I decided to play it cool, hoping she wouldn't say anything that would be embarrassing or make Amelia angry.

"Hello, Danny. How's my favorite handsome little young man today?" Kelly asked as she took the cans from the conveyor belt. She started to ring them up as I took out my wallet. Since Amelia had gone through all the trouble of fixing us food, I decided that I was going to pay for the drinks.

"Uh, pretty good. How about you?"

"Good," she said as she pushed some buttons on the register.

As casually as I could, I looked over at Amelia and the Bluesman with a neutral expression on my face.

Amelia did not look very pleased.

Great, I thought. *I was really making some progress, and now this. Way to go.*

Bark!

I gazed down at Zock, and he was looking at something outside the window that had caught his attention, which he felt the need to bark at. It had been so loud in the quiet store, practically everyone had probably heard it.

Kelly stopped what she was doing so she could lean over the counter and look down. Zock was staring up at her and panting.

"Friend of yours, honey?" she said smiling as she brought herself back up and finished ringing up the transaction. She had called me "honey." In front of Amelia. I could have just died.

"Uh, he's my dog. He's okay. He just didn't want to be left outside. I hope it's okay since we'll be leaving in a few minutes."

"I don't think it will be a problem, sweetie," she said as I gave her the money for the drinks so she could ring up the sale. Now she had called me 'sweetie.' Another term of endearment. In front of Amelia. I really did feel like I was dying. At any other time I would have loved to hear Kelly calling me those things because I had dreamed of it... but not now. Anytime but now.

Kelly gave me the change, and I told her that we didn't need the cans bagged because we were going to put them in my backpack

"Come around the counter for a moment," she said, as she started taking the cans from the plastic binding and, not even thinking about it, I did. When they were all separated, she placed them in and stacked them neatly in my backpack. While she was doing so, I looked over at Amelia to see what she was doing.

She did not have a happy expression on her face.

Great. Kelly was just being nice and she was unknowingly causing me to blow it with my official/unofficial girlfriend.

Once Kelly was done stacking, she zipped up my backpack for me, and I thought that was the worst of it.

"Have a nice day, honey. Come and see me again soon."

I wanted to scream.

I quickly waved good-bye to her, and the four of us proceeded to walk toward the exit. I wanted to smooth things over as quickly as I could, so I looked over at Amelia and smiled. "She's pretty nice, huh?" I said in a casual manner.

"She sure is, 'sweetie,'" she replied in a hard tone as she started to walk ahead of us. I immediately deflated. She was officially mad at me. I looked over at the Bluesman, and it was taking everything he had for him to contain his laughter because it was completely obvious what was going on.

He leaned over toward me so that only I could hear him. "Women. You can't live with them; you can't live without them."

He was absolutely correct. The Bluesman was very wise.

With a sigh and with my head hanging, we proceeded to walk toward our bikes.

Then, as I thought about it, I became angry. I mean, really, what did she have to be mad at? We had spent all day yesterday together and had a wonderful time, and she obviously knew I liked her. Plus, here we were now about to go and spend the day together again. I knew that if it was going to be in any way pleasant, I had to clear this up right now, otherwise it would put a dark cloud over the day and we would all wind up being miserable, all over nothing.

I got off my bike and stood in front of her while she was sitting on hers.

"What's wrong?"

"What do you mean what's wrong?" she said looking directly at me.

"You're mad."

"No, I'm not." She looked away.

"Yes, you are."

"No, I'm not."

"Yes, you are."

"No, I'm not."

I felt like we were playing tennis. This could go on all day. Time for a change.

"Tell me why you're mad. Is it because of Kelly?"

"Oh, is that your girlfriend's name?" she crooned.

"She's not my girlfriend," I moaned. "She's just someone my mom and I see whenever we come up here."

"You must come up here as often as you can."

"No, I don't." Countless trips immediately went through my mind, but she didn't need to know that.

"Then why was she calling you 'sweetie' and 'honey'?"

"She was just being nice. That's her job. She has to be nice to people." The Bluesman's words came to mind.

"Well, she was certainly doing a good job. She even loaded your bag for you. That sure was nice of her," she said sarcastically.

"Amelia, why are you so mad?"

"I'm not mad."

"Yes, you are."

"No, I'm not."

"Yes, you are."

"No, I'm not."

We were doing it again. I had to put a stop to this so we could get underway. "You're jealous," I said and instantly regretted saying it. I honestly expected her to pounce on me right there and beat me up. Even Zock probably wouldn't be able to stop her once she got going.

"What did you say?"

"You're… you're jealous," I said a bit nervously, trying not to show it. I was ready to turn and run if I had to, but I stood my ground.

"I am not *jealous*." She emphasized the last word by crossing her arms in front of her as she looked at me defiantly.

"Then why are you giving me attitude?" I matched her tone. "There's nothing to be mad over. Besides, she's old. She's probably at least twenty!"

"You certainly seem to like her."

"What do you mean?"

"You didn't seem to object to her fawning all over you."

"She was being nice! I told you that!"

"She was being *too* nice, if you ask me."

I was floored. I had absolutely no clue what to say. Girls were a new life form to me, and I knew that they had their own language. Why couldn't it just be like yesterday, when everything was great? Finally, I said, "I never get mad when you talk about the boys you like." I knew it sounded immature even as I was saying it. What can I say? I was desperate.

"What do you mean? When have I ever talked to you about boys?"

"You said that you like David Hasselhoff, the *Knight Rider* guy. Also, David Lee Roth." I really hated that she liked David Lee Roth, not that I was ever going to tell her that. He was a rich rock star, plus he had muscles. David Hasselhoff was just some guy who drove a make-believe talking car. He would probably do nothing after the show was over and go back to Germany or whatever.

"Danny, they're celebrities. That's different."

"How is it different? They're guys, aren't they?"

"I can't believe we're having this conversation," she exclaimed in a way that reminded me of my mom when she and my dad sometimes got into it, usually over something stupid. Like this. "So, you don't have a crush on any celebrities?" she said regarding me with a speculative look.

I couldn't believe it. I was already sinking into a hole that I was digging with every word that I said, and she had just given me a bulldozer to help with the job. How did my dad or any other man put up with this on a daily basis? I was already tired from talking so much. She looked like she could go on forever.

"Uh...well..."

"'Uh, well,' what? Tell me."

"It's not important. You're changing the subject."

"No, I'm not. You're the one who brought it up. Who is she?" she demanded.

"She's just a celebrity. Like you said, it doesn't matter."

"Tell me!"

"Phoebe Cates!" I blurted.

There was a silence for a moment.

"Who?" she inquired.

"*Fast Times at Ridgemont High.*"

"The movie? What about it?"

"She was in it."

"She was? Who was she?"

"She was the girl with the long, dark hair."

It was quiet for a moment as she thought about what I was talking about. Then, her eyes lit up. "The girl who did the topless scene by the pool while that guy was... was... you know what he was doing! Her?"

"Yeah," I said feeling a bit ashamed. I had completely forgotten about that scene. I mean, I hadn't forgotten it, but I had forgotten about it, if you know what I mean. I wonder if she was picturing me doing... that. It was embarrassing.

"She was pretty," she finally said.

I looked at her for a moment, trying to gauge if she was planning on tricking me. Girls are good at that.

"Really?" I said trying to gauge where she was going with it.

"Really. Oh, Danny, it just annoys me that you would flirt with someone in front of me like that. Right in front of me!"

"I wasn't flirting with her at all. Name one moment where there was a time that I was flirting with her. She was doing all of it."

She thought about it for a moment, and I knew I had her.

"Look," I said moving myself over her wheel and holding her hands. "She's just someone that I know whenever I come in to the grocery store. You're someone...someone I really like," I explained and wondering at the same time how it sounded. I was trying to picture what James Bond would do, and I don't think he would ever say anything like that, mainly because he would never have to say anything like that. The girls just threw themselves at him when they weren't trying to kill him.

"Really?" she said. Her tone had softened, and I knew I was hitting it home.

"Really." We just looked at each other.

Then we heard some sniffing and looked over at the Bluesman. He was mock crying, holding his fists under his eyes as he pretended to wipe away tears.

"That was beautiful, you guys, just beautiful. It brought tears to my eyes just watching it, really," he said and then made this huge honking sound that reminded me of Matt Distler.

"Shut up!" we both yelled at him at the same time. We looked at each other and slowly started laughing, the Bluesman joining us.

"Goatman's?" I said to her.

"Goatman's." She smiled that beautiful smile.

I climbed on my bike, and we were off.

128

You cannot possibly imagine how tired I was after all that. Is this what all relationships are like? It's a miracle the human race is still moving along if boys and girls are fighting like this all the time. I remembered how perfect everything had been the day before, and what a good time we'd had, talking and playing air hockey and miniature golf and sitting on the bench on her porch. Then I understood: For all the rough patches a relationship might hit from time to time, it was the times like that that made it all worth it.

I know it may sound stupid, but I felt more grown up at that moment than I ever had in my entire life. Was that what it took to be a grown-up? Fighting with a girl? I really wasn't sure that being a grown-up was such a good thing, then. Who would want to do that all the time? Then again, I supposed it wouldn't be all the time if it was the right girl, and Amelia certainly felt like the right girl, if you know what I mean.

We now had to go back in the same direction that we had come from to get to our destination, but it was worth it because we now had some cold sodas. I knew they were cold because I could feel them pressing up against my back. They actually felt kind of nice, and they kept me cool, even though they were a little bit heavy. I was glad that I'd elected to wear the backpack and buy the sodas despite the little altercation about Kelly. But it actually might not have been such a bad thing. Because of our little talk, I felt that we knew each other better than we ever had before. Progress! It involved having to get into an argument, but it was progress!

We were riding along, and I was feeling really good. In fact, I decided that this was it. This was the day that I was going to pop a wheelie. I could feel it! I got some speed going so that I was now riding right between the Bluesman and Amelia, and once I felt like I was ready, I pulled up on my handlebars and...

I was doing it!

129

I had popped a wheelie and, even more important, I was riding it!

"Hey, guys! Look!" I yelled.

But they were already watching me as I was doing it. Amelia especially had a great view of me, which I had planned, and she looked pretty impressed, if I do say so myself.

"Way to go, Dan!" I heard the Bluesman yell.

Then, all too soon, my wheel came back down and touched the earth again. It had been a truly intoxicating moment, and I was glad that there were people around to witness it, especially Amelia, who was looking at me with a wonderful smile, possibly with the same kind of expression she would have while looking at David Lee Roth. Wow! *This must be what it feels like to be a rock star!*

I knew the Bluesman could do things like that all the time and more, with no problem, and I was almost scared that he was going to...but he never did. I think it was because he knew that I had just had a shining moment in front of my official/unofficial girlfriend, and he didn't want to blow it for me. The Bluesman had always been my best friend, but I don't think that I had ever appreciated him more than at that particular moment. What a great day!

It just occurred to me that I have been mentioning Goatman's all this time and you probably have no idea at all what I am talking about. I guess it does sound like a strange name. To you, I mean. I had first heard about it several years earlier, so I was pretty used to it.

Goatman's was a strange place that, for the most part, was in the middle of nowhere, just open fields. You had to ride out on a long, dirt road to get there, and it was some kind of...place. It was actually kind of hard to describe because I was not exactly sure what it was. I don't think anyone really knew what it was, or had been. Once you finally arrived there, Goatman's was a place that appeared to be at least a hundred years old. It looked like an old, abandoned resort or gaming facility or farm, or a combination of all of those. The arched entrance of it was almost completely hidden because it was overrun with trees and bushes that, once upon a time, were probably well kept.

Once you were inside and started to explore things, the first thing you would see was a long sitting area to your left with a roof stretching over it. It looked like a long, wiry bench with a shelf in front of it that curved around for at least fifty feet. It appeared to have been some kind of shooting range. The thing that made it seem odd was that there was nothing to shoot at because there was no open space in front of it, just some dirt roads that led farther into the complex, and some giant trees and bushes that went on forever. Also, to the left of the long bench once it ended was a rather large pond. Sometimes when we'd gone out there we'd seen some ducks floating on it. We had no idea where they had come from because, like I said, the place was in the middle of nowhere. Maybe that was what appealed to them about it and they thought it was their little secret and they wouldn't be bothered there. On the right side was a large, dark building that appeared to be a barn and looked like it might cave in at any moment because the wood was so decayed and old. We had gone in there several times in the past, and there was really nothing to it, just a large, open space with weeds growing everywhere. However, there was a strange kind of smell. The only way I could think to describe it was age, age and...something else that I just could not place. Maybe I just never wanted to know.

As soon as you entered the facility, there were three dirt roads that you could take to go exploring. Most of it was open area, although at one place – which led me to believe that this used to be some kind of resort – was a giant swimming pool filled with dirt, leaves, and bushes. Just getting to it was like walking through a dense jungle. There was even a small tree that appeared to be struggling to grow in it and was doing a pretty good job. The pool looked like it had not been used in decades because it certainly would have taken that long for it to become overrun with growth like it was. Beside the pool and off to the side was a small bar area with some old, rusty stools in front of it that looked as if it was going to collapse any day, and the sinks behind it were nothing but square, wooden boxes. Built around it was a wooden canopy that was so ancient it would not have surprised me if millions of termites had made it their home. The back of the bar was nothing but empty holes of various sizes where I assumed things like hoses and wires and such were once used for getting drinks out of tanks stored underneath. Huge cockroaches almost the size of my hand were everywhere, and they were usually mad when people came around because it meant the territory they'd claimed as theirs was being invaded.

Along each of the three roads you eventually came to other old, wooden structures of various sizes. One of them had easily been a stable of some sort because of the small, wooden cages inside. I assumed horses were kept there, but who knew? Maybe it had been pigs or sheep, maybe even goats. It was so old there wasn't even a trace of a smell of what kind of animals used to be stored in there except for that strange smell I told you about earlier, which I couldn't place.

Other structures were more of the same. Although, I do remember in one of them that we once found an old horse's saddle and some old tools like some screwdrivers and two hammers lying around. One of them was that old wooden kind that looked like a small block on top of a handle. I remember I picked it up and hit something with it, and it immediately came apart because it was so archaic and weather-beaten, dust exploding everywhere. I think we even found an old, rusty lantern there, also, at one time. Yet in all of our exploring, we had never found any indication of what this place used to be. There were never any signs saying the name of the place or any kind of advertising, nothing. I had often thought of asking my parents about it and seeing if they knew anything, but then they would want to know why I was riding out to the middle of nowhere and would probably go ballistic that I was doing it because a place like that was no place for little boys. So we never found out.

The reason the place came to be known as Goatman's is because of a legend that I always had assumed someone made up, probably a kid. The legend had it that the reason it was called Goatman's was because there was a thing living there that was supposedly half human and half goat. If you looked closely around the area, you would see tracks around the dirt roads that were supposedly the imprints of a goat's feet or hooves or whatever you call them. The weird thing about them was that they were only in tracks of two, not four. I had also heard a legend that said the tracks were two hooves and two footprints that looked human. I myself had never seen any of these tracks, however, so I was not really partial to believing the story. In any case, that's how it got its name – Goatman's.

Anyway, we were on our way there again, but this time with Amelia.

We rode through our neighborhood again until we were on an open road beside a large, white wall that enclosed a subdivision. Eventually, we left the wall behind, and the rest of the street was nothing but open road leading nowhere. Soon, the road ended abruptly and turned to dirt, as though the workers who built it had finally wised up and said, "Hey! There's nothing around here to build a road for. Let's pack up and go home, boys!"

So, there we were. Needless to say, the riding was going to be a little rougher from there on in. The Bluesman and I would not be having any trouble, and because of the kind of bicycle that Amelia was riding, she was able to

133

adjust pretty easily. Still, you could tell that she was not used to riding on that kind of terrain and had kind of an annoyed expression on her face. It crossed my mind that she might decide to want to turn back later on, especially once the road became rougher, but then I thought about the kind of person she was and how badly she wanted to see Goatman's.

We rode for a while, talking about various things like movies and music and other important stuff. As I looked up at the sky, I was very appreciative of how perfect the day was for riding. The sun was out but it was very cloudy. Not the kind of dark sky that is the prelude to rain but just a lot of clouds that blocked the sun. I was very grateful for this because this was a long trip and in the middle of summer. Having the sun beating down on us was something that we really did not want. Also, there was a good, solid wind that was cooling us off. It was not so strong that it slowed us down, just enough to keep us cool.

After about forty minutes or so, we decided to stop and sit down for a break while we ate. We all dismounted our bikes, and Amelia and I took off our packs and got the food out. She took out a sandwich each and gave us each one as I passed around the sodas.

I was undoing my sandwich bag as I watched Amelia about to open her soda. As she did so, I suddenly realized something. We had been riding on a bumpy road and those were carbonated drinks. That could only mean… "Amelia! No!" I yelled.

Too late. The can exploded as soon as she opened it, and Coke foam exploded everywhere. Fortunately, Amelia, as startled as she was, had really quick reflexes and was able to move the can away from her before any of it could get on her. However, half of the contents of her can were now soaking into the ground.

The Bluesman immediately started laughing. Although, all it took was one look from Amelia and he immediately stopped, just like that.

Needless to say, when he and I opened our sodas we were very careful and kept them away from us. However, we each got to drink only half a can because of the exploding. It had not ever dawned on me that bringing sodas would result in something like this, mainly because we had never brought drinks with us. Still, half of a soda was better than no soda. I suppose we could have brought water, but I couldn't stand water. I knew that it was the healthiest thing a person could drink, but water has absolutely no taste to it! Nothing. And, besides, even if we had brought it, it would have been warm. The only thing I hated worse than water was warm water. So, regardless of the situation, sodas ruled, even if they were now mostly warm and we'd lost half the contents of the can.

We sat there and ate for a few minutes, me giving some of my sandwich to Zock. Almost at the same time we all realized how quiet everything was. There was no noise anywhere. Every now and then some birds would fly by, but that was it. It was very peaceful. It was very rare that it was actually that quiet where we lived, even though we lived in the suburbs, which aren't exactly loud. I mean, the Corpus Christi suburbs aren't like New York or anything, where the noise is constant. Sitting there, it made me think of something funny. The people next door had a relative who lived in New York, and he had come down the summer before, for a visit. He was absolutely astounded at how quiet it was compared to back home, and it actually made him nervous. Can you imagine that? Getting away from all that constant racket made him nervous. I'd seen movies that were set in New York, and the noise was constant: traffic, guns going off, and people yelling and screaming. How could anyone miss *that*?

While he was here, our neighbor's relative stayed in a room at the Holiday Inn, the really nice one on the beach out by the Bay Front that my parents and I sometimes went to. They liked to hang out in the small lounge that they had there and have drinks, and I liked playing in the arcade. There was also a small place to play miniature golf at, although it was not nearly as big or fancy as the one at the country club. By the indoor swimming pool, which was nice, and next to a kids' jungle gym, there was one of those shuffleboard games, where you use a long stick to slide a puck along the ground so that it lands on a certain number in a labeled pyramid. It's pretty popular among old people, although kids can enjoy it also. They even had an open space on the other side with some fake plastic grass where a volleyball net was set up. It was a really nice place! I loved it because it had everything! It even had a small gym. We had never stayed there, of course, but I was sure that the rooms were really nice. Just like the arcade at the country club, it could also be very romantic at night, the silence and serenity of it. The entire wall by the pool was glass, so you could look out at the ocean past the beach and see the stars floating overhead. I thought this would be a really nice place to go on a honeymoon or something like that, especially considering that they had a nice restaurant, where the lights were dimmed inside, and each table had a little bowl with a lit candle in it.

Anyway, about the guy. He was so used to hearing noise all the time that he couldn't sleep without it. Before he went to bed every night, he switched on a cassette player that was sitting on the table next to his bed and played nothing but traffic. Can you believe that? A tape of traffic and nothing else! He said it helped get him to sleep. I would think something like that would just keep a person up. I decided New York did not sound like the kind of place where I would want to live if it was so noisy that you actually couldn't do without it.

Anyhow, to get back to our visit to the Goatman's, we talked for a while, and then we were treated to an impromptu concert. The Bluesman stood up and looked at us. "Do you guys like Eddie Murphy?"

"Yes," we both said. I thought he was the funniest guy on the planet! I watched *Saturday Night Live* all the time, mainly just to watch him. My favorite skits were James Brown's "Celebrity Hot Tub," "Buckwheat," and "Mr. Robinson's Neighborhood," which is the ghetto version of *Mr. Rogers' Neighborhood*. Also, he did a really funny impression of Stevie Wonder. I remember he made this short documentary film about how he dressed up like a white guy in a suit and walked around the streets pretending he was white and observing how *supposedly* a white guy is treated in the world compared to a black guy. The funniest moment was when he was riding a bus and once the only black guy that was on it got off at a stop, it immediately turned into a nightclub with music playing and a cocktail waitress serving drinks. Hilarious! Eddie Murphy ruled!

"Okay, check this out," the Bluesman said.

He immediately went into "Ice Cream Man" from *Delirious*. Eddie Murphy had just done a stand-up comedy special for HBO called *Delirious,* which was the funniest thing I had ever seen. There was a skit in it called "Ice Cream Man," about when Eddie was a kid and his experiences with ice cream and the kids in the neighborhood. The Bluesman was now doing it verbatim, right in front of us, word for word. He was doing the different voices and everything! I had never seen him do this before, and it was exactly like watching it on television. The only difference was that the Bluesman is not black nor was he wearing a red leather outfit. Other than that, it was "Ice Cream Man" done exactly like Eddie Murphy. Incredible! I knew the Bluesman was funny, but being as funny as both Robin Williams and Eddie Murphy?

The Bluesman was beyond funny! Both Amelia and I were in awe and could not stop laughing as we were witnessing what was before us. Amelia was even more impressed than I was because she had never seen the Bluesman performing full throttle, like I had on numerous occasions.

As he was doing his routine, I thought how strange the situation was. Here we were in the middle of nowhere, and the Bluesman was putting on a surprise concert for two people. But, I also could not help but thinking how right it seemed at the same time. It was so ridiculous; it could not help but be anything but right, if you know what I mean. I don't know if you have ever been in a situation like that or not, but if you have, you know exactly what I am talking about. Watching him, I could easily imagine him on a stage somewhere doing exactly what he was doing right now in front of thousands of people. That's how mesmerizing he was and, on top of that, he was doing it all so naturally, like it was nothing. More than any other time in my life, I wanted to hurry up and grow up just so I could see what the Bluesman would be doing fifteen or twenty years from now.

His routine came to an end, and Amelia and I immediately gave him thunderous applause, and he did some graceful bowing as he acknowledged his massive audience of two – three including Zock. We talked again for a while about our favorite movies and television shows and had a really in-depth conversation about music. As we were sitting there drinking some more warm sodas, I was happy to see that Amelia and the Bluesman were becoming the best of friends.

We eventually put all our trash in the empty bags and, after I gathered them all up and placed them in my pack, we were off.

It was not going to be much longer, and I would estimate that we were about halfway there by now. The road turned a little bit rougher, but we were all having such a good time we just ignored it and proceeded on.

Then, in the distance, we saw it – Goatman's. It was kind of hard not to miss because it was this massive bundle of tall trees in the middle of nowhere that seemed as if it had appeared in front of us like an oasis. However, I don't think you would ever have mistaken Goatman's for a paradise. As we got closer, it became larger, until we eventually came to a stop in front of the massive, broken entrance of it. It looked like even more of a jungle than I remembered it.

I glanced over at Amelia, and I could tell from the expression on her face that this was not in any way what she had expected. I think she had been hoping to see…I don't know, a really pretty jungle with talking animals or something, and maybe some music playing in the background like in a Disney film. If we were talking movies, I would compare it more to Camp Crystal Lake, where Jason liked to hang out and look for teen-agers to knock off in gory ways. We stood there for a moment, looking around at the entrance. As we were doing so, I looked down and saw something odd. There were tire tracks in the dirt beneath us. They had to be fairly recent because it had rained a couple of days ago and the tracks were really deep. They were obviously truck tires because the tracks were larger than what a car would leave. I casually wondered if there was anyone in there. I mean, why would there be? It's not like there was anything in there that anyone would want. Then again, here I was thinking that, while we had just made a long bike trip to come all the way out here.

"Well, let's head inside," the Bluesman said and pedaled in. We followed him and, not surprisingly, Amelia was last, and she was looking all over the place with a timid expression on her face.

"This place is spooky," she said, scanning the area.

139

"Cha-cha-cha-cha. Ho-ho-ho-ho. Na-na-na-na," the Bluesman whispered loudly, making the sounds that were always in the *Friday the 13th* movies, when a scene was building and Jason was lurking around, about to kill someone. Amelia immediately recognized the sounds and looked at him, indicating that he had better stop or else, so he did. She glanced over at the pond and saw some ducks floating around.

"Oh! Look over there. Let's go see them," she said smiling as she dismounted from her bicycle, and we did the same. The Bluesman and I looked at each other, and our expressions were telling each other the same thing: Only a girl could get this excited over seeing ducks. Still, I was happy that the ducks were here. Goatman's was already spooking her out, and the ducks seemed to put her more at ease. We walked over to the pond and looked at them. There were seven of them, and when they noticed us, they seemed to be annoyed and started to float away. It probably did not help matters any that Zock was staring at them.

"Oh, they're leaving," Amelia said, dismayed. She took off her backpack and unzipped it. Withdrawing one of the bags, she opened it and took out a sandwich. She proceeded to tear little pieces from it and throw them into the pond near the ducks. The ducks looked at the pieces for a moment and then, sensing food, which they were probably desperate for, considering that there was probably nothing to eat around here, they slowly floated toward the sandwich bits and started gobbling them up. I wasn't sure if there were any fish in the pond or not. Considering the environment, it would not have surprised me if it had been filled with piranha. Maybe even the Creature from the Black Lagoon.

"They like it!" she exclaimed as she tore some more pieces and threw them in the pond, the ducks gobbling them up almost as soon as they hit the water. Once all of the pieces were gone, they honked at her in thanks and then floated away around the bushes, where we couldn't see them any longer. "Well, that was fun," she said, and then we walked back to where our bikes were.

"Well, what now?" the Bluesman said.

"What do you usually do when you come out here?" Amelia asked.

"Go exploring. How about we head into the giant building over there and look around?" I offered as I pointed at the large structure to the right that I had mentioned earlier. Amelia looked at it and just stared at it.

"It looks like its going to collapse at any second."

"That's the fun."

"Fun?" she said, looking at me.

"Sure. Where's your sense of adventure? Let's go check it out." We started walking toward it. As we did, something happened that made my day. Amelia was nervous and got close to me so she could hold my hand as we walked. I think it was an unconscious reaction because she was still looking around at the scenery as she did it, but I wasn't complaining. I think she not only was nervous because of the surroundings and the building we were walking toward but was shaken because of the constant buzzing that was in the air. I wasn't sure, but I think it was being caused by the massive colony of crickets that must have inhabited this place. I could only imagine what it sounded like at night, when crickets really like to come out and make that racket that they obviously enjoy for whatever reason.

We came to the decrepit doorway of the structure, and the door that was barely hanging on. Probably just touching it in the slightest would cause it to fall. The Bluesman walked in, and we followed. Because of the decayed wood and all the holes that were everywhere, especially in the arched ceiling, there was a good amount of light, so we had no trouble seeing where we were going.

141

As expected, there was not really a whole lot to see. I mean, I guess it's interesting to see what a building can turn into after decades of neglect, but it's not like there was a party going on inside or anything. Although, as we were walking around the hay-covered floor, I became aware again of the unusual smell that I still could not place. Zock must have noticed it also because he was now standing in one place and sniffing with a queer look on his face. Then, deciding he was tired of waiting on us to do something, he decided to do some exploring on his own.

The sound of his sniffing was the only sound in the place as he walked along the walls, his tail wagging all over the place. Actually, I was pretty happy that I'd decided to bring Zock with us. I knew that Amelia wasn't crazy about him because of his humping habits, but I got a sense that it made her feel a little at ease to have a dog around. I mean, its not like he was one of those big, ferocious dogs like a Rottweiler or a pit bull, but he was certainly not a wimp. I remember one time when I saw Zock get into a fight with a car, and the car backed down! Actually, it just came to a stop because he had been standing in the middle of the street and refused to back down. He started barking at it, and the car backed up and went around him. So, technically, Zock won. At any rate, if there was anyone around, he would be the first to know about it, and he would in turn let us know.

"Hey! Check this out!" the Bluesman said, and we walked over to where he was standing behind a wooden counter that had certainly seen better days.

"What's up?" I asked as we approached him.

He held up an old, rusty machete. He was wearing a smile of appreciation.

"Oh! A knife!" Amelia said startled.

"It's a machete, like the one Jason uses," the Bluesman said as he held onto the grip and looked at it closely.

142

"What's it doing back there? Is there anything else there?" I asked.

"No, this is it."

Amelia looked at it. "Put it down."

"It's all rusty and old, anyway," the Bluesman muttered in a bored tone as he tossed it on the ground. He walked around the counter and started exploring some more. So far, except for the ducks, that had been the most exciting thing we had seen there. "Hey, what's up there?" he said, looking upward.

We all gazed up. We were now looking at what appeared to be a loft of some sort. Off to the side was a wooden ladder that was built against the edge of a platform that led all the way to the ground.

"I wonder what's up there?" the Bluesman inquired.

"Probably a whole lot of nothing," I replied.

"Only one way to find out," he said with an adventurous smile as he headed for the ladder. He placed a foot on one of the steps and shook the ladder to test its strength. "Feels solid." He started to slowly climb it.

"Be careful," Amelia said, looking at him and squeezing my hand tightly.

He continued to climb. As he put one of his feet on a rung with all of his weight, it gave way and splintered in two, and we both gasped. He reactively gripped the rung above him with both hands and saved himself from a fall. It was only about ten feet, but it still would have been a doozy of a fall.

"I'm okay," he said in a joking tone, but we could tell how much it had startled him. He eventually reached the top, climbed onto the platform, and looked around.

"So, what's up there?" I called out to him.

"Just a wide open area. It's pretty cool. There's a window up here, and you can see above the trees. Pretty good view. Come up and check it out."

143

Amelia and I looked at each other, neither one of us really that interested in just seeing a vast jungle. But adventure was why we had come all the way out here, and here was a small adventure.

"Do you want me to go up first?" I asked.

"No, I'll go first," Amelia answered as we walked over to the ladder, and she gripped it as she looked up. Then she slowly began her ascent. My eye was on her the whole time. I was pretty sure that she wouldn't fall if the Bluesman hadn't because she probably weighed less than he did. Then again, that might be a hard call because she was kind of tall and stronger than either one of us, which was kind of embarrassing. Still, she made it safely all the way to the top, and once she was off the ladder, I followed her up until I was standing beside her.

"That wasn't so bad," I said in a cheerful tone, trying to make her feel better. Actually, I was also trying to make myself feel better because I was nervous with each step upward that another rung might break and *bam!* down I would go. Now that we were both safely up, we looked around the empty area. There was nothing but a couple of barrels of hay in the corner, so this must have at one time been a barn where horses or cows were kept. Also, the strange, musty smell was a lot stronger up here than downstairs. We walked over to the window where the Bluesman was admiring the view and gazed outside. Not surprisingly, the glass was long since broken, the shards probably lying on the ground below.

He had been right: It was a pretty nice view. It looked over the direction that we had come from. All we saw was a long, dirt road leading back to the outlay of our neighborhood, which we could barely even see because everything was so far away. It amazed me how far up we were because the climb had not seemed that long, I guess because I was nervous. Still, it was nice to see. However, this was definitely not the kind of place where I would like to be during the night.

I looked back at the barrels of hay, and we walked over toward them.

"I wonder how long these have been here?" the Bluesman said.

"Probably decades," I said absently.

The Bluesman gave it a kick and dust flew up. Also, about a dozen cockroaches immediately scattered from it and started running across the floor.

"Aiiiiiiiieeeeeeeeeeeee!" Amelia screamed, backing away from them before they could get any nearer.

"Well, I think that's a hint and a half that it's time to go," I stated.

"I think so, too," Amelia said as we went back to the ladder and began our descent to where Zock was standing waiting for us. The Bluesman went first, then me, and Amelia went last. I wanted her to go last because, in case something did happen, we would both be down there to do our best to catch her fall. We made our way out of the barn and headed back to where our bikes were parked.

"So, what now?" I said.

The Bluesman said, "Let's go see the swimming pool."

"Swimming pool?" Amelia asked.

"It's not far from here," I explained as we proceeded to make our way through the jungle until we had arrived. Zock had the easiest time because he was smaller than the rest of us and closer to the ground. Nothing really had changed. It was still the same swimming pool filled with dirt and bushes. I noticed that the tree that was in it had grown a little bit. Or, at least it appeared bigger, but it could have just been my imagination.

"I bet this used to be a really nice pool back in the day," Amelia said, looking at it with a trace of sorrow.

We walked over to the bar, and the Bluesman walked behind it and faced us. "So, what will it be, partner?" he said, smiling, as he slammed his hand on the bar. The bar immediately collapsed in a loud heap, dust flying everywhere, and dozens of sizeable cockroaches raced away from their home, which we had destroyed. Actually, it had already been destroyed, but they were probably happy with it. I can't picture cockroaches being very picky about anything.

"Aiiiiiiieeeeeeeeeeeeee!" Amelia screamed as she ran back away from them, with me right behind her. The Bluesman, more startled than anyone, ran from behind the bar so he was now standing beside us. We looked at the caved-in bar and the dust in the air above it as its occupants vacated it.

"Sorry about that," the Bluesman said with an embarrassed grin.

I looked over at Zock, and the way he was standing with his head straight and slightly up caught my attention. His ears were flicking up and down. "Hey, what's up boy?" I asked as I approached him and then looked in the direction he was staring at. There was nothing but trees and thick growth.

Then, we all heard it. There was some kind of subtle rustling in the growth.

"What is that?" Amelia whispered.

"I don't know," I said absently. In all the times we had come out here, we had never encountered any kind of animal expect for the ducks. And the cockroaches, if you wanted to count them.

Zock had not made a sound, but he was still staring into the growth.

Then, as if whatever was making the noise had become aware that it had been heard, it stopped. We stood there for a few minutes and nothing happened.

Finally, Amelia said, "Let's head back."

"No argument there," the Bluesman said as he proceeded in the direction that we had come from, this time at a faster pace. Zock stayed there for a few moments, still staring. Looking at him and the stance he was in, it appeared as though he were challenging whatever had been making the noise. Then, he turned around and followed us.

Once we were back where our bikes were parked, we just looked around and grinned nervously.

"What do you think that was?" Amelia asked me.

"Probably just a squirrel or something," I said, and she relaxed. Actually, I was not sure in the least what it was, but it seemed like the most logical thing, and it made her feel better. I think I had a pretty good idea of what she was thinking right now – we should have just gone swimming at the club again. Truth to tell, that sounded like a really great idea, especially after yesterday, but here we were. We had ridden all the way out here for some adventure and something a little bit different. This was certainly different from a nice country club in the suburbs.

"Well, why don't we go riding around for a while and then come back here and have lunch?" the Bluesman said.

We agreed and then mounted our bikes. The Bluesman led the way down one of the roads, and we were off, Zock happily trailing behind us.

After a while, we came to another structure that was about half the size of the one near the entrance and had only one level. Most of the roof had been eaten away. We walked inside, and there was not really much to see. It was just a wide, open area with a dirt floor and with sprinkles of hay everywhere. Although, in the back corner was an old, white, beat-up refrigerator that looked to be at lest fifty years old. I opened it up while standing as far away from it as I could so I could jump if anything popped out, but there was nothing in it, and once the door opened, a puff of air that sounded like a dying man's gasp leaked out. So much for that.

We went back and mounted our bikes and then talked about which way to go, either explore further or head back

147

to camp. In the end, our stomachs won out, and we began the ride back to camp. For some reason I was really hoping to see the ducks again. Despite some of the cool if uninteresting stuff we had seen, the ducks had been my favorite of the day. Once we were back, we saw that the ducks had returned, and we decided to have lunch on the edge of the pond while we watched them. We opened our packs and passed the food around, being extra careful with the sodas, even though it really did no good and they exploded again. Still, we were all incredibly thirsty, so none of us complained. The ducks kept a respectful distance but were ready to move forward in case some food appeared in front of them again. Zock was especially on his best behavior. He had not so much as barked once and was even leaving the ducks alone. I think it was because he was enjoying watching them as much as we were and knew that if he barked, they would immediately leave. Still, I did not expect them to paddle up to the shore and say hello.

It struck me that this had turned out to be a really nice day. Here I was on an adventure with my two best friends and my faithful dog, sitting by a beautiful pond and having lunch on a pleasant, cool day. Things could certainly be worse. Once the summer ended and we had to go back to school, things would definitely turn for the worse. But right now? Great. Really great.

We finished our lunch and went back to where our bikes were parked behind some bushes and sat down in the shade of the shooting range bench for about an hour.

As we were talking and joking around, we thought we heard something. Everyone must have heard it at the same time because we all stopped talking at the same moment and looked at each other.

"Do you hear that?" I asked.

"What is it?" Amelia said.

"It sounds like… a machine. It's far away, but it sounds like a car or motorcycle or something," the Bluesman offered. He got up and looked around the bush-laden entrance and peered outward with his hand resting above his eyes.

"What is it?" I asked.

"I'm not sure because it's still too far away to tell… but I think it's a pick-up truck."

"A pick-up truck? Coming out here?" I said. Then I remembered the tracks that had been left and I looked down at them. For some reason, they made me uneasy. I mean, it wasn't like I had a reason to feel that way or anything since this place was apparently off limits to nobody. It could be a couple of guys coming all the way out here to do some duck hunting or maybe even some fishing if there were fish in the pond, which I was assuming there were if there were ducks here. Maybe people even came out here to camp, as unusual as that might sound, this being kind of a creepy place. I had heard that campers liked solitude and being in the middle of nowhere, and this certainly fit the bill. I had even heard a rumor that crazy high school kids liked to drive all the way out there so they could have parties and get it on in sleeping bags. Still, it made me feel uneasy. I got up and stood beside the Bluesman and peered toward the racket. Yes, there was something coming toward us, and it did look like a rather sizeable truck. Whoever was driving it, I was pretty sure they couldn't see us because we were so far away, plus the sun was in their eyes, which would make seeing all the way over here even more difficult.

"Let's… let's hide the bikes in the bushes over here," I said, beginning to move toward them.

"What? Why?" the Bluesman asked.

"I…I don't know. I just want to hide them and then for us to get out of the way until we know who they are."

"They're probably just some guys coming out here to do the same thing we're doing."

149

"Danny? What's wrong?" Amelia said, getting up and standing beside me as she looked toward the truck.

"I don't know. I know it sounds weird, but I think we should hide the bikes and ourselves until we know what's going on."

We were all silent for a moment while we looked outward.

"He's right. Let's do it," Amelia said as she walked toward her bike and I followed her, the Bluesman following me. We rolled our bikes behind the bushes and tangled growth behind the long bench, to a place where they would be impossible to see unless you actually walked down the row of coverage and looked for them. The tangled mass was so thick that they did not stand out in any way, and there was still a lot of room for us so we'd be able to peer out, but nobody would be able to see us.

The sound of the truck was getting closer, and we were able to peek through the brush and see it more clearly. It was blue and white and was one of those kinds of pick-up trucks that are huge, the kind that you actually have to place your foot on a step that's built onto it in order to get into the cab — the kind my dad says only men with small wieners drive.

It drew closer, and I looked down at Zock. He appeared as if he were getting ready to bolt toward the truck so he could start barking up a storm. I kneeled down and placed my arms around him so he wouldn't get any funny ideas. Until we knew who these guys were, we didn't want them to know we were here.

The truck, which was really big and had one of those small, windowed carriages that you could install in the loading dock, passed through the entrance area, leaving a trail of dust behind it. I looked at the license plates and saw it was from Arkansas. The window on the driver's side was open, and I could hear the radio playing some country and western song, though I had no clue as to who it was. I

150

was of the opinion that country and western music sucked, so my knowledge of it was very limited. I even liked disco more than country and western, and that's pretty bad, if you know what I mean. Although I did not remember it all, my parents had told me that when I was a kid, my favorite song had been "Rhinestone Cowboy." I really did not know if that was true or if they just said that to try to annoy me. Since they were parents, I wouldn't have put anything past them.

Then, before I could do anything to stop him, Zock barked.

The truck continued for a moment and then stopped in a cloud of dust. Maybe it was fear, but when the red parking lights popped on, they seemed as bright as red suns. I immediately placed my hand over Zock's snout before he could make any more trouble.

The truck had not moved since it stopped.

Then, we all smelled it – McDonald's.

The smell of McDonald's was coming from the truck. Every fast food restaurant has its own particular smell, and I was absolutely sure it was McDonald's because I'd eaten there a hundred times. In fact, if you had placed any fast food item in front of me while my eyes were closed, I would probably have been able to pick it out. That's how good I was.

Then, the driver's side door opened and a guy walked out. He stood there with his hands on his hips, looking around at the area behind him. I immediately recognized him because he was the kind of guy you could never really forget because he was so weird. It was that bald guy who the Bluesman and I had seen in the Maverick Market the previous morning when we were drinking the Slurpees. I remembered how he had been buying an overflowing basket of candy bars, which was weird because it wasn't even Halloween and, call it a strong hunch, but he had not struck me as the kind of guy who had kids. I mean, what kind of girl would…do it…with a guy like that, if you know what I mean.

He was wearing the same large biker jacket as the day before, which was really unusual because this was definitely not jacket weather, and I thought he must be burning up, but he looked fine, and he was still wearing that dopey smile and rapidly blinking all the time. Wouldn't that hurt after a while? All of that blinking?

We all looked at each other, wondering what we should do. If he walked over here and started looking around, he would easily be able to find us. We were fine where we were, but if he started poking around….

Even Zock must have gotten the message about how weird this guy was because he had not made a sound, and it did not feel like he was trying to get away. Now, if a *dog* thought a guy was weird, you can just imagine how weird he must really be.

Then, seeming to come to a decision because he had stopped anyway, he reached into his cab, pulled out a few McDonald's bags, and walked to the back of his truck.

Zock saw the bags and licked his chops. I held onto him extra tight from then on. I knew how he felt because I could have gone for a Big Mac and a cold shake right then myself. The man opened the back door of the carriage and climbed into it.

"What's that guy doing? Is he having lunch?" the Bluesman whispered.

"I don't know," Amelia whispered back, involuntarily squeezing my shoulder. At that moment, I realized what a strong grip she had, but I decided not to say anything.

"I wanna go home!" a young, choked voice yelled from inside the carriage. The voice sounded like a mixture of pain and fright, and we all looked at each other in wonder.

"EattheMcDonaldsitsgoodforyou," we heard the man say in his strange speaking pattern, where he ran all the words together.

"Mister, please take me home," the voice begged. It was kind of far away and sounded so wrenching, it was hard to tell if it was a boy or a girl. From what I could tell, I would estimate the voice to be about six or seven years old.

"EattheMcDonaldsitsgoodforyou," the man said again.

A moment later, he appeared from the carriage and closed the door and locked it. He placed his hands on his hips and looked around again. Man, this guy was big! At first I thought he was looking for where the sound that Zock had made had come from, but then I realized that he was just looking around his surroundings in appreciation as though he were in paradise. If he considered this paradise, I would hate to know what he thought hell was. I mean, some locations of the place were nice, like the pond... and that's about it... but it would certainly never have been mistaken for paradise.

After he had seemingly had his fill, he turned around, walked back to the driver's side, got in, and took off on the trail to the right. We watched him from the brush until we were sure that he would not be able to see us and then walked back into the open, all of us in wonderment.

"What the hell was that all about?" the Bluesman blurted, still looking down the trail and then at us.

"I have no idea," I replied.

"Who was that in the back? It sounded like a little girl," Amelia said.

"You must have better ears than I do because I couldn't tell. Maybe it's his daughter or something," I said as I thought again about what kind of girl could do the you-know-what with him. Probably a redneck who liked country and western music.

"I don't think so. If it was, why wasn't she riding up front with him?"

She had a point, especially since I would think it would be boiling in there. It was just a simple carriage, nothing

153

fancy that looked like it might have air conditioning. She must have been really burning up back there!

"That's a good question. I don't know."

"What's he doing here? Where's he going? What's down there?" she asked.

"I'm not sure. We rode down that trail once for about half an hour, and there was nothing but open fields with weeds taller than us on either side," I explained. "Unless there's something farther down there, I have no clue what he's doing."

"We need to do something," she said.

"Do something? What are we going to do? For all we know, that guy's a monster. He certainly looked like one," the Bluesman said.

"Any man who would lock up a child like that is a monster." Amelia looked down the trail again.

"I agree, but it's none of our business," the Bluesman said.

"What do you mean it's none of our business?" Amelia was genuinely offended. "We need to make it our business. What if he had more than one child in there?"

"Oh. Wow. I hadn't thought of that," the Bluesman muttered.

"Well, now you have something to think about," she snapped.

"Okay, okay. Don't get so mad. What should we do?"

She thought about it for a moment. "I don't know."

"Great. She doesn't know."

"Well...we can't just stand here. We need to do something."

"I agree," I said. "We don't know who that guy was or what he's even doing here. I think we can only assume after what we saw and considering that we're in the middle of nowhere he's doing something bad. I mean really bad."

"That's for sure." Amelia was getting even angrier.

Then, something popped into my head that my mom had reminded me of this morning – all the disappearances of the kids in our neighborhood. Oh, my God.

"Oh, my God. I think… I think I know who that guy is," I said.

"What? You mean you know his name? Who is he?" Amelia said.

"No, I don't mean I know who he is as far as his name goes. Although, I do remember that he said his name was Gordon."

Amelia looked at me with her eyes wide.

"You know him? You know that guy?" she whirled on me as though she was a detective and she was interrogating me.

"We saw him yesterday at the store," the Bluesman said. "He was buying a lot of candy."

"Why didn't you say anything?" she said.

"I just did," the Bluesman said, and she rolled her eyes.

"Anyway, I mean I think I know who he is," I said wanting to get back on track.

They both looked at me like they were trying to figure out a puzzle.

"The disappearances around our neighborhood? The kids?" I prompted.

There was a silence as that realization sank in.

"Oh, God. You think…?" Amelia said, now horrified.

"I think so. I can't think of anything else, and it's the only thing that fits."

"So… he has all those kids somewhere around here?" the Bluesman said.

"I don't know. I'm assuming. I mean, I hate to say it, but I'm not even sure they're alive."

Amelia gasped.

"Like I said, I don't know," I said quickly. "I'm just guessing. I could be completely off."

"And you could be completely on," the Bluesman said.

"So, what should we do?" Amelia asked.

"We could head back home and call the police," I offered.

"And what do we say? We saw this weird bald guy with a speech impediment and we think he's the guy who's been kidnapping kids around our neighborhood? What makes you even think they would believe us?" the Bluesman cried.

"Because they're the police," Amelia said.

"Yeah, and we're kids. Cops hate kids."

Amelia moaned. "They do not."

"Yes they do. They resent having to put up with calls about kids crank calling and knocking on doors and running away and rolling houses with toilet paper and things like that that take up their time when they could be taking care of more important things," he complained.

"He does have a point. They probably wouldn't even believe us anyway. Even if they did, they would want some kind of proof other than 'I saw a weird guy.' On top of all of that, none of us is even supposed to be all the way out here anyway," I said. "If our parents found out about it, especially if this is all just some kind of mistake, we would all be grounded for life!"

We all stared at each other in silence.

Amelia was the first to speak. "Well, we need to do something."

"Okay, how about this?" I said. "How about we find out where this guy went an—"

"What do you mean, find out where he went? For all we know, he's driving a hundred miles away!" the Bluesman blurted. "He could be driving to Mexico!"

"I doubt he's driving to Mexico," I said.

"How do you know?"

"I don't."

"Well then, he could be driving to Mexico. God knows what they do to kids there! I heard that they're so poor

156

over there that they actually eat people who wander across the border for food."

"That's horrible!" Amelia said.

"And it's not true," I said calmly. "Look, I see it as the only thing we can do. We follow the trail until we find something, which I doubt is really that far away, maybe an hour or so."

"An hour?" the Bluesman shouted. It took us about an hour and a half to get here and you want to ride another hour?"

"Here's what we need to do. We need to find wherever he's living, see if he actually is the guy who's been kidnapping the kids, get some proof, ride back home, and then call the police. They'll take care of the rest. Besides, if we do the right thing and save the day, I seriously doubt that our parents will be mad at us. Well, not as mad as they might be if they found out that we had driven all the way out here just for kicks."

"I like it," Amelia said.

"Okay. I'm game," the Bluesman said.

"Fine. Let's go," I said as we walked toward our bikes and mounted them. Once we were all set, we started pedaling down the long road not knowing what we were going to find, and an unspoken thought between us that dreaded what we might.

THE GOATMAN

We had been riding for quite a while and there was nothing in the distance except open fields of rampant weeds and a long dirt road that seemed to be taunting us. None of us had said a word in ages, and the only sound around us was our tires grating on the road. I looked at Zock, and even he seemed to be annoyed and wondering where the heck we were going. The day that had out started so nice, not counting the incident at H.E.B. where Amelia and I had gotten into it, was turning more sour by the moment. Added to this was the fact that we might very well be riding into a very dangerous situation and confronting a person who… was not normal, to say the least.

Also, I felt like someone was watching us. I know how that sounds considering that we were in the middle of nowhere and we would easily be able to tell if anyone was following us either by car or by air, but that's what it felt like.

Amelia looked none too happy and I know the Bluesman was not in the best of moods because he had not cracked one joke since we had left the area where we had been having a pretty darn good time, ducks and all.

Finally, considering the situation and deciding that we were not exactly on a time limit of any kind, I decided to speak.

"Hey, why don't we stop for a while and eat something? Get some rest?"

Without saying a word, the three of us pulled to the right side of the road and dismounted our bikes. We all stretched, and you could hear a few bones cracking as we moved. How's that for tense? We were all thirteen years old, and we already had cracking bones. The Bluesman had a trick where he could crack his knuckles so loudly,

158

you would swear that a machine gun was going off. He did it on both hands but neither of us reacted. However, Zock looked at him oddly and I think was expecting him to do it again. I knew from experience that the Bluesman could do that particular trick only a couple of times a day, and it would be hours before he could do it that loudly again. It wouldn't surprise me if he someday soon developed the early stages of arthritis.

"Oh, God, that feels good," the Bluesman moaned as he locked his hands above his head and stretched. "It feels like we've been riding for hours. How long has it been?"

"Just over half an hour," I said checking my watch.

"What? You have got to be kidding me? That's all?"

"That's all."

He looked down the empty road with a sullen expression on his face. "How much longer do you think we should go?" he said.

"Until we find him," Amelia stated.

"Yeah? Got any idea how long that's going to take? Can you give me an estimate? Look down there," he said gesturing. "There's nothing there!"

"He's out there!" Amelia said sharply.

"Yeah! Somewhere! And, believe me, 'somewhere' is a really relative word in this case."

"So, what do you want to do? Just go back and leave those kids?"

"Amelia, we don't even know for sure that that's what this is. It could just be a...a domestic dispute."

"A domestic dispute? Are you kidding me? You heard that kid in the back of that pick-up. She was in agony and scared out of her mind. That was not a dispute! That was torture!"

The Bluesman didn't say anything and just hung his head.

"So, what? You want to just turn around and forget it ever happened? Is that it? Leave those kids to their fate?"

"Okay, look, I don't want to be the harbinger of death here or anything, but we still don't have all the facts about this. It's all up in the air, and we could very well be going on a wild goose chase. And, I hate to say it, but even if he is the guy, the kids might all be dead."

Amelia just looked at him coldly for a moment and then turned away. She almost appeared as if she were going to cry.

"Look, I'm sorry, but it is a very real possibility. If we find this guy, I just don't want you to be shocked at what we might find. I hate to say it, it's a rotten thing to say or even think, but it could very well be how it turns out."

"I don't think they're dead," I said.

"What? How do you know?" he asked.

"He took time out of his schedule, whatever his schedule is, to stop off at McDonald's and buy that kid food. Why would you feed someone if you were just going to kill them?"

The words hung in the air and I was glad that I had thought of that because Amelia looked a lot more relieved.

"Then, if he's not killing them, what is he doing with them?" Amelia inquired.

"Maybe he's going to sell them on the black market," the Bluesman said.

Amelia moaned in frustration, and I was halfway to hoping that the Bluesman's vocal cords would freeze up for a few hours.

"I saw a special on it on television a few months ago. I think it was *60 Minutes*. It was all about how people take kids overseas and sell them to the highest bidder and th—"

"Enough!" Amelia yelled.

"Well, you don't have to yell," he said in a hurt voice. "I'm just... brainstorming. I'm trying to think of every possibility I can."

"Can't any of them be good for a change?"

"Amelia, what do you want me to say? What could possibly be good about something like this?" he said helplessly.

I hated to say it, but he had a point. What good could possibly come from kidnapping kids?

"Look, we're all feeling tense and worked up right now and it's not doing any of us any good. Let's eat something and rest for a bit and then hit the road again," I suggested.

"Every minute we're standing here could be a minute that he's torturing a kid," Amelia said.

"We don't know that. We don't know anything. What I do know is that if we keep pushing the way we are with the way that we're all feeling, we're all going to collapse, and what good will that do anybody? We'll just take ten minutes or so and then get back to it, okay? Just ten minutes."

"Okay," she finally relented.

We took off our packs and pulled out some food and sodas and passed them around. Hot sandwiches and warm soda. What a feast. Still, I was more concerned about us just taking a break and trying to mellow out than I was about the food. As we sat down and started eating, I thought of something that might be a good laugh. I hated to do it at the expense of Zock, but I was sure he would understand. "Hey, check this out," I said. Zock was now sitting right beside me, and I moved the can I was holding right in front of his face and opened it. Soda immediately sprayed everywhere and Zock, understandably startled, jumped back in shock at the can that had just attacked him.

None of us did anything... and then the Bluesman started to chuckle a little, and it slowly began to build into a full-grown belly laugh that would not stop. I joined him, and shortly after that, Amelia was also laughing. We were now all sitting in the middle of nowhere, not knowing at all what we were going to be facing in the near future and scared to death, and we were laughing up a storm over an exploding soda can. Actually, it was not really that funny, but it was a good example of how starved we were for anything to release the tension and uncertainty we were all feeling. Feeling guilty, I pulled Zock close to me and hugged him, then gave him half a sandwich, which he quickly gobbled up. I knew he had to be really thirsty, and his water dish might as well have been in another universe for all that it mattered right now, so I held the soda can above his head and poured the remaining contents into his mouth. He was so thirsty and caught on to what I was doing so quickly; he pretty much was able to drink every drop of it. Apparently, Zock liked Dr. Pepper as much as I did. We sat around eating for a few more minutes and, with a mixture of reluctance and perseverance, we mounted our bikes and proceeded on.

We rode on in silence but in a slightly better mood for about twenty minutes. Then, from out of nowhere, we heard something in the distance, and we all knew exactly what it was because it couldn't possibly be anything else. We knew because we had heard the same sound just a short time ago: a truck driving on a dirt road, and the familiar rattling it was making as it occasionally hit the odd large collection of rocks or dips in the road as it sped forward. Then, off in the distance, we saw a glint. It was the shining of the glass on the windshield because the sun had decided to come out for a little bit. We all stopped at about the same time and looked at each other. We were pretty sure that he had not seen us yet but not totally sure. One thing we were sure of was that just staying parked out in the middle of the road was not going to do any of us any good.

"Come on," I said. I moved off the road and dismounted my bike as I got close to the weeds. Amelia and the Bluesman were doing the same. I started trying to push my bike into the thick growth of the tall weeds and, with more than a tad bit of effort, was able force my way in and kept pushing onward for about twenty feet. The Bluesman was soon beside me with his bike, but Amelia was having trouble pushing hers because it was so big. We left our bikes to help push it in until they were all sitting next to each other. From this point, our bikes would be impossible to see from the road. Zock had absolutely no trouble at all getting in because he was so small compared to us. We all had no trouble noticing how much hotter everything suddenly was, and the humidity certainly was not helping. You would think being in something resembling shade would make everything cooler, but no. At least the sun was still being mostly blocked out by a cloudy sky or we would barely be able to stay on our feet right now.

Actually, because of the long ride that we were currently undergoing, we might have already been facedown on the road a ways back. Also, I didn't want to say anything, but I was worried about snakes. This seemed like just the kind of turf that would appeal to them. Wasn't that just a wonderful thought? This little adventure was certainly bringing out the best in me.

Amelia was leaning next to me, and I could tell from her expression that she was really nervous.

The sound of the truck was getting closer.

"How far away do you think he is?" she whispered.

"Not far," I whispered back.

"Do you think he'll be able to see us?"

"No, I don't think so. We can barely even see the road now, so there's no chance he would be able to see us, not to mention the fact that he's moving fast and not looking for anyone, anyway."

"I hope so."

As we were waiting for the truck to pass, I peered over and noticed Zock was looking behind us at the wall of weeds and his ears were moving up and down, which meant that he could hear something that we couldn't. Trying to be as subtle as I could so as to not make Amelia notice, I turned my head in the direction that Zock was facing and tried to listen to anything that might stand out. Expect for the truck and a few crickets making that noise that they love so much, there was nothing. All I was doing was staring into some larger-than-life weeds. It made me think of my happy thoughts of the snake again, and I was hoping that the truck would hurry up and pass so we could get out of here. Sweat was covering my face and getting in my eyes, and Amelia and the Bluesman were not faring any better. Zock must have felt like he was in hell because he was wearing a year-round fur coat. Throughout the whole day, time had not moved any slower than the moments we were living in right now.

We could hear that the truck was really near and, from the sound of it, going pretty fast. A few moments later we saw it pass, leaving a trail of dust behind it. We gave it a few minutes and then started to move back out onto the road, and not a moment too soon! I felt like I was on fire, it was so hot! As soon as we were out of the weeds and back on the open road, I moaned in exhilaration. I was now feeling so grateful. I know that sounds odd because we were right back where we started from, but between this and the heat and discomfort from kneeling down in the weeds, not to mention worrying about snakes, this was heaven! It really made a person appreciate the smaller things in life.

"Where do you think he's going?" Amelia asked as she looked down the road, where we could now barely hear the truck.

"I don't know. Wherever it is, he has a long ride ahead of him," I stated.

"Not as long as ours," the Bluesman said in somewhat of a hard tone, and I immediately tried to think of something to say before this started off another argument.

"I just thought of something."

"What?" the Bluesman asked, looking at me while wiping his face with his hands. He was tired, frustrated, and scared. We all were.

"If he's just now making another trip somewhere for whatever reason, the place that he came from must not be that much farther."

We all looked at each other and then down the road where the truck had just come from. As far as we could see, there was nothing but an open road.

"How much longer do you think it is?" Amelia said.

"I would think no more than an hour, maybe less."

"You know that for sure, Einstein?" the Bluesman said.

"No, I don't. But assuming that he didn't just drop the kid off at the place and then immediately hit the road again, I would think that we have to be pretty close to the place."

"The place?"

"What?"

"You said 'the place.' What 'place' are we looking for? Has anyone thought of that? We don't even know what we're supposed to be looking for."

He was right. That was something that had not even dawned on me. I mean, it wasn't like I was expecting a giant castle to appear from a mist with a neon sign in front of it saying "Here They Are! Turn Right Here!" I had just assumed that we would know where it was whatever it was when we saw it. It sounded logical. In a wasteland like this that was nothing but empty fields, anything would stand out.

"I would think it would be…"

"Yes? It would be…."

"Well, think about it. Here we are at Goatman's. Now, think about all the other old, rundown buildings that we've been in. It would have to be something like that, wouldn't it? I doubt there's an apartment complex located all the way down here!"

"How do we know which building?"

165

"Whenever we see a building, we search it. Look how long we've been riding. The next one has to be it. It has to be!"

The Bluesman was quiet for a moment as he scanned the road again.

"And you don't think it's much farther?" he said.

"No, not much farther," I replied, trying to sound a lot more confident than I felt.

"Why do you think he was leaving again?" Amelia said.

We all looked at each other, and none of us had an answer.

"What if… what if he's going to get another kid?" she said.

That really struck us. He could be going back out for any number of reasons but because she had mentioned it, that possibility was now at the top of the list. Needless to say, it did not set our minds at ease. In fact, it made us feel quite the opposite; it made us even more determined to finish this.

"I think we should go. We're wasting time just standing here." I started pedaling. The others did the same, and we were once again on the move.

As were we pedaling, it occurred to me that not only did we have no idea why the man had left again so quickly from wherever his destination was; we had no idea when he was going to be driving back. What if he came back when we were in an area where there was no place to hide? As annoying as the weeds were, they were great cover. If they vanished — which I doubted because they seemed to go on forever but it was still possible to come to an area that was deprived of weeds — what then? I decided not to say anything about it. Amelia and the Bluesman had enough on their minds without me contributing more worries. Besides, trying to think positive, I was hoping we would find the kids, wherever they were, before the man decided to show up again.

We went on for another forty minutes with barely a word spoken between us when the Bluesman suddenly shattered the silence.

"Hey, what's that?"

I had been mainly looking at the road directly in front of me while slumped on my seat as I lazily moved my front wheel from side to side. His sudden exclamation startled me and almost made me lose my balance. I looked ahead and saw nothing but open road. At first, I thought I saw the truck coming right for us, that somehow the guy had circled around another dirt road and was now barreling toward us at a hundred miles per hour with terrible country and western music blaring from his stereo and trying to make us feel even worse as he was determined to run us down.

Then I realized that there was nothing there at all, just more road.

"What are you talking about?" Amelia looked forward. She seemed tired.

"Up there to the right. See it?"

I looked up to where he was pointing and, at first, all I saw was more waves of weeds. Then I saw what he was talking about. In the distance I could see what I thought was the arched roof of something poking out from the middle of nowhere. It seemed to be appearing and reappearing at the same time, as it was lost in the waves. My eyes immediately widened. That was it! It couldn't possibly be anything else!

"I see it!" I said excitedly.

"I see it, too!" Amelia exclaimed with excitement and relief. "Do you think that's it?"

"I think so!" the Bluesman said happily.

We all looked at each other with triumphant expressions on our faces and then started pedaling faster, a renewed strength flowing through us. Even Zock seemed to sense the excitement of what was going on. It was kind of difficult to gauge exactly how far away it was because the road was taking a dip and then coming back up to a more level ground. Also, all the weeds, which at a distance looked quite beautiful, which seems to be an odd thing to say about something as ugly as weeds, made everything very difficult to get a fix on. They almost made the place appear to be a boat that was sailing on some calm, flowing waters like in a painting. It was because of the weeds that the place was almost totally hidden. Whoever this guy was, he had certainly picked the right spot to do…whatever it was he was doing. I shook any kind of thoughts that were dark from my mind and concentrated on good things, as difficult as that was.

Slowly but surely the place seemed to be getting closer as we kept pedaling and, after an eternity, we were finally close enough to see what it was. Like I'd suspected, it was a giant barn. It was old and rundown, but it was in fairly good shape compared to the other places we had seen. Unlike the other places, this place was huge. It was almost the same height as the other barn near the entrance, but it was at least five times longer. Even though it was nothing more than just an old building, it seemed very ominous. I was not exactly sure if it was because of what it looked like or because I knew what was inside. Maybe a little bit of both.

We pulled up to the front of it and looked at the door as it stared down at us as though we were gnats.

"Let's head inside," the Bluesman said getting off his bike.

"Wait!" I said still looking up at it.

"What? We're here. Let's get moving."

"We need to hide the bikes. We don't know when the guy is coming back, and we certainly don't want to tip him off when he gets here that someone has found this place while we're inside and don't know about it until it's too late. He may even have a gun in his truck."

"That's a good idea, Danny," Amelia said and, despite the situation, I couldn't help liking the way she said that when she was looking at me. The entire day had taken a turn for the worse and fallen apart, but it was nice to know that once this was all over, we would still be able to pick up where we'd left off.

"Let's move," the Bluesman said as we pushed our bikes to the wall of weeds off to the side and forced them through. Once they were well hidden, we walked back up to the large door of the place. As we looked closer at it, our faces immediately fell.

There was a bulky silver chain and a large padlock securing it shut, both of them new. If I had any doubt left as to whether this was the place, this little piece of evidence in front of us totally demolished it.

Apparently, whoever this guy was, he was not taking any chances on anyone being able to get inside, even though this place was in the middle of nowhere. Then again, the reverse was also possible. Just like nobody could get in, nobody could get out. Since finally arriving here, none of us had heard anything out of the ordinary, just silence. I did not know whether to consider that a good sign or not.

"Now what?" the Bluesman said, disappointed while looking upward to find any other way of getting in.

"There has to be another way in. This place is so big; it would be stupid to build just one entrance into it. Let's take a walk," I said as we started to walk around the left side of it.

As we did so, I gazed at Zock and saw that he was rooted in place with his head up and staring off into the weeds, his ears slightly moving back and forth again. I looked in the direction he was staring at and saw nothing. Then, I smelled something. It was very faint, but I recognized it. It was that odd smell that I had sniffed earlier when we were back at the other barn. Then again, it could just have been everywhere and I had not noticed it because I had other things on my mind. It could even be coming from this place or something inside it. At any rate, we had more important things to worry about besides sniffing around.

"Zock? Come on, boy," I said. He continued to look off for a moment and then just turned around and caught up with us.

As we were walking the length of the barn, I noticed a large, gnarled tree that looked like it had been burnt to death as some point and was doing everything it could to stay alive. Judging from the appearance of it, it was failing miserably. Its almost bare branches were stretching out in almost every direction as though it were pleading to anyone or anything it could for help.

Sitting next to the tree, almost right beside the barn, was a large contraption. From a distance, we had no idea what it was, although, we could hear a humming coming from it even from where we were, and it became louder as we got closer to it. Once we were standing in front of it, we examined it with perplexed looks on our faces. It was the first mechanical object that we had ever encountered in all of our trips to Goatman's that seemed to be working. Yet again, it was more evidence that this was the place because somebody had to be caring for it and making sure it was running all the time.

"What do you think it is?" the Bluesman asked.

"It looks like some kind of engine or generator or something," I stated.

"What do you think it's for?" Amelia asked.

"Well, if that guy lives here, he's probably using this for power to run whatever's inside. I doubt there's any other way he could get electricity or gas or anything without some kind of power source to run it, and this appears to be it. I'm not sure, but it looks like it's running on gas. It is, smell it? And, look over there. There's a giant gas can," I said walking over toward it.

"Check out this piping," the Bluesman said as he pointed to a length of pipe that was running from the machine, along the ground, and toward the barn. "It runs from this thing to that hole that was made in the barn wall. I bet that guy loaded it in the back of his truck, brought it out here, and then hooked it up."

"So, this is the place, then. I mean, why would this thing be in the middle of nowhere and running if this wasn't the place?" Amelia suggested.

"We have to get inside," the Bluesman said as he spied a door in front of us and went to test it. "Locked," he said disgusted.

"I'm not surprised," I said as I looked up and saw something that caught my attention. "Hey, look up there!"

They all gazed upward to what I was talking about. There was an open window above us. It was so far up; the only way we could possibly get to it was if we had a ladder.

"Well, that's wonderful. Too bad Superman isn't here. I wonder if there's another way in," he said looking down the length of the barn.

"I doubt it. If he was careful enough to lock these two doors, then all the others are probably locked also, if there even are others," I said.

Amelia asked, "So, what now?"

I looked over at the tree and got an idea. One of the branches was set very close to the window. In fact, it was set so close to it, a person could easily jump from it to the window. Then all I would have to do was unlock the door from the inside and let everyone in. Perfect. Maybe this tree wasn't so bad after all.

"I think I have an idea," I murmured, still looking up at the tree. Amelia followed my gaze and immediately saw what I was thinking and then looked at me with her eyebrows raised.

171

"Are you out of your mind? That's at least thirty feet up. You could fall and break your leg!"

"Only if I fell," I said with a grin as I took my backpack off and set it down on the ground.

"It's not funny. That tree looks like it's about to roll over and die. How do you know that branch would even be able to hold you?"

"I don't, but this looks like it's going to be our only way in. Unless you can jump really high, it's the only option," I said walking toward the trunk of the tree.

"Wait a minute!" Amelia said following me. "Why should you go?"

"What do you mean?"

"I mean who elected you to try it and not either of us?"

"Well, I just thought I would do it since I'm the shortest one here, not to mention that I'm a pretty good climber. You've seen me on the monkey bars at school. I'm a whiz," I said proudly.

"I would go, but I'm not really crazy about heights," the Bluesman said, looking up at the branch uncomfortably.

Amelia looked up at the branch again and then back at me with a worried expression. It was settled. I was going to pretend I was Spider-Man. I got a good grip on the trunk and started climbing.

"Be careful," Amelia crooned.

"Being careful is pretty much at the top of my mind," I replied as I grabbed a branch and continued to climb. Fortunately, the tree was loaded with branches, and I was able to make my way up pretty easily. I stopped at one point and looked down. Amelia, the Bluesman, and even Zock were staring up at me in wonder. Amelia had her hands folded over her chest as she was looking at me and, even though I shouldn't have been thinking it because this was not the time to play around, I couldn't help but think how cool I must look right now, risking life and limb and maybe even falling to my death as I was heroically giving

172

my all to save the helpless kid inside. If this wasn't progress, I didn't know what was!

I grabbed another branch and moved up some more. Soon, I was right in front of the branch that led to the window. It looked pretty thick and sturdy, but I wasn't about to take any chances, not with the ground waiting to catch me. Looks could be very deceiving, and the branch thinned out a bit the closer it reached out to the window. Still, seeing that open window so close and yet so far away, it was so tempting to just rush toward it and jump inside.

Exhaling, I started to crawl along the branch and was about halfway there when I thought I heard a cracking sound. I was so pumped up with adrenaline because I was so close to getting us inside I really was not sure if it was real or just my nerves playing tricks on me. At any rate, nothing was getting done by just staying there so I moved onward. I was just a few feet away from the window when the tree branch creaked again. This time it was so loud; I knew it was not my imagination. It was real!

"Danny! Be careful!" Amelia screamed.

"Doing my best," I said back down to them and moved again. Now I could actually feel the branch starting to move slightly downward, and I knew that it would not be able to support my weight much longer because the tree was too old and had gone through too much. That I had gotten this far was practically a blessing. I looked at the window again, and it was closer than ever. If I could just get a few feet closer to it, I would easily be able to leap toward it if I had to. Sweat was covering my forehead and getting into my eyes, and I took a minute to wipe it away. Then I moved, and the branch replied in protest. It was at this time that I realized that the tree probably did not like me very much. This was it. Every second from here on in counted, and I decided to just go for it. I quickly scampered along for as long as I could. I was almost at the end of it when I heard the branch giving away and falling beneath me.

"Danny!" Amelia screamed.

Panicked, I jumped toward the windowsill and was halfway in as I landed on my stomach and grabbed onto the empty air in front of me, grasping nothing. I immediately spread my arms out on either side of me to brace myself in case I started to fall backward. Fortunately, I had landed far enough in that it didn't matter if I didn't grab onto anything to keep from falling. I heard a loud creaking behind me, and I turned around just in time to see the branch slowly break off from the tree and then start to fall to the ground. Amelia and the Bluesman quickly got out of the way and watched the old branch plummet to the ground just a few feet in front of them with a loud crash. I quickly maneuvered myself all the way inside and let myself fall down. For a split second, I thought that there was no floor because it was so dark I could barely see in front of me. Then I hit the floor with a thump and realized that the window had just been set higher than what you would normally find in a house. I got up and peered out the window. It was set so high I had to boost myself up to it and swing a leg over the sill and hold myself in place.

"Are you guys all right?" I yelled down to them.

"Yeah! How about you?" the Bluesman yelled back up to me.

"I'm fine. A bit of a close call, but I'm fine."

"Okay. What now?"

"I'm going to go downstairs and find the door so I can let you in."

"Okay. Be careful in there."

"The thought had crossed my mind," I said as I swung my leg over again and let myself fall. I landed on my feet and just stood there for a moment as I let my eyes adjust to the dark before walking any farther. As my eyes began to get used to the darkness, I realized where I was, or at least where I thought I was. It was a loft, just like in the other barn. There were some scatterings of hay covering the wooden floor, and positioned around the area in various places were barrels of hay stacked on top of one another as if they had been long forgotten, at least half a dozen stacks. I wasn't sure, but I thought I saw a light coming from down below somewhere. By light, I mean a real light, not just the sunlight that was peeking through the cracks and holes on the roof and walls, giving everything around me an eerie look.

Suddenly, something slammed into my face, and I immediately grabbed at it. It was hard to tell what it was because I was so startled and terrified about what was happening, but it felt like I was touching a small, furry animal...with wings! I started yelling and screaming as I was moving around in what probably looked like a rather macabre and deranged dance. The thing on my face was squeaking up a storm, and you can just imagine how much I was loving all of it. What the hell was this thing?

"Danny!" I heard Amelia scream again.

She must have heard me yell out and, because of extenuating circumstances that were presently not under my control, I was unable to answer her.

After a few moments, I lost my balance and fell to the ground in a cloud of dust that made me start coughing and, for lack of anything else to do; starting rolling around and pounding on my face, hoping I hit this thing in a soft place. It must have gotten tired of me hitting it on its back or whatever because it suddenly stopped, and the next thing I knew I could see again. Well, not *see* see because I was still in the dark, but this was a heck of a lot better. I turned my head just in time enough to see something fly out the window.

What the hell is that? I thought to myself as I saw it fluttering away while still blinking up a storm and trying to see clearly. My face felt shredded up. It was probably not as bad as it felt, but I wondered if I was going to be scarred for life and people were going to scream in horror and run away when they saw me coming.

"Aiiiiiiiiiiieeeeeeeee!" It was Amelia.

"Holy crap!" I heard the Bluesman yell.

Oh, no! I thought.

I immediately got up and ran to the window and boosted myself up. The first thing I saw was Amelia running around in a circle with her eyes closed and waving her arms everywhere.

"Get away! Get away! Get away!" she was screaming over and over, which was actually kind of amusing because I couldn't see anything around her. Zock was just standing there watching her, wondering what the problem was and enjoying the show. The Bluesman looked up at me with a shocked look on his face.

"What the hell are you doing up there, man? You're throwing bats at us?" he yelled.

"What? That thing was a bat?" I said in surprise.

"Hell, yeah, it was a bat! And it was pissed! What are you doing up there? Playing with Dracula?"

"No, I was just walking around in the dark and it attacked me."

"Well, stop it," he said, not knowing anything else to say. "Come down and let us in so we can get out of here!"

"Okay," I said as I let myself fall to the ground again. It then dawned on me that that might not have been the only bat calling this place home. For all I knew there was an entire colony hanging upside-down from the ceiling, staring at me right now and getting ready to swarm. It was so dark, I couldn't really see anything, so I decided to just hurry up and find my way downstairs. I wandered over to where the light was coming from and soon found myself on the edge of the loft and looking down into a vast, cavernous area. The light was coming from a lone lamp that was sitting on a desk with a few chairs around it. I started walking around looking for a ladder. There had to be a ladder placed around here somewhere. All I had to do was find it and then I co-

"Whalp!"

I had stepped into an empty part of the floor that I had not seen and thought I was falling and scared to death because I knew how long the drop was from climbing the tree from outside.

"Auuuuuuuggggggggggh!" I was going to die! I was going to break my leg! I was going to break my back! I was going to be paralyzed for the rest of my life and spend the rest of my remaining days in a wheelchair and drinking my meals from a straw because my jaw would be shattered and all of my teeth would be gone and I would be a drooling vegetable staring up at the ceiling all the time like "The Wanderer" and I...

I was sliding down something.

I realized – once I had stopped screaming, that is – that I was not falling but moving down a very steep slide that felt like metal because it was so smooth. It was covered with loose strings of hay, and I could feel the wind whipping into my face. I could not see anything in front of me, and I knew I was going to crash into a wall or a swarm of bats or maybe even Dracula or something even worse, so I put my hands in front of me. At the same time, I realized how foolish this was because whatever I hit, just blocking myself with my hands was not going to help much. Still, it was better that not-

"Mwaaaaaah!"

I was falling again. I was in the open air. The slide had ended and I was now floating in the darkness and about to become up close and personal with the ground. I was desperately hoping that I had fallen close enough to the ground so that it would not hurt so much. I wondered what....

"Uuuuugh!"

I hit the ground, and the wind had been knocked out of me. But, to my surprise, the ground was not really that hard. I mean, it was hard, but not as hard as I had expected it would be. There was something in my mouth. I started spitting it out, and I realized it was hay. I had fallen onto a pile of hay. With a sigh of relief but still blind, I struggled to get up and started to move around and feel my way.

"Uuuuuuurp!"

I fell from the pile of hay and rolled in a heap to the ground. I knew it was ground because it was hard, and I could feel the dirt under my hands. Apparently, my little ride was over, and believe me, I was more than happy about it. In the past ten minutes, I had almost fallen to my doom from a tree, been attacked by a bat, and had almost fallen to my death. Enough was enough. I needed to find the door so we could get started on locating the kids and then get out of here. My eyes were a little more adjusted to the darkness by now, and I could see better — not that there was really that much to see. I got up and, with my hands in front of me, started wandering around in the darkness. I banged into a few things, which I think were tables of various sizes, and the noise all this was making in the large area made any little thing sound like a bomb dropping. It dawned on me that I was certainly glad that that guy was not here right now. He would certainly have heard me before he saw me.

I soon saw the outline of the side door that we had tried to get into because the sunlight was coming through around it. I made my way over there and was able to see a little better than just wandering around in the darkness. Fortunately, it was a just a simple bolt lock, and I was easily able to turn the knob and open the door. The sudden brightness compared to what I had been just experiencing was startling but welcome, and I saw Amelia and the Bluesman standing right in front of me.

"It's about time," the Bluesman said.

"Sorry. I was… kind of busy."

"Oh, are you all right?" Amelia asked as she cradled my face in my hands and examined me.

"I'm fine. Why?"

"You have some scratches on your face."

"Oh, it's nothing," I said. "It's from that bat that I got into a fight with. No big deal."

After I said that, I wondered if maybe it was a big deal after all. Bats are wild animals and carry rabies. I didn't think it had bitten me, but I wasn't sure about scratches. Could a person get rabies from scratches? With the way my luck was going so far, once it got dark and the moon came out, I was going to turn into a vampire and suddenly have an unquenchable thirst for blood.

"Well, we need to get them looked at when we can," she said.

I have to take a little bit of a time out right now to tell you that it felt really good having Amelia cradling my face in her hands. Her hands were really soft, and the way she was looking at me right now, I felt like I was melting. I really thought I was going to get lost in those beautiful eyes of hers.

"Excuse me, Romeo and Juliet. Can we get it on with it?" the Bluesman said as he held out my backpack.

We looked at him, embarrassed, and then I stepped back so they could come in. The Bluesman gave me my pack, and I slipped it on.

"Wow, it's dark in here," Amelia whispered.

"Where's the light switch? There has to be one around here somewhere," the Bluesman said as he started feeling around the rim of the door. "Here it is."

Click.

Suddenly, about twelve bright lights hanging from above came on, and we could see the entire length of the barn. It certainly was jarring to see such brightness in a place that had probably known nothing but darkness for decades. Looking up at the lamps that were hanging from the ceiling, it was obvious that they were new and had been recently installed by someone, more than likely our weird, bald friend with his original mode of communicating.

"Should we be doing that?" Amelia asked.

"Doing what?" the Bluesman said.

"Turning on the light. What if he sees us?"

"We'll turn it off if we see him coming."

"If?"

"Well, 'when' we see him coming. Besides, we need some light to see what we're doing or we're just going to be stumbling around in the dark. It looks like this switch here controls all of them at once and not just one at a time, so it's all or nothing," he said while examining the light switch.

I looked out at the area, and I wasn't sure what to think. It was nothing like I'd imagined. Soon we were all just standing there and staring at our surroundings.

"Wow. This is not at all what I was expecting," I said as we looked around. I had expected to see a barren barn with nothing but dirt floors and maybe some stacks of hay to add to the atmosphere. Instead, it was relatively clean. I mean, it was not as clean as a house would be, but it looked as though someone were making a valiant attempt to make it like one and partially succeeding. Instead of a bare dirt floor, a giant, wide strip of tacky carpet was laid out for a pretty good length before it ran out, and the dirt floor was visible in the distance. It looked used and worn, but it was certainly better than what was lying underneath it. In the section to the right of us was an area that looked like a small apartment. There was a long, brown couch and some beat-up lounge chairs sitting around a glass table that was actually quite beautiful, something that my mom would have liked. However, nothing matched. It was like a person who was partially blind had gone shopping at a pawn shop and had only a minimal amount of cash to spend. Then, something we all noticed at the same time was a television set that was sitting in front of the table and facing the couch and chairs. We walked toward the area, and Amelia, who must have been really tired, fell onto the couch.

"Ow!" she yelped, startled, as she got back up and decided to just sit up instead of lie down.

"What's wrong?" I asked, walking toward her.

"It's the couch. It looks nice and comfy – well, comfy, at least – but it's hard as a rock. Wait a minute," she said feeling where she was sitting. "This area is soft, the middle is hard," she said as she felt one cushion and then another.

"That's weird. You would think it would all be the same," I said, feeling the cushions along with her. "He must have gotten a good deal on it wherever he got it. Nobody would want a piece of junk like this."

The Bluesman was playing around near the television and pushed the button. Surprisingly, it came on, but it was just static.

"Hey! This guy has television. He's all the way out here and he has television. How's he doing that?" the Bluesman said.

I walked over to it and looked at it. It was obvious where he was getting the power from, the machine outside. Whoever this guy was, he was weird, but he certainly did know a thing or two about fixing stuff up, what with the lights and the television and all. He must be a whiz with electronic stuff. Then I noticed something. There was a VCR sitting on a table beneath the television, and I switched it on and a movie appeared. I didn't recognize the movie or anyone in it — none of us did. Apparently, he had fixed this thing up so he could watch movies, and that was it. I looked at the movie boxes stacked beside the VCR, and most of them were cartoons. Did this weird guy sit around on his couch all day watching cartoons? For

181

some reason, I could easily picture it. I turned off the television and VCR, and it was now quiet in the area again.

"Hey, I was watching that," the Bluesman said.

I regarded him in a bored manner and started looking around again. It was at that moment that I realized something I hadn't noticed before: It was cool in here. "Hey, do you feel that?" I asked.

"Feel what?" Amelia asked, still sitting on the couch and leaning back.

"The air in here, do you feel how cool it is? It should be burning up in here, but it's not."

"Hey, you're right. He must have fixed this place up with air conditioning," the Bluesman said. "This guy must be some kind of genius to do all this. I thought he was a retard or something. Maybe he's a... what do you call it? An idiot savant?"

"Maybe. It still freaks me out that this guy must live all the way out here. Check this out," I said as I walked over to a refrigerator that was sitting off to the side, a small, wooden sandwich table sitting next to it with plastic salt and pepper shakers on top of it. A small radio was also sitting on it. I placed my hand against the refrigerator and could feel that it was cold. I opened it up, not knowing what to expect to find. Certainly not what I did find. It was a fully stocked fridge. It was filled with containers of mustard, mayonnaise, ketchup, pickles, and olives. There was also cheese, ham, and turkey. Practically every soft drink I could think of was taking up the second shelf, including Dr. Pepper. On the first one were milk, orange juice, cranberry juice, and grape juice. In the freezer were multiple boxes of TV dinners and ice cream. This guy had everything, and it was all neatly and carefully placed and stacked so that all the labels were in perfect order. Amelia and the Bluesman were now standing beside, me looking at all of this stuff in wonder. Even Zock was interested because his tongue was hanging out.

182

"You could live on all of this stuff for a month!" the Bluesman declared, and I guessed he was right. Just looking at it I was getting hungry. I looked over toward the wall and saw a cupboard sitting next to it. We closed the refrigerator doors, walked over to it, and opened it. It was filled with all sorts of canned goods. Soup, chili, beans, everything! Like the refrigerator, all the cans were perfectly stacked so that the labels were showing. There were even some loaves of bread and some boxes of cereal stacked to the side. This guy may have liked to live in a hovel in the middle of nowhere, but he was certainly a neat freak. It made me wonder what kind of person could be like that? Why would a person choose to live like this? Usually, I could look at a person and imagine the kind of individual he was...or at least, the kind of individual I thought he was. This guy was a total mystery with surprise after surprise.

"Look over there," the Bluesman said, and I followed his gaze.

There was a little area off to the side, and in it was a small machine that appeared to be an oven, but it looked like a giant hot plate or something, not an oven with the four burners on top of it to heat pans up and the large compartment below to put things in it like a pizza or a turkey. No, this was just a small ring on a metal box with a pot sitting on it. I guess that was why he just had simple things he could easily heat up and nothing really fancy. Farther off was a bed sitting vertically by the wall. It was a small bed for one person, and it was perfectly made. Not so much as a crinkle in the sheets, so perfect that it looked like something you would see in a store. Sitting to the left of it was a nice lamp placed on a small drawer, and on the right was a bookshelf filled with rows and rows of hardback and paperback books. On the other side was a dresser that I assumed held various clothes, and sitting next to it on the floor were a pair of boots and a couple of pairs of shoes. On the wall in front of the bed and taped to the wall was a poster of a smiling Heather Thomas, the one where she is in a hot tub and wearing a pink bikini. I looked at the Bluesman. "Looks like the two of you have something in common."

"Very funny," he replied.

I smiled. We left the area, walking back to where the couch and chairs were as we looked at the other side.

What a mess.

The other side of the barn was a complete opposite of the neatness of the living quarters. It was not complete chaos because it looked as though some kind of effort had been made to keep things in order. There were rows and rows of steel tables with all sorts of mechanical equipment sitting on top of them. Most of it was stuff that I could not even hope to guess what it was. but I did recognize components that looked like they might fit in a television set, others maybe a lawnmower or a tractor. There were also what were obviously car parts, maybe even parts for a motorcycle. In fact, sitting on a large table near where we were standing was most of a car motor that looked like it was in the process of being worked on because there were some fine tools scattered all around it. Sitting next to it was a portable radio that had paint splattering all over it. There also seemed to be a faint smell of paint coming from somewhere like it was some kind of auto shop. Off to the side were some giant steel barrels, and next to them were several small containers that said "Gasoline" on them. This was probably his gas supply to keep his machine outside going. Then, sitting beyond all the tables was something that I was surprised that I had missed because it looked so incredible.

"Come on," I said as we walked past the tables until we came to it.

Sitting in front of us and in perfect condition was a shining red '57 Chevy. I mean, the thing was in perfect condition! There was not a mark on it. Even the whitewall tires were spotless and looked brand new! If I was not aware that we were in the middle of nowhere, I would have sworn that we were in a museum. We walked all the way around it, looking at both the body and inside the windows until we were standing in front of it again.

"Will you look at this beautiful creature," I said, marveling at it.

"What a car! And it's just sitting there like it's just...like it's just a regular car!" the Bluesman blurted in a perplexed tone, not able to take his eyes from it.

"So, it's a car. Big deal," Amelia said.

We looked at her with our mouths hanging open, trying to grasp what she had just said.

"This... this is not just a car. 'Just a car' is what my mom drives. This is a vintage '57 Chevy in perfect condition. It's like it just came off the assembly line!" I said, trying to explain to her the importance of what we were in the presence of.

She just looked at us, still bored.

I guess you had to be a guy to fully appreciate the importance of this situation.

"Well, if you two are through professing your love for the car, can we please get back to the reason we're here?" she said.

"Oh, yeah," I said, having completely forgotten. I know that sounds terrible, but I'm sure you understand, especially if you're a guy. I mean, this was important! Anyway, she was right; we had a job to do. We looked beyond the car, and it was just open area until the wall of the barn. There were a couple of stacks of hay, but that was it. We walked back the other way until we were in the living area again.

The Bluesman looked around. "Okay, I'm stuck."

"What do you mean?" I said.

"Where are the kids? I mean, we've walked the entire length of the barn and haven't seen anything. I don't think they're being kept upstairs or you would have seen them," he mentioned as he looked up at the loft that ran the entire length of the barn. "Where are they?"

Good question. Where are they?

"Well," I said, looking around the area and then back upstairs, "they might be up there... somewhere."

"Wouldn't you have seen them earlier?" Amelia said.

"I could barely see what was in front of me, much less the entire loft," I said, still staring upward.

"So, they might be up there?" Amelia said with hope in her voice.

"Could be. I need to get back up there so I can check."

"Okay, where's the ladder?" the Bluesman asked.

"Uh, I don't know."

"What do you mean you don't know? How did you get down?"

"I fell down."

"You fell down?" Amelia said startled. "You fell all the way from up there?"

"Well, I didn't fall down. I was walking around in the dark and I walked onto an empty part of the floor. The next thing I knew I was sliding down a ramp or slide, and then I was flat on the floor. Over there. That's where I came down," I said, pointing to a giant stack of hay with an opening above it.

"Wow," Amelia said, looking at it while imagining what I must have gone through and then back at me. "You must have been scared.

"No, not really," I said, pretending I was Clint Eastwood. Actually, as you well know, I had been terrified, but why bother her with details?

"Look, over there is a ladder leading up to it," the Bluesman said, as we looked to where he was pointing. Leading up to the loft was a wooden ladder and, from where we were, at least, it looked pretty sturdy. I was not really looking forward to another climbing adventure, especially up where I had met my flying friend, but this was why we had come all the way out here. If there was any chance those kids were up there, we had to check. We walked over to it, and I grabbed it. After a few shakes to test its durability and to make sure that it wasn't going anywhere, I started to climb, followed by the Bluesman and then Amelia.

We were soon all standing in a large open area with nothing to see. Remembering what I had just gone through, I quickly looked up at the ceiling and was very happy to find that there was not a small army of bats hanging upside down and staring at us with hungry eyes. I don't know if that one bat I had seen was just a rogue or if there were others hiding anywhere. I wasn't even sure what a bat was doing all the way out here. Were there even bats in Texas? I thought they were just in Transylvania and assorted dark caves. At any rate, all we saw was an empty, dirty floor as we just stood there staring at it looking for any indication that people had been here. I think we were all depressed; we'd been hoping to find the kids up here since they were certainly not downstairs. I wondered if maybe the guy lived here but was storing the kids someplace else. If so, where? This was the only place we had seen for miles. They had to be here. There was simply no other place for them to be.

"Where are they?" Amelia asked in an annoyed tone.

"I wish I knew," I replied as I looked over the edge at the open area. The only interesting thing I saw besides the car was Zock wandering around and sniffing.

"They have to be here. I mean, wouldn't you think they would be? Where else could they be?" the Bluesman said.

"I don't know," I said.

"Maybe we should head back," the Bluesman suggested. Both Amelia and I looked at him.

"What? Why?" Amelia asked.

"Well, we've done everything that we can do here and we haven't found them. We don't even know for sure that they're here. All we do know is that that weird guy is living here for some reason, and I'm sure he must be breaking the law or something, living out here in the middle of nowhere. Maybe he's a fugitive or something. If we tell the police about this, they would have to do something about it, wouldn't they?"

We all thought about it in silence for a moment.

"I don't think it's enough. We still don't know who that guy is. Maybe he owns this place and he's choosing to live out here for whatever reason. He's certainly put a lot of work into it. Maybe having weird living habits is just the way he is, it doesn't mean that he's a fugitive or anything," I offered.

"You're defending him?" Amelia accused, looking at me with wide eyes.

"Of course not. I'm just trying to think of every possible variable. Since we haven't found the kids, we really don't have anything to pin on him, and that means that the police would just tell us to get lost."

"What about the kid in the back of the truck?"

I had forgotten about that. I was so intent on trying to find kids in general, I had forgotten about the single kid we had heard.

"You're right. I don't know if he's a fugitive, but he certainly is kidnapping kids. If we could get a name or picture of him or something that would give us a clue, then the police could look in their database and see if he's in there."

"Maybe there's something downstairs, some bills with his name on them or something. He had to get all of this stuff somehow," the Bluesman said, indicating all the things downstairs.

"I agree. But if he paid with cash for everything, there would be no bills with his name on them; at least I wouldn't think so. The bills we would need to see are the ones for credit cards. He strikes me as too dumb or maybe even too smart to use a credit card because he knows it could be traced. And if he did have the cash to pay for all this stuff, where did he get it? Plus, this is Goatman's, a place in the middle of nowhere. If he's all the way out here, he obviously doesn't want to be found."

"What about mail? How does he get his mail?" Amelia offered.

"Judging by his living habits, he doesn't really strike me as the kind of guy who has a lot of friends. In fact, after seeing him and observing the kind of things he likes to watch like those cartoons, he strikes me as kind of a kid, himself. Maybe that's one of the reasons that he's kidnapping kids, so he has someone to play with."

"Wow. That's weird," the Bluesman said while I knew he was picturing that guy playing jacks or jump rope with little kids. It certainly was a picture.

"Plus, he's supplying his own power, so I doubt he is getting any kind of bills. Besides, I don't recall seeing a mailbox out front," I mentioned.

"So what do we do?" Amelia asked.

None of us said anything and were just looking around the area. As I was doing so, I noticed that Zock had been spending a good amount of time in a certain area and kept sniffing the ground. He was near the living area, near the end of the carpet, so there was nothing interesting to see. Then, looking closely, I noticed that something was sticking out from under the carpet. It could barely be seen, and it was only because of Zock that I had noticed it. Looking closely, I saw what appeared to be some kind of a rectangular shape on the ground…and it appeared to be wood covered with dirt so that it blended in almost perfectly with the rest of the floor.

I pointed at Zock. "Hey, look at that."

"What's he doing?" the Bluesman said.

"I don't know, but it looks like he found something," I said while moving toward the ladder and beginning to descend, hoping for any kind of hope. A few moments later, we were all on the ground, walking toward Zock. He was looking at us as we approached, his tail wagging with excitement. Whatever he had found, he was happy about it. We were now in the area that we had seen from upstairs and looking down at the rectangle. Unless you were looking for it, it would have been almost impossible to spot.

"What is it?" Amelia said.

"It looks… like a door," I replied and then picked up the end of the carpet to look underneath it. "I think it is a door. This is all one piece of wood on the floor, and there's a piece of rope nailed to the other side of it. Help me roll this carpet back," I said to the Bluesman, and we had the entire strip rolled back a few moments later so that the entire rectangle was now visible.

We all looked at each other with trepidation, all of us pondering the same thing: If the kids were here, they might very well be underneath us at this moment. What I was wondering, and I'm not sure if they were wondering the same thing, and I certainly didn't want to say anything, was whether or not they were alive. It would really be a shame to come all this way to rescue these kids and find that they were…well, you know.

"So, what now?" the Bluesman asked, looking at the piece of rope.

"Now, we find out if this is where the kids are," I stated as I gripped the rope with both of my hands and gave it a good yank.

I almost fell off balance because it came up so easily. Judging from the size of it and how it was made of wood, I had expected it to be a lot heavier. Instead, it came up pretty easily. The Bluesman helped me move it aside, and we were all now looking at a wooden staircase that seemed to descend into nothing but darkness.

"Well, are we going to go down?" Amelia finally said.

"I don't know – should we? We don't even know what's down there," the Bluesman offered.

"I don't see any kind of light switch around here," I said, looking around the rim of the staircase. "We would break our necks if we tried to go down in that, especially since we don't know how deep it is."

"Wait a minute," Amelia said as she walked through the living quarters to one of the steel tables. She picked some things up and then brought them back. "I saw these when we were over there earlier," she explained as she gave us each a flashlight and kept one for herself.

"Good deal. Look at Miss Eagle Eye," I said, grinning at her.

"So, I guess this is it. What do you think is down there?" the Bluesman asked.

"Hopefully what we came all this way for." I clicked on my flashlight and shined it down.

We could see the end of the staircase. It was a lot deeper than I thought it would be. If it were a basement in a typical house, I would not have expected it to be more than twenty feet. This looked to be at least forty. Plus, just standing at the top of it, I could get a sense of how large the downstairs area was. It certainly did not feel like a small, cramped area. It also smelled old and new at the same time. This room, or whatever it was, had certainly been used recently.

Taking a breath, I started to slowly descend the stairs, taking them one at a time in case one of them decided to break under my weight. All our flashlights were now on, so things were pretty bright – not that there was really anything to see. We were all gripping the wooden rail very tightly, scared that any moment something was going to happen, maybe even another bat flying out to say hello. In

191

the end, nothing happened, and we were all standing at the bottom, looking back up. Zock was staring down at us and, seeing that nothing had happened to any of us, quickly padded down the stairs. I could tell he was nervous because his ears were constantly moving and he was sniffing like crazy. Watching him, I was suddenly glad that I had decided to bring him. If it weren't for him, we would have never found this door.

The Bluesman was shining his light around, and the beam came to rest on something that interested him.

"Hey, check this out," he said, as he spied a light switch on a wooden post and clicked it on.

The entire area was suddenly lit up with brightness, and we looked around. It was a large room that was probably about a third of the size of what was upstairs. Surprisingly, it was very clean, and it was obvious that a lot more work had been put into making this a more livable area than upstairs. In fact, if I had just woken up in here and you told me that I was under a barn in the middle of nowhere, I would have thought that you were putting me on.

What was unusual about it was what was down here, and all we could do was gape at the surroundings around us. The entire room looked like something you would see at some kind of children's facility or day care center. The walls were painted yellow and baby blue with orange and red stripes streaked through the middle of them, all the way around the room. On the far side of the room was what looked like a play area. There was a small table with small yellow chairs surrounding it, and on the table were a half-finished picture puzzle and a Rubik's Cube. Sitting to the side was a large green beanbag that could be used as a chair. Underneath all of this was a large, yellow shag rug. In the middle of the room and placed against the wall was a medium-sized television set, this one nicer than the other one, facing a small couch and some small plastic chairs of assorted colors that were set on a multicolored circular rug.

Scattered about on the floor were toys such as a plastic fire engine, a couple of Tonka trucks, a Raggedy Ann, more than a few Barbie dolls and their various accessories, some G.I. Joe and Masters of the Universe figures, and vehicles, and some stuffed animals scattered here and there. On the other side of the room was what I supposed was the reading area. There was a small table and chairs like the set across the room. In front of them was a small bookshelf that was filled with assorted books. From where we were standing, I could see that a lot of them were Dr. Seuss and Charlie Brown books. On the table was a coloring book that was open to a picture that was half colored. There were about a half dozen posters thumbtacked to the wall of things like puppies and kittens in amusing positions with funny captions written below the frame. A couple of them were of Snoopy and Woodstock. The floor had been completely carpeted so that not a trace of dirt floor was visible.

To say that we were dumbstruck would be an understatement. I think that I can honestly say that every horrible thought you could possibly have imagined had crossed our minds, even though none of us had wanted to mention them, afraid that they would be true. What we were seeing in front of us was the very last thing we would have expected. In fact, none of us would have expected something like this at all. To a kid who was still in the one-digit mode of life, this would probably be a pretty nice place to hang out. The only bad thing about it was that they were kidnapped and brought here against their will. Finally, the Bluesman decided to speak in his own observant and articulate way.

"What the hell is this crap?" he said, slowly looking around as if he was in a daze.

"That's a good question," Amelia said equally stunned.

"This looks… this looks… like a nice place." I realized, as I was saying it, how stupid that must have sounded. Still, you had to go see it to believe it. If this were a legitimate place that was located somewhere in the neighborhood, they would rake in the business, and parents everywhere would rejoice! Someplace nice to dump the kids off and then go out and have a good time!

"What does this guy do? He kidnaps kids and then he brings them here so he can play around with them?" the Bluesman guessed.

"It looks like it," I said, still looking around.

"Why would he do that?" Amelia asked.

"No clue. Maybe... maybe he just never grew up or something," I suggested, reaching for any kind of an idea that might be a solution to this mystery.

"Do you think that he brings them here to play or does he... you know, molest them?" the Bluesman said with a worried looked on his face.

"I hope not. I am totally at a loss for words. If this were *T.J. Hooker* or *Strike Force* or something, I would think he would just be holding them here and then contacting the parents for ransom demands or something, but all the kids that have disappeared have never been heard from again."

"Where are they?" Amelia said scanning the room.

We all started looking around. We had been so struck by the playroom, we had forgotten about the kids!

"They have to be around here somewhere. They're not upstairs and there's not any other place around where they could have been stored," I said.

"You don't think that maybe he has another secret compartment that he's keeping them in or anything?" the Bluesman suggested.

I thought about it for a moment.

"I doubt it. If there were, Zock would have sniffed it out. They have to be around here. Let's walk around and see what we can find," I said.

We all went off in different directions looking at every little thing that caught our attention. The entire area was one big room with, from what we could tell, no adjoining rooms. I passed a cupboard and opened the drawer. There were items in it that kids would like such as candy bars, which wasn't very surprising, Hostess cupcakes, Twinkies and various kinds of cookies. There was not one healthy item here to eat whatsoever. A kid could develop cavities in a week if they lived here. I closed the door and started walking again. I checked under the staircase and there was nothing but some large empty boxes from Sears. It appeared that Sears was the store where he had picked up all the kids furniture.

Zock was wandering around and he came to a stop in front of a wall and was sniffing at it. I looked at him and wondered why he would be sniffing a wall. It wasn't like there was anything there to see. Amelia noticed him also and walked over to him.

"Find something, Zock?" she asked. He looked up at her, licked his chops and continued to stare at her. She felt around the wall and her hand came to rest on something.

"Hey, look at this," she announced, and the Bluesman and I walked quickly to where she was standing.

"What's up? Find anything?" he said.

"There's a doorknob here," she stated holding onto it with her right hand.

We looked at her hand. She was right. It was a doorknob. It was painted over with the same color as the stripes going across the wall. Because of this, it would have been almost impossible to see. Also, the outline of the door would have been hard to see unless you were looking for it. Since we were now standing right in front of it, we could see the door clearly and the three latches on the left side running the length of it.

"What do you think is in there?" I said.

"I don't know," Amelia said twisting the knob as hard as she could. "It's locked. The kids might be in there," she gasped as she tried the lock again, twisting it this way and that.

195

"Wait! Stop!" I said pulling her hand away from it.

"What? Why? We have to get in there!"

"We don't know what's in there. It could be where the kids are being held; it could be something else. For all we know, there's a pack of wild dogs in there that he keeps for security."

She immediately backed away, frightened.

"I didn't mean to scare you. I have no idea what's behind the door — dogs is just a thought. I seriously doubt it would be dogs because if he did have any, they would probably be upstairs and we would have already met them."

"Well, he certainly went through a lot of trouble to hide the door. Look how perfect it is. We're standing right in front of it, and I can still barely see it," the Bluesman said, marveling at the craftsmanship.

"Then that means he's hiding something," Amelia declared.

"That sounds right. I can't think of any other reason," I said.

"We have to get in there."

"I'm all for it. How do we do it?"

"We could break it down," the Bluesman suggested.

"That only works on television where they use prop doors that are made to shatter so they look cool when they are broken into," I said, and then knocked on the door a few times, "and the way this sounds, it's pretty thick, probably oak."

"Then how do we get in?" Amelia said anxiously and then knocked on the door as hard as she could. "Hello? Is anyone in there? Hello?"

Nothing.

"Maybe the kids aren't in there," the Bluesman said.

"And maybe they just can't hear us because of this door. Or, maybe if they can hear us, something is keeping them from being able to answer."

Amelia looked at me with a fearful expression.

"I'm not saying that's the reason, but it could be a possibility. Maybe they're tied up or have tape over their mouths or something. They might even be knocked out with chloroform."

"How do you think of things like that?" she said looking at me like I was an alien.

"Well don't stare at me like I'm a monster or something. It's what they do on television whenever bad guys kidnap someone."

"You need to start watching some other television shows instead of the ones where all people do is kidnap people and fight and have shoot-outs and car chases."

"Oh? What do you suggest?" I said as the Bluesman and I looked at her expectantly, already knowing the answer.

"Shows like *Dynasty* and *Dallas*. Those are good shows about real life."

"Oh, come on!" I moaned. "You can't be serious? All they do on those shows is cry and double cross each other and sleep with each other's wives. I can take *Dallas* because it has J.R. in it, but that's it. You need to watch *T.J. Hooker* and *The A-Team*. You should even try *V* or *Battlestar Galactica* or *Buck Rogers* when they come on, even *The Incredible Hulk.* Those are good shows. I know you like *Knight Rider*."

"*Knight Rider* is a good show. He helps people."

"He helps people with the help of a talking car. How is that real? I mean, I like the car and the show, but how is it real?"

"I mean besides the talking car, it could be a real show, someone driving around and helping people.

"And T.J. Hooker isn't? He's a policeman. Policemen are real people."

"It's not the same thing."

"Sure it is!"

"You're such a boy!"

"You're such a girl!"

"Excuse me? Can we get back on topic here? I think we were trying to get past this door so we can save the day?" the Bluesman reminded us. I suddenly thought about how ridiculous that little exchange was. Here we are in a dangerous situation in the middle of nowhere and we're arguing about our favorite television shows. You know things are bad when the Bluesman is the voice of reason.

"You're right," I sighed. "Well, it's locked and we can't break it down. Got any ideas?"

He rattled the doorknob for a moment and then kneeled down and examined it.

"I have an idea," he said looking around. "This knob is nothing fancy. The door is a piece of work, but the doorknob shouldn't be a problem."

"What do you mean?" I asked.

"I need to find some essential items," he said.

He started to walk around the room and strolled over to the area where the bean bag was. Then, he got down on his knees and started to peer into the yellow shag rug the table and chairs were resting on and began to walk around on all fours. Amelia and I looked at each other wondering if he had gone crazy. Lord knows that the Bluesman was already kind of far gone to begin with... in a good way, of course. He saw something that he liked and palmed it in his right hand and then started searching again. He apparently found something else he liked because he picked it up and then started walking toward us with a triumphant smile.

"What did you find?" Amelia said.

He opened up his right hand and we just stared at what was in it and then at him.

"Hair pins?" I said.

"Watch the master work," he said as he bent them open to a position that he liked. Then he kneeled down and started inserting them into the doorknob as he moved them around with a look of concentration. He was watching his work and listening at the same time.

Moments passed. The only sound in the room was the sound of the hair pins clinking around in the metal of the lock. My backpack was getting heavy, and I took it off and set it aside, the cans rattling around inside as I laid it on the floor.

"This is harder than I thought," he said with a look of concentration on his face. "I practice all the time on the front door at my house, but this one is a little tricky."

Then the lock snapped, and the door clicked open. We looked at him incredulously.

"How did you learn how to do that?" Amelia was amazed.

"*T.J. Hooker*," he said as he put the hair pins in his pocket and opened the door. I looked at Amelia with a big smile on my face, and she looked at me with a stoic one.

"Did you have anything to say?" I inquired of her.

She ignored me and looked at the unlocked door.

"Well, the door is open and we haven't been attacked by dogs. I guess we should go in," she said.

She opened the door and, surprisingly, we were not met with darkness. We walked farther in and just stopped and stared. The room was about half the size of the playroom, and on the left side was a small, partially tiled area, which I assumed was used for showering. There were no stalls at all for any kind of privacy, just one large area. I didn't see any faucets on the wall, only a large, rolled fire hose placed on the floor that was hooked up to some kind of large pump. The hose and pump actually looked kind of odd because everything in the playroom appeared as if it had just been purchased from a store fairly recently. Yet the pump and the hose looked old and worn, like they belonged upstairs with all the mechanical components on the steel tables. Also, the shower area looked like it was only partially completed, or like someone had been building it and gotten to a certain point and said that was good enough to get the job done.

To the right of us was a long row of small, wooden rooms sitting side by side, each one about half the size of the average bathroom. Each had a thick plate of glass with eight small holes in it about the size of a golf ball. The sides of the rooms were wooden walls so that each room was completely closed off from the others, and the top of the arrangement was a steel vent. In each room were a small sleeping bag and pillow and nothing else. Well, that's not entirely true. In each little room was also a child. There were ten little rooms in all. Eight of them were occupied with young boys and girls. Six of them were asleep, and the other two were busy. A little boy was reading a book, and a little girl was just staring off into space, looking like she was going to cry. None of them had noticed us yet. Looking at the thick glass and taking into account the oak door, it was no surprise that they had not heard us knocking...or if they did, perhaps they had just assumed it was the weird guy working on something in the playroom. A person could start up a motorcycle outside this room and they would probably barely hear it.

I looked at all the faces, and I recognized Tommy Moore, the kid who lived just a couple of blocks down from me who had disappeared a couple of months ago. Tommy was eight years old and always enjoyed making fun of me because he was someone else who could pop a wheelie on his bike, while I was still struggling to do so. Until earlier today, that is. Even though he liked to show off all the time, he was still a good kid, and I knew his parents were worried sick about him.

Now he was right in front of me.

"Oh, my God," Amelia whispered in wonder as she looked at all the poor kids locked in the rooms like prisoners, which was indeed what they were. "Here they are, all them. They're all alive. Thank God."

"We found them, man. We found them!" the Bluesman said with a giant grin on his face as he placed his hand on my shoulder and squeezed it. The smile was infectious because I was now smiling, also. This was probably the single greatest moment of our day, knowing we had found these kids and we were going to do everything we could to get them out of here and back home where they belonged.

Zock walked past us and to the room where the little girl was sitting in a corner. With her knees up to her chin, she was staring into space with a sorrowful look. She noticed something moving near her out of the corner of her eye and looked to see what it was. She was met with a panting Zock gazing at her. Her eyes immediately widened, and she scrambled to stand up straight. I was happy to see that she was fully dressed and not...undressed, which really set my mind at ease. I'm sure that Amelia and the Bluesman felt the same way. She did not look harmed in any way, just scared, and with good reason. She kneeled down and pressed her small hands against the glass. There was a giant smile as her face as she saw Zock, and I could tell that she desperately wanted to get out of her makeshift prison and play with him. She noticed us standing there, and her eyes widened in shock as she quickly stood back up. At first, she backed away, apparently scared that we were friends of the guy who had kidnapped her. Then, perhaps seeing that we were not much older than she was, she approached the glass again and put her mouth in front of the small holes in the glass.

"Please let me out," she said in a heartbreaking whisper. I had expected her to start screaming and crying and frantically pounding on the glass. Instead, she had done the exact opposite. I knew right then that I could not even begin to imagine what she had gone through and, as selfish as it sounded, never wanted to. Zock raised himself up on his hind legs and rested his front paws on the glass so that he was now eye level with the little girl, and she smiled at him again. Zock and the three of us were probably the only other beings besides the other kids and the weird guy who was keeping them prisoner whom she had seen in months.

Amelia rushed up to the glass and yelled into one of the holes, "Don't worry, honey, we're going to get you out of here!"

Her voice had been so loud in the small, quiet room that all the other kids suddenly started to wake up and look to see where it was coming from. Once they saw us standing there, a look of disbelief covered their faces and they all got up and ran to the glass with their hands pressed up against it. Again, I was happy to see that they were all dressed and, from what I could tell, healthy. Whatever this guy was doing with them, he wanted to keep these kids alive.

They started crying and pounding on the glass, the muffled sound of them filling the room, hoping and praying that they were about to be rescued from this ordeal and finally be sent back home to their families. As happy as I was to see them up and about, I was suddenly afraid that they might be heard by the guy before we could get them out of here. Then I remembered that the guy was gone and thanked God for small favors.

It dawned on me that we had no idea when he would be coming back and would have no way of knowing when he did. Still, all we would need was a few minutes more to get these kids out of their prisons and upstairs. I had no idea what we were going to do next, but we could only take this one step at a time and hope for the best. It was blind luck that we had found them in the first place. I was counting on that same luck to get them and us out of here safely. The only one of them who was not screaming was the little girl who was looking at Amelia.

"Are you going to take me home?" she asked through one of the holes in a tired voice and with sleepy eyes.

"Yes we are, honey. How long have you been here?"

"About six weeks."

Amelia's face deflated. Being trapped in this tiny room would be like an eternity in hell, especially for a little girl.

"What's your name?" Amelia said.

"Cindy."

"Cindy, I'm Amelia. Are you okay? Has he... has the man... done anything to you?" she asked. Her reluctant tone plainly said she did not really want to ask but knew she had to. Even just thinking about something like that was sickening.

"No, he doesn't make us do anything nasty. He just likes to watch us play. Sometimes he joins in."

He... he likes to watch you play? Is that what you said?"

"Uh-huh. He lets us out into the other room and watches us play games and color and stuff. Sometimes he plays with us, but he usually just sits and stares with a big dopey grin on his face. He's kind of weird and he talks weird, also. His name is Gordon."

"Yeah, we know about that," the Bluesman said.

"He never hurts us; he just likes to watch us play, and I think it's whenever he leaves to go somewhere that he locks us in here. He's a lot like a kid, but dumb. I think he's retarded or something."

Judging from what we had all seen of him, I think we were all in agreement with her.

"Does...does he take care of you?" Amelia asked, and I knew what she was getting at. If Cindy here had been here for six weeks, then that meant some of the other kids had been here even longer. Yet, they all seemed to be clean and well taken care of. None of them stunk. Even the sheets and pillows appeared to be clean. Also, none of them appeared to be malnourished in any way. They might have been living on only candy and fast food, but at least they were eating.

"I guess, but he's kind of mean about it."

"Mean? How so?"

"He'll take us out of here one by one every day and make us take our clothes off while we go stand over there and take a shower," she said pointing across the room.

"A shower?" Amelia said looking at the area. Like me, she must have noticed that there were not any faucets in the walls of the area, just a drain in the middle of the floor.

"Yeah, he'll spray us with the hose over there while saying 'Timetogetclean,'" over and over. That's how he says it, 'Timetogetclean.' Then, he'll turn away while we put our clothes back on and put us back in our rooms. It's really annoying because the water is so cold, but I guess he means well. He's just dumb, like an old dog."

Amelia was just staring at her, broken-hearted. I couldn't blame her because I felt the same way. At least I was relieved to hear that nothing bad had happened. I mean, as bad as this entire ordeal was, it could certainly have been worse. The way Cindy was describing him, he sounded like a dumb kid who wanted other kids to play with but was also trying to act like a grown-up, maybe even try to do something that he thought a parent would do. Talk about creepy.

"We need to get them out of there," I stated.

"Consider it done," the Bluesman said as he moved to one of the rooms and pressed his hands to the glass, his fingers in the holes and starting to jostle it. It hardly moved at all. "Man, this thing is heavy, and look how thick this glass is."

I walked up beside him with Amelia right next to me as we looked at it, the little girl inside looking at us and waiting for us to let her out. It was then that we noticed that the glass was really a door with three latches on the left side, running the length of it, and a padlock on the right at doorknob level that was secured to a looped piece of metal that was screwed into the wood. The padlock was the largest one that I had ever seen, about double the size you would normally find at a bicycle store. Not only was the body of it large, the actual loop of it was about as thick as my first finger. Looking at all the other rooms, I saw that each had the same kind of lock. We all regarded each other with disappointment, thinking the same thing – we had a problem.

"What are we going to do?" Amelia sounded worried.

"I don't know," the Bluesman said as he raised the lock and looked at it with disgust. "We were so close."

"And we're still close. There's got to be a way to get in there," I said thoughtfully.

"Yeah, it's called a key," the Bluesman said.

"Which we don't have, and I'm assuming that the guy keeps them on him at all times. And even if they *are* here, I have no idea where to look for them," I said scanning the room and seeing nothing of interest.

"Maybe there's some spares upstairs," Amelia suggested.

"If there are, where would we look? We could spend hours up there and not get anywhere," the Bluesman moaned.

"Well, we have to do something," Amelia said, looking at all the kids sadly. They were all quiet now, standing there silently staring at us. They must have heard us talking because they seemed aware that we could not get them out – either that or they had pretty much deduced it for themselves. Otherwise, they would be out of their prisons right now. I was actually surprised that none of them had started screaming or going ballistic like you would expect most kids to do in a situation like this. Instead, they were strangely calm. Scared, but calm. I could not even begin to think what could have been done to them in all this time to make them act this way.

"Did you see any bolt cutters when we were upstairs?" the Bluesman asked.

205

"No, but even if there are any big enough to handle something like this, it wouldn't do us any good," I said looking at the lock I was holding in my hand.

Amelia brightened. "What? Why? That would seem like a good idea."

"It is a good idea and it would work if any of us were Arnold Schwarzenegger," I said.

"What do you mean?" she asked.

"Look how thick this thing is. The strength it would take to use the bolt cutters would have to be Hulk level. Even if Keith and I were both using it and giving it everything we had, there would be no way we could cut through this thing, much less doing it eight times," I sighed.

We all stared at it for a moment.

"I have an idea," the Bluesman said.

"What?" I said.

"Let's break the glass down."

Both Amelia and I looked at him as though he were E.T. coming down the ramp from his spaceship.

"Are you out of your mind?" she finally said.

"What? We don't have the key; it's the only other way."

"If we broke the glass, where do you think it's all going to go once it shatters? It's going to go over the kids and cut them to ribbons!" she yelled.

"Oh…yeah," he said weakly.

"'Oh, yeah,' is right," she replied.

"Even if we did try and break the glass down, we don't have anything that would be able to shatter something this thick," I said tapping it. "Look at this thing. The only way this glass would break is by driving a car through it. I could hit it with a bat and it would probably barely even crack it. God only knows how he got ten of these things down here. Each one of them must weigh a ton."

"Because he's built like Arnold Schwarzenegger," the Bluesman stated.

While still inspecting the lock, my eyes glided over to the looped piece of metal that was screwed to the wood.

Screwed.

I looked at it for a moment, feeling a hopeful grin spread across my face.

"I think I have an idea," I said, inspecting the screws.

"What?" Amelia said.

"Well, we don't have the key and we can't break the glass, but maybe we can unscrew this metal piece here from the wood and then open the doors."

They looked at what I was talking about and grinned along with me.

"That's it, man! That's it!" the Bluesman said as he squeezed my shoulder.

"With all of that junk upstairs, there have to be some tools somewhere. If we can find three four-edge screwdrivers, and each of us work on a door, we should have them out of here in no time."

"Let's go up and look," the Bluesman said as we all three started to leave.

"No! Don't leave us!"

"Come back!"

"Noooooooooooooooo!"

"Please come back!"

"Stay!"

"Where are you going?"

"I want my Mommy!"

All the kids were screaming at once now, terrified that we were going to leave them. I really couldn't blame them. Here we were, the first people they had seen in weeks or months except for the weird guy, and we were leaving them in their prisons.

"Hush! Hush! It's okay," Amelia was yelling with her arms up, trying to calm them down. "We're just going to go upstairs to try to find something to get you out of here, okay?"

207

"Don't go!"

"Stay!"

"Let me out!"

"I wanna go home!"

"Hush! Hush! Okay, I'm not leaving, okay? I'm not leaving! Calm down!" she yelled.

Once she said those magic words about not leaving, they started to calm down.

"You two better go upstairs and look, and I'll stay down here with them," she said to us.

"Good idea," the Bluesman and I said at the same time.

"We shouldn't be more than a few minutes, hopefully," I said, looking at the Bluesman. Then he, I, and Zock left the room, rushing up the stairs and across the living area until we were on the other side of the barn, where all the junk was. "Okay, some tools have got to be lying around somewhere. You take that side and I'll take the other."

"Sounds good," the Bluesman said as we started to quickly look around all the components, searching for the specific tools we needed. Along the way, I found several hammers and some wrenches, but nothing we could use. The Bluesman, I felt, must not have been faring any better, or he would have spoken up. I kept looking, however, and when I finally saw them, I actually thought I was going to faint. Sitting on a table next to what appeared to be two torn-apart fans were two screwdrivers. I rushed over to them and picked them up. Yes! Four-edge screwdrivers!

"Bark! Bark! Bark!"

Shocked by the outburst, I looked over at Zock to see why he was barking so loudly. My first thought was that the guy had wandered in here while we were upstairs, and we had not seen him… but he wasn't here.

"What's he barking at? He scared me to death!" the Bluesman yelled, looking at him.

Zock was standing in place with his head arched up, looking toward the side of the barn, the direction that we had come to get here.

Oh, God, I thought.

I rushed by him and toward a window and looked out. I was surprised to see that it was sunset and getting near dark. We had been at this for hours! Suddenly it felt like this afternoon had been a different lifetime ago, when we were doing nothing but sitting by the pond watching the ducks and having lunch. Now, we had stumbled onto a nightmare!

I tried to see something out of the ordinary that had gotten Zock's attention but didn't see anything. Then I saw it.

Far off in the distance was a pair of headlights... and they were approaching.

"Oh, crap!" I yelled.

"What?" the Bluesman said as he was running toward me.

"The guy! He's coming! I can see his headlights!"

He looked at me in shock.

"You're shitting me!"

"I shit you not!"

"Oh, shit! Amy!"

I dropped the screwdrivers, and we immediately rushed down the stairs and into the playroom and then the prisoner room. Amelia looked at us, startled.

"Did you find them?" she asked.

"We gotta get out of here!" I yelled.

"What? Why?"

"The guy! He's coming!"

"What?" she yelped in surprise.

"The guy! He's coming! We gotta get out of here! We gotta hide!"

"We...we can't! What about the kids?"

209

"We'll deal with them later! Right now, we gotta get out of here and hide or we're dead meat!"

Amelia looked at us and then back at the kids.

"Kids, listen to me. We're going to go, but we'll be right...."

"No!"

"Let us out!"

"Don't go!"

"Don't leave us!"

"Hush! Hush! Hush! Listen, the crazy man is coming back, and we have to hide so we can...so we can find a way to get rid of him and then come back and get you. We'll be back! I promise! But, I need you to do something for me. I need you all to pretend that you never saw us. Don't say anything about us. If the man finds out about us, he might... I don't know, but it won't be good. So I need you all to be good and don't say anything, okay? We'll be back, I promise!" she said as she started retreating away from them.

The look on their faces was heartbreaking, but they seemed to understand the situation, and I could only hope that they didn't say anything, or we were all going to be sunk.

We ran out of the room and made sure the door was locked. Then, as were we running for the stairs, I picked up the flashlights we had set on the floor, turned mine on, gave the other two to the Bluesman and Amelia, and we rushed up the stairs. Working as quickly as we could, the Bluesman and I moved the door back in place, moved the carpet back to where it had been, and then I ran to the side door, where we'd come in, and switched off the light. We were now in darkness, and Amelia and the Bluesman immediately switched on their flashlights.

"Now what?" I heard Amelia say.

I walked through the darkness until we were all staring out the side window.

The headlights were closer now. I guessed he would be here in about ten minutes. Hopefully, he had not been able to tell that the lights in the barn had been on.

"We need to hide," I said.

"Good idea. Where?" the Bluesman said.

I thought about it for a moment.

"We need to stay in here somewhere so we can keep an eye on him. We can do that only from in here," I explained as we walked away from the window and toward something that I remembered. "Here," I said as we were now standing behind a pair of six giant blocks of hay. "This is good. He'll have no reason to come back here, and we'll be able to peek around the stacks and between them."

"Sounds good," the Bluesman said as we all sat down with our legs spread out in front of us, clicked off our flashlights, and listened to the sound of the approaching pick-up truck and the ominous silence of the barn around us. Zock was restless, and I put my arms around him to calm him down and hold him in place. It was only then that I realized how tired I was. I was exhausted! The entire day had drained me, and I could only assume that Amelia and the Bluesman felt the same way. I leaned my head back against the hay and closed my eyes, grateful for this moment of rest.

"Oh, crap!" I suddenly said as I snapped my head back up.

"What?" the Bluesman said.

"I think…"

"You think what?"

"I think I forgot to turn the light off in the play area," I said slowly.

"What? Are sure?" Amelia said.

"I don't…I don't know. I don't remember. Do you remember?"

"No, I don't" she whispered.

211

"I don't know. I want to say yes, but I really don't know," the Bluesman said uncertainly. "Can we go check?"

I thought about it for a moment. I was pretty sure that I had turned them off but not completely sure, and if I wasn't completely sure, then I had to assume that I hadn't.

"Stay here. I'm going to check," I said, getting up.

"Wait! Listen!" the Bluesman said grabbing my arm.

The pick-up truck was pulling in to the side of the barn. There was absolutely no time to run over there, pick up the rug, move the door and check the light, run down and turn it off if it was on, run back up, move the door and the rug, and do it all in the darkness before the guy was inside.

All we could do was hope that my mistake had not jeopardized us all.

We heard the door of the pick-up slam shut and, a few moments later, the crunch of his boots on the dirt outside as he was walking. Then we heard the sound of the front door being opened. A moment later, all the lights snapped on, and we heard his footsteps on the dirt again, and then more muffled ones as he was now walking on the carpet.

Then, he started whistling. The entire barn was filled with the sound of his surprisingly strong whistling, and we all looked at each other oddly as we realized that he was whistling the "Peanuts Theme" from the Charlie Brown television specials. Out of all the infinite number of songs that he could possibly choose from, this one was the most odd. Having heard his taste in music, I would have expected some ear-piercing country and western torture. Although, after observing him and after Cindy telling us about his childlike habits, this song seemed oddly fitting. I was sure that Charles M. Schulz would be glad to have this guy as a fan.

The whistling abruptly stopped, and we all froze, not making so much as a sound. My first thought was that I had left something behind. Did I leave the carpet up? Was the door open? Was something out of place? Could he somehow see us? A million things went through my mind at once. Amelia was squeezing my hand, and we looked into each other's eyes. We were both thinking the same thing: This was it. He had found us.

Then he started whistling again.

We all started breathing again.

Being as quiet as I could, I turned around so I could look between the barrels of hay. I was able to see most of the living area but not him. Then, shifting around, I could see him standing in front of the refrigerator with his back to us. Looking inside it, he pulled out some items. He moved over to the sandwich table, and I was able to see jars of mayonnaise and mustard in his hands; he set them down and then turned on the radio. A horrible country and western song came on. In the vastness of the large barn, it seemed incredibly loud. If I had to choose between this and his whistling, I would rather hear the whistling.

"What's he doing?" the Bluesman whispered.

"I think he's making a sandwich," I whispered back. "He's standing in front of that small table by the refrigerator with some jars he took from it."

"That sounds good. At least his sandwiches are cold."

At that moment, I realized how hungry I was and that my stomach was growling. It was not so loud that you could not hear it unless you were sitting right next to me, but it seemed loud. This struck me as ridiculous: How could I be thinking of food at a time like this? Then, something else popped into my mind. It was almost dark and I was not at home. Once it got pitch dark and I was not home yet, my parents would freak because, as you know, I was not allowed to be out after dark. I'll give you one guess why. In fact, I'll even give you a hint: He's currently engaged in eating a sandwich. I bet all of our parents were worried right now. It was not uncommon for us to hang out all day and then not wander back home until

213

night, especially during the summer, but that didn't mean that our parents didn't expect us to call and check in every now and then to ease their minds. When we got home, I was really going to be in for some big-time trouble. Hopefully, after I explained my side of the situation, they would understand. I mean, come on! Look at this! Wouldn't you give me a break?

He ate his sandwich loudly, obviously chewing with his mouth open, and humming as he did it. Not a song or anything, just a humming noise. It was really weird, and we all looked at each other, wondering about the infinite depths of weirdness that this guy had. There seemed to be no bottom to it. Then, once he was done with that, he opened the refrigerator again and pulled out a can of Dr. Pepper. He popped it open, and we could hear him slurping as he drank it in large gulps. He then let loose with a belch that was so thunderous, Zock actually went into a scared stance looking like somebody was about to kick him. I bet this guy could even give Matt Distler a run for his money...and that's saying something. If we had not been in this situation, it probably would have been quite funny.

I made a silent vow to myself that I was going to stop belching in front of my mom from now on. I wasn't sure if I was going to be able to keep that vow because it really was pretty great fun to annoy her with it, but I was going to try. If this was an example of what I sounded like, it was no wonder it drove her crazy.

"Thatwasgooditstimetoplay," he said to nobody as he moved out of range of my sight. A moment later, we heard the familiar sound of the carpet being moved, and then the door on the floor being lifted.

The Bluesman and I looked at each other, trading silent thoughts. I wondered again if I had remembered to turn off the light. Apparently, we were about to find out.

214

"I'll take a look," the Bluesman said as he peeked around the corner. "He's moving the door," he whispered to us.

Then everything was quiet.

"What's he doing?" I whispered.

"He's... he's just standing there staring down the stairway. The light's on. I can see it from here," he whispered, looking worriedly at me.

"Oh, crap," I muttered.

I felt Amelia squeeze my shoulders, her silent way of telling me that it was all right. But it wasn't all right. How could I have been so stupid? I mean, sure we were scared and in a hurry, but how could I have been so dumb as to miss that? Not only were we in a dangerous situation made even more dangerous now, we also had the kids to worry about.

"DidIforgettoturnoffthelight?" we heard him say in his weird, childish manner.

That it exactly what happened. Please believe it, I thought.

"Sillymealwasyforgettingthings," he said, and then we heard him tromping down the stairs.

We all collectively sighed and sat back and thanked God that this crazy guy thought he had just slipped up. We were no closer to figuring out what we were going to do next, but at least we were still safe.

Then, lying there with my back to the hay, I suddenly realized something, and I straightened up. "Oh, shit!" I gasped.

"What? What's wrong?" Amelia said, jumping and scampering away as she was looking around the floor, probably expecting more cockroaches or maybe rats.

"My backpack! I'm not wearing it!"

We were all quiet for a moment as we thought what this might meant.

"Did you... did you?" the Bluesman said.

215

"I left it downstairs. I took it off and set it by the door while you were working on it, and I forgot to grab it when we ran out."

"Are you sure? Maybe you took it off somewhere else," Amelia said hopefully, but I could tell by the way that she had said it that she did not really believe that.

"No, I remember taking it off. It's down there."

"Maybe he won't see it," the Bluesman consoled.

"How can he not see it? It's right there in the open. We were lucky with the light. Once he sees that and pieces the two together, we're screwed! I'm sorry, guys."

"It's not your fault, man. It could easily have been either of us," the Bluesman said. "We've gotten this far. If he sees it… we'll deal with it"

I didn't say anything, but I was mentally cursing myself. How were we going to deal with a man who was really no more than a kid, yet who could probably fight the Hulk to a standstill?

Minutes passed. Then, we heard a loud tromping coming up the stairs.

He had found it.

The tromping had stopped.

"What's he doing?" I whispered to the Bluesman.

As carefully as he could, he took a quick look around the corner and then turned back to us.

"He's just standing there by the door holding the backpack. He has a huge smile on his face."

"A smile? He's smiling? What's he smiling for?" I whispered.

"Imgoingtofindyou! Imgoingtofindyou!" he said loudly.

The way he said it was scary and made my blood turn cold. I froze in place. If this were a horror movie, you would expect the bad guy in this exact situation to be screaming and bellowing at the moonlit sky about how he was going to find whoever it was that had crossed him, probably a girl because all the horror movies had a final chase scene involving a screaming, crying girl, struggling to get away. And then there would be some kind of chase scene through the woods or the neighborhood with accompanying suspenseful music in the background before the climax, where they faced off against each other.

Instead, the way he was saying it was as though he were a happy child, playing a game, probably hide and seek and he couldn't wait to find us and say 'Tag! You're it!'' Of course, his way of saying it would also probably involve him pounding the crap out of us and then locking us into his little playpen downstairs and adding us to his collection. If not that, then killing us in some horrific manner. Probably with a knife. That seemed to be the most common instrument of destruction in horror movies. Knives were scarier than guns because it was a more intimate and messy way of dispatching somebody. *Happy thoughts, ladies and gentleman! Brought to you live here at Goatman's by Danny Brent! But please call me Dan.*

"I'mgoingtofindyou! Imgoingtofindyou!"

The way he was talking in such a joyous manner, you would have thought he had just come running downstairs to the tree on Christmas morning and found the pony that he had always wanted waiting for him to come and pet it. Thinking about it, I cannot remember the last time that I had heard someone so happy about…anything, which was really sad now that I thought about it. Our fear was giving this guy the time of his life!

"Maybe… maybe he doesn't know that we're still actually here," I whispered. "I mean, he found the backpack, but he doesn't actually know that the person who left it is still in the barn. Plus, he doesn't know how many of us there are."

"That's true," the Bluesman said thinking about it. "Still, you know he's going to look. Eventually, it will dawn on him to look back here."

Then we heard him tromping around on the carpet.

217

"Imgoingtofindyou!Iknowyourehere!Imgoingtofindyou"

"We've got to get out of here. Somehow, we've got to…get him out of here so we can rescue the kids and get home."

"Good idea. Any suggestions?"

I didn't say anything.

"Imgoingtofindyou!Iknowyourehere!Comeoutcomeoutw hereveryouare!"

He sounded like he was farther away, on the mechanical side of the barn. I crawled around Amelia so I could look around the hay and see that way. He was walking in between the tables toward the car, moving his head this way and that. Once he saw that there was nobody over there, he would make his way back and…probably check here.

"Is he coming back?" Amelia said.

"Not yet, but it won't be long."

She was trying to hide it, but I could tell she was trying to keep herself from crying. This was my fault, all of it. It was because of me that we were in this situation, and I felt so terrible about everything. In trying to do the right thing, I had screwed up, and I was going to get all of us killed, not to mention the kids downstairs, who now were forever doomed to their prisons to add to my woes when they thought that help had come at last.

There had to be a way out of this, I told myself. *Think!*

One thing came to mind. It was crazy and stupid, but there was absolutely nothing else that I could think of.

"I'm going to lure him of sight so that you two can get the kids and get out of here," I said.

They both looked at me like I was crazy.

"How are you going to do that?" the Bluesman asked.

I thought about it for a moment and then looked above me. The loft was right above our heads. If I could somehow get him to chase me up there….

218

"What are you looking at?" Amelia asked, following my gaze.

"I need him to chase me up there. While I'm running around and keeping him occupied, you two can get downstairs and save the kids and then get out of here. Keith knows where I dropped the screwdrivers. If I can keep him back far enough from the ledge, he won't be able to see what you're doing. Maybe I can... maybe I can push him off the edge or something."

"Are you out of your mind? That's the craziest thing I've ever heard. All you'll do is get yourself killed," Amelia blurted.

"That thought had occurred to me."

"It's not funny."

"Any better ideas?"

"Why don't you... why don't you make him chase you outside? It's dark and I'm sure you will be able to run faster than him. Plus, you'll find some places to hide."

I thought about it for a moment. It sounded like a good idea. In fact it was a better idea because she was right. It was more open and dark outside. Hiding would be relatively easy, at least easier than upstairs, where there was just hay. They would also have more time to get downstairs and start working on the locks while I was keeping him busy. The only thing that made me worry was that I didn't know whether he had a gun. While we were walking around the barn, none of us had seen any guns, but that didn't mean that he didn't have any. He might even have a rifle or something in his truck. After all, this was Texas, and every other person was armed. Well, that was something I would deal with if I had to.

"Imgoingtofindyou!"

He was making his way back. Okay, this plan was going to have to do because we didn't have anything else. Desperate times called for desperate measures.

219

"Okay. I'm going to get his attention and then run out the side door when he comes after me. Stay behind the hay and swing around it so he can't see you when he runs by. Hold on to Zock so he doesn't chase after me," I said to Amelia.

They both looked at me for a moment.

"Be careful. Try not to let him catch you," Amelia said as she touched my cheek.

"Sound advice," I winked.

Then I ran around the hay and stopped in place.

"Hey, Gordon! Do you want to play?" I yelled at him.

The guy stopped in his tracks when he saw me. A look of surprise covered his face, and then the smile reappeared, along with his rapid-fire blinking. Looking at him standing there, I could see, even though he was still in the mechanical area, that this guy was actually even bigger than I thought, and the knowledge that I had just made a drastic mistake popped into my mind. It was too late to change course now, however.

"YouknowGordon?" he said pointing to himself in a comical way.

"Yes, I know Gordon," I yelled back at him, feeling ridiculous speaking like him.

"HowdoyouknowGordon?"

"Gordon likes to feed kids candy!" I said. It was pretty dumb, I admit, but it was better than going into a long spiel about how Gordon likes to kidnap little kids and lock them up and force them to play while he watches in his own little world.

"Youareakid.Youhavebeenbad.Gordonhastoputyouinwit htheotherkids."

"I don't think so, guy."

"Ihavetoyouareakid."

"Tell you what. If you can catch me, you can put me in with the other kids. Deal?"

"YouwanttoplayagamewithGordon?"

"I'll play any game you want, but you have to catch me first."

"Gordonlikestoplaygames. Heisverygoodatthem."

"You're going to have to prove it!"

We looked at each other for a moment, me not blinking at all and him blinking like a machine gun, still wearing that dopey grin, his head shining in the light. I took a moment to wonder if he polished it with something because it really was shiny.

Then I ran for the side door.

I immediately heard his footsteps behind me and knew that he was running after me. I honestly did not know whether to be happy about this fact or not. I'm sure you understand.

As I ran past the hay, I looked at Amelia, Zock, and the Bluesman out of the corner of my eye and kept going. When I was at the door, I opened it and left it open, ran outside, and kept going. I ran to the other side of his giant truck, the one that you needed a small wiener to drive, and hid behind the front wheel as I peeked over the hood. He appeared in the doorway a moment later, the outline of his large body in the light. I mentally patted myself on the back about this because it meant that he had not seen Amelia, Zock, or the Bluesman. Now that I was keeping Gordon occupied, they could get to work on freeing the kids. After that, I had no clue, but it was progress. I ducked down.

"Imgoingtofindyou! Imgoingtofindyou!"

I decided that silence was the best option at this particular moment.

I heard the crunch of his boots on the dirt. He did not seem to be in any kind of hurry, but I knew he was looking for me in the darkness and listening for any sound that did not belong in these quiet surroundings.

I was so scared, my breathing sounded louder to my ears than a chainsaw. I was trying to control it but was having very little luck. My pulse was racing, and I could feel nervous sweat all over my body. His footsteps sounded like they were getting farther away, and I peeked around the corner of the truck. He must have thought I was hiding behind the tree because that's where it appeared he was walking. I had a small respite.

As terrified as I was, I couldn't help but look at the night sky and notice how beautiful it was. Stars were everywhere, and I could see them so much more clearly all the way out here than in the suburbs because there was no light for miles except for the barn to interfere with the bright clarity of the millions of stars that seemed to stretch out for infinity. The sky was so beautiful, I could not take my eyes from it. Even though I knew I should be watching Gordon and doing everything I could to distract him from going back inside the barn, I had to watch that magnificent sky.

A memory came to mind. About six months earlier, Amelia had been over at my house on a school night. It was a very rare occasion – it was already dark outside, and she wasn't home. Instead, she was with me. I don't know what led to it, but we were lying on our backs on my front lawn, staring up at the night sky. Zock was lying next to me and, at some point, I must have gone back into the house and gotten my portable radio because we were listening to music at a low volume as we talked. A lot of the popular songs of the time were coming on one after another, but I remember two songs by the same artist played back to back – it must have been a twofer day – and those songs really stood out: "Hold on Loosely" and "Caught Up in You" by .38 Special. I remember those songs because it was at that moment that I realized how special this time really was and, even then, I was old enough to realize that moments like this were the snapshots of life that were worth treasuring. There was a quiet calmness in the air, and everything felt serene.

222

Even though we were probably not out there for more than an hour and a half before her mom called, saying it was time to come home, it had felt a lot longer, maybe because I had wanted it to last longer. I remember even as we were lying there in the moment how perfect everything was, just perfect, how it all felt, and I would be more than happy to be doing this every night for the rest of my life with Amelia. And now, just like then, I had picked out my favorite constellation: Orion. I could name all the constellations in the sky, but for some reason, Orion had always been my favorite, and every time I was out at night, it had become my habit to look for it. Sometimes it appeared closer than at other times. On certain nights it even appeared so close that it seemed I could just reach out and touch it... like tonight. *Orion, old buddy, it sure would be nice if you could reach down right now and take us all away from this.*

"Areyouoverhere? Imgoingtofindyou!"

Apparently, that wasn't going to happen. I snapped out of my reverie and came back to the horror of real life and all it had to offer at the moment.

Once he saw that I was not behind the tree or around his generator, which was humming in the night, he would probably make his way over here. In the shadows from the little light that the barn was offering, I could see him making his way down to check if I was there. This guy really was dumb. He was tiptoeing towards the tree even though he had just loudly announced that he was coming for me and that he was going to find me. I strained my neck, wondering if I could see how Amelia and the Bluesman were proceeding with the kids, but I couldn't see anything. I needed for Gordon to get farther away so I could safely get back in there and help.

Then I thought further about it and realized that was a terrible idea. If he saw me go back in there, even if I closed the door and locked it after me, he would be able to get back inside and see what we were doing and put a stop to it. Then we would all be trapped inside together and sunk. Still, I had to see if this was working. I looked on the ground and saw a rock about the size of a golf ball. Hoping this would work, I picked it up, brought my arm back, and hurled it with everything that I had past the tree and generator. I saw it sail into the darkness and into a colony of tall weeds. A moment later I heard it clunk against something and make a loud banging noise. I guess I hit something that was made of metal because that's what it had sounded like.

Gordon immediately raised his head in the direction that the sound had come from.

"Iheardyou! Imgoingtofindyou! Imgoingtowinthegame! HereIcome!!" he announced as he started running off into the darkness. A moment later I heard the weeds being moved around.

I wasn't sure how long this was going to tide him over till he finally realized there was nobody there, but at least for the moment it had worked. With a little bit of luck, he was dumb enough that he'd walk all the way to Dallas looking for me. I decided to risk getting a quick look at the progress Amelia and the Bluesman were making while I could.

With one last look into the darkness, I bolted back into the barn and past the haystacks. The carpet was pulled back, and the wooden door had been moved. As I ran to it, I looked over toward the window and saw that the screwdrivers I had dropped there were gone. That meant my two friends were downstairs working. I knew that progress was going to be slow, but as long as I could keep Gordon busy outside chasing rocks, or me, they would be able to work. I ran down the stairs quickly to the prisoner room so I could look inside. I must have scared Amelia and the Bluesman because they were both standing there with the screwdrivers held out in front of them as though they were guns. The Bluesman was standing in front of Amelia in a protective stance. When they saw that it was just me, they closed their eyes and exhaled.

"Jesus, man! We thought it was the guy!" The Bluesman tried to breathe normally again.

"Sorry. I wanted to see how you guys were doing."

"We just started. This is going to take a long time. It would be a lot easier if we had the keys," Amelia said.

"I wish we had them, but he probably has them in his pocket or jacket or something," I said as I looked at the kids, who were all staring at me. Every one of them was so frightened, it was really hard to look at them. Each was trapped in that little prison that they all so much wanted to finally escape from. "Okay, I'm going to get back upstairs. He's probably figured out by now that it was me throwing a rock into the field to create a diversion. I'll do what I can to keep him occupied. You guys keep working."

They didn't say anything as they each quickly turned to the screws they had been focusing on and started working. I turned around and ran back to the stairs. As I was doing so, I realized that Zock was running after me. At first, I wanted to stop and tell him to go back, but then I thought this might actually be a good thing. Zock might be able to get the weird guy's attention in some way, and I wasn't really worried about Zock because he could run ten times faster than Gordon. I ran back up the stairs and back to the open door. As I ran outside, I was just in time to see the welcome sight of Gordon emerging from the bushes. Even in the semi-darkness, I could see him pretty clearly: He was holding something above his head with his right arm straight. In a bizarre way, he looked strangely like the Statue of Liberty. I decided it was the rock I had thrown, but it just as easily could have been Merlin's crystal ball for all I knew. Then he stopped in his tracks and looked across the area at me. Well, not at me, exactly. He was looking at Zock.

He raised both of his arms in the air in front of him and smiled.

"Doggie!" he yelled happily.

Zock barked at him.

This guy was just too much!

Now he was running toward us.

"Come on, Zock!" I yelled, and then we started running away from him, past his truck.

"ImgoingtogetyouZock!" he yelled.

Wow, he really had good hearing.

We ran the length of the barn, and then I stopped and looked back because I wanted to make sure that he ran past the door and kept running toward us. I was sure that if he happened to look inside the door as he was running and saw that the carpet was unfurled, he would forget about us and run inside to check on his collection of kids. I had to make sure that that didn't happen.

"Come on, Gordon! Come play with us!" I yelled, waving my arm at him as though he were an old friend I was inviting to a party.

"Imgoingtogetyou!" he yelled in a joyful manner as he ran past the door.

Seeing that stage one was over, it was now time to be fleet of foot. I turned around and started running, Zock right beside me. We rounded the corner, pulled in front of the barn, and kept going. I stopped on the other side and heard Gordon's hefty steps before I saw him. Then he suddenly appeared like a runaway train, turning the corner. For someone as big as he was, he really was pretty fast...although I noticed he was already wheezing a bit. I took that as a good sign, hoping that he might even collapse from exhaustion if he was pushed hard enough. But for right now, it was time for more running, and Zock and I took off down the other side.

I guess it was adrenaline, but I was now running faster than I ever had in my entire life. I suppose fear had a lot to

226

do with it, also. As I was running, I was coming toward the side window, where I had seen his headlights approaching, and I sneaked a quick peek inside without stopping. It dawned on me that if we had come this way when we arrived here, I would not have almost killed myself climbing an old, rotten tree and then gotten attacked by a bat. I guess we had just been so worked up about finding the place, none of us had seen the window. Well, at least I was alive. For now, anyhow.

In that quick glance, the place appeared the same as I had left it. Nobody was upstairs, and I wondered how many kids they had freed so far. We arrived at the other end of the barn, and I stopped and looked behind me.

My face fell.

Gordon had stopped and was looking in the window.

Oh, crap! "Hey, Gordon!"

Nothing.

"Hey, Gordon! You... you bald dumbass!"

That got his attention. He was now looking at me with a hurt look on his face.

"DidyoucallGordaonadumbass?"

"Yeah, I did! Dumbass!"

"YoushouldntcurseatGordon!"

"What's Gordon going to do about it, dumbass?"

"Stopthat!"

"Make me, dumbass!"

Gordon actually looked like he was going to cry. I couldn't believe it! What was even worse was that I felt guilty about it. Can you believe that? This guy was trying to kill me, and I felt guilty about hurting his feelings! What a night!

"Hey, Gordon! You don't want everyone to call you a dumbass do you?"

"No!"

"Well if you don't catch me, everyone in the entire world is going to call you a dumbass. No matter where you go, people will say, 'There goes Gordon. He's a real dumbass because he couldn't catch that kid!'"

"No!"

"Yes!"

"No!"

"Yes!

"No!"

This could go on all night...which, I realized, was actually a good thing. If we were standing here having this ridiculous argument, Amelia and the Bluesman could work in peace. And with less danger to me. All right, then!

"Yes!

"No!"

"Yes!"

"Nonononono!" he yelled in an excruciating voice and started running after me again.

Well, so much for that idea. It was good while it lasted.

I resumed my running and was facing the other side, where the tree was, when I turned back and saw Gordon racing around the corner. He must have slipped on something because he couldn't stop his turn. A surprised look came over his face as he tumbled to the ground. He lay there for a moment on his stomach and then slowly turned over and sat up. He was breathing hard and...I couldn't believe it: The guy was starting to cry! It was not coming out in torrents or anything, but he was definitely starting to blubber up. For some insane reason, I felt guilty about it. It was my fault that he was running around all over the place, and it was my fault that he had just crashed to the ground and hurt himself. It was like beating up a dumb animal. If this kept up, I was going to develop a complex. Once this was all over with, I might seriously have to consider seeing a psychiatrist.

I just stood there and stared at him. Eventually, he looked up at me and noticed that I was there and suddenly smiled.

228

"WillyouhelpGordonupsowecanplaysomemore?" he said while holding out his hand. This was not a trick. He was serious.

Unbelievable!

"No, Gordon. If you want to play, you're going to have to get yourself up," I explained.

His smile fell, and he dropped his arm while staring at the ground.

"Letmerestforaminutethenwecanplaysomemore," he said breathing heavily.

"Suit yourself. Take all the time you want," I said, leaning against the barn. I was grateful for this for two reasons: 1.) I was getting tired. The whole day had caught up with me, and I was more tired now than I ever had been in my entire life. Now I knew how the Dallas Cowboys felt after a game against the Steelers. 2.) The longer he stayed collapsed on the ground, the more time Amelia and the Bluesman had to work on freeing the kids. This was a win/win situation.

We stayed there for about five minutes, neither of us saying anything. The only sounds were the crickets and our breathing, at first labored but now easier. I was actually surprised that Gordon didn't ask who I was or where I had come from — the things you would expect a person who was kidnapping kids and bringing them to his hideout to ask. Instead, all he wanted to do was play…once he was rested, that is.

Then, without saying a word, he quickly got up and started running after Zock and me again.

I just as quickly took off, and we were at it once again.

I ran past the door. A quick look revealed no change.

Come on, guys! What's taking so long? I thought.

When I came to the end of the barn, I looked back to see how close or far Gordon was.

He was gone.

Oh, crap! Amelia! I thought.

I ran back to the door and looked inside.

Gordon was standing near the open door on the floor, with his back to me. His arms were hanging by his side, and his head was slightly tilted. He was not doing anything except standing there, probably trying to figure out what was going on. As far as he knew, I was the only kid who was running around. He was probably wondering how I was able to run around the barn with him and open the door on the floor at the same time. He was also probably wondering how anyone had found the little hideout where he kept his playmates.

I knew that his little reasoning session would not last long. There was only one thing to do.

Taking a deep breath, I ran into the barn toward Gordon. As soon as I was near enough to him, I jumped up and slapped the back of his bald head as though I were giving someone a high five, completed my jump several feet in front of him, and came to a stop. The impact had made a loud smacking sound, and Gordon was now holding his head with his hands and looking at me with a dumbstruck expression.

"YouhurtGordon!" he yelled.

I didn't know what to say, so I didn't say anything.

"YouhitGordon! JustlikeDaddyusedtodo!"

I really didn't know what to make of that. What I did know was that Gordon was no longer smiling — in fact, he had a huge frown on his face. Apparently, Gordon had Daddy issues.

"Imgoingtogetyou!" he screamed and started running toward me.

As you probably have guessed, I took this as my cue to run, also. I ran toward the mechanical area in between the tables and heard Gordon running behind me. It may have been my imagination, but it sounded like he was running faster now. This did not set my mind at ease. Apparently, his anger had given him fuel for fire, and he was now in peak form. I felt absolutely wasted, and I didn't know what to do because I couldn't keep this up for much longer. If I led him outside again, that would be great for Amelia and the Bluesman, but it would mean certain death for me because we would be out in the open again. I had to find something else.

I was now at the end of the table, right in front of the '57 Chevy, and ran around it to the left, so that I was now heading toward the living area again. This time, I did not even bother trying to look behind me – I could hear that Gordon was pretty close. Like in a horror movie, I was imagining his claw reaching out for my shirt collar just inches away, about to pull me, screaming, into the darkness, where I would never be seen again because he had devoured me, bones and all. I could see the open door to my right, and my mind raced, considering what to do now, since I knew that heading out there was the worst thing I could possibly do. Then, just ahead of me, I saw the ladder leading up to the loft. This had been my original idea. Amelia had said that it was crazy, and I had believed her, but apparently, crazy was going to have to do for now. Putting on a burst of speed and not breaking stride in any way, I grabbed the ladder and quickly scampered up like a terrified monkey, which was basically what I was.

As I was climbing, I felt Gordon's hand graze my foot, and then I heard a loud thump as he came back down. I continued to race up the ladder and didn't stop moving until I was all the way up. Once I was standing straight up, it took everything I had to stay on my feet, and you cannot imagine how grateful I was for this moment of rest. I took a few breaths and then looked over the ledge.

Gordon was standing there, bent over, with his hands on his knees. Apparently, his little adrenaline rush was over. Zock was looking up at me while keeping his distance from Gordon.

I needed to get his attention, or he might forget about me and head to the play area downstairs. I picked up two large handfuls of hay and dropped them on him. He immediately looked up at me. "Dontdothat!"

I picked up some more and did it again.

"Isaiddontdothat!"

"What are you going to do about it?"

"Imgoingtogetyou!"

"How are you going to get me if you're down there?"

"Illwaitforyoutocomedown."

"Why would I come down if I know that you're waiting for me?"

That seemed to stump him because he didn't say anything.

"Gordon, are you a dumbass?"

"Imnotadumbass! StopcallingGordonadumbass!"

"If you just stay down there and don't come up here and try to catch me, that makes you a dumbass!"

"Sayswho?"

"Says everyone! If you don't come up here, then everyone will know you're a dumbass because I'm going to tell them!"

"No!"

"Yes!"

"No!"

"Yes!"

Here we go again.

"No!"

"Yes!"

"Noyouwontnoyouwontnoyouwont!" he bellowed as he started climbing up the ladder.

Looking down at the top of Gordon's bald head and seeing it get larger as he got closer was one of the most ominous things I have ever seen. I felt like I was in a disaster movie. I was the earth and he was the moon, on a collision course with me. Unfortunately, there were no missiles in the air to stop it like in that Sean Connery movie. I think it's called *Meteor*. If you haven't seen it, you should check it out.

Meanwhile, it was time for me to hide.

I ran behind one of the stacks of hay and crouched down behind it as I listened to Gordon proceed up the ladder. A moment later, I heard the thump of his feet moving across the wooden floor and then stop.

"Imgoingtofindyou!"

Back to square one, ladies and gentleman.

I heard him thumping around. His footsteps sounded like they were getting farther away and I peeked around the hay barrel I was behind and saw him. He was about forty feet away with his back to me. He started walking in that direction and then, for no reason I could determine, he suddenly whirled around and started walking in the direction that I was in. I held my breath as I listened to him, trying to gauge from his footsteps where he was. As he was moving, I moved also, being as careful as I could not to let my footsteps be heard. I was now on the other side of the hay barrel, and I peeked around and saw Gordon again. He was about thirty feet away, standing next to another hay barrel. Suddenly, he raced around it and stopped.

"Imgoingtofindyou!" he said.

Needless to say, I did not retort with a smart remark at this particular moment, even though it was an absolutely golden opportunity.

He moved to another hay barrel straight on, and then darted to the right of it.

"Yourenotthere!" he said in a disappointed tone, stating the obvious.

Not letting that daunt him, he proceeded to move in the opposite direction toward another barrel of hay. Then, in somewhat of a comical routine, he quickly ran around it with   quick   steps,   twice   screaming "ImgoingtofindyouImgoingtofindyou!"

He stopped and then ran around it again in the opposite direction hoping that if he changed his strategy, I would suddenly appear as if I were a ghost.

This guy really was a piece of work.

He was now standing still again and looking down at the other barrels of hay, pondering what to do. I silently said a *thank you* to whoever it was who had left all of these hay barrels that were up here because they were definitely saving my life. Then, apparently coming to the conclusion that I was not in that direction, he turned around and started walking back to the side where I was.

I held my breath and got ready to run. Pulling back so he couldn't see me, I listened to his footsteps so I could gauge where he was, and moved as he moved. I was now on the other side of the barrel and peeked around it. Gordon was walking toward the other assorted barrels in front of him that he had already checked. I guess he'd forgotten he'd already done that. Gordon did not strike me as the type of person who had a long-term memory about certain things. Suddenly, he whirled around and ran to the barrel where I was and swung to the right, where I had been just seconds ago, and stopped.

Silence.

I heard him take another few steps to the other side.

Silence.

"Imgoingtofindyou!"

Sooner or later, I'm sure you will, I thought, as I stood there, braced against the hay.

Then I heard him turn around and walk off, and I closed my eyes in relief. There were half a dozen barrels on the other side that he could look around, searching for me, and I would have a chance to rest.

He suddenly turned around, ran back to my barrel, and appeared on the other side before I could do anything.

We were now staring directly into each other's eyes.

"Ifoundyou!" he declared with joy, his arms up in the air. This was really the first time that I had ever really seen him up close and in the light. He still had that same idiotic grin on his boyish, idiot face. That was nothing new. What I noticed now was that on his left wrist, he had a tattoo of the cartoon character Mighty Mouse, and I could not help but stare at it. I thought Mighty Mouse was weird. I mean, a super hero mouse that went around saving people while singing opera? It sounded kind of "funny" to me, if you know what I mean. At any rate, it was time to leave.

"Yes you did! See you later!" I yelled.

I bolted into a fast run toward the other side, and I could hear his footsteps close behind me.

Up ahead were four stacks of hay barrels, and I ran for them. Once I was past the last one, I whirled to my left and ran around it, Gordon right behind me. I ran the length of them and then turned around to my left, so I could run around it again.

We ran round and round these barrels four times, and I felt like I was in a Tom & Jerry cartoon. I'll give you one guess which character I felt like. Because I was smaller, I was able to move faster and gain some distance between us. Then, I noticed that I did not hear Gordon's footsteps anymore and kept running. When I came around the barrel again, I saw something horrifying.

Gordon was standing there in place with a large smile and his arms out as though he were going to give me a big hug.

Thinking quickly, I decided to chance a ridiculous stunt, a stunt that always seemed to work in the movies when children were running wild but always seemed ludicrous in real life.

I kept running and then hit the floor feet first, ducked, and slid between his legs on the loose hay strands that were lying around, barely making it. Then, in a quick motion, I got up and kept running. If I had been only one inch taller, I would have crashed right into him.

Looking back, I saw Gordon turn around with an awestruck look on his face and then start running after me. I could not believe how lucky I had been tonight, and how cool that little stunt must have looked. More than several times I should have been dead, if not at least severely injured. Yet, here I was still alive and on the run.

If Amelia could see me now! I bet she would have gotten a real laugh about my sliding between Gordon's legs. My dad always says that making a girl laugh is the first step toward getting her attention.

Right now, I certainly had Gordon's full and undivided attention.

I kept running, and it dawned on me as I looked ahead that I was coming toward the wall and there were no more barrels of hay to hide behind or swerve around.

This was it. I was sunk, and there was no way that even someone like Gordon would fall for that sliding stunt again.

I almost thought about just jumping off the loft and hoping that I landed on something soft, but at the same time realized how insane that idea was even as I was thinking it. I may have been scared out of my mind, but I certainly did not have a death wish.

However, maybe I could land on Zock. Just kidding.

I was running out of floor.

Just then, something dawned on me – the slide.

It was coming up, and it was the only option I had available. It was now right in front of me, and I jumped up so that I was now going down it feet-first, sliding down. Now that I could actually see, for the most part, where I was going, it was not as scary as my first adventure, when I was in the dark. I was hoping that Gordon would not follow me and that he would either just stay up there or, if he really felt the need to play with me some more, take the ladder.

No luck.

I heard a loud thump and then heard him sliding down after me.

"Wheeeeeeeeeeeeeeeeeeee!"

Incredible! I was fleeing for my life, and this guy thought he was at Astroworld! Now that I thought about it, I wished I were at Astroworld also! At least none of the rides there included a large, dumb maniac intent on killing me. If I wanted that, I would just go back to school and annoy a teacher.

We slid the rest of the way down until we were about to come to the end. I knew what was coming and prepared to roll so I could get back on my feet at quickly as possible. The slide ended, and I was in the air for a few seconds before I came crashing down into the pile of hay. I rolled down, got on my feet, and started running, all in one swift motion. A moment later, I heard Gordon crash down with a loud thump and then roll to the ground.

"Thatwasfunletsdoitagain!" he proclaimed.

"You go ahead! Have fun!" I yelled as I proceeded to run.

Gordon immediately got up and gave chase. We were running down the length of the barn, and I passed the ladder that went up to the loft. I looked back and saw Gordon running toward me. I half-hoped that he was serious about wanting to go on the slide again and that he was going to climb the ladder for a repeat performance.

No luck. He kept on coming.

Apparently, he would rather play with me some more than go on the slide again. Lucky me.

No knowing what else to do, I kept running forward and was bent on opening the front door and running outside again. It was not my first choice, but maybe I could hide in the weeds or in the back of his truck or something.

I collided with the front door and turned the latch. It wasn't opening. *Oh, crap!* I thought.

237

I savagely turned the latch on the door, but it wasn't budging. I couldn't see a lock of any kind, and I wondered what the hell was keeping it from opening. My eyes were scanning everywhere at once.

Then I heard Gordon's footsteps, and I turned around. He looked like a rhinoceros charging toward me. All that was missing was a giant horn.

My luck had run out. This was it.

No! I thought. This wasn't it. Amelia and the Bluesman were depending on me to keep this lunatic occupied so they could free those kids. I was not going to let them down. I refused to let them down!

I did the only thing I could think of.

"Gordon! Stop!" I yelled, holding out my hand to him in the halt position as though I were a school crossing guard.

To my utter amazement, he actually did.

"IthoughtyouwantedtoplaywithGordon," he said, looking at me with expectant eyes and breathing heavily.

"Uh, I do," I said, at a total loss as to what to do next. This was an insane night, and I decided to do an insane thing. It wasn't like I had anything to lose. "Simon says to do this!" I said, as I raised my arms above me with my fingers spread out.

With a giant grin on his face, he did exactly that.

I could not believe it. I simply could not believe it. Here it was right in front of me, and I still could not believe it. Here I was playing Simon Says with a giant grown man who had serious mental problems and liked to collect children and hold them in makeshift cages for kicks. Hey, whatever works. At this point, I wasn't picky.

"Simon says do this!" I said as I brought my arms down to my sides at shoulder length.

He did just that.

"Simon says to this!" I said as I kept my left arm out straight but covered my chest with my right hand.

238

Gordon at first covered his chest with both of his hands and then quickly realized his mistake and put his left arm back out. I decided not to penalize him about it, which I am quite sure that you understand. In fact, I was really not quite up on the rules of this game. If someone messed up like that, what happened? It would be something to look into later…if there was a later.

"Simon says do this!" I said, bringing both my arms up above me again, and this time jumping up and spreading my legs apart.

Gordon did the exact same thing to a tee and, the way he was grinning, was having an absolutely marvelous time.

"Thisisfun!" he said.

"It sure is!" I yelled back, indulging him. "Simon says do this!" I said, as I brought my legs back together while bringing my arms to my sides while he did the same.

While we were playing a rousing game of Simon Says, I noticed that Amelia had quietly sneaked up the stairs with a weird look on her face and her mouth hanging partially open. I completely understood. She had probably heard the game and wondered what was going on, me and this guy playing Simon Says. Seeing it actually happening in front of her was even weirder.

Seeing Amelia, an idea began to form. It was risky and crazy had no possible reason to work, but this entire night had been crazy. Might as well add to the fun. The doorway on the floor was behind Gordon and to his left, so he hadn't seen her. If I could get Gordon to play a few more rounds of Simon Says, and Amelia was clued in to what I was doing, we might get out of this.

"Simon says do this!" I said, as I stayed facing him, and walked to my right and then stopped. He did the same thing, and was now standing right in front of Amelia, about ten feet in front of her, but with his back still to her. "Simon says do this!" I said, raising my arms all the way above my head, and he did the same. I could see Amelia behind me with that same weird expression on her face, quietly mouthing, 'What are you doing?'

Now was the moment of truth.

"Simon says do this!" I said, as I started walking backward.

Gordon started doing the same and, much to my relief, Amelia clued in to what I was doing and immediately walked to the top of the stairs and got on her hands and knees so the side of her body was facing him.

So far, so good. I kept walking, and so did Gordon.

Then, he backed into Amelia and, understandably startled, started to lose his balance as his arms starting wildly flailing everywhere. I thought this was it because he was now at that point where he was falling backward but still at that point of being able to right his fall if he moved quickly. Seeing that he was about to save himself, I quickly ran forward and slammed into him, pushing with everything I had. It was like running into a brick wall, he was so large and strong.

Still, it was enough, because he was toppling over Amelia and going down.

As he was doing so, I looked behind him and was able to quickly see the Bluesman at the bottom of the stairs. He had a startled look on his face as the monster was toppling toward him.

Gordon tried to grab me as I pushed him, a terrified look on his face, but I used my momentum to keep running forward and to the right side of the opening, as I watched a surprised Gordon tumble down the stairs end over end. I saw his head hit a stair, and there was a sickening *bonk* sound. Then, before he could completely get out of the way, Gordon landed on the Bluesman's leg, and they fell to the floor. The Bluesman quickly got up and scrambled away from him and got on his feet. When he did so, he yelped in pain and grabbed at his ankle. Apparently, Gordon's tumble down the stairs had injured the Bluesman.

240

But the stunt had served its purpose, because Gordon was now sprawled on his back, knocked out cold. At least I thought he was out cold. He might be dead for all I knew…though I hoped not. I know that sounds strange considering that the guy was trying to kill me, or at the very least make a prisoner to add to his collection, but I hoped he wasn't dead.

I leaned down and helped Amelia up. "Are you all right?"

"I'm… I'm fine," she answered, though she grabbed at her side a bit. "I think I sprained my back a little, but I'll live."

I hugged her, and she hugged me back, and we stayed like that for awhile.

"I'm glad you came up at that time and picked up on what I was trying to do. Otherwise, I would have been sunk."

"I'm glad that I could assist you, kind sir," she said, and we both laughed. We then parted so we could look at each other and into each other's eyes.

As we were doing so, it dawned on me that this was a perfect time to just grab her gently, pull her to me, and then kiss her. It was a perfect moment. Working together, we had just foiled the bad guy, and this was an intimate situation caused by a surge of excitement. It was absolutely perfect. It didn't get any more perfect than this. Action heroes live for moments like this! I was going to do it. Right now, I was going to give her the best kiss that she ev-

"Ooooooooh, God!" the Bluesman moaned from below.

"Keith!" Amelia yelped, and then she turned around and rushed down the stairs, me following and Zock following me. All thoughts of kissing had gone from my mind. My best friend was in trouble, and he needed help.

He was leaning against a wall as we rushed over to him.

"What's wrong?" I asked.

241

"My ankle. When that guy came tumbling down, he landed on me before I could get away. He must weigh a ton!"

"Can you walk?" I said as I looked down at the injured leg. He put some weight on it.

"Ow! I think the best I can manage is a pretty decent hobble. What the hell were you doing? First you throw bats at us and now the guy? Are you trying to kill us?" he said grinning.

"I'm sorry," I said. "I didn't mean for that to happen."

"Oh, hey! Don't worry about it. I'm just messing with you. Besides, you stopped the bad guy. All you had to do was throw him down the stairs to do it!" he laughed.

"I guess so," I said as we all turned around and looked at him, lying there with his eyes closed. Even from where we were standing, we could see a huge knot on his bald head.

"Do you think he's dead?" Amelia said.

That was a good question. It was time to find the answer. I walked over to him and regarded him for a moment. Then, I leaned down and pressed my hand against his neck.

At that moment, I expected him to open his eyes, grab at me, and say, "Gotcha!"

Instead, he just lay there as I tried to see if he had a pulse.

"Danny, what are you doing? Trying to wake him up?" Amelia said, startled.

"I'm trying to see if he has a pulse. This is how they do it on *T.J. Hooker,*" I said. I left my finger pressed against him for a few more moments and then backed away from him. "He's alive. He's going to have a huge headache when he wakes up, but he's alive."

"He's alive? How long until he wakes up?" the Bluesman asked.

Another good question. Unfortunately, I did not have an answer. It could be an hour from now; it could be ten

242

minutes. We needed to get things moving and get out of here as quickly as we could. Which reminded me...

"How many kids have you gotten free?" I asked.

They both looked at each other and then at me.

"Well?"

"Uh, maybe you should take a look for yourself," Amelia said.

I looked at her for a moment and then walked to the prison room. As I entered, I stopped in shock.

All the kids were still in their prisons. The doors were still locked shut.

I heard Amelia and the Bluesman behind me and turned around.

"What the hell have you two been doing all this time? I've been running around like a madman trying to stay out of reach from that guy, and you haven't gotten even one kid out?"

"Hey, man! It's not our fault! Look at these things!" The Bluesman produced a screw as long as my pinkie. "I was able to get three of them out and Amelia got two. These things are really screwed in there tight, and there are four per latch! My hands are already hurting!"

I understood. Even with the three of us working together as fast as we could, we could easily be here for hours. We needed the keys. That was the only way we were going to be able to get these kids out in any reasonable amount of time. Then I realized something. "Hey, that guy probably has the keys in his pocket."

They both just looked at me.

"Well?"

"You want to go digging around in that guy's pockets?" the Bluesman asked.

"Not really, no." I saw all the kids silently looking at me. "But it's the only way to get them out of there. Come on."

243

We walked back into the play area. The guy was still out cold – at least for right now. We slowly approached him, me on one side and Amelia and the Bluesman on the other. We kneeled down beside him. "Okay, let's check his jacket first. You check that side and I'll look over here," I said, gently touching his jacket to see if that would wake him up. When it didn't, I reached farther inside while looking back at Amelia.

She had not moved on inch.

"Amelia, I know you're scared, but I need some help here. Look, he's out cold. Just reach in his jacket and check. We need to move as fast as we can and get out of here before he wakes up, okay?"

Without saying another word, she slowly reached into the inside of the guy's jacket while keeping an eye on his face the whole time so she could bolt if he even so much as blinked. I can't say I blamed her. I was ready to run across the room in a second myself if he moved. I dug around inside the pocket on my side and felt something. I pulled it out and was dismayed to see that it was a G.I. Joe action figure. I'm not sure, but I think his name was Snake Eyes, that Ninja guy.

Amelia gasped, and I looked at her, immediately thinking that Gordon was now awake and had grabbed her. That was not the case, but she was frozen; then she slowly pulled her hand from the jacket.

In her fingers was a key ring with at least a dozen keys on it. "I found it!" she said.

"Great!" I said as I took them from her and raced back to the prison area, Amelia following me and the Bluesman hobbling behind her. Zock trailed in too, and we were all together again. I looked at the keys: They were all silver and pretty much looked the same except for the fact that the teeth marks on them were all a little different. They were not labeled in any way, so I was going to have to try each key on each lock until I came to the one that worked.

244

Working as quickly as I could, I started inserting different keys into the locks until I came to the one that opened that particular lock and unsnapped it, then proceeded to the next one, and kept doing so until all the locks were now undone. What a stroke of luck! Something that would have taken painstaking hours was now taking mere minutes! We were on our way!

Within no time we had the doors to the prisons open and were pulling the kids out. Not surprisingly, most of them were crying with relief at having their freedom again, their nightmare finally over. However, some of them were just standing there quietly and watching the three of us work, still not able to fully grasp the concept that they were finally free. There was one little girl who had apparently fallen head over in heels in love with Zock and was kneeling down beside him and stroking at him. Looking at him, I could tell that he loved the attention. Zock always did have a way with the ladies... except Amelia.

Once they were all free, I laid down the law. "Okay, kids? We're going to get you out of here and then get you home, okay? My name is Dan, this is Amelia and over here is...the Bluesman." I had been about to say 'Keith', but then I'd thought of using his nickname because it might interest the kids and fascinate them. Why would a person be called "The Bluesman"?

It seemed to work; they were all looking at him with interest. Maybe they expected him to pull out a guitar and serenade them. On the other hand, maybe they expected him to dress up like John Belushi or Dan Aykroyd and start singing "Soul Man." At any rate, it kept them quiet, which was what I wanted.

The worst was over, but we were not out of the woods yet. "Okay, I need all of you to keep quiet and stay together because we're going to go upstairs now, okay?"

None of them moved. I was absolutely shocked. If I were them, I would be running out of here as fast as I

245

could, the first chance I got. In fact, that was what I had been doing for the past twenty minutes or so.

"Is...is Gordon out there? Is he going to come get us and lock us up again?" a little girl with long brown hair asked.

"No, honey. Gordon's...Gordon's gone. He's not going to bother you anymore. Promise," I consoled.

The little girl smiled, and this must have set them all at ease because we all started slowly walking from the prison room into the play area, holding hands in one long train.

As soon as we approached the stairs, the kids all stopped and looked in fear at the unconscious Gordon lying on the floor. I was happy to see that he was still out cold, but I wasn't sure how long this was going to last. We needed to move.

"Come on, kids," it's all right. He's not going to bother you. Just walk around him and up the stairs. Come on," Amelia coaxed them, helping each kid one by one past Gordon's unmoving body, urging them up the stairs, and then following the last one. Once that was done, I put the Bluesman's arm around my shoulders, and we walked up together. Well, I walked; he more or less hopped.

Finally! We were home free!

"Okay, now what?" the Bluesman asked, and we looked at him. "Well, we got them out of there — now how do we get them and us home?"

"That's a good question," I said looking around. It wasn't like we were near a bus stop or anything.

"Hey, let's call the police!" he offered.

I looked at him. "How?"

"What do you mean, how? With a telephone!"

"Did you see any power lines all the way out here? There is no telephone," I said solemnly.

"Oh, yeah."

"It sure would be nice if we had a portable phone like something they would use on *Star Trek*. Imagine that. A cordless phone that you could carry in your pocket because it's no bigger than your hand and you could call anywhere in the world with it," I said dreamily.

"Yeah, right! That's *Star Trek*! Like something like that is ever going to be really invented. If it ever is, it won't be until the year 2030 or something," the Bluesman moaned.

I had to agree with him. Still, it would be a nice little invention that would certainly come in handy.

Right now, however, we needed to get back on track and stop daydreaming. I scanned the area, and something caught my eye. The beautiful thing that caught my eye was cherry red and sitting on the other side of the barn. I smiled.

Amelia looked at me and then followed my line of sight and then gazed back at me.

"Oh, no!" she moaned.

"Yes," I said.

"No!"

"Yeeeeeees," I said in a lustful voice as I started walking toward it, the others following me.

"Danny! Are you crazy? You've never driven a car in your entire life!"

"It's not so hard. I watch my parents do it all the time. Besides, my dad has even let me at the wheel once or twice."

"Were you sitting behind the wheel or sitting shotgun and just holding onto it?"

"Uh, sitting shotgun," I mumbled.

"That's not the same thing!"

"Sure it is. The only difference is that now I'll be sitting behind the wheel and using the gas pedal and... that other thing."

"You mean the brake?" she said in a skeptical voice. "That's what it's called."

"Oh, yeah. I knew that."

247

"Danny, I'm not going to let you do this. It's suicide! You'll get all of us killed!"

"No, I won't. Besides, it's not like we have any other choice, unless you want me to try driving that monster truck out there. I probably wouldn't even be able to see over the dashboard. This is all we have. The only other option is to walk. Do you want to spend the whole night walking in the dark? We wouldn't get back until next week!"

She was quiet for a moment as she just stared at me.

"You just want to drive that stupid car!"

"No, I don't!"

She looked at me.

"Okay, you got me. I want to drive the car. But it's also the only way to get out of here, right?"

She turned toward the car and sighed.

"There you go!" I said in triumph.

We had arrived at the car, and I wrapped my hand around the handle to the front door. I have to admit, I actually trembled with delight touching this beautiful work of art, especially knowing that in just a few moments I would actually be driving it! I could already picture all of us piled inside of it, listening to the radio as we were headed home. It was too bad it wasn't a convertible; then we could put the top down and feel the wind in our faces as we headed back. That would be really cool. Still, I wasn't complaining. I opened the door, and the smell of it immediately hit me. It was beautiful! It smelled like a new car! I don't know where the car came from, or if Gordon had rebuilt it or stolen it or what, but it looked and smelled brand new. Letting the smell of it bless my nostrils, I sat down in the seat and placed my hands on the wheel. While doing that, I also adjusted the seat and the mirrors to my liking. I was ready to go!

"Okay, hop in. We're leaving!"

All the kids cheered as they started to moved toward the car.

"Wait a minute! Wait a minute!" Amelia said, stopping them. Then she turned her attention back to me. "Haven't you forgotten something?"

I looked at her and tried to think of what I could possibly be forgetting. We had the kids, Gordon was knocked out and we had a car to get back home in. What else could we possibly need? I shrugged my shoulders helplessly.

"Have you ever heard of a little thing called 'keys'?"

"Oh…yeah," I replied.

"Oh, yeah," she said

"Well, let me check," I said as I pulled the key ring from my pocket and looked to see if the ignition key was there and sorted through them. "It's not here."

We all regarded each other as we thought the same thing – Gordon had them.

"I guess we should go search Gordon," I said as I got out of the car. "Come on." I took a few steps before I realized that Amelia was not following me. "What?"

"I'm not going back down there! What if he wakes up and grabs us?"

"He won't wake up."

"How do you know that?"

"Because I do."

"How?"

"Because I do."

"How? And don't say 'because I do' because you don't."

What could I say? She had me.

"Look, we have to get the keys, and he probably has them. I'm going to need some help turning him over if they're in his back pocket."

"I'm not going anywhere near his back pockets!"

"Will you come on? Time's a wasting!"

249

"No!"

"Yes!

"No!"

"Yes!"

"No!"

I couldn't believe it. I felt like was in a rerun. The kids were all smiling. They thought it was hysterical, like something you would see on *Three's Company*.

"Fine, I'll be back in a minute," I said as I walked off toward the doorway. A few moments later, I heard some footsteps behind me. Turning around, I saw Amelia following me. I let her catch up with me, and we walked the rest of the way in silence. When we got to the doorway, we looked down and were able to see Gordon's legs sprawled out on the floor.

"Okay, he's still out cold. Let's hurry up and get the keys so we can get out of here." I preceded Amelia down the stairs and slowly approached Gordon, kneeling beside him. I wanted to make sure he was still out, so I decided to try something. "Hey, Gordon!" I yelled into his face.

Amelia immediately got up and started running. She then stopped when she realized what had happened and looked at me in shock.

"What are you doing? You scared me to death!"

"Sorry. I wanted to make sure he was still out."

"You could have at least warned me what you were going to do!"

"Sorry. I just thought of it."

"You still could have told me!"

"Can we get on with it, please?" I said as I searched his jacket pocket again while Amelia squatted down and tentatively did the same on the other side. We then checked his front pockets and found nothing. "Okay, they must be in his back pocket. Let's check my side first. "I'll push and you pull." We grabbed Gordon's arm and shifted him toward her.

250

"This guy is so heavy! Can you get to the back pocket, yet?" she asked.

"Just a little more," I wheezed, moving him over until I had access to his back pocket. I held him in place as I felt it and sighed.

"Well?"

"It must be on the other side. Push him back toward me, and I'll pull."

We shifted Gordon again until she had access to his back pocket and started feeling around. She had a look on her face as though she was touching a slug and then an expression of surprise appeared as she was digging.

"Did you find it?" I asked.

She pulled her hand away from him and jangled a key ring with a half dozen keys on it. Some of them were long – car keys!

"All right!" I exclaimed as we shifted him onto his back. I took the key ring from her and looked at it. A perplexed expression spread across my face when I looked at a picture that was dangling in a small piece of hard plastic. It was a group photo of *Duran Duran*.

"Look. The two of you have the same taste in music," I joked.

She just looked at me, not saying anything.

"Hey! Are the two of you all right down there?" the Bluesman yelled from upstairs, startling us.

"Yeah, we'll be up in a minute!" I yelled back and then got up.

As we did so, we heard a light moan and froze.

We looked back at Gordon, and he was motionless…but he had moaned. Not a good sign.

"We have to get out of here," I said. We immediately ran up the stairs and saw the Bluesman waiting for us.

"I thought I heard you yell something and hobbled over here," he said.

"It was just Danny screaming in his face to see if he was awake," Amelia said, annoyed, while looking at me.

"I had to see if he was awake, didn't I?" I protested.

She just rolled her eyes in frustration, and then we all made our way back to the car. I got into the driver's seat and was about to start it up.

"Wait a minute," Amelia said. "Aren't you forgetting something?"

"What? We have the key. What more do we need?"

She looked behind me and held her arm out as though she were presenting something. I looked behind me and immediately noticed what she was talking about.

The double doors were shut. They needed to be opened before we could get the car out.

"Oh," I said and got out of the car. She just closed her eyes and shook her head as I walked toward the doors. I looked at the door for a moment and then realized something. "I don't believe it!"

"What? Is there another lock?" the Bluesman asked.

I turned around and just looked at him with my mouth hanging open like I was in pain.

"What? What's wrong?"

"There's no lock here!" I said as if I were a caveman and I had just discovered fire.

"You're kidding!" he blurted in disbelief.

There was no lock! After all that trouble with climbing the tree, almost falling to my death, falling down the slide in the dark and being assaulted by the bat, the back door had been unlocked the whole time! We could have avoided all of that if we had just walked all the way around and checked the back! I guess Gordon did not see the need to put a lock on the back door if the front and side doors were already locked. Moaning, I gave each of the doors a hard shove and was able to open them both up pretty easily. Soon there was plenty of room to back the car out. Still in

252

somewhat of an irritated mood, I walked back and got in the car and started it up.

At the sound of that beautiful engine purring, my bad mood instantly vanished and a huge smile crossed my face. This little moment right here had made it all worth it. As I was sitting there revving the engine, I casually wondered if they would let me keep the car once we got the kids safely back home and took care of everything with the police. I mean, it wasn't too much to ask, right? All I had to do was wait a few years until I was old enough to get my license, right? We could find a place to store it, right? My parents would be all for it because they wouldn't have to spend a dime on a new car, right? It wasn't like I was stealing it or anything, right? Well, that last part might be a bit of a problem, but I felt sure something could be worked out, right? Think of all the fancy dates that I would be able to take Amelia on in a few years. No more just riding our bikes somewhere or depending on our parents for rides. I would be a mobile man! With a car like this, I would be the talk of the school! I would be the envy of everyone! I wou-

"Danny?"

I heard someone calling my name and looked at Amelia, realizing that she was talking to me. I blinked a few times and just looked at her.

"What?"

"I said are you all right? You had a dazed look on your face like you were daydreaming or something."

"Oh. I was just thinking about something. Okay, everyone hop in!" I yelled and all the kids started walking toward the car.

"Wait a minute! Wait a minute!" she said stopping them.

"What? What's the problem? The car's running. Let's go!"

"We are not getting into that car until you back it out. You've never even driven before! How do we know that you won't kill us all?"

"Oh, now you're just being dramatic. I am not going to kill anybody. It's not like I'm going to be racing at Daytona or anything."

"Just back the car out and get it outside and then we'll get in," she said, still blocking the kids from the car.

"Fine," I agreed as I closed the door and then looked in the rearview mirror to make sure that there was nothing behind me. All I could see was open land. This was going to be easy, and then we could be on our way.

"Be careful. You don't know how powerful the engine on this thing is," the Bluesman said, gazing at it. "The way it sounds, there must be some kind of monster under the hood."

"That's just the way it sounds. Clear the way so I can back it out," I said and they did as I found the switch for the headlights and turned them on. Looking at the gear shift, I found the reverse option and shifted the gear into the right position. Then, I lightly touched the gas pedal.

Roooooaaaaaaaaaaaaaaarrrrrrrrrrrrrrrr!

"Oh, God!" The car immediately streaked backward, catching me completely by surprise. I looked at everyone; they were looking at me the same way. I slammed my foot onto the brake pedal and could feel the car skidding on the dirt. The next thing I knew, I was falling back, and the night sky became my focal point of vision. Then I heard a crash, and the entire car came to a stop and I flopped around in the seat before I was still.

What happened? I thought, blinking and shaking my head.

"Danny! Oh, God! Danny? Are you all right?" I heard Amelia yell and then saw her a moment later looking down at me through the windshield, both her and the Bluesman and some of the kids as well. "Danny? Are you okay?"

"I'm… I'm fine. What happened?" I muttered still trying to grasp why I was looking up at her.

"You tore off and couldn't stop in time. You're in a ditch. Are you okay? Can you get out?"

"Yeah… yeah, I think so," I said as I reached over, unlocked the door and pushed it open. It immediately closed and I had to open it and keep it open with my arm as I struggled to get free. As I placed my leg out, I realized that it was dangling in the air. I looked down, and the ground was a couple of feet below me. She was right. I was in a ditch. Placing both of my legs in front of me, I let myself fall from the car. I landed on the slanted side of the ditch and then struggled to make my way up. The Bluesman and Amelia grabbed my hands to help me up, and then I turned around and looked at my car.

The front wheels of my beautiful car where in the air a couple of feet off the ground. I almost felt like crying.

"My beautiful car," I wailed. They looked at me as if I were crazy.

"The car? Man, screw the car! You could have died!" the Bluesman exclaimed.

"My beautiful car," I said again. I began to almost sniffle as I realized that all of my dreams were now dust. Then I looked at it more closely. Actually, the damage was not really that bad from what I could see. The back of it was probably a little banged up, but it could be repaired, right? It probably wouldn't cost that much if it was just some bodywork, right? There was nothing wrong with the engine, right? I would still be able to take it cruising once I was sixteen and got my license, right? I would be able to take Amelia out on a real date and we cou-

"Danny, are you okay?" Amelia said looking at me closely.

"I'm fine, why?"

"You look like you're about to cry. Are you sure you're okay?"

255

"I'm fine. I was just...thinking," Sadly, I looked at the two front headlights of the car, staring at me as if in accusation. The car was mad at me, I could tell. It would probably never forgive me. I might not be able to help it now but the very least I could do was turn it off. I carefully made my down the ditch again.

"What in the world are you doing?" Amelia called out to me.

"Getting the key. No sense in just letting her stay here running," I said as I crawled back in the car, turned off the lights, retrieved the key, and then made my way back. "Well, I guess we should head for the truck," I stated as I started walking.

Amelia grabbed my shoulder and whirled me around.

"What?" I said in surprise.

"Are you out of your mind? You almost killed yourself driving that car and now you want to try to drive a truck that's as big as a tank?"

"That was just the car. Now I know what to expect."

"Danny, no!"

"Yes!"

"No!"

"Yes!" I said as I started walking down the aisle.

"Danny!" Amelia said catching up with me. "No! You're going to wind up killing yourself and all of us too!"

"Well, I'm not exactly crazy about it, but what other choice do we have? We don't have any other way back."

"Let's wait till morning."

"What good will that do? Either way, we still have to make our way back. We might as well do it now. Besides, can you imagine how worried our parents are? Not to mention that those kids want to get home as soon as they can."

"Danny, there has to be some other way that we can—" Auuuuugggggghhhhhhhh!"

We stopped in surprise and fright and looked to where that loud noise had come from.

Gordon was racing toward us with his arms outstretched, and he looked none too happy. He had just emerged from the doorway like a creature from the depths, and on seeing us – me especially – he went into a total rage. Apparently, playtime was over. Killing time was in.

"Get out of here!" I yelled at Amelia while still watching the approaching Gordon.

"What? What about you?"

"It's me he wants. If I can get him to chase me again, it will keep him away from you and the kids."

"Then what?"

"I'll think of something," I said as I took off and raced for the side door, leaving Amelia looking after me.

As I was about to head out the door, I turned around and was happy to see that Gordon was running after me. Well, not exactly happy about it, but at least he was bent on capturing me instead of the kids.

I raced out the door into the night and immediately headed to my left toward the front of the barn. As I was about to round the corner, I heard Gordon run out the door and chanced a quick glance at him.

What I saw was pure, unleashed rage. Even in the semi-darkness I could see it in his eyes. Gordon was beyond angry, beyond furious. He had probably never been this angry in his life, and I was the culprit who was responsible for it. I guess everything that he had been through tonight had been bad enough, but pushing him down the stairs had been the absolute limit. I knew that if he got his hands on me, I was going to be dead. No more games, no more quick or clever escapes – dead.

I ran faster.

So did Gordon.

"Youhurtmyhead!" he bellowed. I could hear in his voice how hurt he really was, and not just physically.

257

There was emotional pain as well. I got the feeling that Gordon came from a place where this sort of thing used to happen on a fairly regular basis but had thought that he had somehow escaped it and put it behind him...until he met me. In his demented mind, I had been a playmate of his, and I had betrayed him, probably the worst betrayal of his life. I still had no idea who this guy was or where he had come from, but I did know that it was from a place of pain...of that I was sure. He had appeared to be in his mid-thirties, but it was hard to tell because he was bald and yet, on the other hand, he acted so much like a child. If this was what he was like now, I could not even begin to imagine what his childhood must have been like.

"YouhurtmyheadnowI'mgoingtohurtyou!" he cried.

There was no doubt in my mind that if Gordon got his hands on me, I would not even begin to understand the meaning of hurt until I was feeling the last few moments of my life ebb away as he strangled or pummeled me to death.

We were now on the other side of the barn, racing into the darkness, and I had absolutely no idea what to do. There was no place to hide, no place to run to, and the way he sounded, he was not about to give up until he had me.

I rounded the corner and, as I was doing so, I took a moment to rejoice that Amelia and the Bluesman must have closed the doors. That would certainly keep Gordon's attention on me, and I guess you could imagine how outrageously happy I was about that. I also noticed the car sticking out of the ditch, the front of it appearing as if it were a submarine making an emergency return to the surface. It really made me sad to see such a beautiful car in that kind of position.

"Youbrokemycar!" Gordon screamed at me.

Apparently, he was even more upset about that than I was. Lucky me. If I was not absolutely positive that he was angry at me before, this certainly confirmed it in no uncertain terms.

I ran to the wall of weeds on the other side and started running beside them, hoping that maybe I could somehow dive into them and hide before he could find me…but I knew that that was just a fool's dream because he would easily see me and be on me in no time.

I was getting tired… so tired. If I could just rest for a few minutes I would be ever so grateful. Just a single minute would be enough.

I was slowing down.

Even as I was still trying to pour it on as much as I could, I was aware that I was slowing down and I couldn't do anything about it. The entire day had taken its toll on me, and Gordon still sounded like he could run a marathon, he was so angry.

I stumbled on something that was on the ground for a split second and lost my footing. I was quickly able to straighten myself and stay on my feet, but it had cost me because Gordon was nearer. My breaths were coming in quick heaves, and they were getting shorter. My heart felt like it was going to explode. If I didn't stop soon, I was scared that I was going to have a heart attack or something. It wouldn't surprise me. I was so terrified and so tired, I doubted anyone would be able to take much more of this.

It felt like I could actually feel Gordon's breath on my neck, and the hard tromp of his steps on the dirt sounded like cannons.

Then, it finally happened.

I fell. I collapsed onto the ground in a heap of dust and cried out in despair when I did so. I was so disappointed in myself. Everyone was depending on me, and I had let them down, and now I was about to get myself killed in the process. Even as I fell, I hoped that Amelia and the Bluesman would somehow find a way to save themselves and the kids and get out of here. They were both smart, they would find a way; they had to find a way! Surely all of this had not been for nothing? We were going to give everyone closure to this nightmare and a happy ending. Wasn't that how it was supposed to work?

Gordon's footsteps had stopped, and I could tell that he was standing right behind me. I slowly turned around and looked up at his looming figure. He had already been so big to begin with. Now he was larger than life and he was going to be the last thing that I ever saw.

"Imgoingtokillyou!" he screamed while pointing at me with a large, quivering finger that looked an awful lot like the barrel of a gun in the darkness.

Amelia, I love you. I wish I had gotten the chance to tell you that when I had so many perfect opportunities, but I threw them all away. All of those moments when we were together and I could have just said it, but I never did. I would like to hope that even though I never did get around to saying those words, you know how I felt, anyway. It would have been so nice to have kissed you just once.

Gordon bent toward me with his giant hands open and I closed my eyes.

Then I heard some frantic wrestling of the weeds.

"Auuuugggggghhhhhhiiiiiiiiiieeeeeeeeeeeeeee!"

The scream was so blood-curdling and so laced with pain and agony, I almost thought that…well, I didn't know what to think because I had never heard anything like it in my entire life. I'm glad that I hadn't because it was the kind of scream that could penetrate a person's senses and haunt them for years to come.

I opened my eyes and looked up.

At first, I didn't know what I was looking at, and I had to keep myself from blinking because my mind was telling me to shut my eyes, but I was willing them to stay open because I could not tear them away from what was in front of me.

Something had Gordon.

He was fighting to get out of the grip of something that was even bigger than he was, and I saw that his feet were dangling off the ground. I quickly tried to think of something that could lift a guy who looked to be at least two hundred and twenty pounds like he was nothing off the ground and nothing came to mind.

I looked at what was wrapped around Gordon.

Two monstrously muscled arms that looked to be covered with some kind of white fur were gripping him. Gordon was savagely trying to free himself from the arms and pounding on them, shaking his entire body, trying to get free, and the arms still held him steadfast. I saw them tighten around him, and in the silence of the night heard the sound of Gordon's ribs snapping and popping and his agonizing screams as they did.

I was so frozen with fear and mesmerized with what was happening right in front of me, even if I had thought of getting up and running away, I don't think I would have been able to do so.

My eyes looked upward, and I saw something that actually made me gasp.

Up above Gordon, I could see the head of whatever it was that was holding him and slowly squeezing him to death.

It was the giant head of a goat.

Even as I was seeing it, I couldn't believe it. I know that it was dark outside with very little light, but it was a real head of a goat. There was no way a mask could be that realistic, I don't care how many good make-up people live in Hollywood.

The goat's head had a weird quality to it, as though it were...blended with something. That's when I realized what it was – it was also the face of a human being because the dark eyes looked totally human. As monstrous as the face was, the eyes had a quality that could only be found in a human being. I don't know if you would call it intelligence because he also had the look of a wild, savage animal, but there was definitely something human there.

261

There was also a pair of giant, brown swirled horns on his head that curled at the tips, and it was only then that I smelled that familiar scent that I had smelled all through the day at certain places.

It dawned on me with alarming suddenness what I was looking at.

The Goatman.

He was real.

He was real, and he was standing right before me. Even more than that, he was saving me.

With a savage grunt, he pulled Gordon into the weeds and disappeared. Everything was silent for a moment.

Then, the weeds started rustling again in a torrent, and I heard more snapping of bones and Gordon's screams. I knew with certainty that he was dying. A person could only make inhuman noises like that when they were being faced with imminent death and they could not do anything about it. It made me think of an image of someone who was literally being slowly pulled apart while every bone in his body was being crushed at the same time, and even that would not begin to really describe it.

Even after all the things that he had done and everything that he had put me through, I could not help but feel sorry for him, and I started crying as I heard what I knew were going to be his final screams.

Then there was silence. I lay there, afraid to get up, afraid to even move. I noticed that even the crickets were now quiet. It was the most utterly, completely silent moment of my life. I didn't think it was possible for the world to be this quiet. I wondered if this was what an astronaut felt like when he was drifting in space and for a brief moment had a portion of the universe all to himself.

The weeds started to rustle again, and I kicked away not sure what to expect.

The figure emerged from the weeds again and stood before me. He appeared to be at least seven feet tall. With

Gordon no longer blocking him from view, I was able to see his full body. His head and arms were just as I described but even more ominous in appearance since I could see them in full view. His chest was enormous and looked like the body of a man and covered with what looked to be hair. Not wool or anything small and curly, but white, fine hair. Further down below his waist, his body began to transform into something resembling an animal, and the hair began to become darker and coarser. His legs were incredibly huge, too huge to be just legs. That's when I realized that they were not just legs; they were haunches. They looked so powerful and so muscular; it would not have surprised me if the figure before me was capable of running a hundred miles an hour. It was difficult to tell in the dark...but I think his feet were huge, black hooves. I thought how impossible that must be to be able to support a body that large with just a pair of hooves, no matter how large and spread-out they were.

Not knowing what to do, I just stayed there on the ground as if I were paralyzed and looked up at him while holding my breath, not able to take my eyes from him.

We stayed there, staring at each other, for what seemed like a small eternity.

Then, with a small movement of his head as if he were saying, "You're welcome," he turned back around to the weeds and disappeared into them. I heard them rustling for a while as the figure was moving through them, and it gradually dimmed until I could not hear anything at all except for some crickets that had apparently decided it was once again time to take up their never-ending symphony.

He was gone.

Just as suddenly as he had appeared, he had vanished.

Still trying to understand and comprehend what I had seen and now realizing that I was actually still alive, I slowly got up and walked over to where the Goatman had been standing.

Two giant hoof prints were barely visible in what little light was coming from the barn. I looked into the wall of weeds and almost thought of running after him to...I don't know, thank him, I suppose. But I also knew that it would be a waste of time because I would never see him again. For all I knew, I was the only person who had actually ever seen him. This was his home, and it had been invaded. He had done what he had to do to set things to right, and saving me had been part of what needed to happen, no more. Still, I was grateful to him, and I owed my life to him because I would certainly be dead right now if he had not chosen to appear. I would repay him by respecting his wishes to be left alone and let him live in peace.

I slowly got up, walked back to the barn and into the much welcome light as I entered the doorway.

As I started to walk back to the area where the car was, where I had left everyone, I realized that there was nobody there. At first, I began to panic because I thought that somehow Gordon had gotten to them. Then I realized how impossible that was. Gordon was dead. I looked around the barn some more and tried to call out for them, but all that came out was a hoarse gasp. For some reason, the barn felt like a different place now. I don't know why because it didn't make any sense – it was still the same place we had discovered just a small time ago. Still, for some reason, it felt different now, like some kind of weight had been lifted from it.

I then realized the only place that Amelia and the others could be and started walking toward the doorway. As I looked down, I didn't see anything but the stairwell leading into the area, but I knew that they were down there. Amelia and the Bluesman would have done anything to protect the kids and themselves from Gordon, even if that meant going back down there. I slowly walked down the steps and saw nothing but an empty play area. They had do be down here – it was the only place they could possibly be because the only other place they could have gone would be outside, and I would have seen them when they left. On top of that, there was no way that Amelia and the Bluesman – especially him, with his injured ankle – were going to start walking toward home in the darkness in the middle of the night, no matter how badly they wanted to get out of here. That would have been crazy. Then again, this had been a crazy night.

I looked around some more, and that's when I noticed that the door to the prison area was shut. We had left it open when we left. I walked over to it and turned the handle, expecting it to be locked, but when I turned it, it wasn't. Of course it wasn't locked. Why would it be? The lock was made to keep the people that were inside from being able to exit, not vice versa. I opened the door and was met with a horde of screams that made me jump and almost start running. That's how much the choir of fright had startled me. Even though I was dead tired, I was still ready to run some more if I had to. Fortunately, those days were over, and I hoped that I never had to run again. Well, maybe not ever. There was now going to be plenty of time in the future for me to say something to Amelia that annoyed her so she could run after me and beat me up. That would be nice and, truth to tell, I couldn't wait.

They were all huddled on the other side of the room sitting down and holding each other, all of them perfectly safe. After the initial fright, they realized that it was me standing before them like an old scarecrow.

"Danny?" Amelia said in surprise as she let go of the two little girls who had been gripping her just as tightly.

"Hey," I gasped as I shuffled toward them, my eyes barely open.

"Oh, my God!" She got up and rushed toward me.

"Oh, man! What happened?" the Bluesman asked as he did the same. Both of them were now coming for me.

"What a night," I said.

That's when my body finally said, "Enough is enough," and I collapsed into their welcoming arms.

AFTER THE GOATMAN

When I woke up, my eyes fought to stay closed, and I felt like I should just go back to sleep and stay that way for a hundred years. The first thing that I thought of was that it was a school day and I just wanted to stay in bed, hoping that my parents would just forget about me and let me sleep in. Then I suddenly remembered what had happened and where I was. My eyes immediately snapped open, I bolted up with a gasp, and I looked around, starting to take rapid gulps of breath. Once I saw where I was, I began to calm down. I was in one of the little rooms with some sheets covering me and a pillow tucked beneath my head.

In a flash I remembered. Gordon. The Goatman. Walking back in here and finding them and then collapsing in their arms. Apparently, they had made a bed for me and left me to sleep it off. I looked at my watch to see what time it was, but it was a waste of time. Sometime throughout all the running around it had gotten broken and the front of it was smashed. Great. I loved this watch!

Sighing, I slowly got up and winced in pain as I felt every muscle in my body cry out in protest, especially my legs. Still, I tried to get up and slowly succeeded. Zock must have sensed I was up because he walked into the room, looked at me, and started bathing me with his tongue. I didn't stop him. As far as I was concerned, this was the best wake-up call that I had ever had.

"Hey, boy. Glad to see me?"

More tongue action.

"Believe me, I feel the same way," I said as I petted him for a while, then got all the way up and made my way to the play area.

It seemed like any average day in a nursery.

267

The kids were at various play stations, talking or coloring or reading. Two of them were sitting quietly in front of the television, watching cartoons. Most of them were in the process of eating something or, from the look of various wrappers and discarded boxes lying around, had finished eating. It was all junk food, of course, but I don't think their parents would mind them gorging on it. Besides, they would all be eating their fruits and vegetables again soon enough. Of that I was sure.

Amelia was sitting on a small chair, reading out loud to a couple of the kids, who were spread around her and listening attentively. I recognized the story: "Little Red Riding Hood." Out of all the fairy tales that she could have been reading, I found that one to certainly fit the occasion. I looked around the room and saw that the Bluesman was passed out cold on the giant bean bag. One of the kids was standing across from him and throwing little wads of paper at his face, giggling as they bounced off and fell to the floor. The Bluesman was so lost in sleep he didn't even notice. The sight made me smile, and it certainly did feel good because it felt like such a long time since I had actually had a reason for a genuine, solid smile.

"Danny!"

I turned, and Amelia was looking at me in surprise.

"Hey," I said as I playfully waved at her.

She put her book down and immediately rushed over to me. Her proclamation had been so loud; it had even woken up the Bluesman and certainly with a start. He then looked at himself and wondered why there were little pieces of paper all over his chest and scattered on the floor around him. Then he got up and hobbled over with a grin on his face.

We all hugged each other tightly, not wanting to ever let go.

"Hey, guys. It's good to see you again," I said.

"You, too, man. You, too," he said, squeezing me hard.

268

"Oh, Danny, we were so scared to death when you ran out of the barn and Gordon ran after you. We didn't know what to do, so Keith and I started getting all the kids down here. A few minutes later, we heard this loud scream. At first, I was so scared that it was you, but then I realized that it must have been Gordon."

"How?"

"I recognize your screams from beating you up all the time. That wasn't you."

"Oh."

Then they let go of me, and we all looked at each other.

"Dan, what happened? We haven't left the room since you came back down," the Bluesman said.

"How long was I out?"

"About two hours. You must have been really tired."

"I'm still really tired," I said with a lousy attempt at a joke.

"Danny, what happened up there?" Amelia said as she touched my shoulder. "Where's Gordon? We were scared that he was going to come down here at any moment. We've only been in this area for just over an hour because the kids were getting bored just sitting in there. What happened?"

I thought about it for a moment, I mean really thought about it. Should I tell them about what I saw? Should I tell them about the Goatman and what happened? It would have sounded crazy. Heck, if someone had told me about it, I would have thought that they were crazy. Still, these were my two best friends and because of this, because of everything that had happened tonight, I knew that there was now going to be a bond between the three of us that would never be broken. What we had now, we would have for life. Things were going to happen in our lives that might take us in different directions as we grew up, but a part of us would always be the little kids we were now. That's really true of everyone, if you want to be honest about it,

269

even if some people don't want to admit it. I may not know a lot in my thirteen years of life on this earth, but of that I am certain. In the end, I decided not to tell them, at least not for now. Maybe sometime in the future when we could all look back on this with a clear head, knowing that it was finally behind us, but not now.

"He's gone," I finally said. "He won't be coming back."

At first, I thought they were going to bombard me with questions and want all the details from the moment I ran out of the barn to the time that I reappeared and almost fell on my face in front of them. They must have seen something in my eyes or face, though, that told them that while there was more, something I wasn't telling them, it was something I wasn't ready to talk about. So they didn't ask. For that moment alone, among the countless moments we had already shared and the many wonderful more we would share in the future, I will always be grateful to them for that.

"Okay," the Bluesman said as he smiled and patted me on the shoulder.

Amelia just looked at me. I knew that she wanted to know what had happened, but because I wasn't saying anything, and knowing how this experience had affected me, I think she realized that she did not want to know...at least for now.

"So, I guess we should look into getting back home," the Bluesman suggested, gazing around the room at all the kids, who were involved in whatever it was that they were doing. Looking at them right now, it was hard to believe that some of them had not been home in months because they were being held captive by a... I don't know exactly what he was. A lunatic? I'm certain that at least a part of him was that, but there had certainly been other forces at work in that damaged mind of his. I'll probably never know. Or maybe I was just telling myself that because I didn't *want* to know.

"What should we do?" Amelia asked

"Well, we could take the truck," I said, and Amelia looked at me with wide eyes. "Just kidding. We got this far, I certainly do not want to drive us into another ditch or worse. With my luck, I would probably wind up somehow driving us to the moon."

"What are we going to do, then? Nobody knows that we're out here, so it's all up to us to get out of this place," the Bluesman said.

I thought about it for a moment and came to the only reasonable conclusion I could think of.

"I'm going to get on my bike so I can get help and then bring them out here," I said.

They both looked at me like I was crazy.

"Danny, are you kidding me? Look at you! You can barely stand up! After everything that you've been through, you want to ride all the way back home during the night? What if you collapse on the road or something? We would never even know!" Amelia said.

"I won't collapse. I feel great!" I said of making a show of standing up straight and stretching out my shoulders. I can honestly say that my performance was a lot better than what I actually felt, but I really did not see any choice in the matter, especially since I still considered all of this my fault. Maybe it all would have happened this way anyway, but that didn't matter now. What's done was done and I needed to finish it.

"Danny, you can't...."

"It's the only thing to do," I said as I began to head for the stairs. Amelia grabbed my shoulder and whirled me around with eyes ablaze. Wow. She was really angry!

"And why should it be you? Why should you be the one to go?"

"I'm the only on who can," I said.

"Oh? And why are you the only one?"

"Well, for one thing, Keith's ankle is shot. That's going to keep him from riding. And as for the other..." I said looking down beside her, and Amelia followed my gaze.

Cindy was holding onto her left hand, and it was completely obvious that she was not going to let her go. In fact, in the short time that I had been conscious, I had noticed that pretty much all the kids had been gravitating toward Amelia. If she tried to leave them, they would probably all have a fit! She looked down at Cindy and then back at me and completely understood.

"Okay, fine. You win. But why does it have to be now, Danny? Why not wait until morning when you're better rested?"

"I'm telling you, I feel great right now. That little nap really did work some wonders!" I said, making another show. "Besides, I would rather do it now at night when it is cool out than during the day when the sun is beating down on my back. Don't you think that that's the better option?"

"What I can see is that no matter what I say, you're going to have an answer for it. You're such a boy!"

"You're such a girl!"

"Before you go, I want you to eat something."

"Oh, come on! I'm wastin—"

"I mean it. You haven't had anything to eat in hours and you've been running around so much, you've probably lost ten pounds!"

"Amelia, I need to get start—"

"If you don't eat something I'm going to beat you up, and then how far will you get?"

"Fine, Mommy. I'll eat something," I said, which made the kids laugh. I walked to the refrigerator and pulled out a Dr. Pepper. Truth to tell, I really was thirsty. I snapped opened the cold can and gulped down the entire thing in record time. Then, without even thinking about it, I immediately let loose with the loudest belch that I had ever

272

released. It wouldn't have surprised me if everyone in Corpus Christi had heard it and was looking toward the skies. All the kids were now huddled around us and had been watching us argue. When they heard me belch, they all looked at me with shocked expressions and then started laughing hysterically. It was probably the first time that they all had had a real laugh in quite some time. Even the Bluesman was laughing and applauding at the same time, which caused me to start laughing.

Amelia was just looking at me with a stoic expression on her face, which immediately caused me to stop once I noticed her.

No sense in upsetting the little woman if you can avoid it, my dad always said.

Then, wanting to hurry up and get going, I saw Amelia's backpack on the floor. I opened it and ate a few warm sandwiches plus a few of Gordon's candy bars. Then I had another Dr. Pepper, this time without the belch, much to the disappointment of the kids.

"Happy?" I said to her.

She just folded her arms and looked at me. That was about the best I was going to get for right now.

Then, with all that done, the two of us proceeded to walk up the stairs together.

"Amelia?" Cindy wailed running after her.

"I'll be right back, promise," she said lovingly to her as she kissed her on the head. This seemed to console her because she just smiled at her. Then Cindy looked at me and then back at Amelia, and her smile grew even wider. I suspected that even as young as she was, she thought that Amelia and I were boyfriend and girlfriend. What can I say? I suppose she was right, even though we had not made it official or anything, if you know what I mean.

We left the kids in the charge of the Bluesman and proceeded up the stairs and outside to the area where we had hidden our bikes, Zock following us. I pulled mine out and then set it down so Amelia and I could look at each other. There was a full moon out, and I noticed how beautiful she looked in it. I thought back to that night when we were lying outside on my lawn talking and listening to the radio and made a promise to myself that there would be more nights like that in the future.

"You be careful," she ordered.

"You know me – I'm always careful," I said with a wink. The events of tonight had obviously proved otherwise, but it seemed like a cool thing to say. This did not seem to satisfy her in the least. I don't really blame her. If she had seen even half of the stunts I had pulled since we'd arrived there, she probably would refuse to even let me out of her sight ever again. (Now that I thought about it, I felt that wouldn't really be such a bad thing.)

Then, deciding that this was the perfect moment and it would never get any more perfect than this, I moved close to her, put my arms around her, and kissed her.

At first, she seemed to be surprised, and she tensed up. Then I felt her wrap her arms around me as she kissed me back, our lips pressed against one another. Even though it could not have lasted more than a few seconds, I felt like we had been kissing for hours, and I never wanted to let her go, it felt so good.

Also, my lips were nowhere close to getting all mangled up by her braces. They might have if I had used my tongue, which was gross, but a first kiss should be strictly romantic and not gross. Here I was doing it, and it all felt right. I certainly wasn't a pro or anything yet, but it surely felt right. All that worrying for nothing! What a moron I am!

Finally, we parted and looked at each other once again.

"I guess I better get going," I said.

"I guess so," she said softly.

I mounted my Mongoose and looked down beside me. Zock was staring up at me, fully expecting to keep me company on my trip.

"You ready to go, boy?"

"Bark!"

With one last look at Amelia standing there watching me nervously, I started pedaling and we were off.

I turned onto the road and looked down at it. There was nothing but darkness ahead of me, but the light from the full moon at least provided something. I kept looking back at the barn, and every time I did, the dim light it emitted was fading farther into the distance. After a while, it was completely gone, and it was just me and Zock making our way back home.

The stars certainly looked beautiful, and I kept looking up at them with a lazy grin on my face. It might have been my imagination, but I felt that Orion was hovering right above me on purpose so he could keep his eyes on me. The only sounds in the darkness surrounding me were the sound of my tires whirring on the ground, Zock's collar jangling as he ran beside me, and the symphony of the crickets.

I wish my watch still worked. I should have borrowed Amelia's or the Bluesman's before I left. Then again, I probably didn't really want to know what time it was because I would be looking at the watch every five minutes and it would just make time seem to run slower. Still, I wondered what time it was. I knew our parents must be worried sick. I wondered if they had called the police or were just frantically calling all of my friends, wondering where I was. I really hated having to put them through this. It was tough enough raising a kid without my having to add to it. I bet they had to be really climbing the walls. Mom, especially.

I started to pedal faster.

I wondered what Amelia's mom would think after all this was over because it was my fault that she was with me and trapped in the middle of nowhere. Would she be mad? Mad would probably be an understatement. If I was a parent and Amelia was my daughter and some kid had put her through all this, I would certainly be mad. Then again, I thought I might cut myself a break. However, I realized there was the strong possibility that I was being biased because I am that kid in question. Worries raced through my head: *What if they ban me from ever seeing her again? That would be horrible! What if we never get to go out on a date? What if I never get to take her out to dinner or a movie in my new car that needs to be fixed up and stored somewhere until I turn sixteen? What if I don't get to take her to the prom? Or, worst of all, what if her family moves away and I never see her again? Her parents might even get a restraining order in case I went looking for her, which I probably would because she's my girlfriend and all.*

I was getting tired.

This was a really stupid idea. What had I been thinking? After everything that I had done today, what sane person would take it upon himself to do what I was doing right now?

I could barely stand up before I left the barn, and here I was pedaling my bike in the darkness in the middle of nowhere. I was exhausted, and I wasn't even at the entrance to Goatman's yet. I still had a good hour and a half to go after that! What if I collapsed right here? Nobody would ever know. I would never see Amelia or the Bluesman again. I would never see my parents again, either. They would just find me here face-down in the dirt, covered with all sorts of bugs feeding on me, maybe even a few snakes and a couple of crows to add to the effect. That would be the picture that would be on the cover on the front page because pictures like that sell copies. The more gruesome, the better.

Plus, because I was a kid, it would make it even more gruesome and heart-wrenching, tug at the old heartstrings. The media would have a field day with it! Eventually, they would find the kids and it would all come out what had happened. I would be hailed as a hero! A legend! Live fast, die young, just like James Dean. James Dean was actually not much older than myself when he died. Of course, he had a car, unlike me. I have a bicycle.

I bet they will name a high school after me. They do that with heroes, you know. That would be really cool. Then again, maybe that wouldn't be so cool. I would technically be responsible for making thousands of kids hate me because they were sitting in school bored out of their minds. Instead of being a hero, I would be hated and shunned. Kids everywhere would curse me and my name and I would become synonymous with the devil. I would really hate that because I'm basically a good kid. Really, I am. My parents really lucked out.

Wow. I was getting really tired now. My legs felt like taffy. I wondered how much longer I would be able to take this. Sooner or later I was just going to keel over and collapse. I knew it. A person can only take so much, and I'm going....

Wait a minute! Was that...? *Yes!* The entrance to Goatman's! I could see the outline of it in the darkness. There was the giant barn looming to my left, and right in front of me was the entrance. My eyes grew wide with anticipation as I kept pushing. Then, once I soared through the entrance like a captured bird finally freed of its cage, I couldn't help but start laughing. I know that sounds ridiculous because laughing was the absolute last thing a person should be doing right then in my situation, but I did, and it felt so good. Zock must have shared my enthusiasm because he barked a couple of times. I knew that I still had a long way to go, but I was now halfway there and the worst part was over. If I could get this far, I could certainly push a little bit more and get us home and finally put an end to this horrible little adventure that we would soon be able to put behind us. Feeling renewed by this little victory, I started pedaling faster as I looked up at the starlit sky and the beautiful moon guiding my way as I breathed in the cool night air.

That may have been a mistake.

Now I was *really* tired.

I had been pedaling for I don't know how long because, as you well know, I did not have a watch. Well, I had one, but it was broken. I'll give you one guess why and who is responsible for that and, no, it is not Mike McCluskey. Although, he is probably fast asleep on a lumpy cot in a jail somewhere, and I was about to pass out. Did I mention that I am a good kid? If I am such a good kid, why am I in the middle of nowhere in the middle of the night and about to pass out from exhaustion because a lunatic has been chasing me all night? Answer me this, why don't you?

Mike McCluskey had a destructive streak in him second only to Hitler. It wouldn't surprise me if there was a 666 somewhere under his hair somewhere. Last Christmas, his favorite hobby was going around the neighborhood, unscrewing the little colorful light bulbs that people had strewn all around their houses and then throwing them up in air so he could watch them explode on the street. Then there was Halloween. He would go up to a person's front door where a pumpkin was sitting and kick the face of it in. He would also steal bags of candy from little kids, then offer to sell it back to them. Mike loved egging people's houses and he was an expert toilet paper roller, covering a tree so well you would think it had just snowed during the night. Mike would even use toilet paper to mummify cars.

He loved crank-calling people. He would get some poor old lady on the phone and, in a surprisingly adult voice, tell her that she was a lucky winner and had just won a trip to Hawaii, that she should get up bright and early tomorrow and be at the airport at 6:00am where one of his representatives would be waiting for her. Once he even got a little kid on the phone and convinced him that his parents were dead.

Mike loved firecrackers. He loved them so much that he had to share them with the neighborhood dogs by throwing them at them and watching as they recoiled in terror when they popped.

So, yes, my parents certainly did luck out. Come to think of it, I had not seen Mike in quite awhile. I wonder if he was in jail right now. My Dad knew about Mike and he said that kids like him grew up to be either criminals or politicians, one not really that much different from the other.

If I don't get home soon, I may very well pass out. No fooling this time. They might find me dead and staring up at the sky with my eyes open and a look of horror on my face. This is how people look when they are being visited by the Grim Reaper. Speaking of which, I wonder how the Grim Reaper got his job. Was he born into that position or did God just tell one of his angels that he was not making his quota compared to the rest of his other angels and because of it he was now going to spend the rest of eternity as the Grim Reaper? Maybe he was elected. Maybe there is a general election every four years and a new Grim Reaper is appointed at that time. I wonder how many terms a person can serve as the Grim Reaper. Thinking about it, I really do not think that that it is a job that anyone would want. I certainly wouldn't want it, going around and taking people's souls and bringing pain to everyone around them as the person they love dies. That would really suck. Only a sick person would get off on doing something like that, someone like Mike McCluskey. I bet he would love it! I bet he was the kind of guy who would really get a kick out of clai—

Wait a minute… Lights! I could see a row of streetlights ahead of me in the distance! That meant I was now pretty close to the neighborhood. Civilization once again! Here we go!

279

Amazingly, I found the energy to start pedaling fast again and bent forward on my handlebars like a jockey on a horse. I wondered if this was what that guy who rode Seabiscuit felt like. Probably not. A horse could move a lot faster that what I was doing right now. Maybe I should have taken the truck. I could have at least tried. I mean, sure I had wrecked the car, but that had just been a trial run. Everyone messes up on the trial run. Just imagine, if I had taken the truck, I would already be there by now. Well, maybe. There's a good chance I would have just found another way to wreck, and then I would have felt even worse about wrecking another automobile, and I would still be riding my bike right now.

I was getting closer, slowly but surely.

Actually, this was worse than not seeing any lights. You might think it would be a good thing, but it wasn't. Because I could see the lights in front of me, I now could gauge how fast or, I should say, how slowly I was going. It was taking forever to get there! I felt like a turtle! It this was what turtles felt like, you could have it! As an experiment, I decided to close my eyes as I was pedaling. No, I had not gone crazy. My reasoning was that if I kept my eyes closed for a while, maybe just opening them every now and then to look at the ground below me to make sure that I was still on the road, a lot of time would have passed and by the next time I looked up, the houses would be closer, and I would feel better. Get it? Sound reasonable? I tried it for I do not know how long because I do not have a watch, a working watch, and then looked back at the houses hoping they would be right in front of me.

They were still far away!

They were closer, but not close enough to be considered "close," if you know what I mean.

Okay, no more games. It was time to get serious. Just concentrate on making it and think good thoughts, and this would be over before I knew it. I stared at the ground beneath me thinking of anything that would keep my mind occupied. Song lyrics, movies, television shows, girls (don't tell Amelia that), anything!

Then, it happened. I was now driving on pavement!

My wheels had gone from that knock-a-round sound of driving on the dirt road to that sudden nice, smooth hum of driving on the pavement. Plus, it was so quiet out right now, the humming was a lot louder than it would usually be.

"Yes!" I yelled in triumph, and it echoed into the night. Zock barked his approval as he scampered along beside me.

We still had a ways to go on the empty, abruptly ending street before we entered the neighborhood, but this was massive progress! I had done it! Against all the odds of collapsing in the dark somewhere and gasping my last breath while staring up at the stars, I was now back in the neighborhood and would soon be finding some help.

There was now a massive white wall to the right of us. The other side was empty fields where, across it, I could see the lights of all the other houses. In front of me, I could see a long strip of power lines and lit streetlights that seemed to stretch on forever down the street. It was actually all really nice to look at and take in. Romantic, even, if you know what I mean. Then, the entrance to this subdivision finally came up and I swerved to my right and into the yard of the first house I came to. Wow. What a nice house. I quickly got up off my bike and ran to the porch, rang the doorbell several times and then leaned on the door with the side of my head and hands on it as I tried to catch my breath.

I must have fallen asleep because I was suddenly falling to the linoleum floor and hit it with a smack, my hands involuntarily covering my head so they took the brunt of the impact. It still hurt, though.

"What the hell is this?" I heard an older man say in a perplexed voice.

"Honey? Who is it?" I heard a woman's voice ask that sounded like it was in front of me on the top of some stairs.

"I don't know. Some crazy kid and a dog."

I'm not crazy, mister. I'm just tired. You would be too if you had gone through the day that I had. Believe me.

"Son? Are you okay? Son?" I heard his voice say as I felt one of his hands on my shoulder and trying to turn me around.

I tried to say something to him in a coherent fashion, but all that came out was...

"Buuullllllllaaaaaaaawwwwwaaaaaaaaa..."

"What?" he said.

I don't blame you, mister. I wouldn't have understood that either. I needed to focus. Even though I was so tired that I just wanted to sleep for a week, I had finally made my way here, and I just had to push a little more. I focused my thoughts and tried again.

"Kidnapper... kids... Goatman's... prison... barn...." I moaned.

"What did he say?" the woman's voice said as I heard her walking down the stairs.

"I'm not sure. Son? Are you okay? Are you hurt? Do you need help?"

All very good questions, but not what I was trying to get across. I strained to turn myself all the way over so that I was now lying on my back and looking straight up at him. He was a guy who appeared to be in his fifties. He had mostly white hair and was wearing a pair of black-rimmed glasses that made him look like Clark Kent. He was also wearing a red robe and some white pajamas underneath it. Wow. It must really be late. I had probably woken them both up from a sound sleep. *Sorry about that. I wouldn't have done it unless it was really important.* It was time to try again.

"Found the kidnapper...who took those kids...all the way out...Goatman's..."

282

There was a silence for a moment and I closed my eyes. They were so heavy.

"Honey, did he just say what I thought he did? Did he say that he had found the kidnapper who has been taking all the kids?" the woman asked.

"I... I think so," I heard the man say as I felt his hands on me, one on my shoulder and the other on my cheek. I looked up at him again, and he was kneeling beside me, his face just inches away from mine. "Son? Son? Can you hear me?"

"Yeah... kind of..." I mumbled.

"Honey, pick him up and place him on the couch. Look at the poor dear. He's exhausted! He must have...he must have gotten away from him somehow," the other voice said.

I felt myself being lifted up in a strong grip and then I was flying. The next thing I knew, the ground beneath me was so very soft. I could sleep for a week right here.

"Son? I need you to wake up. I know you're tired but this is important. I need you to stay with me here. Please."

"O...kay," I struggled to say as I opened my eyes again and regarded him. He looked like a nice man, just like my dad.

"What's your name?"

"Danny...Brent."

"Danny Brent. Go look in the phone book and see what you can find under 'Brent'."

"Okay," I heard the woman say and then the sound of her feet tapping on the floor as they moved into the distance.

"Danny? Listen to me, son. I need to be clear on this. I need you to repeat what you just said. Can you do that for me? Come on, son. Stay with me."

"Okay. Amelia... and I... and the Bluesman... we rode out to Goatman's... don't tell Mom or she'll be mad... ground me... we found the kids at... barn... all eight of

283

them... fine... Gordon...kidnapper... dead... rode back to tell everyone... get help... Amelia... help... tired...."

"Son, I need to understand. I need to be clear. Are you telling me that you know where all the kids are that have been kidnapped from the neighborhood? That they're all alive and in a barn somewhere and you came back to get help for them? Is that it?" he said urgently.

"Okey-doke," I said, just like Christopher Lloyd on *Taxi*. That guy really was a loon.

"Oh, my God!" I heard the woman say in an awestruck voice. I guess she had come back. "We need to call the police!"

"Do it! After that, we'll call his parents and then get to work on finding those kids!"

"Honey? Danny?" I heard the woman's voice say again and I could smell some kind of lotion on her. This time it was nearer. I opened my eyes, and there she was. She looked kind of like Barbara Eden, although older. "How are you feeling? Can I get you anything?"

Only one thing came to mind.

"Dr. Pepper."

"He wants a Dr. Pepper?" the male voice said.

"Yes."

"We don't have Dr. Pepper. We have Coke," he said.

"Honey, we have Coke. Is that all right?"

"Yeahhhhhhh..."

"Okay, I'll be right back," I heard her say as she got up. "I found a 'Brent' that's in this neighborhood. I'm going to call the police and then his parents."

"Okay," the male voice said.

"Danny? I'll be right back with a Coke, okay?"

"All right..."

But in the end, it didn't matter. I had finally passed out.

"Danny? Danny Brent?"

Was someone saying my name? Amelia calls me Danny. I prefer to be called Dan because it sounds more mature, but I really don't mind when she calls me Danny. People call her both Amelia and Amy, and she is fine with either one. Although she hates to be called names like "Track Tooth" because of her braces. She has beaten me up for it many a time.

"Danny? Wake up, son. I need you to wake up, now," a male voice ordered.

It dawned on me that it must not be my dad waking me up to go to school because his voice sounded different. I opened my eyes halfway.

There were two police officers in front of me. One of them was standing up and the other was kneeling down in front of me. He had a hard face like a Marine.

Police officers. Cool!

"Danny?"

"Yeah?" I said sleepily.

"Danny, I'm Officer Peske and this is my partner, Officer Hudson."

"T.J. Hooker?"

"Uh, no, Danny… he's not with us right now. Do you know where you are at this moment?"

"Someone's house? A nice woman was talking to me. Coke."

"That's right, Danny. You were talking with Mr. and Mrs. Peterson. Do you remember that?"

"Yeah."

"Good. Now, Danny, according to them, you arrived at their house about twenty minutes ago and you mentioned that you have knowledge of the kidnappings that have been happening in this neighborhood for the past several months. Is this true?"

"Yeah."

I heard some murmuring among the four of them.

"Okay, Danny? I need you to wake up, son. Come on. I know you're tired and you look like you've been through an ordeal, but we need you to focus."

"Okay," I said trying really hard to wake up and do my best to help him. "My parents?"

"Mrs. Peterson called them and they're on their way here right now."

"I am going to be so grounded!"

Somebody laughed and I heard Mrs. Peterson say "shush!"

"Well, we'll put in a good word for you Danny, okay? Now, where are the kids? Where did you come from?"

"Goatman's."

There was a moment of silence.

"What did he say?" a male voice said.

"Danny? Did you say Goat Man's?"

"Yes."

"What is Goat Man's, Danny?"

"It's a place... a dark place where we go to hang out from time to time."

"Where is it, Danny? Where is 'Goat Man's?'"

"When the road ends, keep on going and you will eventually come to it. It's really far away."

"When the road ends keep on going...? Is the kid giving us some kind of riddle? This is no time to fool around!"

"I think I know what he's talking about," I heard the other policeman say and then heard him move closer. His voice sounded younger. "Danny? This is Officer Hudson. When you say, 'when the road ends," do you mean the road on the other side of the wall where the street ends and there's a dirt road?"

"Yes. Goatman's is out there. About an hour and a half ride on our bikes."

"You said 'our'. Are some friends of yours out there with the kids?"

"Yes, sir."

286

"Okay, Danny. Thank you. You rest for a moment. I know what he means. That road on the other side of the wall that leads out into the fields is what he's talking about. Apparently, there's a barn or something out there where the kids are being kept. For some reason, it's called 'Goat Man's.'"

"You're sure?"

"I don't see that he can possibly be talking about anything else."

"Okay. Mr. and Mrs. Peterson? We're going to have to make some calls and get some assistance out here. If this is what I believe it is, we're going to need some more help."

"Okay, officer. Would you and your partner like some coffee?" Mrs. Peterson asked.

"That would be really nice, sir. Thank you."

Ding-dong!

"That must be his parents," Mrs. Peterson said as I heard her footsteps going away.

"Ohhhh...I'm going to be in so much trouble," I mumbled. I was starting to finally wake up. I think fear had a lot to do with it.

Officer Hudson chuckled and kneeled beside me. He was really muscled up! I wish I had muscles like that!

"I think I'll be able to help you out with that, son. If what you've done tonight is what I think it is, you've just become quite the hero."

"A hero?" I repeated in a daze. "Just like Superman."

"Exactly like Superman. Here, I think this is for you," he said as he gave me a cold can of Coke. I would have preferred a Dr. Pepper because I'm a Dr. Pepper man, but this would certainly do. My throat felt like sandpaper. I took the Coke from him and gulped it all down in record time. This might very well have been the most delicious drink that I had ever tasted.

"Danny! Oh, baby!" I heard a familiar voice say. I looked over and saw my mom and dad rushing toward me.

287

I was happy to see that they did not look mad at all. More worried than anything else. Officer Hudson got out of the way and my mom immediately leaned over and grabbed me and held me tight, my dad also joining in. "Where have you been? We've been scared senseless! Why are you so dirty? Why is your face so scratched up? What's happening?" Then, apparently not to me, "We got a call that he showed up here about to collapse, and we rushed over. What's happening? Is he in trouble?"

"Mr. and Mrs. Brent? I'm Officer Hudson, and standing over there on the radio is my partner, Officer Peske. We were called over here by the Petersons because we have reason to believe that your son may have located the children who have been kidnapped from this neighborhood in the past several months."

Momentary silence.

"What? Honey, is this true?" my mom said, looking at me.

"Uh, yeah," I mumbled as I took another drink from my can and then remembered that I had already ingested all of it.

"I'm... I'm sorry, I don't understand."

"Apparently, your son and some friends of his went out riding somewhere and came upon the location where the kids are being held. We're waiting on a team to get here and then we're going to head out there. We're going to need your son to help us out some more once we leave."

"Um...okay," she said more than a bit dumbfounded.

"I'm sorry, Mom. I'm sorry, Dad. We were just going out for a little adventure and... well, we found the kids and the guy who kidnapped them and there was a bunch of running around and trying to lose him and I wrecked the car and Amelia and the Bluesman are still waiting out there for me with the kids because I went to get help and I wanted to drive the truck but I thought that would be really dumb and then I got on my bicycle...."

"Honey, honey, it's all right. I don't...we don't fully understand what's going on but...apparently you did a good thing. You just sit back and rest."

"I'm... I'm not in trouble?"

My mom and my dad looked at each other and then back at me.

"Of course not, Dan," my dad said.

"I'm not grounded?"

"We'll... talk about that later."

Considering the circumstances, that was probably as good as it was going to get.

"Mrs. Peterson? Can I please get another Coke?" I said, wanting to change the subject.

"Of course, dear. I'm sorry, would you two like anything? It looks like it's going to be a long night," she said to my parents.

"I guess so," my mom laughed nervously. "Cokes would be fine, thank you."

As we sat there waiting for the other cops to arrive, and since I was now more awake, I explained to the officers exactly what Goatman's was and what had been happening since we arrived there. I told them everything that had happened since we arrived there: lunch, the ducks, eating by the pond, and the exploring that we did. Then I told them about Gordon and how we had seen his giant truck and how we had heard the kid's voice in the back, which was why we had followed him to the barn where the kids were being held. I explained to them how we had found the play area and then the prison area and about all the running around that I did with Gordon chasing me while Amelia and the Bluesman were trying to free the kids. My mom and dad looked at me in amazement, not saying anything, and I knew that once this was all over I was really going to be in for it. I told them about the stunt that Amelia and I had pulled, how Gordon had fallen down the stairs and gotten knocked out and how we had gotten the

289

keys so we could finally get the kids out. I have to admit, I really did come off sounding like a superhero. All that was missing was a fancy costume.

The only thing I left out was the part about the Goatman and how he had saved me. That was something I would never tell anyone. Maybe I would someday, but not now. The way my parents were looking at me, I don't think they would be able to handle that since they both looked like they were both about to have heart attacks. Oh, I did mention the part about the car and wondering what it was doing there and how I had put it into a ditch when I tried to drive it. The damage didn't look too bad and only needed a little bit of body work to be as good as new. Was there any way I could have it once this was all over? Any chance of that happening?

"Uh, we'll look into it, Danny," Officer Hudson said, and the way he had said it, it made all of my hopes go running down the tubes. Now I was just going back to depending on my bike. How was I supposed to take a girl out on a decent date with just a bike?

Ding-Dong!

"And here we go," Officer Peske said.

Mrs. Peterson went to answer the door and, because I wanted to see what was going on, we all followed her.

"Oh, my!" Mrs. Peterson said as she opened the door. There were four more police officers at the door and, on the street in front of the house, I could see four more police cars, two ambulances, and there was even a fire truck! All of them had their lights on, even though the sirens were silent, and the entire area was awash in a swirl of colors. Off to the side, a news van was parked, and some lady I recognized from television was holding a microphone and talking into a camera. I looked at the police officers, and they were gazing at her with annoyance. Apparently, they had been hoping that the news people would not find out about this — at least, not so quickly.

"Mr. and Mrs. Brent? I'm going to need to borrow Danny for the trip so he can ride in the car and show us where we're going. Do you mind?" Officer Hudson said.

"Um, no, of course not, I guess," my mom mumbled as she looked at my dad.

Then it struck me as to exactly what he was saying. "Do I get to ride in the police car?" I asked, excited.

"Yes, you do, Danny," he said.

"Awesome!"

"Honey," my mom said, embarrassed, as she looked at me and then at the officers. Judging by the grin on their faces, this was something that was pretty common.

"Mr. and Mrs. Brent? I hate to be in such a rush but we really should get going. Plus, I want to keep Danny away from the press and get him in the car," Officer Peske said.

"I understand. Thank you," my mom replied. "Do you mind if we follow you in our car?"

"I suppose asking you to wait here would just be a waste of time."

My parents just looked at him, not saying anything.

"I thought so. Okay, Danny. Let's go," he said as he, his partner, and I left the house. They walked with me in the middle so that they could shield me from the television lady. I don't know what the big deal was. I thought it would be pretty cool to be on television. Although, I probably didn't look my best right then. Maybe they had a make-up department with them that could fix me up, I groggily wondered. They might even be able to figure out a way to make me looked more muscled up.

We were soon standing beside the police car, and I peered inside. It looked really cool! There was so much cool stuff inside; I didn't know where to start looking. A real police car. Just like on *T.J. Hooker*! All the kids at school were going to be so jealous!

Officer Peske got into the driver's side, and Officer Hudson was opening the back door for me. It was only

291

then that I noticed that Zock had been trailing behind me the whole time.

"Um…"

"Yes, Danny?"

"Do you mind if I ride up front? That would be really cool."

"I'm sorry, Danny. I can't do that. Regulations."

"That's all right. It's still cool." Zock and I got in the back seat, and then Officer Hudson closed the door after me. I'm pretty sure that Zock wasn't supposed to be there with me, but they were being nice enough to give him and me a break. Once he was settled in the car, Officer Peske spoke some technical stuff into the radio. Once he was done, he put the car into gear. I still couldn't get over it: a real police car!

"Okay, let's go," he said as he pulled out. When we came to the main street, he took a left; we were now proceeding back along the same route that I had just come from, the large, white wall now on my left again.

"Is this the way, Danny?" he said, looking in the rearview mirror at me.

I looked forward through the safety wiring that was separating the back seat from the front and gazed ahead into the darkness. I immediately felt a chill run through my body, and for one split second, I was more scared than I had ever been before all that night. It fully dawned on me right at that moment that we were heading back to where it had all begun, back to where I had almost gotten killed and seen something…that I was hoping I would never see again.

It was also where the kids and the Bluesman were waiting for us to take them home.

And Amelia.

"Danny? You alright?"

"What? Oh, yeah… yeah. This is the way. Just keep going straight."

We were moving along smoothly and then, all of a sudden, we hit the dirt road and the familiar sound of tires on dirt was beneath me once again. Even though I was in a car now instead of on my bike, it strangely sounded the same.

I turned around and looked behind us. Wow! It looked like a convoy was following us. All the cars still had their lights going on even though there were no sirens, which I was very happy about. Right now, as glad as I was that this was almost over and the kids would be back home and I would see my friends once again...all I wanted was quiet. That might seem strange to say because I had just experienced several hours of quiet time to myself, as if I were the last person on the face of the earth, and there was no longer any such thing as daylight in my own, strange world, but I wanted to feel some peace and just...take it all in, come to terms with all of it.

I sat back in the seat and just stared out the window as we made our way back to Goatman's, Zock's head in my lap and me petting him. The radio squawked every now and then, but the two cops were both ignoring it. From time to time, each of them would ask me something about what had happened, especially about Gordon, and I would absently answer them. Because, my voice probably sounded weird, they asked me more than once if I was all right, and I assured them that I was. I just needed to find a calm place and center myself. I think I freaked them out because I saw them looking at each other.

They probably thought that I was in shock or something but I wasn't. I was just...going with it. I was fully aware of everything that was happening around me but at the same time I felt as if I were someplace else watching it all from another perspective, a perspective that wasn't quite as real. I suppose it's kind of like what a person feels like when they are watching television and know that everything is happening because it was all in a script that someone has written and it is really all make-believe, but this was real life. Real life was a lot scarier because things like this really did happen, were happening right now.

Even though I was in a car now instead of riding my bike, the trip was seemingly taking longer, which was weird because we were going ten times faster. I looked out the window and saw the full moon again and, looking farther out, saw Orion and the rest of the millions of stars that were endless miles away and were so much above petty and monstrous things like this.

Then we slowed down because we were coming to the entrance of Goatman's. Officer Peske turned on his bright lights and eased the car slowly in, then came to a stop when he saw the three roads in front of us.

"Okay, Danny, which road?"

"The one on the right."

"You sure?"

"Yes, sir," I said looking down it. I realized that I was holding my breath and had to concentrate to stop doing it.

"Okay," he said as he put the car back into gear, and we proceeded down the road, our personal convoy following us.

It would not be much longer now. Soon it would all be over and we could all get back to our normal, safe lives.

I must have dozed off because when I opened my eyes, my head was leaning against the window, with Zock's head still in my lap. I looked around the area and ahead of us, instantly recognizing where we were. We were just coming down the small hill where we had spotted the barn so long ago. My eyes fluttered a few times with anticipation and I leaned forward toward the wiring.

"We're almost there," I announced. I must have startled them because Officer Peske's head turned in surprise.

"You sure, Danny?"

"Yeah, look," I said as I pointed and, if you looked closely, you could see some of the light that was coming from where the barn was. He immediately got on his radio and said a lot of technical stuff, and I kept leaning forward, not really paying attention to him, lost in thought about finally seeing my friends again.

The light was looming ahead of us like it was taunting us until, finally, we were there.

We pulled up alongside Gordon's truck. As we did so, Officer Peske looked at the license plate and read it off to someone on his radio. Then, we all came to a full stop and doors everywhere behind us were opening and thumping closed. I got out of the car, letting Zock get out first. I was still inhumanly tired, and I knew the excitement of what was happening was the only thing that was keeping me on my feet. When this was all over I was probably going to sleep for a week.

Then, I remembered where Gordon was, and they would probably want to know about that. I tapped a nearby police officer on the arm and explained to him where I thought Gordon was without going into any detail about the Goatman. He thanked me and got hold of another police officer and, with their flashlights on, proceeded to where Gordon was lying. I watched them disappear into the weeds. As I did so, I wondered if by any chance the Goatman was watching us, was watching me in particular. If he was out there, he could be anywhere, and I was pretty sure that he was not going to let himself be seen again. I was very glad of that, but a small part of me was also sad because, as hideous as he may have been, he did save my life.

Officers Peske and Hudson gathered in a group with the other officers and discussed some things while looking at the barn. A couple of firefighters and some paramedics also came into the group, and it seemed like everyone had something to say.

What was everyone standing around for? We were here! *Let's go! Let's go!*

"Okay, Danny?" Officer Hudson said. "You gave us a good layout of the place, but we would like you to come in with us. Stay back behind us and let us go in first. Do not at any time move ahead of us. If I tell you to do something, you immediately do it without question, okay?"

"Yes, sir."

"Okay, let's go," he said. They started moving forward to the side door and, moments later, I was in the barn again. As I was walking into the place and the familiar surroundings that I had left such a long/short time ago, I felt the familiar chill run through me that I had felt while in the police car. How could I be cold in the middle of summer? It was completely baffling. Then again... I suppose it wasn't really cold that was chilling me.

They stood around for a few minutes, checking the place out. Like the three of us previously, they were amazed at the layout of the area, half a nice makeshift living quarters and the other half a workshop of some kind. One of the officers said something into his radio and, a few moments later, about half a dozen people with dark jackets walked into the barn and started going over the living area with little pieces of equipment, I guess looking for hairs and fingerprints and stuff like that to find out who Gordon was.

I tapped on Officer Hudson's arm and then pointed to the doorway that led downstairs. He nodded and alerted the other officers in the group, and we all proceeded toward it. They looked down the stairway for a moment, and we all heard the same thing. The television was on, and there was some talking that could barely be heard. I wasn't sure, but I thought I heard Amelia's voice. Although, I realized that could just be wishful thinking because I so much wanted to see her again — I wanted to see everyone again.

As they started walking down the stairs, Officer Peske silently instructing me to stay back, I noticed that they were all holding on to their gun holsters. Though the guns were still holstered, it looked like the cops were ready to draw them at a moment's notice and start blasting. I know they were just doing their jobs, and the only stuff I knew about police work was just from watching television and movies, but I hoped they didn't scare the kids, looking like they were ready for a shootout.

"Hello? Is there anyone down here?" Officer Peske said as we were going down, me last. In fact, I was still standing at the top with Zock.

"Hello?" I heard the Blueman's familiar voice say.

"Keith!" I whispered to myself, and I felt a smile curve my lips.

A moment later, I saw him appear at the foot of the stairs, looking up at the police officers with his mouth open. "Police! Cool!" he exclaimed.

"Son? Are you Keith?" Officer Peske said.

"You came! You know who I am! Did Dan send you?"

"Yes, he did," Officer Peske said, looking behind him and up at me. The Bluesman followed his gaze; when he saw me, his eyes lit up. The other officers descended into the room, and I walked down the stairs until the Bluesman and I were standing in front of each other. We immediately hugged each other.

"You did it, man!"

"Yeah, I did," I whispered, still amazed that I actually really had done it, and then we let go of each other.

"Did you get to ride in a police car?" he asked.

"Yeah, I did," I said in a bit of a cocky voice, and in the back of my mind, even though I felt a little guilty about it, I thought, *Let's see you top that!*

"Cool!"

I smiled and looked around the room. Some of the kids were lying down asleep, which I suppose wasn't surprising, and the various police officers were going around the room, waking them up. When the kids saw the officers, their eyes went wide with excitement because they now knew for sure that it was all over and they would soon be home again. A

297

couple of the officers disappeared into the prison area, which I knew they would be spending a lot of time in, and as I looked around the room, I saw Amelia standing there with a couple of the kids, watching everything that was going on. She saw me and smiled, and I immediately moved toward her and hugged her.

"You came back," she whispered.

"Of course I came back. I had to come and get my girlfriend, didn't I?"

She laughed, and we held each other tighter and stayed like that awhile as we listened to the confusion around us.

"You did it, Danny. I was so scared that you were going to collapse on the road somewhere, and I would never know. You were so tired when you left here. How can you possibly still be awake right now?"

"I think I'm running on pure adrenaline and nothing else. When we get back home, you probably won't see me for a week because I'll be asleep the whole time."

"You and me both," she laughed.

"And me three," the Bluesman said as Amelia and I stepped back from each other and I looked at the Bluesman's boyish, smiling face. We all came together in a group hug and held each other. I guess the exhaustion was really hitting me hard because I started crying right there and could not stop. I felt like a real wimp because heroes are never supposed to cry. Superman doesn't cry. T.J. Hooker doesn't cry... but then, I thought, they aren't real, and I was, and real people cry. I looked up and both Amelia and the Bluesman were crying also. And you know what? It felt great. I know that sounds weird, but it really did. I think that the tears had wanted to come out of all of us hours ago, but because we all had had a job to do, we had repressed the crying or something. I don't know, it's not like I'm a shrink or anything, but that's what I think. Now, case closed.

"Amelia?"

We looked down and saw Cindy looking up at us. Well, she was actually looking at Amelia. Keith and I just happened to be there.

"Yes, honey?" she said as she bent down toward her.

"Will I ever see you again? Are you still going to be my friend?"

"Oh, of course I will, honey. We'll see each other all the time," she said as she hugged her.

Watching her, it suddenly struck me that Amelia was going to make a great mother someday. I mean, I was sure that that was going to be really far off...but she was going to be a really good mother. What a weird thought, of all the things to be thinking right then.

"Danny?"

I glanced over and saw Officer Hudson looking at me. "Yes?"

"We're probably going to be here for a while. Do you want to take the kids upstairs with you? We need to start asking them some questions, alert their parents, and make sure that they are all right. How would you like to be my deputy for the evening and take care of that?"

I look at him, wide-eyed. Now I was wide awake again! "Wow! Cool! Do I get to carry a gun?"

"Sorry, Danny. Maybe next time," he said with a grin.

"Okay. Oh, by the way. The car is parked – or, I should say 'resting' – behind the barn."

"We'll look into it."

I continued to look up at him.

"I'll see what I can do, Danny, but I'm not promising anything," he sighed.

"That's cool. Thanks, Officer Hudson," I said as I held my hand out.

"Call me Darren," he said as he took it.

Cool! I was on a first name basis with a policeman!

We gathered the kids together and walked up the stairs. As soon as we were in the living area again, I looked around and could not help but be amazed.

There were at least thirty people wandering around!

Where had they all come from? I guess word gets around whenever something juicy is going on.

"Danny?"

I turned my head and saw my mom and dad walking toward me. They each hugged me and asked me again if I was all right, fidgeting over me. It was kind of embarrassing to have my parents fawning all over me like that because Amelia was standing right there watching and everything, if you know what I mean. Then again, it was also kind of neat.

We made our way out of the barn together, and I looked over at the endless trail of headlights and silent police lights that were filling the night sky with their colors. I knew that they were here to help, but it kind of made me upset because now the beautiful stars, which had been my only friends all that time besides the moon and Zock, were not as clearly visible anymore.

Something must have happened, and calls must have been made because there were now a lot more cars and trucks than when I was at the Petersons' house. I wondered if the *National Enquirer* was here. Those guys would probably turn this thing into some kind of alien invasion or maybe the return of Bigfoot. Now that I thought about it, they wouldn't be too far off base with the Bigfoot thing. More like Goatfoot.

Almost immediately after my exiting the barn with the kids, about a dozen police officers and paramedics surrounded us, asking various questions, and especially if we were all right. The kids were frightened of all the strangers and huddled around Amelia, the Bluesman, and me. Once they saw that the people meant them no harm, though, they slowly went with them, especially once they were told that they would soon be with their parents again. In fact, most of the parents were probably on their way here right now, breaking all sorts of speed limits. I can't say that I blame them.

"Amelia?" Cindy said, looking up at her and still holding on to her arm.

"It's okay, honey. The nice lady just wants to make sure that you're all right," Amelia said in a consoling way as she looked at the paramedic and then back at Cindy. "You go with her, and I'll find you later, okay?"

"Okay," she said with a childish smile, even though it was perfectly obvious that she did not want to leave Amelia.

Then the lady reporter I had seen in front of the Petersons' place was rushing toward us with a determined look on her face, and a camera guy trailing her. If she had been carrying a gun instead of a microphone, she would have looked exactly like a soldier. Well, not *exactly* like a soldier because she was attractive and done up and everything, but you probably know what I mean about people who work on television and how flawless they have to look, especially news people who never have a hair out of place.

"Hello. Are you the three kids who discovered where the kidnapped kids were being held?" she almost shouted with excitement. I guess this is what they mean when a reporter is "sniffing out a story."

"That's us," the Bluesman said.

"Great! How would you like to be on television?"

"Cool!" the Bluesman immediately said.

"My name is Kendra Carrington, I'm with Channel 3 KIII TV3. What's yours?"

"The Bluesman."

"I'm sorry?"

"Uh, it's Keith. Keith…Richards."

She looked at him for a moment. "Are you serious?"

301

"Yes, I'm serious," he said in a depressed tone.

"I love The Rolling Stones."

"Yeah, both you and my parents," he said in the same depressed tone.

"Well, I think it's a nice name," she said with a smile and, since she was pretty attractive, the Bluesman immediately perked up.

"Cool! By the way, is Joe Gazin here?"

"No," she said, still smiling. "Joe is at the station right now. In fact, he's probably going to be watching me interview you."

"Cool!"

It was at this point that that I thought that the only word in the Bluesman's vocabulary was 'cool.'

"Okay, we're going to set up the camera, I'm going to give an introduction, and then I'm going to ask you a few questions about what happened. Just relax and be natural, okay?"

"Okay," he said, winking at Amelia and me. It was at this moment that I felt a moment of dread. The Bluesman was capable of taking anything and turning it into a joke.

"Three...two...one...and we're rolling," the cameraman said, pointing at Kendra as the camera aimed at the two of them, a bright white light spreading all over the area.

"Hello, this is Kendra Carrington, live in the secluded outskirts of a suburb of the city. I'm speaking with Keith Richards, at the scene where the kidnapped children were being kept. He and his two friends were responsible for finding the location earlier today and reporting it to the police just a short time ago. We're speaking with the police officers, who you can see in the area behind me. This barn is the location where the kids were being kept by a lone man, who at this time has not been identified, although we are told he is now deceased. Mr. Richards, can you tell us anything more about this situation and what you have gone through tonight?"

"Hello. Uh, it actually wasn't just me. My friends Amelia and Dan were also involved. There they are behind us," he said as he turned around toward us, and we waved at the camera. I noticed that Amelia seemed to be particularly taken with it and was seemingly watching everything the woman was doing. She really seemed interested in what was going on, taking everything in. "In fact, Dan – he's my best friend – is the real hero here. He rode his bike all the way back in the dark so that he could get help and call the police. If it wasn't for him we would all be stuck here right now."

"What an incredible story. You three certainly have gone through quite the ordeal tonight."

"I guess you could say so. Say, are we live right now?"

"Yes, we are," she said smiling. She sure did have nice teeth.

"I thought so," he said as he turned around and smiled at us. Then, he faced the camera again and immediately went into "Ice Cream Man."

Amelia and I looked at him in shock and then started laughing because we thought it was hysterical! He was doing it exactly the way he had done it earlier, switching voices and characters and everything. The news lady was looking at him in shock. She simply could not believe it! Here she was trying to do a serious interview about a dire situation, and the Bluesman was turning it into a stand-up routine! She tried to stop him, but all he did was get louder. Then she tried to get the cameraman to stop, but he must have been enjoying it as much as we were because he kept his camera on Keith.

Eventually, the Bluesman's routine was put to a halt, and the reporter switched to interviewing both Amelia and me. I guess the interviews went well, if not as funny, and later on, we saw ourselves on television, but the clip of the Bluesman doing the Eddie Murphy bit was the clip that was being shown most often. However, the few curse words that he said were bleeped out.

(When the summer eventually ended and we were back in school, the Bluesman became even more famous than when the school year had ended. The legend of the Bluesman had grown tenfold! Now there was no stopping him and, as before, I could easily imagine him doing exactly what he had been doing in front of the camera, but in front of millions of people.)

We finished answering some more questions from random people and letting the paramedics check us out to make sure we okay. One of them put some kind of ointment on my face to help with the scratches that my friend the bat had left earlier, and it really stung! But, like they say about any kind of medicine, if it tastes bad, it must be good for you. The Bluesman was keeping the kids entertained with jokes and impressions. I guess the excitement of being on television had really fired him up because he was now wide awake and entertaining his audience like there was no tomorrow. To my delight, someone thought to bring soft drinks and donuts (which I guess was no surprise, if you know what I mean), and I was now in possession of a very welcome Dr. Pepper.

Things were starting to mellow out a bit, and I guess I was finally able to realize that all of this was finally over. I mean, I was sure there would be odds and ends to take care of as time went on, but the worst of it was over. With Zock beside me, I wandered around to a quiet area beside the barn away from the lights and people, where there was not as much confusion, and it was more tranquil. I was able to get a good look at the stars once again, and I looked up at them and then at the open fields beyond me.

I wondered if he was still out there.

I mean, I was sure he was, but there was no reason for him to ever appear again because his home was now safe, and I was sure that he would be more than happy once we all left.

So, I guess that was that.

"Hey? You feeling all right?"

I turned around and saw Amelia standing there, holding a can of Coke. I held my hand out to her, and she walked over and took it. Then, without saying anything, I immediately kissed her, and this time she must have been expecting it because she did not act surprised in any way. We parted and smiled at each other, and then looked up at the sky.

I noticed that we were standing in an area that, for some reason, was a very nice patch of soft, green grass, just like my yard. I looked at Amelia, and she instantly knew what I was thinking because she must have thought that night was as special as I did.

We lay down on the grass and looked up at the stars together, Zock by my side, and it was just like it had been back then. The only difference was that there was no radio to listen to...well, that and the fact that we were now holding hands.

Life was certainly good. There might have been a certain altercation along the way, to say the least, but it was now the best it had ever been, and I had no complaints whatsoever.

Well, maybe just one.

I never did get the car.

EPILOGUE

Time moved on, as it tends to do and, after all these years, one thing that I have learned is that once you are an adult and living in the real world, time seems to move a lot faster than when you are a kid. A hell of a lot faster.

We enjoyed the rest of the summer in peace and fun except for having to put up with the odd interview here and there and, for a while, we were all local celebrities. The story even got some national attention because of the severity of it. It was weird, thinking that people as far away as California and New York were watching me on television and reading about what I had said in interviews. But, after a while, things died down because there always seemed to be another disaster for people to focus their attention on, which would take the place of the last one...at least, until the next one popped up. Such is life.

We returned to school after summer was over, but two things had changed: 1) We were all more popular, which was kind of hard to deal with, at least as far as I was concerned but not for Keith. The legend of the Bluesman had grown so much that he now was more or less the king of the school. Also, the girls were all over him, much to the chagrin of all the jocks. 2) I officially had a girlfriend now.

Amelia and I were now a couple, and we dated for the rest of the time we went to Tom Brown Junior High, and eventually when we transferred to Carroll High School, and it was all great. She and the Bluesman were the best friends that I have ever had, nobody else coming close. We were bonded, now and forever. By the way, remember all the complaining I was doing when I went to Tom Brown? That was absolutely nothing compared to high school! Well, I guess a lot of it was the same – there just seemed to be more of it, also added to the fact that people were making a valiant effort to act more grown up, most of them failing miserably. These are the people who are going to be running the country someday? I weep for the future.

Amelia and I even wound up going to the prom together (by now, her braces were long gone, and she was even more beautiful, which I didn't think could be possible), and it was an absolutely wonderful night. We danced, we talked, we laughed – it was all perfect. Well, almost perfect. I had a used car that my Dad had helped me buy to get me around. It was by no means as nice as that '57 Chevy that I was so much in love with, but at least it was not a bicycle. If I recall correctly, the Bluesman had three dates for the prom, all four of them showing up together and having a wonderful time. I still do not know how he managed to do it.

After high school, things changed because we would all soon be eighteen and would legally be adults, no longer kids. A part of our lives would be over and it was time to begin a new chapter in a brave new world.

The Bluesman and I had a long talk that lasted into the night when it was getting near to graduation because he was still unsure of what he wanted to do in life. The only thing he enjoyed was telling jokes and making people laugh. As I had mentioned then, that handful of years ago, I suggested that he should get into show business.

When we were about to transfer to Carroll and the Bluesman was thinking about what classes to take, Amelia suggested that he should get involved in the drama club since he was so funny. At first, he was reluctant to do it, but with some more coaxing from the two of us, he eventually did. And, you know what? He was awesome! He was in practically every production that the school put on, and he was good in every one, but he especially excelled in anything having to do with comedy. When our final year ended, he was voted "Most Likely to Make the World Laugh."

And he eventually did.

After he graduated, I suggested that he should head out to Hollywood and give it four or five years and see what happened, and he did. He started doing stand-up comedy at all the local clubs, and began to build up quite a following. He was getting a lot of attention but was discouraged that he really didn't seem to be getting anywhere, and we talked on the phone frequently. I told him to keep his chin up and stick it out because I believed then, as I still do now: Nothing can stop the Bluesman. Within a couple of years, he was already a working actor and getting roles in movies and television shows. He had done it, just like I knew he would. Now, among all the films and network shows that he has been involved in throughout the years, he is currently famous for being the star of the number-one sitcom on the air right now. Looking at the wasteland that television is with all of that reality-TV garbage that is currently polluting the airwaves and slowly killing the brain cells of America, I think that that is quite an accomplishment.

You are probably not sure of whom I am talking about, even though the story may sound familiar. I do not blame you. Because he always hated his name and did not want to put up with constant Keith Richards jokes, he changed it. You probably know him as Keith Rivers. Ring a bell, now? I thought it might.

To this day, Keith is my best and dearest friend. In fact, I was the best man at his wedding, and he was the best man at mine, and we are always calling each other up or e-mailing each other. The three of us get together several times a year, and whenever he e-mails me, he always ends it as, "Your Friend Forever- The Bluesman," a private joke between us because once he left Corpus Christi, he left that "The Bluesman" moniker behind. Now, it is just for us.

Well, that is not completely true. He is currently involved in making a comedic film where he plays a school teacher, and one of the troublesome kids in his class is known as "The Bluesman" because he likes to spontaneously burst into song.

Gee, I wonder where they got that idea from.

Zock died when he was seventeen, which is pretty old for a dog, and I cried like a baby when he did. Throughout the years, I had taken numerous pictures of him, both alone and with me beside him. I still keep a framed picture of him on my desk so I can look at him from time to time when I am working and remember all the good times we had together. In fact, Zock had a habit of mingling with all the female dogs around the neighborhood through the years, and I guess the best way to put it is that Zock got around. The world is now populated with little Zocks so, in a way, you could say that the spirit of Zock lives on. I miss you, guy.

I have never owned another dog. Once you have had the best, there is no real hope of ever replacing him, so why even bother trying? Although, my son, Robert, has been making some very subtle/loud hints about wanting a dog... and he does have a birthday coming up....

After I graduated, my father got a job offer in Houston, and we moved there shortly after school was over. Both Amelia and I were heartbroken because we knew that we would hardly ever see each other again. Sure, we would be able to talk on the phone, write letters, and maybe see each other occasionally, but it would not be the same. She took an interest in broadcasting and majored in that when she went to school. Also, she won quite the number of beauty pageants and did countless dozens of commercials and ads in the Texas area over the years. She is now the weather person at the same station that interviewed us at the barn so long ago and she sees Joe Gazin on a regular basis. Also, along the way, she developed quite the number of male fans, and her fan club is quite sizeable. I will give you one guess who manages her website for her. She eventually got married but, unfortunately, it did not work out, and they got divorced five years later. However, it did work out for someone else.

I eventually went to school in Houston and, like the Bluesman, really did not know what I wanted to do. Like my father, I majored in accounting, simply because I thought that it would be fairly easy to land a job once I was in the real world. Well, I did get a nice job fairly quickly, and I was finally a working, responsible adult. There was only one problem: I hated it.

When I went to school, I decided to take some of what I was saying to the Bluesman to heart and apply it to myself. I minored in creative writing, since I always did seem to have some ideas floating around in my head for whatever reason and, throughout the years, I doodled around with some short stories here and there. Not surprisingly, I quickly wearied of the 9-5 world and decided I wanted to do something else that was more interesting, and started working on an idea that I had whenever I had some spare time. It took quite a while to complete it because working people have very little spare time. This was definitely not like being a carefree kid. Those days were way over.

I guess it should come as no surprise to you that I eventually became a writer. The fact that you are reading this right now is a pretty good tip-off. I have currently written seven books, three of which have been made into some pretty decent movies. In fact, Keith and I are currently working together on an idea for a screenplay, and things look pretty good. Not surprisingly, it is a comedy, and most of it incorporates memories and events of our childhoods... kind of like this. Keep an eye out for it.

I never found out the full details about Gordon. I don't think anyone ever did. From what little I was able to find out; he was a high-functioning autistic who had escaped from a mental asylum in Georgia two years before he was killed here in Texas. The fact that he was able to stay under the radar as long as he did was nothing short of a miracle... or, a curse, whichever way you want to look at it. Apparently he was very skilled with just about anything mechanical, and he had actually rebuilt that car I was so much in love with. Where he learned how to do all of that or how he even learned to drive will always be a mystery. How he found out about Goatman's is even more of a mystery. He came from a rich family, which has remained anonymous, but rumor has it that it was a large family with lots of brothers and sisters, which I guess in some way explains why he had taken up child collecting, to somehow, in some warped way, reconnect with a family, since his own had rejected him.

I guess that also explains how he was able to come into so much money to buy all of that equipment, more than likely emptying an account somewhere before the family even had any knowledge that he had escaped. I suppose that that is all that anyone will ever know about him, unless someone from the family takes it upon themselves to speak up about him, which I seriously doubt will ever happen. I have wondered oftentimes throughout the years if his family had any kind of involvement in the political arena. After all, he was found in Texas, if you know what I mean.

Regarding Amelia, we have been married for going on eight years now, and we have two beautiful children, a boy and a girl named Robert and Allison, and I could not possibly be happier. I think I realized even when I was a kid that she would always be the love of my life, and I love her more with each passing day as much as the first time we kissed...or when she beat me up. In fact, we tend to have a habit of sitting outside on our back porch with the radio going on (an '80s station) and talking while we stare up at the stars. From time to time, the Bluesman even joins us when he can find some time to get away. Sometimes we travel up to Los Angeles to visit him, and no matter what he is involved in at that moment, he always finds time to hang out with us. Like I said, the three of us were bonded for life.

And the Goatman? I never saw him again. In fact, this is the first time that I have ever spoken about him to anyone besides Keith and Amelia. For over twenty years this has been a secret among only the three of us. I can only assume that he is still out there somewhere, but I don't know. A part of me does not want to know. The other half...? I have never been out to Goatman's since that last little adventure and am not even sure that that area is still even there. If it is, and it has not been developed into a subdivision or something, I will be surprised.

I only mention it because I want some kind of closure to something I have been carrying around with me for over two decades, and the best way for me to do that is to write about it. Now it is finally over.

Well, I have to go. There are things around the house to take care of, and if my wife comes home and sees that they are not done, there is a good chance that she might beat me up.

I love it!

Made in the USA
Lexington, KY
01 June 2018